The Pearl

THE PEARL

*Three
Erotic
Tales*

WORDSWORTH CLASSICS

The paper in this book is produced from pure wood
pulp, without the use of chlorine or any other substance
harmful to the environment. The energy used in its
production consists almost entirely of hydroelectricity
and heat generated from waste material, thereby
conserving fossil fuels and contributing little to the
greenhouse effect.

This edition published 1995 by
Wordsworth Editions Limited
Cumberland House, Crib Street
Ware, Hertfordshire SG12 9ET

ISBN 1 85326 609 4

Typeset in the UK by Antony Gray
Printed and bound in Denmark by Nørhaven

❧ ❧

Contents

❧ § ☙

*Lady
Pockingham
or
They All
Do It*

*Giving an
Account
of her
Luxurious
Adventures,
both before
and after
her
Marriage
with
Lord
Crim-Con*

❧ § ☙

Introduction

To the Reader,
Very little apology will be needed for putting in print the following highly erotic and racy narrative of a young patrician lady, from whose adventures I feel assured every genuine lover of voluptuous reading will derive as much or more pleasure as has your humble servant.

The subject of these memoirs was one of the brightest and most charming of her sex, endued with such exquisite nervous sensitiveness, in addition to an unusual warmth of constitution, that she was quite unable to resist the seductive influences of God's finest creation; for God made man in his own image, male and female, created he them; and this was the first commandment, 'Be fruitful, and multiply, and replenish the earth' (Genesis 1, 28).

The natural instinct of the ancients instilled in their minds the idea that copulation was the direct and most acceptable form of worship they could offer to their deities, and I know that those of my readers who are not bigoted Christians will agree with me, that there cannot be any great sin in giving way to natural desires, and enjoying, to the utmost, all those delicious sensations for which a beneficent Creator has so amply fitted us.

Poor girl, she did not live long, and in thoroughly enjoying her few brief years of butterfly life, who can think her wicked?

The scraps from which my narrative is compiled were found in a packet she had entrusted to a devoted servitor, who, after her sudden and premature death at the early age of twenty-three, entered my service.

As author, I feel the crudeness of my style may be a little offensive to some, but hope my desire to afford general pleasure will excuse my defects.

THE AUTHOR

Part One

My dear Walter,

How I love you! but alas! you will never know it till I am gone; little do you think, as you wheel me about in my invalid chair, how your delicate attentions have won the heart of a poor consumptive on the verge of the grave. How I long to suck the sweets of love from your lips; to fondle and caress your lordly priapus, and feel its thrilling motions within me; but such joys cannot be; the least excitement would be my death, and I can but sigh as I look at your kind loving face, and admire the fine proportions of my darling, as evidenced by the large bunch of keys you always seem to have in your pocket; indeed you look to have a key of keys, whose burning thrusts would unlock any virgin cabinet.

This is a strange fancy of mine (the writing for your perusal of a short account of some of my adventures); but one of the only pleasures left me is to indulge in reveries of the past, and seem to feel over again the thrilling emotions of voluptuous enjoyments, which are now denied to me; and I hope the recital of my escapades and follies may afford you some slight pleasure and add to the lasting regard with which I hope you will remember me in years to come. One thing I ask of you, dear Walter, is to fancy you are enjoying Beatrice Pokingham when you are in the embraces of some future inamorata. It is a pleasure I have often indulged in myself when in the action of coition, and heightened my bliss by letting my fancy run riot, and imagined I was in the arms of someone I particularly wished for, but could not come at. My income dies with me, so I have no cause to make a will, but you will find notes for a few hundred pounds enclosed with this outline of my adventures, which is all I have been able to save. You will also find a fine lock of dark brown hair, which I have cut from the abundant *chevelure* of my mons Veneris; other friends and relatives may have the admired curls from my head, your memento is cut from the sacred spot of love.

I have no memory of my father, the Marquis of Pokingham, and entertain doubts as to whether I am really entitled to the honour of claiming him as a parent, as he was a used-up old man, and from papers and letters, which passed privately between him and my mother, I know that he more than suspected he was indebted to his good-looking footman for the pretty baby girl my mother presented to him. Indeed, he says in one note that he could have forgiven everything if the fruits of her intercourse with James had been a son and heir, so as to keep his hated nephew out of the estates and title, and wished her to let him cultivate her parsley bed for another crop, which might perhaps turn out more in accordance with his wishes. The poor old fellow died soon after writing that note, and my mother, from whom this dreadful consumption is transmitted to me, also left me an orphan at an early age, leaving me her jointure of £20,000, and an aristocratic title which that amount was quite inadequate properly to support.

My guardians were very saving and careful, as they sent me to school at eight years of age, and only spent about £150 a year for schooling and necessaries, till they thought it was time for me to be brought out in the world, so that I benefited considerably by the accumulated interest of my money.

The first four years of my school passed away uneventfully, and during that time I was only in one serious scrape, which I will relate, as it led to my first taste of a good birch rod.

Miss Birch was rather an indulgent schoolmistress, and only had to resort to personal punishment for very serious offences, which she considered might materially affect the future character of her pupils, unless thoroughly cut out of them from the first. I was nearly seven years old when I had a sudden fancy for making sketches on my slate in school. One of our governesses, Miss Pennington, was a rather crabbed and severe old girl of five-and-thirty, and particularly evoked my abilities as a caricaturist, and the sketches would be slyly passed from one to the other of us, causing considerable giggling and gross inattention to our lessons. I was infatuated and conceited with what I considered my clever drawings and several admonitions and extra tasks as punishment had no effect in checking my mischievous interruptions, until one afternoon Miss Birch had fallen asleep at her desk, and old Penn was busy with a class, when the sudden inspiration seized me to make a couple of very rude sketches: one of the old girl sitting on a chamber utensil and the other of her stooping down, with her clothes up to ease herself, in a rural setting. The first girl I showed them to almost burst with laughter, and two others were so anxious to see the cause of her mirth that they were actually stooping over her shoulder to look at my slate when, before I could possibly get to it to rub them off, old Penn pounced upon it like an eagle, and carried it in triumph to the now alert Miss Birch, only to be further chagrined by the amused smile which our principal could not repress at first sight of the indecent caricatures.

'My young lady must smart for this, Miss Pennington,' said Miss Birch, with suddenly assumed gravity; 'she has been very troublesome lately with these impudent drawings, but this is positively obscene; if she draws one thing she will go to another. Send for Susan to bring my birch rod! I must punish her whilst my blood is warm, as I am too forgiving, and may let her off.'

I threw myself on my knees, and implored for mercy, promising 'Never, never to do anything of the kind again.'

MISS BIRCH – 'You should have thought of the consequences before you drew such filthy pictures; the very idea of one of my young ladies being capable of such productions is horrible to me; these prurient ideas cannot be allowed to settle in your mind for an instant, if I can whip them out.'

Miss Pennington, with a grim look of satisfaction, now took me by the wrist, just as Susan, a stout, strong, fair servant girl of about twenty, appeared with what looked to me a fearful big bunch of birch twigs, neatly tied up with red velvet ribbon.

'Now, Lady Beatrice Pokingham,' said Miss Birch, 'kneel down, confess your fault, and kiss the rod,' taking the bunch from Susan's hands, and extending it to me as a queen might her sceptre to a supplicant subject.

Anxious to get over the inevitable, and make my punishment as light as possible, I knelt down, and with real tears of penitence begged her to be as lenient as her sense of justice would admit, as I knew I well deserved what she was going to inflict, and would take care not to insult Miss Pennington again, whom I was very sorry to have so caricatured; then I kissed the rod and resigned myself to my fate.

MISS PENNINGTON, maliciously – 'Ah! Miss Birch, how quickly the sight of the rod makes hypocritical repentance.'

MISS BIRCH – 'I quite understand all that, Miss Pennington, but must temper justice with mercy at the proper time; now, you impudent artist, lift your clothes behind, and expose your own bottom to the justly merited punishment.'

With trembling hands I lifted my skirts, and was then ordered to open my drawers also; which done, they pinned up my dress and petticoats as high as my shoulders; then I was laid across a desk, and Susan stood in front of me, holding both hands, whilst old Penn and the

French governess (who had just entered the schoolroom) each held one of my legs, so that I was what you might call helplessly spread-eagled.

Miss Birch, looking seriously round as she flourished the rod – 'Now, all you young ladies, let this whipping be a caution to you; my lady Beatrice richly deserves this degrading shame, for her indecent (I ought to call them obscure) sketches. Will you! will you, you troublesome, impudent little thing, ever do so again? There, there, there, I hope it will soon do you good. Ah! you may scream; there's a few more to come yet.'

The bunch of birch seemed to crash on my bare bottom with awful force, the tender skin smarted, and seemed ready to burst at every fresh cut. 'Ah! ah! oh!!! Oh, heavens! have mercy, madame. Oh! I will never do anything like it again. Ah – r– re! I can't bear it!' I screamed, kicking and struggling under every blow, so that at first they could scarcely hold me, but I was soon exhausted by my own efforts.

Miss Birch – 'You can feel it a little! May it do you good, you bad little girl; if I don't check you now, the whole establishment would soon be demoralised. Ah! ha! your bottom is getting finely wealed, but I haven't done yet,' cutting away with increasing fury.

Just then I caught a glimpse of her face, which was usually pale; it was now flushed with excitement, and her eyes sparkled with unwonted animation. 'Ah!' she continued, 'young ladies beware of my rod, when I do have to use it. How do you like it, Lady Beatrice? Let us all know how nice it is,' cutting my bottom and thighs deliberately at each ejaculation.

Lady Beatrice – 'Ah! oh! ah – r – r – re! It's awful! Oh I shall die if you don't have mercy, Miss Birch. Oh! my God I'm fearfully punished; I'm cut to pieces; the birch feels as if it was red hot, the blows burn so!'

Then I felt as if it was all over, and I must die soon; my cries were succeeded by low sobs, moans, and then hysterical crying, which gradually got lower and lower, till at last I must have fainted, as I remembered nothing more till I found myself in bed, and awoke with my poor posteriors tremendously bruised and sore, and it was nearly a fortnight before I got rid of all the marks of that severe whipping.

After I was twelve years of age they reckoned me amongst the big girls, and I got a jolly bedfellow, whom I will call Alice Marchmont, a beautiful, fair girl, with a plump figure, large sensuous eyes, and flesh as firm and smooth as ivory. She seemed to take a great fancy to me, and the second night I slept with her (we had a small room to ourselves) she kissed and hugged me so lovingly that at first I felt slightly confused. She took such liberties with me, my heart was all in a flutter, and although the light was out, I felt my face covered with burning blushes as her hot kisses on my lips, and the searching gropings of her hands in the most private parts of my person, made me all atremble.

'How you shake, dear Beatrice,' she answered. 'What are you afraid of? you may feel me all over too; it is so nice. Put your tongue in my mouth, it is a great inducement to love and I do want to love you so, dear. Where's your hand? here, put it there; can't you feel the hair just beginning to grow on my pussy? Yours will come soon. Rub your finger on my crack, just there,' so she initiated me into the art of frigging in the most tender loving manner.

As you may guess, I was an apt pupil, although so young. Her touches fired my blood, and the way she sucked my tongue seemed most delicious. 'Ah! Oh! Rub harder, harder – quicker,' she gasped, as she stiffened her limbs out with a kind of spasmodic shudder, and I felt my finger all wet with something warm and creamy. She covered me with kisses for a moment, and then lay quite still.

'What is it, Alice? How funny you are, and you have wetted my finger, you nasty girl,' I whispered, laughing. 'Go on tickling me with your fingers, I begin rather to like it.'

'So you will dear, soon, and love me for teaching you such a nice game,' she replied, renewing her frigging operations, which gave me great pleasure so that I hardly knew what I was doing, and a most luscious longing sensation came over me. I begged her to shove her fingers right up. 'Oh! oh! How nice! Further! Harder!' and almost fainted with delight as she at last brought down my first maiden spend.

Next night we repeated our lascivious amusements, and she produced a thing like a sausage, made of soft kid leather, and stuffed out as hard as possible, which she asked me to push into her, and work up and down, whilst she frigged me as before, making me lie on the top of her, with my tongue in her mouth. It was delightful. I can't express her raptures, my movements with the instrument seemed to drive her into ecstasies of pleasure, she almost screamed as she clasped my body to hers, exclaiming, 'Ah! Oh! You dear boy; you kill me with pleasure!' as she spent with extraordinary profusion all over my busy hand.

As soon as we had recovered our serenity a little, I asked her what she meant by calling me her dear boy.

'Ah! Beatrice,' she replied, 'I'm so sleepy now, but tomorrow night, I will tell you my story, and explain how it is that my pussy is able to take in that thing, whilst yours cannot at present; it will enlighten you a little more into the Philosophy of Life, my dear; now give me a kiss, and let us go to sleep tonight.'

❦ *Alice Marchmont's Story*

You may imagine I was anxious for the next night to arrive. We were no sooner in our little sanctum, than I exclaimed, 'Now, Alice, make haste into bed, I'm all impatient to hear your tale.'

'You shall have it dear and my fingers, too, if you will but let me undress comfortably. I can't jump into bed anyhow, I must make the inspection of my little private curls first. What do you think of them, Beatrice? Off with your chemise, I want to compare our pussys,' said she, throwing off everything, and surveying her beautiful naked figure in the large cheval glass. I was soon beside her, equally denuded of covering. 'What a delightfully pouting little slit you have, Beatrice,' she exclaimed, patting my mons Veneris. 'We shall make a beautiful contrast, mine is a light blonde, and yours will be brunette. See my lithe curly parsley bed is already half an inch long.' She indulged in no end of exciting tricks, till at last my patience was exhausted, so slipping on my *chemise de nuit*, I bounced into bed, saying I believed it was all fudge about her having a tale to tell and that I would not let her love me again, till she had satisfied my curiosity.

'What bad manners to doubt my word,' she cried, following me into bed and taking me by surprise by uncovering my bottom and inflicting a smart little slapping as she laughingly continued, 'There, let that be a lesson to you not to doubt a young lady's word in future. Now you shall have my tale, although it would really serve you right to make you wait till tomorrow.'

After a short pause, having settled ourselves lovingly in bed, she began:

Once upon a time there was a little girl about ten years old, of the name of Alice; her parents were rich, and lived in a beautiful house, surrounded by lovely gardens and a fine park; she had a brother about two years older than herself, but her mama was so fond of her (being an only daughter), that she never would allow her little girl out of her sight, unless William, the butler, had charge of her in her rambles about the grounds and park.

William was a handsome, good-looking man about thirty, and had been in the family ever since he was a boy. Now Alice, who was very fond of William, often sat on his knee as he was seated under a tree, or on a garden seat, when he would read to her fairy tales from her books. Their intimacy was so great that when they were alone, she would call him 'dear old Willie', and treat him quite as an equal. Alice was quite an inquisitive girl, and would often put Mr William to the blush by her curious enquiries about natural history affairs, and how animals had little ones, why the cock was so savage to the poor hens, jumping on their backs, and biting their heads with his sharp beak, &c. 'My dear,' he would say, 'I'm not a hen or a cow; how should I know? don't ask such silly questions'; but Miss Alice was not so easily put off, she would reply, 'Ah! Willie, you do know, and won't tell me, I insist upon knowing, &c.,' but her efforts to obtain knowledge were quite fruitless.

This went on for some time till the little girl was within three or four months of her twelfth birthday, when a circumstance she had never taken any notice of before aroused her curiosity. It was that Mr William, under pretence of seeing to his duties, was in the habit of secluding himself in his pantry, or closet, from seven to eight o'clock in the morning for about an hour before breakfast. If Alice ventured to tap at the door it was fastened inside, and admittance refused; the keyhole was so closed it was useless to try and look through that way, but it occurred to my little girl that perhaps she might be able to get a peep into that place of mystery if she could only get into a passage which passed behind Mr William's pantry, and into which she knew it used to open by a half-glass door, now never used, as the passage was closed by a locked door at each end. This passage was lighted from the outside by a small window about four feet from the ground, fastened on the inside simply by a hook, which Alice, who mounted on a high stool, soon found she could open if she broke one of the small diamond panes of glass. She felt sure that if she waited till the next morning she would be able to find out what Willie was always so busy about, and also that she could get in and out of the window unobserved by anyone, as it was quite screened from view by a thick shrubbery seldom entered by anyone.

Up betimes next day she told her lady's-maid she was going to enjoy the fresh air in the garden before breakfast, and then hurried off to her place of observation, scrambled through the window regardless of dirt and dust, took off her boots as soon as she alighted in the disused passage and silently crept up to the glass door, but to her chagrin found the panes so dirty as to be impervious to sight; however, she was so far lucky as to find a fine large keyhole quite clear, and two or three cracks in the woodwork, so that she could see nearly every part of the place, which was full of light from a skylight overhead. Mr William was not there, but soon made his appearance, bringing a great basket of plate, which had been used the previous day, and for a few minutes was really busy looking in his pantry book, and counting spoons, forks, &c., but was soon finished, and began to look at a little book, which he took from a drawer. Just then, Lucy, one of the prettiest housemaids, a dark beauty of about eighteen, entered the room without ceremony, saying, 'Here's some of your plate off the sideboard. Where's your eyes, Mr William, not to gather up all as you ought to do?' William's eyes seemed to beam with delight as he caught her round the waist, and gave her a luscious kiss on her cheek, saving: 'Why, I keep them for you, dear, I knew you would bring the plate'; then showing the book, 'What do you think of that position, dear? How would you like it so?' Although pleased, the girl blushed up to the roots of her hair as she looked at the picture. The book dropped to the floor, and William pulled her on to his knee, and tried to put his hand up her clothes. 'Ah! No! No!' she cried, in a low voice; 'you know I can't today, but perhaps I can tomorrow; you must be good today, sir. Don't stick up your impudent head like that. There – there – there's a squeeze for you; now I must be off,' she said, putting her hand down into his lap, where it could not be seen what she was after. In a second or two she jumped up, and in spite of his efforts to detain her, escaped from the pantry. William, evidently in a great state of excitement, subsided on to a sofa, muttering, 'The little witch, what a devil she is; I can't help myself, but she will be all right tomorrow.' Alice, who was intently observing everything, was shocked and surprised to see his trousers all unbuttoned in front, and a great long fleshy-looking thing sticking out, seemingly hard and stiff, with a ruby-coloured head. Mr William took hold of it with one hand, apparently for the purpose of placing it in his breeches, but he seemed to hesitate, and closing his right hand upon the shaft, rubbed it up and down. 'Ah! What a fool I am to let her excite me so. Oh! Oh! I can't help it; I must.' He seemed to sigh as his hand increased its rapid motion. His face flushed, and his eyes seemed ready to start from his head, and in a few moments something spurted from his instrument, the drops falling over his hands and legs, some even a yard or two over the floor. This seemed to finish his ecstasy. He sank back quite listless for a few minutes, and then rousing himself, wiped his hands on a towel, cleared up every drop of the mess, and left the pantry.

Alice was all over in a burning heat from what she had seen but instinctively felt that the mystery was only half unravelled, and promised herself to be there and see what William and Lucy would do next day. Mr William took her for a walk as usual, and read to her, whilst she sat on his knee, and Alice wondered what could have become of that great stiff thing which she had seen in the morning. With the utmost apparent innocence, her hands touched him casually, where she hoped to feel the monster, but only resulted in feeling a rather soft kind of bunch in his pocket.

Another morning arrived to find Alice at her post behind the disused glass door, and she soon saw Mr William bring in his plate, but he put it aside, and seemed all impatient for Lucy's arrival. 'Ah!' he murmured, 'I'm as stiff as a rolling pin at the very thought of the saucy darling,' but his ideas were cut short by the appearance of Lucy herself, who carefully bolted the door inside. Then rushing into his arms, she covered him with kisses, exclaiming, in a low voice, 'Ah! How I have longed for him these three or four days. What a shame women should be stopped in that way from enjoying themselves once a month. How is he this morning?' as her hands nervously unbuttoned Mr William's trousers, and grasped his ready truncheon.

'What a hurry you are in, Lucy!' gasped her lover, as she almost stifled him with her kisses. 'Don't spoil it all by your impatience; I must have my kiss first.'

With a gentle effort he reclined her backwards on a sofa, and raised her clothes till Alice had a full view of a splendid pair of plump, white legs; but what riveted her gaze most was the luscious looking, pouting lips of Lucy's cunny, quite vermilion in colour, and slightly gaping open in a most inviting manner, as her legs were wide apart, and her mons Veneris which was covered with a profusion of beautiful curly black hair.

The butler was down on his knees in a moment, and glued his lips to her crack, sucking and kissing furiously, to the infinite delight of the girl, who sighed and wriggled with pleasure, till at last Mr William could no longer restrain himself, but getting up upon his knees between Lucy's legs, he brought his shaft to the charge, and to Alice's astonishment, fairly ran it right into the gaping crack, till it was all lost in her belly; they lay still for a few moments, enjoying the conjunction of their persons, till Lucy heaved up her bottom, and the butler responded to it by a shove, then they commenced a more exciting struggle. Alice could see the manly shaft as it worked in and out of her sheath, glistening with lubricity, whilst the lips of her cunny seemed to cling to it each time of withdrawal, as if afraid of losing such a delightful sugar stick; but this did not last long, their movements got more and more furious, till at last both seemed to meet in a spasmodic embrace, as they almost fainted in each other's arms, and Alice could see a profusion of creamy moisture oozing from the crack of Lucy, as they both lay in a kind of lethargy of enjoyment after their battle of love.

Mr William was the first to break the silence: 'Lucy, will you look in tomorrow, dear; you know that old spy, Mary, will be back from her holiday in a day or two, and then we shan't often have a chance.'

LUCY – 'Ah; you rogue, I mean to have a little more now, I don't care if we're caught; I must have it,' she said, squeezing him with her arms and gluing her lips to his, as she threw her beautiful legs right over his buttocks, and commenced the engagement once more by rapidly heaving her bottom; in fact, although he was a fine man, the weight of his body seemed as nothing in her amorous excitement.

The butler's excuses and pleading of fear, in case he was missed, &c., were all of no avail; she fairly drove him on, and he was soon as furiously excited as herself, and with a profusion of sighs, expressions of pleasure, endearment, &c., they soon died away again into a state of short voluptuous oblivion. However, Mr William was too nervous and afraid to let her lie long; he withdrew his instrument from her foaming cunny, just as it was all slimy and glistening with the mingled juices of their love, but what a contrast to its former state, as Alice now beheld it much reduced in size, and already drooping its fiery head.

Lucy jumped up and let down her clothes, but kneeling on the floor before her lover, she took hold of his limp affair, and gave it a most luscious sucking, to the great delight of Mr William, whose face flushed again with pleasure, and as soon as Lucy had done with her sucking kiss, Alice saw that his instrument was again stiff and ready for a renewal of their joys.

LUCY, laughing in a low tone – 'There, my boy, I'll leave you like that, think of me till tomorrow; I couldn't help giving the darling a good suck after the exquisite pleasure he had afforded me; it's like being in heaven for a little while.'

With a last kiss on the lips, they parted and Mr William again locked his door, whilst Alice made good her retreat to prepare herself for breakfast.

It was a fine warm morning in May, and soon after breakfast Alice, with William for her guardian, set off for a ramble in the park; her blood was in a boil, and she longed to experience the joys she was sure Lucy had been surfeited with; they sauntered down to the lake, and she asked William to give her a row in the boat; he unlocked the boathouse, and handed her into a nice, broad, comfortable skiff, well furnished with soft seats and cushions.

'How nice to be here, in the shade,' said Alice; 'come into the boat, Willie, we will sit in it a little while, and you shall read to me before we have a row.'

'Just as you please, Miss Alice,' he replied, with unwonted deference, stepping into the boat, and sitting down in the stern sheets.

'Ah my head aches a little, let me recline it in your lap,' said Alice, throwing off her hat, and stretching herself along on a cushion. 'Why are you so precise this morning, Willie? You know I don't like to be called Miss, you can keep that for Lucy.' Then noticing his confusion, 'You may blush, sir, I could make you sink into your shoes if you only knew all I have seen between you and Miss Lucy.'

Alice reclined her head in a languid manner on his lap, looking up and enjoying the confusion she had thrown him into; then designedly resting one hand on the lump which he seemed to have in his pocket, as if to support herself a little, she continued: 'Do you think, Willie, I shall ever have as fine legs as Lucy? Don't you think I ought soon to have long dresses, sir! I'm getting quite bashful about showing my calves so much.' The butler had hard work to recover his composure, the vivid recollection of the luscious episode with Lucy before break-fast was so fresh in his mind that Alice's allusions to her, and the soft girlish hand resting on his privates (even although he thought her as innocent as a lamb) raised an utter of desire in his feverish blood, which he tried to allay as much as possible, but little by little the unruly member began to swell, till he was sure she must feel it throb under her hand. With an effort he slightly shifted himself, so as to remove her hand lower down on to the thigh, as he answered as gravely as possible (feeling assured Alice could know nothing): 'You're making game of me this morning. Don't you wish me to read, Alice?'

ALICE, excitedly, with an unusual flush on her face – 'You naughty man, you shall tell me what I want to know this time: How do babies come? What is the parsley bed, the nurses and doctors say they come out of? Is it not a curly lot of hair at the bottom of the woman's belly? I know that's what Lucy's got, and I've seen you kiss it, sir!'

William felt ready to drop; the perspiration stood on his brow in great drops, but his lips refused to speak, and Alice continued in a soft whisper: 'I saw it all this morning, Willie dear, and what joy that great red-head thing of yours seemed to give her. You must let me into the secret, and I will never tell. This is the monster you shoved into her so furiously. I must look at it and feel it; how hard it has got under my touch. La! What a funny thing! I can get it out as Lucy did,' pulling open his trousers and letting out the rampant engine of love. She kissed its red velvety head, saying: 'What a sweet, soft thing to touch. Oh! I must caress it a little.' Her touches were like fire to his senses; speechless with rapture and surprise, he silently submitted to the freak of the wilful girl, but his novel position was so exciting he could not restrain himself, and the sperm boiled up from his penis all over her hands and face.

'Ah!' she exclaimed. 'That's just what I saw it do yesterday morning. Does it do that inside of Lucy?'

Here William recovered himself a little, and wiping her face and hands with his handkerchief, put away the rude plaything, saying, 'Oh! My God! I'm lost! What have you done, Alice? It's awful! Never mention it again. I mustn't walk out with you any more.'

Alice burst into sobs.

'Oh! Oh! Willie! How unkind! Do you think I will tell? Only I must share the pleasure with Lucy. Oh! Kiss me as you did her, and we won't say any more about it today.'

William loved the little girl too well to refuse such a delightful task, but he contented himself with a very short suck at her virgin cunny, lest his erotic passion should urge him to outrage her at once.

'How nice to feel your lovely tongue there. How beautifully it tickled and warmed me all over; but you were so quick, and left off just as it seemed nicer than ever, dear Willie,' said Alice, embracing and kissing him with ardour.

'Gently, darling; you mustn't be so impulsive; it's a very dangerous game for one so young. You must be careful how you look at me, or notice me, before others,' said Mr William, returning her kisses, and feeling himself already quite unable to withstand the temptation of such a delicious *liaison*.

'Ah!' said Alice, with extraordinary perception for one so young. 'You fear Lucy. Our best plan is to take her into our confidence. I will get rid of my lady's-maid, I never did like her, and will ask mama to give Lucy the place. Won't that be fine, dear? We shall be quite safe in all our little games then.'

The butler, now more collected in his ideas, and with a cooler brain, could not but admire the wisdom of this arrangement, so he assented to the plan, and he took the boat out for a row to cool their heated blood, and quiet the impulsive throbbings of a pair of fluttering hearts.

The next two or three days were wet and unfavourable for outdoor excursions, and Alice took advantage of this interval to induce her mother to change her lady's-maid, and install Lucy in the situation.

Alice's attendant slept in a little chamber, which had two doors, one opening into the corridor whilst the other allowed free and direct access to her little mistress's apartment, which it adjoined.

The very first night Lucy retired to rest in her new room, she had scarcely been half an hour in bed (where she lay, reflecting on the change, and wondering how she would now be able to enjoy the butler's company occasionally), before Alice called out for her. In a moment she was at the young lady's bedside, saying: 'What can I do, Miss Alice, are you not warm enough? These damp nights are so chilly.'

'Yes, Lucy,' said Alice, 'that must be what it is. I feel cold and restless. Would you mind getting in bed with me? You will soon make me warm.'

Lucy jumped in, and Alice nestled close up to her bosom, as if for warmth, but in reality to feel the outlines of her beautiful figure.

'Kiss me, Lucy,' she said; 'I know I shall like you so much better than Mary. I couldn't bear her.' This was lovingly responded to, and Alice continued, as she pressed her hand on the bosom of her bedfellow, 'What large titties you have, Lucy. Let me feel them. Open your nightdress, so I can lay my face against them.'

The new *femme de chambre* was naturally of a warm and loving disposition; she admitted all the familiarities of her young mistress, whose hands began to wander in a most searching manner about her person, feeling the soft, firm skin of her bosom, belly, and bottom; the touches of Alice seemed to fire the blood, and rouse every voluptuous emotion within her; she sighed and kissed her little mistress again and again.

ALICE – 'What a fine rump! How hard and plump your flesh is, Lucy! Oh, my! what's all this hair at the bottom of your belly? My dear, when did it come?'

LUCY – 'Oh! pray don't, miss, it's so rude; you will be the same in two or three years' time; it frightened me when it first began to grow, it seemed so unnatural.'

ALICE – 'We're only girls, there is no harm in touching each other, is there; just feel how different I am.'

LUCY – 'Oh! Miss Alice,' pressing the young girl's naked belly to her own, 'you don't know how you make me feel when you touch me there.'

ALICE (with a slight laugh) – 'Does it make you feel better when Mr William, the butler, touches you, dear?' tickling the hairy crack with her finger.

LUCY – 'For shame, miss! I hope you don't think I would let him touch me' – evidently in some confusion.

ALICE – 'Don't be frightened, Lucy, I won't tell, but I have seen it all through the old glass door in his pantry. Ah! you see I know the secret, and must be let in to share the fun.'

LUCY – 'Oh! My God! Miss Alice, what have you seen? I shall have to leave the house at once.'

ALICE – 'Come, come, don't be frightened, you know I'm fond of Mr William, and would never do him any harm, but you can't have him all to yourself; I got you for my maid to prevent your jealous suspicions and keep our secret between us.'

Lucy was in a frightful state of agitation. 'What! has he been such a brute as to ruin you, Miss Alice! I'll murder him if he has,' she cried.

ALICE – 'Softly, Lucy, not so loud, someone will hear you; he's done nothing yet, but I saw your pleasure when he put that thing into your crack, and am determined to share your joys, so don't be jealous, and we can all three be happy together.'

LUCY – 'It would kill you, dear, that big thing of his would split you right up.'

ALICE – 'Never mind,' kissing her lovingly, 'you keep the secret and I'm not afraid of being seriously hurt.'

Lucy sealed the compact with a kiss, and they spent a most loving night together, indulging in every variety of kissing and tickling, and Alice had learnt from her bedfellow nearly all the mysterious particulars in connection with the battles of Venus before they fell asleep in each other's arms.

Fine weather soon returned, and Alice, escorted by the butler, went for one of her usual rambles, and they soon penetrated into a thick copse at the further end of the park, and sat down in a little grassy spot, where they were secure from observation.

William had thoughtfully brought with him an umbrella, as well as a great coat and cloak, which he spread upon the grass for fear Miss Alice might take cold.

'Ah! you dear old fellow,' said Alice, seating herself, and, taking his hand, pulling him down beside her. 'I understand everything now, and you are to make me happy by making a woman of me, as you did Lucy; you must do it, Willie, dear, I shall soon make you so you can't help yourself,' unbuttoning his trousers and handling his already stiff pego. 'What a lovely dear it is; how I long to feel its juice spouting into my bowels; I know it's painful, but it won't kill me, and then, ah! the heavenly bliss I know you will make me feel, as you do Lucy when you have her; how will you do it? will you lie over me?'

William, unable to resist her caresses and already almost at spending point, makes her kneel over his face, as he lay on his back, so that he may first lubricate her maiden cunny with his tongue. This operation titillates and excites the little girl, so that she amorously presses herself on his mouth as she faces towards his cock, which she never leaves hold of all the while; he spends in ecstasy, whilst she also feels the pleasure of a first virgin emission.

'Now's the time, Alice dear, my affair is so well greased, and your pussy is also ready; if I get over you I might be too violent and injure you; the best way is for you to try and do it yourself by straddling over me, and directing its head to your cunny, and then keep pressing down upon it, as well as the first painful sensations will allow; it will all depend on your own courage for the success of the experiment,' said William.

ALICE – 'Ah! you shall see my determination,' as she began to act upon his suggestion, and fitting the head of his pego into her slit, soon pressed down so as to take in and quite cover the first inch of it.

Here the pain of stretching and distension seemed almost too much for her, but she gave a sudden downward plunge of her body, which, although she almost fainted with the dreadful pain, got in at least three inches.

'What a plucky girl you are, my dear Alice,' said William, in delight. 'As soon as you can bear it, raise yourself up a little, and come down with all your force. It is so well planted, the next good thrust will complete my possession of your lovely charms.'

'I don't care if I die in the effort,' she whispered, softly. 'Never mind how it hurts me, help all you can, Willie dear, this time,' as she raised herself off him again, and he took hold of her buttocks, to lend his assistance to the grave girl.

Clenching her teeth firmly, and shutting her eyes, she gave another desperate plunge upon William's spear of love, the hymen was broken, and she was fairly impaled to the roots of his affair. But it cost her dear, she fell forward in a dead faint, whilst the trickling blood proved the sanguinary nature of Love's victory.

The butler withdrew himself, all smeared with her virgin blood, but he had come prepared for such an emergency, and at once set about using restoratives to bring her round, and presently succeeded in his efforts; her eyes opened with a smile, and whispering softly, Alice said – 'Ah! that last thrust was awful, but it's over now. Why did you take him away? Oh! put him back at once, dear, and let me have the soothing injection Lucy said would soon heal all my bruised parts.'

He glued his lips to hers, and gently applying the head of his pego to her blood-stained crack, gradually inserted it till it was three-fourths in; then, without pressing further, he commenced to move slowly and carefully. The lubricity soon increased, and he could feel the tight loving contractions of her vagina, which speedily brought him to a crisis once more, and with a sudden thrust, he plunged up to the hilt, and shot his very essence into her bowels, as he almost fainted with the excess of his emotions.

They lay motionless, enjoying each other's mutual pressures, till Mr William withdrew, and taking a fine cambric handkerchief, wiped the, virgin blood first from the lips of her cunny, then off his own weapon, declaring, as he put the red-stained *mouchoir* in his pocket, that he would keep it for ever, in remembrance of the charms she had so lovingly surrendered to him.

The butler prudently refrained from the further indulgence in voluptuous pleasure for the day, and, after a good rest, Alice returned to the house, feeling very little the worse for her sacrifice, and very happy in having secured part of the love of dear and faithful William.

How suddenly unforeseen accidents prevent the realisation of the best plans for happiness. The very same day, her father was ordered by his medical adviser to the South of Europe, and started next morning for town, to make the necessary arrangements, taking the butler with him, leaving Alice's mama to follow as soon as the two children were suitably located at school.

Lucy and her young mistress consoled each other as well as possible under the circumstances. But in a few days, an aunt took charge of the house, and Alice was sent to this school, and is now in your arms, dear Beatrice; whilst my brother is now at college, and we only meet during the holidays. Will you, dear, ask your guardians to allow you to spend the next vacation with me, and I will introduce you to Frederick, who, if I make no mistake, is quite as voluptuously inclined as his sister.

Part Two

I will pass over the exciting practices myself and my bedfellow used to indulge in almost every night, and merely remark that two more finished young tribades it would have been impossible to find anywhere.

I had to wait till the Christmas vacation before I could be introduced to Frederick, who, between ourselves, we had already devoted to the task of taking my virginity, which we did not think would prove a very difficult operation, as with so much finger frigging, and also the use of Alice's leather sausage, which, as I learnt, she had improvised for her own gratification, my mount and cunny were wonderfully developed, and already slight signs of the future growth of curly brown hair could be detected. I was nearly thirteen, as one fine crisp morning in December we drove up to the Hall on our return from school. There stood the aunt to welcome us, but my eyes were fixed upon the youthful, yet manly figure of Frederick, who stood by her side, almost a counterpart of his sister in features and complexion, but really a very fine young fellow, between seventeen and eighteen.

Since hearing the story of Alice's intrigue with William, I always looked at every man and boy to see what sort of a bunch they had got in their pockets, and was delighted to perceive Mr Frederick was apparently well furnished.

Alice introduced me to her relatives, but Frederick evidently looked upon me as a little girl, and not at all yet up to the serious business of love and flirtation, so our first private consultation, between Alice and myself, was on how best to open his eyes, and draw him to take a little more notice of his sister's friend.

Lucy, whom I now saw for the first time, slept in the little room adjoining Alice's chamber, which I shared with her young mistress. Frederick had a room on the other side of ours, so that we were nextdoor neighbours, and could rap and give signals to each other on the wall, as well as try to look through the keyhole of a disused door, which opened direct from one room to the other, but had long since been locked and bolted to prevent any communication between the occupants.

A little observation soon convinced us that Lucy was upon most intimate terms with her young master, which Alice determined to turn to account in our favour.

She quickly convinced her *femme de chambre* that she could not enjoy and monopolise the whole of her brother, and finding that Lucy expected he would visit her room that very night, she insisted upon ringing the changes, by taking Lucy to sleep with herself, and putting me in the place of Monsieur Frederick's ladylove.

I was only too willing to be a party of this arrangement, and at ten P.M., when we all retired to rest, I took the place of the *femme de chambre*, and pretended to be fast asleep in her snug little bed. The lock of the door had been oiled by Lucy, so as to open quite noiselessly, but the room was purposely left in utter darkness, and secured even from the intrusion of a dim starlight by well-closed window curtains.

About eleven o'clock, as nearly as I could guess, the door silently opened, and by the light of the corridor lamp, I saw a figure, in nothing but a shirt, cautiously glide in, and approach the bed. The door closed, and all was dark, putting my heart in a dreadful flutter, at the approach of the long wished for, but dreaded ravisher of my virginity.

'Lucy! Lucy!! Lucy!!!' he whispered, in a low voice, almost in my ear. No response, only the apparent deep breathing of a person in sound sleep.

'She hasn't thought much about me, but, I guess, something between her legs will soon wake her up,' I heard him mutter, then the bedclothes were pulled open, and he slid into bed by my side. My hair was all loose, the same as Lucy's generally was at night, and I felt a warm kiss on my cheek, also an arm stealing round my waist and clutching my nightdress as if to pull it up. Of course I was the fox asleep, but could not help being all atremble at the approach of my fate.

'How you shake, Lucy; what's the matter? Hullo! who's this; it can't be you?' he said rapidly, as with a sigh and a murmur, 'Oh! oh! Alice,' I turned round just as he pulled up my chemise, clasping my arm firmly round him, but still apparently lost in sleep. 'My God!' I heard him say, 'It's that little devil of a Beatrice in Lucy's bed; I won't go, I'll have a lark, she can't know me in the dark.'

His hands seemed to explore every part of my body; I could feel his rampant cock pressed between our naked bellies, but although in a burning heat of excitement, I determined to let him do just as he liked, and pretend still to be asleep; his fingers explored my crack, and rubbed the little clitoris; first his leg got between mine, and then presently I could feel him gently placing the head of his instrument in the crack, and I was so excited that a sudden emission wetted it and his fingers all over with a creamy spend. 'The little devil's spending in her sleep; these girls must be in the habit of frigging each other, I believe,' he said to himself again. Then his lips met mine for the first time, and he was quite free from fear on that account as his face was as beardless as a girl's.

'Ah! Alice!' I murmured, 'give me your sausage thing, that's it, dear, shove it in,' as I pushed myself forward on his slowly progressing cock; he met me with a sudden thrust, making me almost scream with pain, yet my arms nervously clung round his body, and kept him close to the mark.

'Gently,' he whispered, 'Beatrice, dear, I'm Frederick, I won't hurt you much; how in heaven's name did you come in Lucy's bed?'

Pretending now to awaken for the first time with a little scream, and trying to push his body away from me, I exclaimed, 'Oh! Oh! How you hurt! Oh! for shame, don't. Oh! let me go, Mr Frederick, how can you?' And then my efforts seemed exhausted, and I lay almost at his mercy as he ruthlessly pushed his advantage, and tried to stop my mouth with kisses. I was lost. Although very painful, thanks to our frequent fingerings, &c., the way had been so cleared that he was soon in complete possession, although as I afterwards found by the stains on my chemise, it was not quite a bloodless victory.

Taking every possible advantage, he continued his motions with thrilling energy, till I could not help responding to his delicious thrusts, moving my bottom a little to meet each returning insertion of his exciting weapon (we were lying on our sides), and in a few moments we both swam in a mutual flood of bliss; after a spasmodic storm of sighs, kisses and the tender hugging pressure of each other's limbs, we lay in a listless state of enjoyment, until suddenly the bedclothes were thrown, or pulled off, then slap – slap – slap, came smarting smacks on our bottoms, and Alice's light, merry laugh sounded through the darkness, 'Ha! Ha! Ha! Ha! Mr Frederick, is this what you learnt at college, sir? Here, Lucy, help; we must secure and punish the wretch; bring a light.'

Lucy appeared with a candle and locked the door inside at once, before he could have a chance of escaping, and I could see she was quite delighted at the spectacle presented by our bodies in conjunction, for as I had been previously instructed, I clung to him in apparent fright, and tried to hide my blushing face in his bosom.

Frederick was in the utmost confusion, and at first was afraid his sister would expose him, but he was a little reassured as she went on, 'What shall I do? I can't tell an old maid like aunt; only to think that my dear little Beatrice should be outraged under my very eyes, the second night of her visit. If papa and mama were at home, they would know what to do; now I must decide for myself. Now, Frederick, will you submit to a good whipping for this, or shall I write to your father, and send Beatrice home disgraced in the morning? And you will have to promise to marry her, sir! Now you've spoilt her for anyone else; who do you think would take a *cruche cassée* if they knew it, or not repudiate her when it was found out, as it must be the first night of her marriage. No, you bad boy, I'm determined both to punish you and make you offer her all the reparation in your power.'

I began to cry, and begged her not to be too hard, as he had not hurt me much, and in fact had, at the finish, quite delighted my ravished senses.

'Upon my word,' said Alice, assuming the airs of a woman, 'the girl is as bad as the boy, this could not have happened, Beatrice, if you had not been too complaisant, and given way to his rudeness.'

Frederick, disengaging himself from my embrace, and quite unmindful of his condition, started up, and clasping his sister round her neck, kissed her most lovingly, and the impudent fellow even raised her nightdress and stroked her belly, exclaiming, as he passed his hand over her mossy mount, 'What a pity, Alice, you are my sister or I would give you the same pleasure as I have Beatrice, but I will submit to your chastisement, however hard it may be, and promise also that my little love here shall be my future wife.'

ALICE – 'You scandalous fellow, to insult my modesty so and expose your blood-stained manhood to my sight, but I will punish you, and avenge both myself and Beatrice; you are my prisoner, so just march into the other room, I've got a tickler there that I brought home from school, as a curiosity, little thinking I should so soon have a use for it.'

Arrived in Alice's own room, she and Lucy first tied his hands to the bedpost, then they secured his ankles to the handle of a heavy box, which stood handy, so as to have him tolerably well stretched out.

ALICE, getting her rod out of a drawer – 'Now, pin up his shirt to his shoulders, and I will see if I can't at least draw a few drops of his impudent blood out of his posteriors, which Beatrice may wipe off with her handkerchief as a memento of the outrage she has so easily forgiven.'

The hall was a large house, and our apartments were the only ones occupied in that corridor, the rooms abutting on which were all in reserve for visitors expected to arrive in a few days, to spend Christmas with us, so that there was not much fear of being heard by any of the other inmates of the house, and Alice was under no necessity of thinking what might be the result of her blows. With a flourish she brought down the bunch of twigs with a thundering whack on his plump, white bottom; the effect was startling to the culprit, who was evidently only anticipating some playful fun. 'Ah! My God! Alice, you'll cut the skin; mind what you're about; I didn't bargain for that.'

ALICE (with a smile of satisfaction) – 'Ho! Ho! did you think I was going to play with you? But, you've soon found your mistake, sir. Will you? will you, again take such outrageous liberties with a young lady friend of mine?'

She cut him quite half a dozen times in rapid succession, as she thus lectured him, each blow leaving long red lines, to mark its visitation, and suffusing his fair bottom all over with a peachlike bloom. The victim, finding himself quite helpless, bit his lips and ground his teeth in fruitless rage. At last he burst forth: 'Ah! Ah! You she-devil! Do you mean to skin my bum? Be careful, or I will take a rare revenge some day before long.'

ALICE, with great calmness and determination, but with a most excited twinkle in her eyes – 'Oh! You show temper, do you? So you mean to be revenged on me for doing a simple act of justice, sir? I will keep you there, and cut away at your impudent bottom, till you fairly beg my pardon, and promise to forgo all such wicked revengefulness.'

The victim writhed in agony and rage, but her blows only increased in force, beginning to raise great fiery-looking weals all over his buttocks. 'Ah! Ha!' she continued. 'How do you like it, Fred? Shall I put a little more steam in my blows?'

Frederick struggles desperately to get loose, but they have secured him too well for that! The tears of shame and mortification stand in his eyes, but he is still obstinate, and I could also observe a very perceptible rising in his manly instrument, which soon stood out from his belly in a rampant state of erection.

ALICE, with assumed fury – 'Look at the fellow, how he is insulting me, by the exhibition of his lustful weapon. I wish I could cut it off with a blow of the rod,' giving him a fearful cut across his belly and on the penis.

Frederick fairly howled with pain, and big tears rolled down his cheeks, as he gasped out: 'Oh! Oh! Ah! Have mercy, Alice. I know I deserve it. Oh! Pity me now, dear!'

ALICE, without relaxing her blows – 'Oh! You are beginning to feel properly, are you? Are you sincerely penitent? Beg my pardon at once, sir, for the way you insulted me in the other room.'

FREDERICK – Oh! Dear Alice! Stop! Stop! You don't let me get my breath. I will! I will beg your pardon. Oh! I can't help my affair sticking up as it does.'

ALICE – 'Down sir! Down sir! Your master is ashamed of you,' as she playfully whisks his pego with her rod.

Frederick is in agony; his writhing and contortions seem excruciating in the extreme, he fairly groans out: 'Oh! Oh! Alice, let me down. On my word, I will do anything you order. Oh! Oh! Ah! You make me do it,' as he shuts his eyes, and we see quite a jet of sperm shoot from his virile member.

Alice dropped her rod, and we let down the culprit who was terribly crestfallen.

'Now, sir,' she said, 'down on your knees, and kiss the rod.'

Without a word, he dropped down, and kissed the worn-out stump, saying: 'Oh! Alice, the last few moments have been so heavenly. It has blotted out all sense of pain. My dear sister, I thank you for punishing me and will keep my promise to Beatrice.'

I wiped the drops of blood from his slightly bleeding rump, and then we gave him a couple of glasses of wine, and allowed him to sleep with Lucy, in her room, for the rest of the night, where they had a most luscious time of it, whilst Alice and myself indulged in our favourite touches.

You may be sure Frederick was not long before he renewed his pleasures with me, whilst his sister took pleasure in our happiness; but she seemed to have contracted a penchant for the use of the rod, and, once or twice a week, would have us all in her room, for a birch seance, as she called it, when Lucy or myself had to submit to be victims; but the heating of our bottoms only seemed to add to our enjoyment when we were afterwards allowed to soothe our raging passions in the arms of our mutual lover.

Christmas came, and with it arrived several visitors, all young ladies and gentlemen of about our own ages, to spend the festive season with us; our entire party consisted of five gentlemen and seven ladies, leaving out the aunt, who was too old to enter into youthful fun and contented herself with being a faithful housekeeper, and keeping good house, so that after supper every evening we could do almost as we liked; Alice and I soon converted our five young lady friends into tribades like ourselves, ready for anything, whilst Frederick prepared his young male friends. New Year's Day was his eighteenth birthday, and we determined to hold a regular orgy that night in our corridor, with Lucy's help. Plenty of refreshments were laid in stock, ices, sandwiches and champagne; the aunt strictly ordered us all to retire at one A.M. at latest, so we kept her commands, after spending a delicious evening in dancing and games, which only served to flush us with excitement for what all instinctively felt would be a most voluptuous entertainment upstairs.

The aunt was a heavy sleeper, and rather deaf, besides which Frederick, under the excuse of making them drink his health, plied the servants first with beer, then with wine, and afterwards with just a glass of brandy for a nightcap, so that we were assured they would also be sound enough; in fact two or three never got to bed at all.

Frederick was master of the ceremonies, with Alice as a most useful assistant. As I said before, all were flushed with excitement and ready for anything; they were all of the most aristocratic families, and their blue blood seemed fairly to course through their veins. When all had assembled in Alice's apartment they found her attired in a simple, long *chemise de nuit*. 'Ladies and gentlemen,' she said, 'I believe we are all agreed for an out and out romp; you see my costume, how do you like it?' and with a most wicked smile, 'I hope it does not display the contour of my figure too much,' drawing it tightly about her so as to show the outline of her beautiful buttocks, and also displaying a pair of ravishing legs in pink silk stockings.

'Bravo! Bravo! Bravo Alice! we will follow your example,' burst from all sides. Each one skipped back to his or her room and reappeared in mufti; but the tails of the young gentlemen's shirts caused a deal of laughter, by being too short.

ALICE – 'Well, I'm sure, gentlemen, I did not think your under-garments were so indecently short.'

Frederick, with a laugh, caught hold of his sister's chemise, and tore a great piece off all around, so that she was in quite a short smock, which only half-covered her fair bottom.

Alice was crimson with blushes, and half inclined to be angry, but recovering herself, she laughed, 'Ah! Fred, what a shame to serve me so, but I don't mind if you make us all alike.'

The girls screamed, and the gentlemen made a rush; it was a most exciting scene; the young ladies retaliated by tearing the shirts of their tormentors, and this first skirmish only ended when the whole company were reduced to a complete state of nudity; all were in blushes as they gazed upon the variety of male and female charms exposed to view.

FREDERICK, advancing with a bumper of champagne – 'We've all heard of Nuda Veritas, now let's drink to her health; the first time we are in her company, I'm sure she will be most charming and agreeable.'

All joined in this toast, the wine inflamed our desires and there was not a male organ present that was not in a glorious state of erection.

ALICE – 'Look, ladies, what a lot of impudent fellows, they need not think we are going to surrender anyhow to their youthful lust; they shall be all blindfolded, and we will arm ourselves with good birch rods, then let it be everyone for themselves and Cupid's dart for us all.'

'Hear, hear,' responded on all sides, and handkerchiefs were soon tied over their eyes, and seven good birch rods handed round to the ladies. 'Now, gentlemen, catch whom you can,' laughed Alice, slashing right and left into the manly group, her example being followed by the other girls; the room was quite large enough and a fine romp ensued; the girls were as lithe and active as young fawns, and for a long time sorely tried the patience of their male friends, who tumbled about in all directions, only to get an extra dose of birch on their plump posteriors before they could regain their feet.

At last the Honourable Miss Vavasour stumbled over a prostrate gentleman, who happened to be the young Marquis of Bucktown, who grasped her firmly round the waist, and clung to his prize, as a shower of cuts greeted the writhing pair.

'Hold, hold,' cried Alice, 'she's fairly caught and must submit to be offered as a victim on the Altar of Love.'

Lucy quickly wheeled a small soft couch into the centre of the room. The gentlemen pulled off their bandages, and all laughingly assisted to place the pair in position; the lady underneath with a pillow under her buttocks, and the young marquis, on his knees, fairly planted between her thighs. Both were novices, but a more beautiful couple it would be impossible to conceive; he was a fine young fellow of seventeen, with dark hair and eyes, whilst her brunette style of complexion was almost a counterpart of his; their eyes were similar also, and his instrument, as well as her cunny, were finely ornamented with soft curly black hair, with the skin drawn back, the firey purple head of his cock looked like a large ruby, as, by Frederick's suggestion, he presented it to her luscious-looking vermilion gap, the lips of which were just slightly open as she lay with her legs apart. The touch seemed to electrify her, the blushing face turned to a still deeper crimson as the dart of love slowly entered the outworks of her virginity. Fred continued to act as mentor by whispering in the ear of the young gallant, who was also covered with blushes, but feeling his steed fairly in contact with the throbbing matrix of the lovely girl beneath him, he at once plunged forward to the attack, pushing, shoving, and clasping her round the body with all his strength, whilst he tried to stifle her cries of pain by glueing his lips to hers. It was a case of *Veni, vidi, vici*. His onset was too impetuous to be withstood, and she lay in such a passive favourable position that the network of her hymen was broken at the first charge, and he was soon in full possession up to the roots of his hair. He rested a moment, she opened her eyes, and with a faint smile said, 'Ah! It was indeed sharp, but I can already begin to feel the pleasures of love. Go on now, dear boy, our example will soon fire the others to imitate us,' heaving up her bottom as a challenge, and pressing him fondly to her bosom. They ran a delightful course, which filled us all with voluptuous excitement, and as they died away in a mutual spend, someone put out the lights. All was laughing confusion, gentlemen trying to catch a prize, kissing and sighing.

I felt myself seized by a strong arm, and a hand groped for my cunny whilst a whisper in my ear said: 'How delightful! It's you, dear little Beatrice. I can't make a mistake, as yours is the only hairless thing in the company. Kiss me, dear, I'm bursting to be into your tight little affair.' Lips met lips in a luscious kiss. We found ourselves close to Alice's bed, my companion put me back on it, and taking my legs under his arms, was soon pushing his way up my longing cunny. I nipped him as tightly as possible; he was in ecstasies and spent almost directly, but keeping his place, he put me, by his vigorous action, into a perfect frenzy of love. Spend seemed to follow spend, till we had each of us done it six times, and the last time I so forgot myself as to fairly bite his shoulder in delight. At length he withdrew, without telling his name. The room was still in darkness, and love engagements were going on all round. I had two more partners after that, but only one go with each. I shall never forget that night as long as a breath remains in my body.

Next day I found out, through Fred, that Charlie Vavasour had been my first partner, and that he himself believed he had had his sister in the mêlée, which she afterwards admitted to me was a fact, although she thought he did not know it, and the temptation to enjoy her brother was too much for her.

This orgy has been the means of establishing a kind of secret society amongst the circle of our friends. Anyone who gives a pressure of the hand and asks: 'Do you remember Fred's birthday?' is free to indulge in love with those who understand it, and I have since been present at many repetitions of that birthday fun.

Part Three

We returned to school, and I kept up a regular correspondence with Frederick, the letters to and fro being enclosed in those of Alice. Time crept on, but as you can imagine as well or better than I can relate all the kinds of salacious amusements we girls used to indulge in, I shall skip over the next few years till I arrived at the age of seventeen; my guardians were in a hurry to present me at Court, and have me brought out in hopes that I might soon marry and relieve them of their trust.

Alice was so attached to me that since my first visit to her home, she had solicited her aunt to arrange with my guardians for my permanent residence with her during my minority, which quite fell in with their views, as it enabled me to see more society, and often meet gentlemen who might perhaps fall in love with my pretty face.

Lady St Jerome undertook to present both Alice and myself; she was an aunt, and mentioned in her letter that unfortunately a star of the first magnitude would also be presented at the same drawing-room, but still we might have a faint chance of picking up young Lothair, the great matrimonial prize of the season, if he did not immediately fall in love with the beautiful Lady Corisande, and that we should meet them both at Crecy House, at the Duchess's ball in celebration of the presentation of her favourite daughter, for which she had obtained invitations for us. For nearly three weeks we were in a flutter of excitement, making the necessary preparations for our debut. My mother's jewels were reset to suit the fashion of the day, and every three or four days we went to town to see our Court milliner.

In company with Alice and her aunt, we arrived at Lord St Jerome's town residence in St James's Square, the evening before the eventful day; her ladyship was a most charming person of about thirty, without family, who introduced us before dinner to her niece, Miss Clare Arundel, Father Coleman, the family confessor, and Monsignore Berwick, the chamberlain of Pio Nono. The dinner was exquisite, and we passed a delightful evening, amused by the quiet humour of the confessor, and the sparkling wit of Monsignore, who seemed studiously to avoid religious subjects. Miss Arundel, with her beautiful pensive, violet eyes, and dark golden brown hair, seemed particularly fascinated by the sallies of the latter, whilst there was a something remarked by both Alice and myself, which led us to suspect the existence of some curious tie between the two ecclesiastics and the ladies of the household.

Lord St Jerome was not in town. At our special request, Alice and myself shared the same room, which opened into a spacious corridor, at one end of which was a small chapel or oratory. Our minds were so unsettled by the thoughts of the morrow, and also hopes of meeting some of our old friends in town, especially the Vavasours, that sleep was quite banished from our eyes; suddenly Alice started up in bed, with, 'Hist! there's someone moving about the corridor.' She sprang out of bed, and softly opened our door, whilst I followed and stood close behind her. 'They're gone into the oratory,' she said. 'I saw a figure just in the act of passing in; I will know what is going on; we can easily slip into some of the empty rooms, if we hear anyone coming.'

So saying, she put on her slippers and threw a shawl over her shoulders, and I followed her example; ready for any kind of adventure, we cautiously advanced along the corridor and soon arrived at the door of the oratory; we could hear several low voices inside, but were afraid to push the door ajar for fear of being observed.

'Hush!' whispered Alice, 'I was here when quite a little girl, and now remember that old Lady St Jerome, who has been dead some time, used to use this room next to the chapel, and had a private entrance made for herself direct from the room into the oratory. If we can get in here,' she said, turning the handle, 'we shall be in a fine place to see everything, as the room is never used, and said to be haunted by the old lady.' The door yielded to her pressure, and we slipped into a gloomy room; we were just able to see a little by the light of the moon.

Alice led me by the hand, having closed the door behind us; a cold shiver passed over my frame, but plucking up courage, I never faltered, and we soon found a little green baize door, bolted on our side. 'Hush!' she said, 'this opens into quite a dark corner, behind the confessional box,' as she gently withdrew the bolt, and we then noiselessly entered the chapel into a little kind of passage, between the box and the wall, and fortunately protected from observation by a large open-work screen, which completely hid us, but afforded quite a good view of the interior of the chapel. Guess our astonishment when we beheld both Lady St Jerome and her niece in earnest conference with the two priests and overheard what passed.

FATHER COLEMAN – Well, Sister Clare, the Cardinal has ordered that you are to seduce Lothair, by all the arts in your power; every venial sin you may commit is already forgiven.'

MONSIGNORE, addressing Lady St Jerome – 'Yes, and Sister Agatha here will assist you all she can; you know she is a nun; by the modern policy of Holy Church, we allow certain of the sisters to marry when their union with influential men tends to further the interests of the Church; the secret sisterhood of Ste Bridget is one of the most powerful political institutions in the world, because unsuspected, and its members have all sworn to obey with both body and soul; in fact, Sister Clare, this holy sisterhood into which we have just admitted you, by this special faculty from his Eminence, will permit you to enjoy every possible sensual pleasure here upon earth, and ensure your heavenly reward as well.'

The bright light shows us plainly the blushing face of Clare Arundel, which is turned almost crimson, as the confessor whispers something to her. 'Ah! No! No! No! not now,' she cried out.

MONSIGNORE – 'The first act of sisterhood is always to do penance directly after admission, and you have taken the oaths to obey both in body and mind; Sister Agatha will blindfold you, throw off your robe, and submit your body to the mortification of the flesh.'

Lady St Jerome quickly removed the dressing-gown in which her niece was enveloped, and left the fair girl with nothing but her chemise to cover her beautiful figure; the bandage was speedily adjusted over her lovely eyes, and she was made to kneel on a cushion, and rest her arms and face on the rails of the altar. Father Coleman armed himself with a light scourge of small cords, fixed in a handle, whilst her ladyship turned up the chemise of the victim so as to expose her bottom, thighs, legs and back to his castigation; then she withdrew, and seated herself on the knee of Monsignore, who had made himself comfortable in a large chair close to the victim; he clasped her round the waist, and pressed his lips to hers, whilst their hands seemed to indulge in a mutual groping about each other's private parts.

The scourge fell upon the lovely bottom; each stroke drawing a painful sigh from the victim, and leaving long red weals on the tender flesh.

The confessor continually lectured her on her future duties, and made her promise to do all his commands.

The poor girl's bottom was soon scored all over, and dripping with blood; the sight of this seemed to inflame the others, so that the confessor's affair stood out between the opening of his cassock, whilst Lady St Jerome spitted herself on the pego of Monsignore, and rode a most gallant St George as he sat in the chair.

THE CONFESSOR – 'Now, sister, for the last mortification of your flesh, you must surrender your virginity to the Church.' Saying which, he produced several fine large cushions, took the bandage from her eyes, and laid her comfortably on her back for his attack, with an extra cushion under her buttocks, in the most approved fashion. Then kneeling down between her thighs, he opened his cassock, and we could see he was almost naked underneath. He laid himself forward on her lovely body, and whispered something in her ear, which was apparently a command to her to take hold of his lustful weapon, for she immediately put down her hand, and seemed (as far as we could see) to direct it to her crack herself. She was evidently fired with lust, and longing to allay the raging heat of the part which had been so cruelly whipped, for she heaved up her bottom to meet his attack, and so seconded his efforts that he speedily forced his way in, and the only evidence of pain on her part was a rather sharp little cry, just as he entered to break through the hymen. They lay for a moment in the enjoyment of the loving conjunction of their parts, but she was impatient, putting her hands on the cheeks of his bottom, and pressing him to herself in a most lascivious manner; just then Monsignore and Sister Agatha, who had finished their course, got up and, the one with the scourge and the other with a thin cane (after first lifting up his cassock and exposing a brown hairy-looking bottom), began to lay into Father Coleman in good earnest. Thus stimulated, and begging and crying for them to let him alone, he rammed furiously into Miss Clare, to her evident delight; she wriggled, writhed and screamed in ecstasy, and gave us such a sight of sensual delirium as I have never seen before or since. At last he seemed to spend into her, and, after a while, withdrew himself from her embrace, reluctant though she seemed to release him.

We could see they were preparing to leave the chapel, so thought it time to make our retreat.

Next day we were presented, and nothing in the manner of the lively Lady St Jerome, or the demure Miss Clare Arundel, would have led anyone to imagine the scene that we had witnessed in the small hours of the morning.

In the evening we were all at the Duchess's ball. Lord Carisbrooke, to whom I was specially introduced, was my partner in the set, in which danced Lothair and Miss Arundel as *vis-à-vis* to Lady Corisande and the Duke of Brecon.

By and by the hero of the evening led me out for the Lancers, and afterwards we strolled into the conservatory, quite unobserved; his conversation was much livelier than I had expected, for Lady St Jerome had represented to us that he was seriously bent on religion, and about to join the Romish Church. The conservatory was large, and we strolled on till the music and laughter seemed quite at a distance, and coming to a seat with a delightful fountain in front of us we sat down; just as he was observing, 'How delightful it is to withdraw from the whirl of gaiety for a few minutes,' we heard some light footsteps approaching, those evidently of a very loving couple; the lady was heard to exclaim, with a saucy laugh, 'Ah! No! How dare you presume so; I would never be unfaithful to Montairy even in a kiss', there was a slight struggle, and, 'Ah, Monster, what a liberty!' and we heard the smack of lips upon a soft cheek; and then, 'Oh! No! Let me go back,' but the gentleman evidently remonstrated, as I could hear him say, 'Come, come, compose yourself, dear Victoria, a little, there is a seat here by the fountain you must rest a moment.'

LOTHAIR, with a start, whispered – 'They must not catch us here, they'd think we had been eavesdropping; let's hide ourselves and never say a word about it,' dragging me by the hand around a corner, where we were well screened by the foliage of the delicious exotics.

My heart was in a flutter, and I could perceive he was greatly moved. We stood motionless, hand in hand, as the lady and gentleman took possession of the cool seat we had just vacated; the latter proved to be the Duke of Brecon. I could see them plainly, and have no doubt Lothair did also.

LADY MONTAIRY – 'Now, sir, no more of your impudent pranks. Pray let me recover my serenity.'

The Duke knelt down and took her hand, which she affectedly tried to withdraw, but he retained it, saying:

'Dearest Victoria, pity my passion. How can I help loving those killing eyes, and luscious pouting lips. That very fact of its being wrong makes my determination the greater to enjoy you the first opportunity. It is useless to resist our fate. Why has the god of love given me such a chance as this?'

She turns away her head with affected prudery, but not a blush rises to assert her horror at his speech. One hand presses her fingers to his lips; but where is the other? Under her clothes. He first touches her, ankle, and slowly steals it up her leg. She fidgets on the seat, but he is impetuous, and soon has possession of her most secret charms. Her languishing eyes are turned on him and, in an instant, he is on his legs, and pushing her clothes up, displays a lovely pair of legs in white silk stockings, beautiful blue garters with gold buckles, her thighs encased in rather tight-fitting drawers, beautifully trimmed with Valenciennes lace. His lips are glued to hers at the same instant, and his hands gently part her yielding thighs, as he placed himself well between them. It is but the work of an instant. He places her hand on the shaft of love, which he has just let out, and it is guided into the haven of love. Both are evidently too hot and impetuous, for it seems to be over in a minute.

She hastily kisses him, and puts down her clothes as she says: 'How awful; but I could not resist Your Grace without disordering all my dress. It's been quite a rape, sir,' with a smile. 'Now, let's make haste back before we are missed.' He kisses her, and makes her agree to an assignation, somewhere in South Belgravia, for the morrow, to enjoy each other more at leisure, and then they are gone.

It would be impossible to describe the agitation of my partner during this short scene; Lothair seemed to shiver and shudder with emotion, I was also all of a tremble, and nestled close to him, my arm designedly touching the bunch in his trousers, always so interesting to me; I could feel it swell and seem ready to burst from its confinement; he nervously clasped my hand, and was speechless with emotion all during the scene which I have described; as soon as they were gone he seemed to give a gasp of relief, and led me out of our hiding place. 'Poor girl,' he said, 'what a sight for you, how I trembled for my own honour, lest the scene should make me lose my self-control. Ah! wretched woman, to betray her husband so!' Then looking at me for the first time he said, 'Do you not think it is best for a man never to marry?'

Used as I had been to such things, his terrible emotion made me quite sympathise with him, and my own agitation was quite natural, as I replied, 'Ah! my lord, you little know the ways of the world; I saw a more awful scene than that which we have witnessed, only last night, enacted by men sworn to perpetual celibacy, and you yourself were mentioned as a victim of their infernal plot.'

'My God! Lady, pray tell me what it was,' he ejaculated.

'Not now, we shall be missed, do you know any place where I can have a private conference with your lordship? If so, meet me tomorrow afternoon at two o'clock, in the Burlington Arcade. I shall come disguised,' I answered.

He hastily wrote the assignation on his tablets, and we made haste to return to the saloons from which we had been absent quite twenty minutes. A little while after, as I was sitting by the side of Alice, whispering my adventure in her ear, Lady Montairy, to whom I had previously been introduced, came and seated herself by my side. 'Ah!' she said with a sly look, 'you're in a fair way to carry off the great prize; my sister Corisande will stand no chance.'

'I've only danced one set with him,' I replied, demurely.

'Ah!' she laughed, 'it was not the Lancers I referred to, but your quiet stroll into the recesses of the conservatory. You had quite a lover's *tête-à-tête*.'

'But we did not indulge in a *Pas Seul*, as you did with His Grace,' I laughed, enjoying her confusion. She was speechless with surprise, her eyes fairly started with affright, and I hastened to reassure her, 'I'm your friend, dear Lady Montairy, your secret is safe with me, and I hope you will not make any remarks in connection with myself and Lothair.'

She squeezed my hand nervously, and asked, 'Do you remember Fred's birthday? I was not there, but my brother Bertram was with his cousins the Vavasours, and passed as their brother Charlie, who happened to be too ill to go with them. I'm initiated into your society. We shall meet again,' she added with a smile; 'I must go now to keep my engagements.'

The supper was a fairy feast, except for its substantial reality, and we returned home to Lady St Jerome's charmed with everything, and especially with the fine prospect we seemed to have of future enjoyment.

Next day I made an excuse to go out alone to pay a visit to an old schoolfellow, and two o'clock found me sauntering through Burlington Arcade. Lothair was there to the minute, and gently whispered in my ear, as I was looking in a doll shop, 'Now, this is really kind of Your Ladyship, and proves you can be depended on; I have made a most excellent arrangement, we have only to step across the road to the Bristol Hotel in Burlington Gardens, where I have ordered luncheon for myself and cousin, in a private apartment, and they know me too well to pry into my affairs.'

The chambermaid attended me in the bedroom, and as soon as I had laid aside my cloak, hat, &c., I rejoined Lothair in the adjoining apartment, where a sumptuous luncheon was set out.

Lothair, whose shyness of the previous evening seemed considerably dispelled, most gallantly insisted upon my partaking of refreshment, before a word of my communication should be uttered. 'Besides,' he said, 'a little champagne will give you courage, if it is at all disagreeable; the scene last night was such a shock to both of us that if you now prefer to be silent I won't press you about what you mentioned in the excitement of such a moment.'

His conversation was very lively all through the repast, and when we had nearly finished I asked him to ring for a little milk, which was brought to me; he was at the moment abstractedly examining the debris of a *paté de foie gras*. I poured part of the milk into two champagne glasses, and slyly added about ten drops of tincture of cantharides, with which Alice had provided me, to his portion. 'Now, my Lord,' I said, 'I challenge you to pledge me in a glass of my favourite beverage, champagne and milk, I think it is delicious,' pouring out the fizzing wine, and handing him the glass, which I first touched with my lips.

His eyes sparkled with delight as he drained it to the bottom, and flung the empty glass over his shoulder, exclaiming, 'No one shall ever put their lips to that again; it was indeed a challenge, Lady Beatrice, after which nothing but the reality will satisfy me.' Then rising, he persisted in claiming the kiss I had, as he alleged, challenged him to take.

'Now,' he continued, drawing me to a sofa, 'let us sit down and hear the awful communication you hinted at; who were those wretched men?'

'Monsignore Berwick and Father Coleman,' I replied; 'did you ever hear of a secret sisterhood of Ste Bridget, the nuns belonging to which devote both soul and person to the service of the Church?'

'No, never, but go on,' said Lothair, so I continued: 'These nuns are all aristocratic ladies, who devote themselves, as I said, implicitly to the interests of Holy Mother Church, satisfying and appeasing the lusts of her priests, as well as marrying any influential man they think they can lead by the silken tie of matrimony; such, my lord, are Lady St Jerome and Miss Arundel.'

'Incredible,' exclaimed Lothair, 'but I cannot doubt your word, dear Beatrice – permit me to call you that,' his eyes looking amorously at me and evidently already slightly moved by the exciting dose I had given him. I took his hand in mine – it was feverishly warm – then looked him full in the face: 'My dear lord, I would not have been here if for one moment I had thought you could doubt my word.'

'Call me Lothair, darling, throw away all awkward reserve,' he said, putting his arm around my waist, and giving me another kiss on my cheek, 'go on; tell me all about those fiendish priests who have been plotting to ensnare me.'

'Take my advice, Lothair,' I went on, 'you will find Miss Clare quite changed, her demure and reserved aspect turned to alluring and captivating glances; the Cardinal's orders are positive that she is not to spare even her honour if necessary, but that is an article I saw her surrender to the confessor.' Then I described to him the scene we had witnessed in the chapel, which, added to the effects of the tincture, seemed quite to work him up to a state of amorous excitement.

'Honour! Honour!' he exclaimed, excitedly. 'Alas! dear Beatrice, last night I felt able to lose life rather than that, and now it's gone, fled like a shadow, but what is it after all, but a mean, mistrustful shame; you must be mine, I can't restrain the fire of love which is consuming me; the very sin makes the idea more delicious.' My faint efforts were useless, he was a fine strong young fellow; in an instant I was thrown backwards on the sofa, and his hands took possession of my longing cunny; the furor of lust was upon him, but I made a fair show of resistance, and seemed only to yield to force, shutting my eyes as if afraid to see how he was exposing himself.

He roughly forced my thighs apart, and as he threw himself upon me, I could feel the hot soft head of his cock forcing its way between the lips of my vagina. I struggled and contracted myself as much as possible, and as I had previously well bathed the parts in a strong solution of alum and water, he experienced as great tightness and difficulty in penetration as if I had really been a virgin. My subdued cries of pain were real, for his big affair hurt me very much, but he gradually won his way, which was at the last moment facilitated by a copious spend.

'Ah! Darling; how delightful,' he cried, as he lay with his weapon up to the hilt, throbbing and enjoying the lascivious contractions to which I now treated him.

His lips were fixed to mine, the soft velvety tip of his tongue was a titbit I could not refuse, and I sucked it till I almost choked for want of breath. He spent again under the stimulating emotions with which I inspired him. He lay still for a few moments as we recovered our breath, then, with an upward motion of my buttocks, I challenged him to go on.

It was a most erotically voluptuous love engagement. I could not exhaust him; he was continually shooting his love juice into my very insatiable womb, and it was more than an hour before either of us would consent to a cessation of the game.

All that time we had been as closely joined together as the Siamese twins, only one heart and one soul seemed to animate us, whilst we were constantly returning the flow of sperm one after the other in the most thrilling manner.

After we had washed and refreshed ourselves, he begged my forgiveness for his impulsiveness, and promised to make me his wife, but I recalled to him his words of the previous evening: 'That it was better for a man never to marry,' and that for my part I thought that such sweet liaisons could never be enjoyed by 'married people'.

'Ha! ha!' I laughed. 'You have the two nuns of Ste Bridget to enjoy. Be advised by me, and seem to fall into their traps. I will introduce you to another secret society which you have little idea of. It is devoted to the pleasure of love, without being under the control of a lustful priesthood. You shall meet me again this day week and tell me how you get on.'

He parted from me very lovingly; and on my return to St James's Square, I found that Lady Montairy had brought an invitation from the Duchess for us to spend a few days at Crecy House before our return to the country.

'How delightful,' said Alice. 'The Duke has gone to Paris on business, and the Duchess is often indisposed; we shall find ourselves in Paphian bowers.'

Lothair dined with us that evening, but neither of us betrayed, by word or look, the new link between us.

Miss Arundel was attractive, and even alluring, in her manner towards him. Her face was all smiles as she addressed him in tones of sympathy, even of tenderness. Bewitching enough to turn the head of any less susceptible (even than Lothair) to the influence of the softer sex. She looked divine, dressed in a wondrous white robe, garlanded with violets just arrived from Paris; on her head a violet wreath, deep and radiant as her eyes, which admirably contrasted with her dark golden brown hair.

I could see he was fascinated. He asked us all to drive down to Richmond and dine with him the next day, but Alice declined for me and herself, alleging as a reason the short time we had to stay in town, and that we should at once have to avail ourselves of the Duchess's invitation, and with Lady Jerome's permission would remove to Crecy House early in the morning.

I could see this plan afforded them infinite satisfaction. So next day saw us welcomed at Crecy House by Lady Bertha St Aldegonde on behalf of the Duchess, who was confined to her room. Lady Montairy conducted us to our apartments, and dismissing the attendants as soon as possible, she embraced me first, and then Alice, saying: 'How nice of you two dears to come so soon. You're just in time for a most important ceremony. Tomorrow Mama thinks we are all going to the Academy, but in reality it is quite a different place. The fact is, Corisande is going to be received as a member of the Paphian Circle, as we call the society which you helped to originate. St Aldegonde, indifferent and "ne'er do well" as he seems, is the life and soul of it; Bertha indulges him in everything. Jealousy is unknown in our family. You will meet Bertram, Carisbrooke and Brecon all there. We only want Lothair to make it perfection, as Corisande means to taste and try which she likes best.'

ALICE – 'But surely we're not obliged to wait till tomorrow. Can't you, Victoria, give us a little party in your room tonight?'

'Yes,' she answered. 'But only a hen party; ourselves and Corisande. My room is the next to yours. The gentlemen will be at the clubs. St Aldegonde never will have a woman at night, and says the morning is the proper time, because his cock always stands best on an empty stomach before breakfast.'

The indisposition of the Duchess was a good excuse for all the ladies of the family to retire early, and after having dispensed with the lady's-maids, we met in Lady Montairy's chamber, all attired *'en robes de nuit'*.

Bertha St Aldegonde was a really splendid woman, a dark brunette of a fully developed figure, prominent dark flashing eyes, and a most sensual chin. Victoria Montairy was also a fine woman, with a very beautiful classic cast of countenance, whilst the darling Corisande seemed more beautiful than ever, for want of ornament, in her spotless *chemise de nuit*.

Alice and I both kissed her with rapture, which she lovingly responded to.

'Now, what is the programme?' said Alice to Lady Bertha.

'St Aldegonde and Montairy are both keeping themselves in reserve for the grand ceremony of tomorrow,' she replied; 'what weak things these men are; as if we wanted to be kept in reserve. Why, Victoria and myself never get enough; the more we have the more we seem to require, and the less able they become to satisfy us. Talk about women's rights, they ought to compel husbands to find substitutes, when they can't do it for us.'

'Well, if you have a pair of good godemiches, Beatrice and myself will try and satisfy you a little, whilst dear Corisande shall keep us up to the work with a good rod,' said Alice.

The godemiches were brought forth, and proved to be of monstrous size, to our ideas; they were made of the finest vulcanised india-rubber, beautifully moulded and finished, with all appendages complete; we strapped them on as soon as they were charged with a creamy compound of gelatine and milk. All were stripped to the buff.

Lady Bertha took me on her knee, kissing me lusciously, and

handling the dildo as if it had been alive. 'What a fine fellow,' she laughed, 'but not a bit too large to please me.' Meanwhile my fingers were busy, nipping and pinching her clitoris; she glued her lips to mine and fairly sucked my breath away, excited by my touches which had caused quite an erection of her finely developed clitoris. She drew me on to a couch, and I thrust the affair into her already spending cunny, her bottom responded to every shove, whilst I felt the smarting cuts of the birch which Corisande was applying alternately to myself and Alice; it was most delicious. I responded with all my ardour to the loving caresses of Lady Bertha, who clasped me firmly by the buttocks, whilst with two fingers of the right hand she frigged both my bottom and cunny at once; Alice and her partner were quite forgotten; I thought I had never experienced anything so delicious in my life. The combination of emotions quite carried me away, the lovely woman bounding under me in rapture, our luscious kisses, the warmth and exquisite titillations of my fundament arrangements seemed such an acme of bliss that when I made the godemiche spend into her my own nature seemed to melt into a sea of lubricity.

After a few moments I entreated her to be the gentleman, and let me have her stiff clitoris, which I was sure could give me great pleasure. 'Certainly, dear,' she said, 'I often do it to Victoria; throw off the dildo.' As quickly as possible we changed places, and I begged her first to bring herself forward over my mouth that I might kiss her pussy, and caress that exciting clitoris of hers. It was done at once, and I had a glorious view of the paraphernalia of love. A splendid mount covered with glossy black hair; the serrated vermilion lips of her cunny slightly parted, from which projected quite four inches a stiff fleshy clitoris as big as a man's thumb. I opened the lips with my fingers, passed my tongue lasciviously about the most sensitive parts, took that glorious clitoris in my mouth, rolling my tongue around it, and playfully biting with my teeth; it was too much for her, with a cry of 'Oh! Oh! you make me come, darling!' she spent profusely all over my mouth and chin.

She sank down upon me, and I opened my legs to admit her. 'Now it's my turn to repay the delicious pleasure I owe you,' she sighed, kissing me rapturously, and sucking my tongue into her mouth, so that I could scarcely catch my breath; with her fingers she opened my slit as wide as possible, then directing her clitoris to the passage she seemed to stuff lips and all in, then closed my affair upon it, holding them together tightly with her hand. I can't express to you how novel and delightful this conjunction was to me; we were both so heated and excited, our spendings seemed to mingle together and add to our erotic fury; without separating for a moment she rubbed and pushed about inside of me, the lips and hair of her cunny titillating the sensitive parts in a most thrilling way. We swam in a sea of lubricity, whilst Corisande added to her sister's enjoyment by the stimulating effect of her rod.

At last all was over, and we retired to rest, and did not rise till late next morning. Refreshed by a cold bath we had only just time to breakfast and prepare for our visit to the Academy. We drove to Burlington House, but only stayed half an hour, entered the carriage again and were driven to a large house facing the Thames, in Cheyne Walk; it was detached, and stood back in its own grounds.

We were received at the door by a quiet-looking old lady, who was the housekeeper and manager to the Paphian Circle; she ushered us into a large drawing-room, which occupied nearly all the space of the first floor, being supported in the centre by elegant fluted columns of black and gold; the whole apartment looked like a hall of the veritable Alhambra; the windows were closed by gorgeous black and gold curtains and, although it was daylight outside, light was provided by a constellation of wax tapers artistically arranged all round the walls.

The Duke of Brecon was there as a novice, with Bertram and Lord Carisbrooke as sponsors; Lords Montairy and St Aldegonde, with several other gentlemen and ladies, were also present. Alice and myself were overwhelmed with compliments as being two of the original founders of the society.

Lord St Aldegonde, as president, now asked Corisande and the Duke if they pledged their words to keep all the secrets of the Paphian Circle, remarking that oaths were quite useless, as he felt sure those who introduced them had every faith in their honourable intentions. Being answered in the affirmative, and having shaken hands with them, he requested all to prepare for dancing, as no one else was expected.

The company retired to the dressing-rooms, and in a few minutes we were all back in the drawing-room, everyone in a state of nudity with the exception of silk stockings, garters, and elegant dancing shoes. To prevent jealousy or any undue preference there was a deep box on a sideboard, where the refreshments stood; in this box were deposited slips of parchment, each bearing the name of one of the gentlemen present, and the ladies had each to draw for her partner in the first waltz, and the *pas de deux* after it. Corisande drew Lord Carisbrooke, and my prize was St Aldegonde.

I must not omit to mention that one of the ladies would get a slip with 'Piano' on it, and the last gentleman had to turn over the music for her. This fell to Lady Bertha, who was a brilliant pianist and at once struck up a well-known favourite from the Argyll Rooms, and we were instantly in motion. It was far more exciting than the blindfold romp on Fred's birthday; she kept us going till one by one, the couples subsided on the inviting couches, which stood around the room; my partner was in a brilliant state of erection, but he whispered to me, 'Not yet, Beatrice dear, we must see to Corisande.' Everyone seemed to act without the necessity of orders; all the couples ranged up in a semi-circle round the couch where Carisbrooke was caressing and kissing her, whilst the beautiful girl, her eyes languishing with love, was sighing and looking at his fine cock, which she held in her hand. 'Now, love,' said the gallant, 'as a novice you must kiss every gentleman's affair, and then we will initiate you into the mysteries of Venus.' Corisande, all blushes, took each throbbing pego tenderly in her hand and softly kissed the velvet heads. 'Now, Brecon,' said my partner, 'you do the same to the ladies, and that part of the ceremony will be over.'

'With pleasure, on my knees,' said the Duke, and we each presented our cunnies to his lips. Carisbrooke now gently inclined Corisande backwards, and put a soft pillow under her bottom, then proceeded to place himself in position; but unable to restrain his excitability, he spent all over her lovely mossy mount and belly, some of the sperm going quite up to the alabaster globes which adorned her heaving chest.

He blushed with shame and vexation, whilst Corisande was crimson, and gasping with excited expectation.

Lady Bertha, who was the coolest of the company, at once wiped all the sperm off her sister's belly with her fingers, with which she lubricated her crack; then taking hold of His Lordship's affair, directed it properly to the longing gap of love.

'Shove away. Shove, my boy. Heave up your bottom to meet him, dear,' she laughed, giving Corisande a good sounding slap on the side of her buttocks with her other hand.

With a furious plunge, the dart of love made its effort just at the right moment. The collision with her hymen was most destructive, the virgin defences gave way as with an awful shriek of pain, she lost all consciousness. He completed the conquest of his victim's virginity, and then lay soaking, and trying to revive her sensibility by his lascivious throbbing inside of her, whilst we applied salts and restoratives to bring her round.

She very speedily came to herself, evidently forgetting the fearful pain of her ravishment; there was a delightful languor in her eyes, as she patted his bottom and hugged him to her bosom. He responded to the gentle challenge, making her revel in all the delights of coition, and never withdrew his blood-stained priapus till they had mutually spent several tunes.

My partner now led me to a couch, as the others dispersed on the same kind of business. He was still as stiff as ever, and I longed to feel him within me, but, to my surprise, he mounted the reverse way upon me, presenting his bottom to my face and asked me to press my firm bubbies together, so that his cock might spend between them whilst he gamahuched me. It was a luscious position, and I lent all my ardour to second his fancy, and his lascivious tongue made me spend in delight just as his sperm deluged my bosom and belly.

Alice had had Lord Montairy.

After this, the gentlemen's names were replaced in the box, and the ladies made another selection, but in case of anyone drawing the same partner a second time, she had to return the slip and draw another.

Thus we passed a most delicious afternoon, refreshing ourselves from time to time with champagne and ices, or something more substantial, for the worship of Venus and Priapus requires continual stimulation with the most invigorating viands.

In this short sketch of my adventures it would be impossible to describe everything at great length, but I can assure you the ladies fairly exhausted the gentlemen before they allowed themselves to be driven home to dinner.

Part Four

I must now return to my liaison with Lothair; he had promised to meet me again in a week, when I hoped to hear the particulars of his drive to Richmond.

We lunched again at the Bristol Hotel, and without having recourse to the tincture I found him almost as hot and impulsive as before. 'Ah! Beatrice,' he said, as we lay exhausted on the sofa, after a series of delicious encounters, 'I cannot express half the gratitude and devotion I ought to have; for you, not satisfied with making me happy yourself, quite unselfishly advised me how to enjoy the two nuns. But first tell me of that Society of Love, which you promised to introduce me to, and then you shall have my adventure.'

So briefly I described to him the Paphian Circle, and took his promise to allow me to introduce him at the next seance.

'I know,' he said, 'you thought me quite captivated by Miss Arundel, but I never forgot your advice, and resolved to seem to lend myself as a proselyte, accept all the advantages they might offer as baits, and get a thorough insight into all the plans of the Jesuits before I open their eyes, but it is a game that will last a long time. Now, as to the Richmond drive. Lady St Jerome and Miss Arundel were most vivacious and alluring, as we drove down by road; then we had a beautiful row on the river whilst waiting for dinner, which we sat down to with excellent appetites. I plied the two ladies with wine, and requested them as a special favour not to leave me to myself at dessert, as I did not smoke, and there were no other gentlemen present. Everything was sparkling and agreeable, religion seemed to be avoided by mutual consent, the ladies had withdrawn from the table to a sofa in a recess, where their faces were screened from the light of the brilliant chandelier; they had each had two or three glasses of champagne and seemed very careful not to exceed the limits of decorum, when, taking a fresh bottle, I challenged them to drink to the prosperity of the Christian Church.

' "Ah!" said Miss Arundel, with flashing eyes, "but what Church do you refer to?"

' "Dear ladies," I replied, "you shall word the toast as you please, and I will drain a real bumper to it in your company."

' "Then," said Clare, "we drink to the prosperity of the Holy Roman Catholic Church, and long life to His Holiness Pius IX."

'Their eyes sparkled, and both seemed unusually excited.

' "What would we not do to assure your conversion, dear Lothair," said Lady St Jerome. "Come and sit between us whilst we talk seriously to you."

'I sat down on the sofa, and being well flushed with wine, impudently put an arm round each of their waists, and said, without thinking. "Ah! that's mere nonsense; but in truth, I would sell both body and soul for the happiness you and your niece could confer on me."

'Miss Arundel drew a deep sigh, but Lady St Jerome softly whispered, as she laid one hand on my thigh, most awkwardly near to an important member, "Ah! what do you mean? Join our Church, and there is nothing we will deny to you."

' "Nothing! nothing! you will get indulgences and dispensations for everything then," whispered Clare, as she laid her head on my shoulder.

' "No! no traffic with priests; I want my indulgence from you, dear ladies, and if you care for my soul, now's the time to save me; drive me away in unsatisfied desperation, and such a chance will never occur again. Ah! how awfully I am tempted by the proximity of such charms!" I exclaimed, falling on my knees, and clasping their legs, as I hid my face in Clare's lap.

'They were both trembling with emotion, and I was equally agitated, but I seemed to guess from their looks and manner towards me that the present moment was too favourable for them to let slip.

'Lady St Jerome was the first to speak. "Dear Lothair, we do indeed pity your distress. Oh! Oh! for shame, sir, what liberties! Will you? Will you, promise us?" as she fidgeted about in confusion, feeling my hand slowly advancing up her legs beneath the clothes; both my hands were busy, but Clare had closed her thighs, and firmly stopped my advance in silence, whilst her aunt's ejaculations seemed to encourage me more and more.

' "By all that's sacred, I promise everything you may demand of me; they shall receive me into the Church, as soon as they please, if you two will but be ministering angels to my impulsive passions," I cried, taking advantage of her confusion to gain complete possession of the grotto of love.

' "Clare, dear," sighed Her Ladyship, "can we possibly sacrifice ourselves for a nobler purpose? By now subduing his carnal lusts, we shall also draw a lost sheep to the foot of the cross."

'I felt Miss Arundel's tightly compressed thighs relax in their resistance, and she gave a spasmodic sigh as I victoriously advanced my rude hand also to her mossy retreat. "Ah! how delicious to have possession of a double set of the loveliest charms; I will kiss you, and enjoy you by turns," I said in rapture, at the prospect before me.

LADY ST JEROME – 'Excuse me a moment, dear Lothair, Clare is all blushing confusion, let me spare her modesty as much as possible,' as she rose and locked the door, then almost turned out the gas.

'Pulling up her skirts, I threw Miss Arundel backwards on the sofa, and releasing my bursting weapon, threw myself between her yielding thighs, as I exclaimed, "You have indeed relieved me of making an invidious selection, as I cannot restrain the heat of my passion, Clare must be the first victim to it."

'It was almost, if not quite, dark in the recess where we were, but my lips sought those of the lovely girl, her entire frame seemed to quiver under me, and she gave a faint shriek as the head of my cock first touched the lips of her cunny. "Courage, darling," I whispered in her ear, "I won't hurt you more than I can help; open your legs, and give way to me as much as you can, you suffer for a noble object." As if I did not know she had already lost her virginity.

'Lady St Jerome had now returned to the sofa, where she encouraged Clare to bear the dreadful pain with all her fortitude. Then Her Ladyship took my affair in her hand, saying, "Let me, dear Lothair, direct you right. I'm a married woman, and know exactly how it ought to be done." Her touch only added to my excitement. She kept drawing the foreskin back, and took care to present the head rather above the proper entrance to the vagina, to make me think the resistance I felt was genuine, but it gave me infinite pleasure, and made Mr Pego spend all over the entrance of Clare's longing cunny. At last, after great difficulty, they let me fairly in, and I begged Her Ladyship still to keep her hand there and stimulate my exertions. I spent three times, each time more excitedly than the last, whilst the dear girl was a constant flood of lubricity, and seemed to melt with love, clinging to me with all the tenacity of her voluptuous furor.

'At last, notwithstanding her entreaties for me to go on, on, on, I managed to withdraw, as I told her she would leave nothing of me with which to repay all her dear aunt's kindness. "But, Clare darling," I said, "I will still give you pleasure with my tongue." So I made her give way to Lady St Jerome, who eagerly slipped off some of her skirts, as she said, to give me greater freedom, but in reality so that she might enjoy herself more. Her pussy was quite wet with spendings, which had flowed in sympathy with our enjoyment.

'Miss Clare was an apt pupil, and quickly arranged herself over her aunt's face, so as to present her excited cunny to my lips.

'Lady St Jerome had an extraordinary gift of contraction in her vagina, it took hold of my cock, like a delicately soft hand, with a frigging motion, as she wriggled and met my thrusts, of the most delicious kind. I grasped and moulded her lovely breasts with both hands, for she held me convulsively to her body, and I had no necessity to clasp her myself. Our conjunction was so exciting that I spent again immediately, under the touches of what I called her invisible hand, then steadying myself I revelled in love and lubricity for more than half an hour, both the dear ladies gasping, sighing, and sometimes when they spent giving vent to subdued shrieks of pleasure and dearment. Clare seemed quite as excited as her aunt, who I found was frigging her bottom-hole and rousing all her lustful propensities to the utmost with a disengaged hand, as soon as she found I was so safely rooted in herself that one arm could hold me.

'I can't tell you how we finished, for there seemed to be no end to it; however, about eleven o'clock we apparently awoke from a kind of delicious lethargy, into which we had all fallen, and we soon sufficiently composed ourselves to ring for the carriage and start for town; on the plea of keeping out the chilly night air, the windows were put up, and I had one or the other of then astride of my lap and spitted on the shaft of love till the noise of granite pavement under the wheels of the carriage warned us of the near approach to St James's Square.

'I have promised not to marry, but expressed my wish to be received into the Church by the Holy Father himself soon after Christmas, when I will visit Rome on purpose; this will give me plenty of time to carry on my game, and prove to the Jesuits that I am now quite equal to the tricks they played on me, when they had me down at Vauxe before, and imposed on the weak senses of a poor boy, quite green to the ways of the world. I can love Clare, when I don't think of it, but if I do I should hate her even in the midst of our love transports.'

Our time in town was getting short, so at my suggestion Bertram and St Aldegonde arranged an early day with Lothair, for his initiation to the Paphian Circle.

We were still at Crecy House, and this time the affair was managed under cover of a small private party at the Duke of Brecon's, where we dismissed our carriages, and then drove out in those of His Grace for a country excursion, which of course only extended to Cheyne Walk. Everything was in readiness, and Lothair being admitted as usual, we quickly appeared in the garb of Madre Natura as before. Partners were drawn for the first dance; my lot fell to the Duke of Brecon, whilst Lothair was drawn by Alice, and Lady Corisande presided at the piano, where her brilliant execution helped to add to the excitement engendered by the lascivious motions of the dance, in which, when the gentlemen changed partners with us as they went through the figure, they gave our bottoms a fine smarting spank, which we repaid by sharp little slaps on their extended cocks, soon getting tremendously warm and excited over our quadrille, and at the conclusion could scarcely restrain ourselves sufficiently to allow Lothair to give the usual kiss all round to our palpitating cunnies.

I noticed Lady Bertha very busy whispering to everyone, and soon found out that she was proposing a little bit of extra fun for us, of which the novice was of course to be the victim, whilst both pleasure and profit would accrue to the Paphian Circle.

The kissing ceremony was over, and then Alice told him he had yet another little penance to perform before he could be admitted to full rights of membership, pointing to a fine 'Berkeley Horse', which was being wheeled into the centre of the drawing-room, a thing something like a common pair of steps, only covered with red baize, and provided with a cushioned footboard for the victim to stand on, whilst his hands were well stretched above his head, so as only to allow of his standing on tiptoe. Lothair in his simple ignorance stepped up gallantly and was instantly secured by his wrists to the topmost rings of the horse.

St Aldegonde, grinning with delight, tightened the cords unmercifully, making Lothair expostulate with him at the painful tension.

'That's nothing, my boy,' said St Aldegonde, 'don't cry out before you're hurt. Wait until you feel the rods tickle and warm your posteriors, it will do you good, as it did me; it's the most invigorating thing in the world; ask Bertha if I did not give her all she required that night.'

All the company were now furnished with beautiful bunches of long thin elegantly tied-up birch.

ALICE, stepping to the front – 'Now, sir, mind you answer all my questions under pain of severe punishment. In the first place none but orthodox members of the English Church can be admitted to the Paphian Circle, and a member has just hinted to me that you are going to Rome, and may be a Jesuit in disguise. Now, my lord, what do you say to that?' giving his bottom a smart cut, which made him wince with pain, and left a long red mark across the white skin of his manly buttocks.

LOTHAIR – 'My God! you punish without waiting.'

Before he could finish speaking all the ladies attacked him with their rods, raining a perfect shower of painful cuts on his helpless bottom, exclaiming, 'Answer! Answer!! Answer!!! No prevarication! Don't spare him! &c.,' whilst the gentlemen, who stood behind, cut into the fair bottoms of their partners, calling out, 'Pass it on to him; cut away, ladies, he's a Jesuit, &c.'

Lothair at first lost his breath, but soon shouted out lustily, 'Hold! Hold!! It's not true! Don't kill me!'

His bottom and back were scored all over, and little drops of blood trickled down from places where the skin was broken.

ALICE – 'Well, my lord, pray excuse our virtuous indignation, if you are not really a Jesuit. But how about a Cathedral you intend to build for them, eh?' cutting him several deliberate strokes as she was speaking, each one making him quiver under its smarting force.

LOTHAIR – 'Oh! My God! How do you know that? I've only had the plans drawn.'

ALICE – 'But, my lord, allow me to drive the thoughts of such a foolish thing from your mind. Can you not think of some better applications for your money? Will you promise me not to make yourself a fool?' cutting harder and harder every moment, till he fairly howled with pain, ejaculating –

'Ah! Oh! Damme! How cruel of you Miss Marchmont! Ah – for God's sake let me off now. I – I – won't do it; I give my word for that.'

ALICE – 'Beg my pardon instantly, my lord, or you shall feel what cruelty really is like. Cruel indeed! to a young lady who is only doing a painful duty!' catching hold of a fresh rod, and slashing his bleeding bottom with all her might.

Lothair writhes his body about in dreadful pain, and his fine cock stands out rampantly in front, in a most outrageous state of stiffness, the head quite purple from the extraordinary pressure of blood which distends it. 'Ah! ah! oh! oh! I do beg your pardon, I'm sure you will forgive me, and let me off now,' he groans in agony.

ALICE – 'I've only a trifling thing to ask you, now you have apologised. My duty is far more painful and disagreeable to me than it can possibly be to you; bodily suffering cannot for a moment be compared to anguish of mind,' as she still cuts into his raw-looking posteriors, and looks round delightedly on the spectators for encouragement, then goes on again. 'If you're not going to build that Cathedral, will you devote a fourth part of what it would have cost to the building of a proper temple for the meetings of our Paphian Circle?'

LOTHAIR, gasping in pain – '*Oh! Oh! Yes! That I will*, £50,000, if you will let me down at once!'

There was a general clapping of hands all round, and cries of, 'Enough! Enough! He's a good boy now,' and then there was a scuffle all round to secure victims, which were mostly of the weaker sex, but Ladies Bertha and Victoria, by the aid of diplomacy, had got both their husbands prisoners on a sofa and were lashing into them most unmercifully, laughing and shrieking out, 'Keep the game alive! Keep the game alive!'

Alice had meanwhile let down poor Lothair, who was into her in a moment, to the dear girl's great delight, both of them frequently spending and screaming with ecstasy.

My partner threw me across his knee, and made my bottom smart under his loud slaps. I screamed and struggled desperately, and at last equalised matters by grasping his stiff cock, and making him feel that two could play at the game of inflicting pain. He cried a truce, and I speedily righted myself, sitting up with my bottom in his lap, and his pego right up into my vitals. He clasped his arms round me, taking one globe of my bosom in each hand, which he moulded delightfully with his fingers as I rose and fell on his tight-fitting shaft, leaning back my head so as to meet his kisses and give him my tongue. This was a delicious position, his spendings seemed to shoot with extraordinary force into my womb, and my own helped to make quite a stream of sperm, which spurted all over his thighs at each insertion, and fairly drowned the hair round the roots of his pego.

St Aldegonde and Montairy were having each other's wives for a change after their whipping, but cunt seemed decidedly at a discount with them, as each of them was indulging in a bottom-fuck, which those ladies seemed to relish immensely, and to add to the voluptuous excitement of the scene, the darling Corisande struck up 'They a' Do't' to the tune of 'A Man's a Man for a' That'.

> The grit folk an' the puir do't,
> The blyte folk and the sour do't,
> The black, the white,
> Rude an' polite,
> Baith autocrat an' boor do't.

For they a' do't – they a' do't,
The beggars an' the braw do't,
Folk that ance were, and folk that are –
The folk that come will a' do't.

The auld folk try't,
The young ane's do't,
    The blind, the lame,
    The wild, the tame,
In warm climes an' cauld do't,
    For they a' do't, &c.

The licensed by the law do't,
Forbidden folk and a' do't,
    And priest and nun
    Enjoy the fun,
    And never once say nay to't.
    For they a' do't, &c.

The goulocks an' the snails do't
The cushie doos and quails do't,
    The dogs, the cats,
    The mice, the rats,
E'en elephants an' whales do't.
    For they a' do't, & c.

The wee bit cocks an' hens do't;
The robbins an' the wrens do't,
    The grizzly bears,
    The toads an' hares,
The puddocks in the fens do't.
    For they a' do't, &c.

The boars an' kangaroos do't,
The titlins an' cuckoos do't,
    While sparrows sma',
    An' rabbits a'
In countless swarms an' crews do't,
    For they a' do't, &c.

The midges, fleas, and bees do't,
The mawkes an' mites in cheese do't,
An' cauld earthworms
Crawl up in swarms,
An' underneath the trees do't,
For they a' do't, &c.

The kings an' queens an' a' do't,
The Sultan an' Pacha do't,
An' Spanish dons – loup off their thrones,
Pu' doon their breeks, an' fa' to't.

For they a' do't, they a' do't
The grit as weel's the sma' do't,
Frae crowned king
To creeping thing,
'Tis just the same – they a' do't!

Her clear melodious voice sounding distinctly through the apartment had such a thrilling effect that we all joined in the chorus at the
end of each verse, and never before felt so excited or saw such a scene
of delicious wantonness as was displayed on every side, till at last
exhaustion compelled us reluctantly to give up the engagement, and
after a short rest we returned in the carriages to the Duke's mansion, as
if we had only had an afternoon's drive.

This was altogether a memorable day, for as soon as we got back to
Crecy House, Corisande whispered to me that as the gentlemen had all
been fairly used up, her sisters had resolved to have an evening to
ourselves whilst the gentlemen were in Parliament or at their clubs
recruiting their enervated abilities by wine, smoke and cards. We
might be sure of them till six a.m. at least, and the afternoon had left us
all in such a burning unsatisfied state that they had impressed into our
service four handsome young fellows, two footmen and two pages, who
had never yet been admitted to any freedom with their mistresses, but
Lady St Aldegonde had already sworn them to secrecy as to what they
might see in the evening, and given her instructions to have everything
prepared in her own private drawing-room, so as to be ready as soon as
the rest of the establishment had retired for the night.

It was past ten o'clock when we arrived home, but Bertha was so
clever, it was all devised and ordered in a few minutes, the footmen and
pages little suspecting the scene they were to be introduced to when

taking their oaths of secrecy. Everything promised a deliciously enjoyable affair, especially as we had to undertake to seduce them to our purposes.

In less than an hour and a half, it was all ready; the Duchess was still keeping her room, so Bertha dismissed all except John, James, Charles and Lucien (the latter a fine handsome French page) as well as two pretty lady's-maids, Fanny and Bridget. There were five of us ladies who sat down to a game of cards, for which the party was ostensibly designed, all of us very lightly attired in the most *négligé* style as if quite indifferent to any little exposures we might make of our charms.

'My luck is dead this evening,' exclaimed Lady Montairy, throwing her cards down; 'I shall be ruined if I sit here; what do you say to a dance; let's get the servants to join us for fun; come Lucien, have a waltz with me round the room, I feel so low spirited I don't care what I do to drive it away.'

'Fie, sister! how you make the boy blush, but I wouldn't mind a dance myself if it were not for the thing getting known,' replied Corisande.

'Let's have a downright spree for once; John, James, and all of you will keep it secret; I should so like to know how you enjoy yourselves downstairs,' laughed Bertha.

'Your Ladyship's slightest wish is binding upon us,' replied John, most respectfully, speaking for the others, 'and I am sure none of us would betray such a secret, when ladies condescend to a little familiar fun with their domestics.'

Bertha seated herself at the piano, and everything was cleared out of the way for a waltz. Lady Montairy led off with Lucien, I proposed to Charles, a very handsome youth of seventeen, whilst Alice and Corisande had the two good-looking footmen, John and James, for partners, Bridget and Fanny making a female couple.

What fun we had, how flushed and excited our partners looked as we clung to them in the voluptuous evolutions of this inspiring waltz, as the strains of Lady Bertha's talented execution seemed to thrill through our souls; the young fellows quite delighted us by their easy graceful motions and manners, having evidently profited by their everyday experience in seeing their superiors conduct themselves in society.

At last we stopped from sheer exhaustion, Lady Montairy giving Lucien quite an amorous kiss, as she led him to a sofa, pretending she did it to put him at his ease, and we all followed her example, my partner excitedly returning my embrace with ample interest and ardour, his hot burning lips sending a thrill of desire through my frame.

Pretending to wish to cool myself a little I walked him into the next room, which was only lighted by the brilliant moon, and we opened the window, which looked out over a lovely garden, and then sat in a rather dark recess to enjoy the slight breeze which was loaded with perfume of flowers and had a soft sensuous effect on my excited nerves. I longed to enjoy my young partner, but did not exactly like the idea of being the first of the party to break through the slight barriers that still existed in favour of decency, although I knew perfectly well it was intended to be done by Lady Bertha and her sisters; still they seemed so slow in arriving at a thorough explanation with their company that I could wait no longer. 'Charles,' I whispered, 'do you know what love is? Have you ever had a sweetheart?'

'No, my lady, I never had a chance yet, as I look at all the beautiful creatures, and think how hard it is that I dare not kiss one of them. Dear lady, did you but know the intense pleasure your lips afforded me just now you would not think that kiss was thrown away, as I expect you did it in fun,' he responded with emotion.

'Silly boy,' I laughed in a whisper, 'to think that should make you so happy; why I don't mind giving you another here in the dark, if it is such a pleasure, and costs me nothing,' kissing him again in a very amorous manner. He clasped my heaving form to his bosom, and I could feel quite a shiver of delight rush through his trembling frame.

'What makes you tremble so, Charles?' I asked in the most innocent manner, laying my hand carelessly on his thigh just where I hoped to make an important discovery. Nor was I displeased to touch the engine of love which my hand gently prodded, as if quite unconscious of anything wrong. What a start he gave as he exclaimed, 'I am so ashamed, oh lady, you have driven me mad,' then suddenly letting his rampant love dart loose, it stood throbbing and spending over my hand, whilst I seemed to be unable to realise what I was doing.

'Oh; darling! Oh, Beatrice! Forgive me! What pleasure!' he seemed to gasp out, kissing me rapturously, and taking all sorts of liberties with my bosom, which he was moulding and pressing with his hands.

'What am I doing? Pray Charles, don't be so rude,' I said hastily, dropping the hold of his affair, and pretending to want to free myself from his embrace, but the amorous lad had gone too far to release his prize, and almost quicker than I can relate it, his hands were under my skirts, forcing their way to the very shrine of love itself.

My partner was far too impetuous to heed my faint remonstrances, and in spite of all I could do to keep my thighs closed his venturesome hand soon took possession of my heated cunny. 'If I die I must have you, darling lady,' he whispered in my ear, as he suddenly forced me quite back on the sofa, and tried to raise my clothes.

'Ah! No! No! I shall faint. How your violence frightens me!' I sighed, trying to smother my desires by simulating helplessness, and then feigning unconsciousness I promised myself a rare treat by allowing him to think I really had fainted, which, no doubt, would urge him to take advantage of the moment to riot unrestrained in the enjoyment of my most secret charms.

It was almost dark in the shadowy recess where the sofa on which we were was situated. 'She's quite gone, the darling!' I heard him say to himself, as he gently parted my relaxing thighs, 'I'll kiss it first.' Then I knew he was kneeling between my legs, and I felt his fingers gently parting the lips of my cunt. 'How I must have excited her, she's been spending!' he went on, then I felt his lips right between the nymphæ as he kissed me rapturously just on the excitable little clitoris. What a thrill of desire it sent through my frame, as it made me literally quiver all over with emotion, so that I could scarcely refrain from clasping his head with my hand, or nipping his dear face between my thighs.

This only lasted a few moments, but for what seemed awfully long in my excitable state my cunt was spending and throbbing under the voluptuous titillations of his velvety tongue. Heavens how I wanted to feel his prick inside me! and could not have feigned my fainting state another instant, but the moment my lips were in the act of parting to implore him to fuck me at once he started to his feet, pushing my thighs as wide apart as possible, and directly I felt the hot head of his cock placed to the mark; slowly and gradually he pushed his way in, as contracting my usually tight affair I made it as difficult as I could for him to achieve possession. How he kissed my lips, calling me 'Darling lady, dear Beatrice, oh, you love, what pleasure you give me!'

I felt him spend a torrent of his warm essence right up to my vitals, and then lie still upon me, exhausted for the moment by the profuseness of his emission.

Still apparently in the state of inanimation, and without opening my eyes, I made my cunt nip and contract on his throbbing prick as it was soaking within me, in such a manner that he was almost immediately aroused from his delicious lethargy, and recommenced his movements, exclaiming to himself, 'What a love of a girl; even in her fainting state, the love pressure of her cunt responds to the action of my prick. What pleasure it would be if I could but arouse her to sensibility!' as he kissed me over and over again rapturously, quickening his stroke till my blood was so fired I could no longer impose upon him, but suddenly threw my arms around the dear boy's neck, whilst my amorous kisses responding to his silently assured him of the delight he was affording me.

'Here they are, the sly things, why Beatrice is the hottest of the lot, see she has got Charles well in her,' laughed Lady Bertha, bringing a light into the room, and followed by all the others, looking very excited, and as if some of them at least had been doing the same; in fact I could see the front of John's trousers were undone, whilst the flushed face of Lady Montairy, and the delighted manner in which she clung to the handsome young French page, assured me that she at least was on the best of terms with her partner, added to which, in the background, Bridget and Fanny seemed as loving as any of them from their damask cheeks and sparkling eyes.

Charles was dreadfully confused, and I felt that the surprise was taking all the vigour out of him, so with the greatest presence of mind, I threw my legs over his buttocks and embraced him more firmly than ever, as I exclaimed, 'It's this naughty fellow, my dear, who has taken such liberties with me that I fainted from fear, and now that he is in complete possession of my virginity and has aroused all my passions to the highest pitch, he wants to withdraw; slap his bottom well for me, and make him now complete my pleasure, after satisfying his own greedy lustfulness!'

He struggled hard to get away but I held him tightly, whilst all of them slapped him without mercy, making him fairly bound in the saddle to my great delight, more especially when I soon found him swelling up to quite an unnatural stiffness, till his prick was almost breaking my quim, and he was furiously fucking with all his might, as he cried out for them to leave off and let him do it properly.

The noise of the slaps on his bum seemed to give me intense delight and I never remember having had a more delicious fucking, which as he had spent twice previously lasted a long good bout, till we both came together, almost frantic with delight as our mutual essences were commingled at the same moment.

'There, don't let me catch any two of you slipping away by themselves again,' said Lady Montairy, as she gave a last tremendous slap, which fairly made the poor fellow bound under her hand, in spite of his exhaustive spend. 'It spoils half the fun, when some are so sly, and pretend to be mock-modest when at the same time they are quite or more inclined for the sport than anyone.'

We all returned to the drawing-room and refreshed ourselves with champagne, jellies and other reinvigorating delicacies, as we laughed and bantered the four young fellows and the two lady's-maids about their sweethearts and love experiences, till Bertha wrote all the names of the female members of our party on slips of paper, which she said she would hold for the boys to draw their prizes, declaring that Bridget and Fanny, if drawn, should submit to be fucked, although they protested their virginity and determination to keep it for the present, much as they enjoyed the other fun.

First of all she asked us to assist her in stripping our cavaliers quite naked, in order that we might enjoy the sight of their adolescent beauties (John, the eldest, being only nineteen). They were finely formed young fellows, but the splendid proportions of Master Charlie's penis carried off the honours of the evening, being more than eight inches long and very thick. My lady friends were in ecstasies at the sight, and almost made the other three young fellows jealous by each wishing he might draw them for a partner.

'Now there shall be no deception or cheating; I've a novel idea how the lots shall be drawn,' said Bertha, drawing up her clothes till she showed the beautiful lips of her luscious cunt, just peeping out between the slit in her drawers as her legs were wide apart; then drawing me close to her side she gave me the slips of paper and whispered in my ear to arrange them in her cunt with the seven ends just sticking out. It was soon done, then our gentlemen had to kneel down in front and each draw his paper with his mouth.

This was a jolly bit of fun. Bertha looked as if she would have liked to be fucked by all four instead of merely having them draw lots from her gap, which was so tickled as they drew out the papers that she actually spent under the novel excitement.

John drew Bridget; James, Lady Montairy; Charles, Bertha, whilst I was lucky enough to get the handsome Lucien, who had been eyeing me with a most amorous leer, which you may be sure did not in the least offend me.

Corisande and Fanny were told to fit themselves with a couple of most artistically moulded india-rubber dildoes of a very natural size and not too large, which Lady St Aldegonde said her husband had procured for the purpose of having his lady bottom-fuck himself occasionally, when he wanted extra stimulation. 'And now my dear, they will be very useful in enabling you to give these nice youths the double pleasure as they enjoy their partners.'

The ladies were now also divested of everything, till the complete party were in a state of buff, excepting the pretty boots and stockings, which I always think look far sweeter than naked legs and feet.

The interest centred in the engagement between Bertha and Charles, as the others were all anxious to see the working of his fine prick in her splendid cunt. He was in a very rampant state of anticipation, so she laid him at full length on his back on a soft springy couch and, stretching across his legs, she first bent down her head to kiss and lubricate the fine prick with her mouth, then placed herself right over him and gradually sheathed his grand instrument within her longing cunt, pressing down upon him, with her lips glued to his, as she seemed to enjoy the sense of possessing it all. I motioned to her bottom with my finger, and Fanny, understanding my ideas, at once mounted up behind her mistress and brought the head of her well-cold-creamed dildo to the charge against her brown-wrinkled bottom-hole, at the same time clasping her hands round Bertha, one hand feeling Charlie's fine prick, whilst the fingers of her other were tickling the fine clitoris of our mistress of the ceremonies. It was a delightful tableau, and it awfully excited us all when they at once plunged into a course of most delicious fucking. Fanny was as excited as either of them as she vigorously dildoed her mistress, and kept her hands stimulating them in front. Corisande now attacked Fanny behind with her dildo, delighting her with frigging combined.

How they screamed with delight, and spent over and over again, it is impossible to describe, but I had got Lucien's fine prick in my hand as we were kissing and indulging in every possible caress. It throbbed in my grasp as I repeatedly drew back the foreskin, till at length fearing he would spend over my hand, I sank back on a sofa, and drew him upon me, guiding his affair to my longing cunt, whilst he clasped me round the body and kissed more ardently than ever. I could see all that was going on round the room, Lady Bertha still riding furiously on Charles, stimulated by the double exertions of Fanny and Corisande, and watched with delight the frenzied enjoyment of the lady's-maid, as she handled and felt how Charles was going on in front, whilst her young mistress's dildo almost drove her to distraction by its exciting movements in her bottom. Lady Montairy was riding James as he sat on a chair, but John was being quite baffled by his partner Bridget, who wriggled and avoided every attempt of his cock to get into her, as she kissed and allowed him any liberty except the last favour of love.

At last we all finished. 'Now,' said Lady Bertha, 'we will rest and refresh ourselves a little, and then we will see to Bridget and Fanny having their maidenheads properly taken; meanwhile I will tell you a little adventure I once had down at Brentham a few months after my marriage. Well, you must know St Aldegonde wanted to represent the county in Parliament, and a general election was expected very soon, indeed it was rumoured the dissolution would occur almost immediately, so no time was to be lost, and there was one great landowner, who if we could but secure him to our side we were sure of carrying the day. He had been an old admirer of mine, and had been much chagrined at my lordship's success in obtaining my hand, and we both knew he was almost certain to throw all his influence into the opposite scale. We were just going to bed one night, and about to fall asleep after a beautiful fuck (it is nice when first married) when a sudden idea made me quite laugh, it seemed so good.

'St Aldegonde was quite anxious to know what I had been thinking of. "My love," I said, kissing him (I don't often do that now, except when I want to wheedle him out of something), "would you mind giving a bit of my cunt to secure your return for the county?" "Why, Bertha darling, just at this moment nothing would make me jealous, as you've sucked the last drop of spend from my cock," he said, with a yawn, and then realising my idea, he continued, "Do you mean Mr Stiffington, my love; it's a bright idea, if you do, and damned cheap way of buying him, besides cunt could never be reckoned bribery."

'The prospect of adventure, added to the good I might do for my husband, made me volunteer to do it, and as secrecy was everything, we determined that I should go down to Brentham disguised as a servant.

'Next day we started apparently to go to Paris, but I left St Aldegonde at the railway station, and started off to Brentham by myself after changing my dress at a hotel. The housekeeper at Brentham was the only person whom I took into my confidence, but of course she did not know all.

'She passed me off as a niece from town, who had a holiday for a few days, and I mixed with the servants as one of themselves; the idea that I could be Lady Bertha never entered their heads, as I was supposed to be gone abroad for a tour.

'Without delay she got the coachmen to drive me over to Mr Stiffington's place, Manly Hall, with a note to that gentleman on some special business, which I must deliver with my own hands.

'The gentleman was at home, and I was soon ushered into the library, where he was attending to his letters or other business, after breakfast, about 11 o'clock in the morning.

' "Well, young woman, let me have the particular letter you brought from Brentham; why couldn't a groom have done as messenger? By Jove! you're a nice looking girl though!" he said suddenly, seeming to notice my appearance.

' "If you please, sir," I said, blushing, "I'm Lady Bertha's maid, and bring a very important note from Lord St Aldegonde."

'He was a fine handsome fellow of about thirty-five, full of life and vigour in every limb; his eyes looked me through and through, then suddenly penetrated my disguise, as he exclaimed, "Ah, no, you're Lady Bertha herself, what is the cause of this mystery?"

'I was all confusion, but he told me to sit down and tell him without reserve what I wanted, as he drew me to a sofa and seated himself by my side.

' "Your vote and interest to secure my husband's return for the county,' I said in a low voice, "we know you can turn the scale, so I ventured to solicit your influence in person."

' "But how can you expect me to be otherwise than hostile to a man who deprived me of your beautiful self," he replied. "Why did you jilt me for a lordling?'

'I looked down in pretended distress, as I answered with an almost inaudible voice, "If you only knew our family necessities, it would soothe your wounded self-respect; it was the prospect of his dukedom which sealed my fate against my own feeble will, and now it is my duty to further his interests in every way."

' "Dear Bertha,' he exclaimed excitedly, "do I really hear right, would you have preferred me, can you not pity my unrequited love, won't you even favour me with a smile as I look in your face?" taking my hand and covering it with impassioned kisses. "I would support your husband, but – but I must be bribed – let me think what you shall give me, dearest; of course he's had your first virginity, but I must have the second, it will cost him nothing, and no one need know."

'He was growing quite impetuous; with one arm around my waist, whilst he covered my blushing face with the most ardent kisses, I could feel his other hand wandering over my bosom and my thighs, as he felt them through my dress, then taking one of my hands he forced me to feel his standing cock which he had let out of his breeches, the mere touch of which sent a thrill of desire through my whole frame as I sank backwards in an assumed faint.

'He jumped up, fastened the door, then went to a drawer, from which he took a small book and a little box; then kneeling down by my side he gently raised my clothes, kissing my legs all the way up, inside or outside of my drawers as he could get at them, and parting my thighs opened the slit in my drawers, till he had a fair view of my pussy. "What a sweet little slit, what soft silky down it is ornamented with," I could hear him say as he pressed his lips to my mons Veneris, then I could feel his fingers parting the lips of my cunt with the greatest tenderness to enable him to kiss the little button of love. This was too much, I pressed his head down with my hands, as I spent over his tongue with a deep drawn sign of pleasure. "She's mine, how she likes it, the touches of my tongue have made her come!"

' "Look, darling," he continued, as he rose to his feet, "I thought a few delicate kisses would revive you if properly bestowed in the most sensitive place, but I don't mean to have you there; this book will show you the most delightful avenue of bliss, and open up to your ravished senses heavenly bliss you have hither had no conception of."

'Keeping my clothes up, and making me retain hold of his priapus in one hand, he showed me a series of splendid little drawings in the book, all illustrating the way to enjoy bottom-fucking. He could see I was tremendously excited, so lost no time in placing me on my hands and knees on the sofa, then anointing my tight little bum-hole with some ointment from the box, and putting some also on the shaft of his prick, he made me push my bottom well out behind, with my legs wide apart so as to give him every facility, but "Ah! Ah! No, no, I can't bear it!" I exclaimed, the tears fairly starting to my eyes as I felt the first advance of his lovely engine, forcing its way through the tightened orifice; the pain was like a number of needles pricking the part all at once. I can describe the sensation as the sphincter muscle gradually relaxed in no other way. He frigged me deliciously in front all the while, pushing so firmly and getting in in such a gentle manner behind that I seemed to love him more and more every moment, and longed for him to accomplish his task and complete my enjoyment, as the very pain seemed a percursor to some extraordinary bliss; nor was I disappointed; the pain was soon succeeded by the most delicious sensations as his movements stirred me up to the highest pitch of excitement, and he never withdrew till we had spent thrice in rapturous ecstasies, screaming with delight and almost losing our lives from excess of enjoyment.

'Thus my mission was successful, and his lordship became a Member of Parliament.'

This tale had worked us all up, so that we were mutually groping each other's privates, and as soon as Bertha had finished we seized Fanny and Bridget; but too much of the same thing being rather tedious to read, I will only say that John and Charles took their virginities in splendid style when the girls really found no more nonsense would be tolerated.

This was my last adventure in town, and in the next part I shall go on to relate what happened after my marriage with Lord Crim-Con, which took place shortly afterwards.

Part Five

I now come to a most important epoch of my life, which at once sealed my matrimonial fate.

We were to leave town the next day, and were taking a morning walk in Kensington Gardens with Lady St Jerome, when who should suddenly meet Her Ladyship, and demand an introduction to her charming young friends (meaning myself and Alice), but a tall hand-some-looking old fellow of thirty, with the most wicked pair of dark eyes I had ever seen.

Lady St Jerome appeared to have a most sinister smile upon her face as turning to us she said, 'My dears, allow me to present you to the Earl of Crim-Con, the most gallant gentleman of the day, but be careful how you accept his attentions.' Then seeing a rather savage look cross his countenance – 'Pardon me, my lord, if in introducing you to Lady Beatrice Pokingham and Miss Alice Marchmont, I caution them to beware of such a dangerous lover; they are under my protection at the moment, and I should fail in my duty if I did not.'

The angry flush was but momentary, being instantly replaced by a most agreeable smile, as he replied, 'Thanks, thanks, my dear cousin, but your piety always makes you so hard on my little foibles. Will nothing ever make you believe I have honourable intentions; you know how often I have asked you to try and find me a nice little darling wifey-pifey, who would lead me with her little finger, and keep me out of mischief.'

'You might have found a good wife long ago, you miserable hypocrite,' retorted Her Ladyship; 'you know that a certain place is said to be paved with good intentions, and that is where all yours will go to, my lord, I fear; but I only caution my young innocent friends here.'

'Ah, hem, I think I know that warm place you allude to, just between the thighs, is it not, my lady?'

Lady St Jerome blushed up to her eyes as she exclaimed, in an apparently angry tone, 'Now, this is really unbearable, that Your Lordship should at once commence with your obscene innuendoes; my dears, I am so ashamed of having introduced you to such a horrible specimen of modern society.'

'A truce, I will really be on my best behaviour, and try not to offend the most delicate ideas again,' he said with great seeming earnestness, 'but really cousin, I do want to be married and kept out of harm. Now I suppose these two young ladies are eligible parties, do you think either of them would have a worn-out *roué* like me?'

'Really, my Lord, you are incorrigible to go on so and talk like that before two young ladies at once,' expostulated our cicerone.

'Ha, you don't believe me, cousin, but, by God, I am not jesting; you shall see presently, just wait a moment,' he said, then taking out his pocket-book, he pencilled something on two slips of paper which he held in his hand, with the ends slightly projecting. 'Now, cousin, just draw one and see which it is to be.'

'Only for the fun of the thing, to see what you mean'; then she pulled one of the slips from his hand, exclaiming with a laugh as she looked at it, 'Beatrice, you are to be Lady Crim-Con if you will take such a scapegrace for better or worse.'

His Lordship – 'I really mean it, if you will have me, dear lady; may I call you Beatrice? What a happy name, especially if you would make me happy.'

It is impossible to write how I felt at that moment; I knew that he was rich, with a great title – and despite his bad reputation, that was a most tempting bait to a comparatively portionless girl.

Somehow he took my arm, and Lady St Jerome, with Alice, walking in front, seemed to go any way but direct home, in order to give His Lordship every facility to urge upon me his sudden courtship. I can't tell you how it happened, but before we reached the house, I had promised to have him, and in less than a month we were married.

I need not trouble about the wedding ceremony, but at once give some account of the first night I had with my spouse. When I first mentioned him, I spoke of an old man of thirty; that is exactly what he was, and although still a handsome fellow, one would have guessed him to be fifty at least.

His youthful vigour had been expended long ago, by constant and enervating debauchery, and now instead of being able to enter the lists of love in a genuine manner, he had a perfect plethora of disgusting leches, which he required to be enacted before he could experience sensual excitement.

Our first night was passed at the Lord Warden Hotel, Dover, as we were on our way for a continental tour.

During our short courtship I had never allowed him the slightest liberty, as my common sense told me that such a man would discard the most beautiful girl if he could but take advantage of her before marriage.

Well, then, the ceremony at St George's, Hanover Square, where the nuptial knot was tied, was scarcely over, and we had just taken our seats in the carriage to return to Lady St Jerome's house, from which I was married, when he gave me a rude kiss, and thrusting his hands up my clothes, seized upon my cunt in a very rough manner, as he laughingly told me not to pretend to be prudish, as he knew I was a little whore, and had had Lothair and lots of other fellows, in fact that was the reason he had married me, and meant I should be a damned little bitch to him, and do everything he required, which a virtuous girl might object to. 'Besides,' he added, 'I always looked out for an orphan who had no blasted parents to complain to. There, don't cry like a fool,' as he saw the tears of mortification run down my crimson face, 'you have only to pander to my curious tastes a bit, and we shall be happy enough.'

I felt his advice the best I could take at the moment; his evident knowledge of my intrigues gave him such an advantage that I dried up my tears and resolved to make the best of a bad bargain, and I returned his kiss as lovingly as possible, and begged him 'not to be a bad boy before other people', and he would find me everything he could wish.

I must have been very nearly screwed that night before I retired to bed to await His Lordship's coming. I got in between the sheets perfectly naked in accordance with his orders, and commenced frigging myself at once, inflamed by the many bumpers of champagne he had made me drink in his company to various obscene toasts which he constantly proposed, such as, 'A stiff prick for a randy cunt,' 'Here's to a girl who would rather be buggered, than not fucked at all,' and one in particular, which awfully excited my ideas, viz.: 'Here's to the girl who likes to frig herself before you till she spends, then suck your prick to a stand, and prefers to have you in her tight wrinkled bum-hole rather than anywhere else.'

Presently he entered the room, with a hiccup; as he pulled the bed-clothes off me, he exclaimed, 'You're a damned pretty little bitch, Beatrice, and being nearly drunk, my dear, you see my cock happens to stand for once; we will make the best of it. I had the whites of a dozen raw eggs in some milk this morning, and just now a cup of chocolate with half a dozen drops of the tincture of cantharides to make me randy for once.'

His coat, trousers and everything were thrown off in a trice, till he was as naked as myself, whilst his eyes had an almost demoniac kind of glare, so unnaturally brilliant did they look just then.

Springing on the bed, 'Ha,' he exclaimed in a husky voice, 'my little beauty has been frigging herself and spending. Suck my prick or I'll kill you, you little bitch!' he said savagely, as he reversed himself over me, and plunged his head between my thighs, where he at once commenced to suck my quim most deliciously, whilst I nested his rather long prick (it was not very thick), between my bubbies, pressing them together with my hands so as to make him fuck me there, whilst I was so excited that I readily kissed and took his balls in my mouth.

He was so furious in his gamahuching that he continually made me feel his teeth quite sharply, as he bit the clitoris and nymphæ, growling out, 'Spend, spend, why don't you come, you little bitch?' getting more outrageous and cruel every moment, till his bites made me shriek with agony as I writhed about, and deluged his mouth with quite a profusion of my creamy emission.

'A devilish good spend that,' he murmured between my thighs, 'but I have made your poor cunny bleed a little!' as he seemed to enjoy licking up the sanguineous mixture.

'Now suck my prick,' he said with renewed fierceness, turning round and presenting it full in my face. 'You're a cheating little bitch, and I mean to have you dog fashion.'

I took that long prick in my hands, frigging the shaft as hard as I could, whilst I just titillated the ruby head with my tongue till I felt it was tremendously distended and as hard as iron.

'Jump up quick, on your hands and knees, you little whore,' as he gave me a couple of tremendously smarting smacks on my buttocks, loud enough to have been heard a long way off – only our bedroom was at the end of a corridor, the whole of the rooms in that part of the hotel having been taken *en suite* for us.

Turning up my rump as desired, I thought it was only a fancy of his for entering my cunt that way, but he suddenly spit on the head of his long stiff affair, and presented it to my astonished bum-hole, as he exclaimed with a chuckle of delight, 'I'm going to fancy you're a boy, and take the only maidenhead you have left, your cunt will do another time, but it must be a virginity on a wedding night!'

'Ah, no, no, no, you shan't do that to me!' I cried out in fright.

'Nonsense, you little randy bitch, shove your arse out, and let me get in, or I'll pay you back dreadfully, and pitch you out of the window into the sea, and say you committed suicide through over-excitement!'

My fright increased, I was really afraid he would murder me, so I resigned myself to my fate, and clenched my teeth as I felt the head of his prick like a hundred little pins forcing its way within my tightly contracted vent hole. At last he got in, then withdrawing his hands from my mount where he had been tearing and pulling the hair to increase my pain, he placed both arms round my neck, and beginning slowly, fucked my bottom most voluptuously, till with a scream of delight I spent again in perfect ecstasy as I felt the delicious warmth of his spendings shooting up my fundament.

Being so over-excited by the means he had taken to prepare himself for our *noces*, he retained his stiffness, and never gave up possession of my bottom till we had come together a third time.

As soon as he withdrew his long limp cock, now reeking with a mixture of spendings and soil, he at once secured me to the bedposts with some silken cords before I could get away, or was well aware of his purpose.

'Now, my pretty boy, I have got you nicely, and will whip another cockstand out of you as soon as I have sponged off all the effects of our late *enculade*,' he said, bringing some cold water and a sponge in a basin; he laved and cooled my heated parts, till I began to feel quite grateful to him. At last he sponged himself, and wiping himself and me with a fine soft towel, proceeded to select his instruments of flagellation from a long leather case, which I had supposed only held a gun.

He showed them to me delightedly, then selecting a fine switch of horse hair mounted on a cane handle, he began to whip me with it between my thighs, and on the lips of my cunt in a most exciting manner, till I was so carried away with emotion that I begged he would fuck me properly to allay the longing irritation of my burning cunt.

'My prick isn't stiff enough yet, but I'll suck your spendings for you, my beautiful randy little tit,' he cried out, falling on his knees and twisting my body round so that he could get at my cunt. How delightful the thrusts of his tongue were to me in my excited state. I wriggled about in ecstasy, and getting one foot on his prick gently rolled it on his thigh under my sole, till I felt it was getting enormously stiff again, and at the same moment almost fainted away from excess of emotion, as I delighted my lecherous husband by another copious spend.

I thought he was going to fuck me properly now, his engine was so rampant, but instead of that he turned my back to him once more, and selecting a fine light birch rod, made of three or four twigs only, elegantly tied up with blue and crimson velvet ribbons, he commenced to flagellate my tender bottom. How his light switch seemed to cut and weal the flesh at every stroke! It was in vain that I cried for mercy as the tears of real agony rolled down my cheeks; he only seemed the more delighted, and jeered at me upon the effects of every cut, telling me first how rosy my bottom looked, then, 'now you bitch, it's getting fine, and red, and raw, it's bleeding deliciously!' till at last the rod was used up, the splinters lying all about the floor and bed; then throwing it aside he again assaulted my poor bottom-hole, apparently more and more delighted as he gave me pain, forcing his entrance as roughly as possible; however, when he was fairly in I soon forgot everything under the influence of his ecstatic moves, till I could remember no more, and suppose I fainted; he must have released my bonds and allowed me to sink on the bed, for when I awoke the sun was streaming in at the window, and His Lordship was snoring by my side.

His treatment on my wedding night was comparatively mild to what he afterwards made me go through, but his penchant for getting pleasure out of me soon seemed to wear off – although now and then he would fit me with a dildo and make me bugger him behind, whilst I frigged him with my hands in front till he spent.

Another of his amusements, and one which seemed to afford him particular delight, was to show me all his collection of bawdy books, drawings and photographs, till he could see I was awfully excited, and then he would jeer at me about being married to a used-up old fellow like himself, didn't I wish I could have Lothair now, &c.

One day having amused himself this way with me for some time he made me lie down on a sofa, and tying a bandage over my eyes, fastened my hands and feet so that I could not move, then throwing my clothes all up he tickled and frigged me with his fingers till I was quite beside myself with unsatisfied desire and begged him to fuck me, or at least to fetch his dildo and give me some kind of satisfaction.

'It really is a damned shame to tease you so, my little whore,' he laughed, 'so I will get the dildo out of my cabinet in the next room.'

He was scarcely gone many seconds before he returned, and I felt his fingers opening the lips of my cunt, as I thought to insert the dildo, but instead of that it was his prick, and throwing his arms around me he seemed to be more vigorous than usual, his cock swelling and filling my longing gap in a manner I had never felt it before. I spent in an ecstasy of bliss, as I murmured my thanks in endearing terms for the pleasure he had afforded me by such a delicious proof of his manliness.

Presently a strange hand seemed to be feeling his prick and thrusting a pair of fingers into my cunt alongside of his still vigorous engine.

'Ah! Oh! I Oh!! Who is that?' I screamed from under my skirts, which were thrown over my face.

'Ha! ha!! ha!! She pretends to think I've been fucking her when she must have known it was James all the time!' I heard him laugh, as at the same moment all the obstructions were removed from my face so that I could really see it was the young butler on the top of me, with his prick still in full possession, and just beginning to run a second course.

'Kiss her, put your tongue in her mouth, my boy! Fuck! Fuck away! or it will be the worse for your arse!' exclaimed His Lordship, who was handling his balls with one hand, and slapping his rump furiously with the other. 'See how she pretends to be ashamed; it's quite delightful, Lady Beatrice, to see you can still blush.'

I screamed and protested against the outrage, but James's delicious motions soon made me forget everything, and recalled to my mind the orgy we had with the servants at Crecy House, and in imagination I was again in the arms of the wondrously developed Charlie.

We spent a second time, but he kept his place and continued the love combat with unabated vigour, and His Lordship seeing that I was quite carried away by my feelings, and responding to his man's attack with all my naturally voluptuous ardour, released both my hands and feet so that I might thoroughly enjoy myself.

'Hold tight James,' he cried out, 'she's so high spirited, you'll get unseated, but the little devil needn't think she's to have this treat all to herself!'

Saying which he mounted on the sofa behind the young butler, and I could see his long prick was now as stiff as possible, and he seemed to have a rather easy task in getting into his man's bottom, no doubt having often been there before; but wanting some extra excitement on this occasion, he had sacrificed me to his catamite, in order to bring himself to the necessary pitch by seeing all our lascivious movements.

You may be sure that after this James and I were upon the best of terms, His Lordship introducing him to our bedroom at night, and joining us in every kind of wantonness; he even once contrived to get his long thin prick into my cunt alongside of James's as I was riding a St George; it gave me the most intense pleasure, and immensely delighted them both by the novel sensation, and by the idea of having achieved an apparent impossibility.

After this Crim-Con seemed to get quite blasé and indifferent to everything we did, and even insisted on sleeping by himself in another room, leaving us to ourselves. However, both myself and paramour were not so blind as to believe he was quite used up, but consulting together we came to the conclusion that His Lordship had fallen in love with my young page, a youth of fifteen, who had only recently entered my service, and slept in a small room at the end of a long corridor in which both our bedrooms were situate.

He always locked himself in when going to bed, as he said, for fear I would not let him alone, so to determine the mystery one night we floured the whole length of the corridor, and in the morning were rewarded by seeing the marks of His Lordship's footsteps, both going and returning from the page's room.

We did not want to spoil his fun, only to enjoy the sight of it, and reap a little extra excitement if possible from the scene, so next day we examined the ground, and found that a small room next to that occupied by the page exactly suited our purpose, being furnished as an extra bedroom for visitors; we had only to make some good peepholes to enable us to sit or kneel on the bed and see everything.

After retiring to bed at night (James and myself had been in the drawing-room all evening going through the most exciting and lascivious ideas, to amuse His Lordship, who contented himself by leisurely watching our love gambols, smoking his cigar, and evidently keeping himself in reserve for something by and by), instead of settling ourselves between the sheets we adjourned to the spare room, next to that in which Reuben, the page, slept.

We were too soon for His Lordship as, on applying our eyes to the peepholes, we found the boy's room was yet in the most profound darkness; so as the night was warm, and there was no necessity for covering, we reclined upon the bed to await the coming of Crim-Con; meanwhile we amused ourselves by kissing and toying with each other's parts, till my handsome butler, notwithstanding the previous hard work of the evening, was in a most rampant, impatient state, and would fain have cooled his ardour within my longing cunt but that would have spoilt all, as our transport would have been certain to be overheard by the page, and thus prevent all our anticipated sight-seeing.

Just as I was whispering to him to keep quiet, we heard a match struck in the next room, and applying ourselves to the holes, were much astonished to find Reuben was not alone, there was the butler's assistant, a rather tall fair youth of sixteen, with whom we had never reckoned in our calculations; he had always such a cold, reserved respectful manner, even to James, that we never for a moment gave him a thought as likely to be mixed up with a Lordship's amusements.

Reuben lighted a couple of the candles, then turning to his companion, who was lying on the bed frigging slowly his standing prick, as if keeping it in a state ready for use, said, 'Will, it's time His Lordship was here now, what a good job I broke away from you just now, or you would have spent and spoilt all; he likes to see us looking ready and randy, but if he thinks we have been fucking or frigging by ourselves he would damn us, and bolt off in a rage.'

Reuben and Will were both quite naked, and there was a great contrast between the youths, for while the latter was rather slim, tall and fair, the former was a regular Adonis in figure, beautifully plump, with a rosy face, dark hair and dark fiery impetuous eyes; his prick was also in a fine state of erection, and neither of them had more than a suspicion of downy hair around the root of their pricks.

'What a fine fellow you look Rube, no wonder His Lordship seduced you; besides, you are a dear unselfish chap for introducing me into the fun, won't I fuck you gloriously when he is here to see us. I love you warmer, hotter than ever I could the prettiest girl in the world! And then, too, think of how well it pays!'

Here the two boys lay down on the bed fondling each other's pricks and kissing mouth to mouth, sucking tongues, and twining about in the most amorous manner, till I fully expected every moment to see them spend, but they stopped suddenly, a step was heard outside, the door creaked on its hinges, and His Lordship appeared with a large table lamp in his hand.

'Hold, hold hard, you randy rascals!' he exclaimed, 'I believe you've been and had your fun already. If you have, you buggers – ' he hissed between his teeth, in a frightfully suggestive manner, which seemed almost to terrify the boys, who paled slightly for a moment, and then both of their faces flushed crimson.

Rube was the first to answer. 'Oh no, my lord, we have been too careful only Will was just telling me his love, and how gloriously you should see him fuck me.'

'Bravo! So he shall, my dear, and I will suck your darling pego, and find out if you have been deceiving me.'

He placed his lamp on a small table at the foot of the bed, so that the room was now excellently well lighted, then seating himself on the bed he opened his dressing-gown, showing his long limp prick; then he took the pair of them on his lap and they sat on his naked thighs whilst he kissed them, thrusting his tongue into their mouths, or handled and compared their two charming pricks.

This was only a little preliminary toying; presently, asking Rube if the cold cream was under the pillow, he threw aside his only vestige of a garment, and stretched himself on his back on the bed.

'Now my plump little beauty,' he said, addressing the page, 'kneel over my breast, and give me your prick to suck, and now Will, mount behind him, and I will put your tool to his arsehole.'

James's assistant was too ready to need a repetition of the welcome order, he was there in a moment, his hard cock quite eight inches long, battering against the tight dark wrinkled nether hole of his love.

His Lordship was so eager for work that he scarcely had taken Rube's seven inches between his lips before his fingers were busy with the lubricant on Will's prick and the page's bottom, directing the former's delighted tool so cleverly to the mark that almost immediately he completed his insertion up to the roots of the hair, and was revelling in the delicious sensations and pressures to which his love treated him.

His Lordship sucked excitedly at the morsel in his mouth, and we could just hear him mumbling out, in a half-choked voice, 'Beautiful! Fuck! Go on quick. Spend, spend! Ah – r – r –,' as we could see Rube's dark eyes full of fire, and his prick stiffen and shoot its juice into Crim-Con's mouth, till the drops of thick creamy spend fairly oozed from his lips as he still sucked and smacked them with great gusto; besides, we could see his own prick rising into quite a manly state.

Will fucked into his love's bottom with fury, and seemed to spend almost at the same time, and so exhaustively that he must have fallen backwards had he not clung round Rube's neck.

We were not idle whilst this exciting scene was enacted under our eyes. James instinctively wetted the head of his prick and my bum-hole with spittle, and soon drove his great machine through the narrowest gate of Paradise. Its movements were indeed heavenly, blissful. I never before felt such an acme of pleasure, the sight before me, the soul stirring movements behind, and our mutual emissions almost made me groan in an agony of delight.

A perfect frenzy of lust seemed to take possession of my body, I could see His Lordship's prick was now finely erect, and the two boys were alternately kissing and sucking him.

Whispering my paramour to follow me, I quickly rushed from our concealment into the room where they were. As the door was not locked and before they could recover from their surprise, I threw myself on my back on His Lordship's belly, almost taking the breath out of him by my sudden weight on his stomach and regardless of his 'Damned Hellish Bitch' and other exclamations of displeasure. I fixed his stiff prick in my bottom-hole in triumph, nipping and squeezing, and wriggling my bum about on him as James with his tool in an awfully excited and distended state took possession of my hot raging cunt.

The boys seemed quite to understand my ideas, as they each of them knelt and presented their pricks for me to fondle, whilst Crim-Con, still cursing and swearing at me for a 'Damned Hellish Bitch, &c.', groaned under our weight, but I could feel he was thoroughly enjoying it, as his prick stiffened more and more every moment, under the delightful movements and pressures to which I treated him; besides, the membrane between his prick and James's was so slight that it was almost like two cocks rubbing together in my cunt.

I frigged the boys till their eyes almost started from their heads from excess of emotion and they spent over the firm round globes of my bosom, but I still kept them stiff, alternately kissing the head of one or the other prick whilst Crim-Con's hands tickled their balls, and frigged their arseholes till we made them nearly mad.

I had never felt my husband's long thin prick so well before, and James's affair was so distended by the excess of lustful excitement that I was gorged to repletion, and yet felt that I wanted more, more, more! Had I been cunt all over I should have wanted every hole well filled by a good stiff one. What a delicious moment. Ah! ah! if I could but die like that! I seemed transported to another world, my senses were leaving me, I was indeed in Paradise!

I remember no more of this extraordinary scene, but James told me next day they were frightened as I went off into such a deathlike faint they had to carry me to my room and use restoratives till I gradually breathed a little and sank into a restless kind of sleep, that I had bitten both the boys' pricks till they were sore and bleeding. 'As for His Lordship,' he added, 'I am afraid he is as good as dead, he was so exhausted Dr Spendlove had to be fetched, and he fears the worst.'

This was too true. His Lordship only lived forty-eight hours, whilst I have never been well since. The extraordinary excess of lubricity that night seemed to have quite undermined my constitution, and I have gradually declined from that time. I was advised to be very careful how I indulged in venereal pleasures in future, but in spite of my weak, nervous, excitable nature, I have found it impossible to quite abandon those pleasures which seem to me to give the only real foretaste of the future Paradise; regardless of declining strength, whenever the opportunity offered I have indulged in the delights of love myself, or in seeing others do it.

The executors settled everything whilst the incoming earl, to show his appreciation of their services in furthering his interest, made most lavish provision for James and the two youths, as he afterwards told me that he considered they helped him to the title and estates a good five or ten years before he could reasonably expect to have come into them.

'And do you not think, my lord,' I asked him when he told me this, 'that I also deserve your thanks, where is your gratitude to little Beatrice?'

He looked at me in a curious kind of way. He was a handsome young fellow of eight and twenty, but married to death by a fair fat wife, who besides having a fortune of her own had already blessed him with nine children, and a prospect of blessing him with many more.

'I can't make you out, Robert,' I went on to say, 'you're so different from your poor brother, and so content with the same thing every day; every look, every smile you have is for that splendid wife of yours. He was for flirting with and having every pretty woman he came across; what sort of a heart can you have, you have never seemed to pity me for my loss?'

He was so handsome, and I so disliked the new Lady Crim-Con, that I resolved to seduce him, and gratify both pique and passion at the same time.

'What are you driving at, Beatrice dear, I'm sure you puzzle me?'

'Ah! you know how delicate and how lonely I am, and never even to give a brotherly kiss of sympathy . . . I know Her Ladyship hates me, but I shall be gone to Hastings in a few days,' I said, bursting out into sobs as if my heart would break, the tears from my downcast eyes dropping upon one of his hands which he had placed in a deprecating kind of way on my lap as he sat by my side.

He kissed me tenderly on the forehead, more like a father, as he said, 'I'm sure I only wish I knew how to cheer you up, my dear.'

'My dear,' that sounded quite a little affectionate and as if the ice was breaking, so throwing my arms round his neck, I kissed him passionately in return for his fatherly salute, sobbing out in a low broken voice, 'Oh, Robert, you do not know what it is to be left dull, miserable, and all alone in the cold, cold world, can you not spare me a little, only a little of those loving smiles your wife must be quite surfeited with?'

He gave a soft sigh, and I felt an arm steal round my waist, as he very tenderly drew me close to him, and did not seem at all loath to receive my kisses, which were getting yet more impassioned.

'If you do give me a kiss, what will Her Ladyship lose?' I whispered.

A perceptible tremulousness seemed to vibrate through his form as our lips at last met in a long, loving kiss. It was quite plain I had at last excited his amorous sensuality, which had previously been so dormant in his respectable married bosom.

'Now, I love you Robert, dear, and you needn't mention such an indifferent thing to Lady Cecilia,' I whispered, when at last our lips parted.

'A slice from a cut loaf is never missed, you know Beatrice,' he said, as he smilingly held me at arm's length, and gazed into my blushing face, and continued, 'besides, I can easily make it up to her, so she will lose nothing.'

'Your loaf is pretty well sliced dear,' I replied, 'considering how many children you have to eat bread and butter, Robert.'

Again he drew me to him, and we exchanged the most lascivious kisses as I sat on his lap. This billing and cooing was so effective that I very soon felt his prick stiffening quite perceptibly under my bottom. His face flushed, and an extraordinary fire beamed in his usually quiet eyes; we understood each other at once. Without a word he inclined my unresisting form backwards on the couch, and as I closed my eyes, I felt him raising my clothes, his hands stole up my thighs till he gained the seat of joy. My legs mechanically opened to give him every facility, in a moment he took advantage of my tacit invitation, and I felt the nose of a fine battering ram at the entrance of my widowed cunt.

The desire for a really good fuck had been consuming me for some days, and I could not resist the impulse, however immodest it might seem to him, of putting my hand upon his glorious engine of love, and directing it into love's harbour myself. It was in, I was gorged to repletion, spending, sighing with delight, almost before he could make a move.

Opening my eyes, I could see he was delighted at my ecstasy. 'Ah, you darling man, my darling Robert, you don't know what it is for a young widow to be deprived of the natural solace of her sex. Now, push on my boy, and let us be thoroughly happy, let us mix our very souls in love's emission, and then tell me if you can spare one a few crumbs of your cut loaf now and then.'

A very few thrusts brought down my love juice again, and I also felt him shoot a tremendously warm flood of his essence into my longing cunt. Our lips were joined in fierce loving, tongue-sucking kisses, whilst I threw my legs over his buttocks, and heaved up my bottom to meet his manly action with the most libidinous abandon.

Her Ladyship was out with the carriage, and we were quite safe for a couple of hours at least; still, considering his family duties, I made him keep a shot or two in reserve for the night, as he contented himself by kneeling down and worshipping at the shrine of love, where he had just been paying his tribute to Venus, exclaiming in ecstasy, as he examined or kissed the various charms, 'What a love of a cunt! How small and tight! What a charming *chevelure*, &c.!'

A day or two after this, to our mutual delight, Lady Cecilia was summoned into the country, to attend on her mother's sick bed.

My room was next to theirs, so at night it was a very simple thing for him to slip into bed with me. I found he knew very little about ornamental fucking, himself and wife having strictly adhered to the plain family style, which had produced such fruitful results. My ridicule of his ignorance made him quite ashamed of his want of knowledge, especially when I introduced him to the delights of bum-fucking, and he faithfully promised me that when Her Ladyship returned, he would insist upon his marital rights over every part of her person, and so steer clear of babies in future, and that if I only made a good peephole I might see all his fun with Lady Cecilia.

Delighted with my conquest, I determined to persuade him to degrade his wife in every possible way, that I might enjoy the sight of it. So I initiated him into every possible style of enjoyment, till I had the satisfaction of knowing that the hitherto respectable husband was completely changed into a lustful libertine.

The Earl was as good as his promise. 'My Robert,' as I called him in our loving intercourse, was so well schooled that he was quite equal to the assertion of all his rights as a husband by the time Lady Cecilia returned home.

After dinner, on the evening of her arrival from the country, he found me sitting alone in the conservatory, and sitting down by my side, whispered in my ear how delighted he was at being able to have a last word of advice with me before retiring to rest with his, no doubt, rather expectant spouse

'You have so drained me, last night and early this morning, dear Beatrice,' he said, putting his arm round my waist, and meeting my ready lips in a long breathless kiss. 'Nothing but some extraordinary excitement will enable me to do justice to her expectations. I must fuck her at least three or four times after such a long absence; how shall I be equal to the occasion?'

'Have me first,' I replied, 'whilst she is seeing the children put to bed, there is plenty of time; it will give you zest for the fun to come, the idea of taking the virginity of her maiden bottom-hole will excite you enough, and the more she resists and gets indignant, the more you will enjoy it.'

I had been gently stroking his prick outside his trousers; my touch was magical, it stiffened immediately, and when I let the impatient prisoner out of his confinement, I thought I had never before seen his priapus so distended and inflamed with lust as at that moment.

Rising up, I first stooped to give the engine of love a warm kiss, and then, keeping it in my hand, raised my clothes and, turning my bottom to his belly, spitted myself on the loving object, opening my legs and straddling over his lap so as to get the very last fraction of its length into my heated cunt. We sat still for a moment or two, enjoying the mutual sensations of repletion and possession so delightful to each of the participators in a loving fuck, before commencing those soul-stirring movements which gradually work our heated desires to that state of frenzied madness which can only be allayed by the divinely beneficent ecstasy of spending and mingling the very essences of our nature.

The idea that I was robbing his hated wife of her just expectations added such piquancy to our loving conjunction that I literally moaned or whined with delight, as I twisted my head round in the act of emission, so as not to lose the luscious kiss which is such an extra pleasure in those supreme moments of our happiness.

He did not come at the same time, but stopped and rested a moment or two, then rising, and keeping me still impaled on his dear prick, without losing place even for a single second, he laid my body face downwards on a little table which stood handy, and then recommenced his delicious moves, with his hands under me in front, frigging and tickling my cunt, till I almost wrenched myself away from him by the violence of my convulsive contortions. Suddenly drawing quite out, with another plunge he drove the head of his tool into the smaller orifice, which is so delightfully near and convenient when in the position in which he had me.

'Ah! Oh – oh – oh – oh – o – o – o – oe!!' I screamed, swimming in lubricity as I felt him so gorging my bottom, whilst his busy fingers were adding to my erotic madness by the artistic way in which they groped within my spending cunt. 'Oh, heavens, Robert, Robert! Do, do come darling! There, ah – re, I feel it, how deliciously warm!' I murmured excitedly, as his flood of boiling seed inundated the gratified and sensitive sheath which enclosed him so tightly.

After recovering from our transports, we conversed about how he should proceed with his wife, his prick all the while as stiff as a policeman's truncheon, till at last fearing Lady Cecilia might surprise us, I went into the drawing-room and played the piano whilst he smoked his cigarette amongst the flowers in the conservatory outside the window.

Her Ladyship pretending fatigue (we knew what she was in a hurry for), the family retired rather earlier than usual to rest, but I took care to be at my peephole before Cecilia and Robert entered their bedroom.

As it was a habit of his to go over the lower part of the house, and see everything safe for himself before going to bed, his lady came first and at once commenced to undress.

She was about the same age as her husband, a vastly fine, fair woman, rather above the medium height, light auburn hair, slightly golden in tint, deep blue eyes, set off by dark eyebrows and long dark lashes, a full mouth, richly pouting cherry lips, and a brilliant set of pearly teeth; then as she gradually unrobed herself, her various and luscious charms quite fired my lascivious blood, as one by one they stood revealed to my earnest gaze. What magnificent swelling breasts still round and firm, and then as she lifted her chemise over her head, and exposed the lovely whiteness of her belly (still without a wrinkle, as she had easy confinements and never suckled her children, for fear of spoiling her figure), set off below by a bushy mons Veneris, covered with light curly silken red hair, through which I could just perceive the outline of her slit.

Now she stood before a cheval glass, surveying herself at full length, I could see a blush cross her beautiful face, as she seemed almost ashamed to look at her own nakedness. Then a self-satisfied smile parted those cherry lips and displayed the sparkling pearls of teeth, as she patted the shiny marble skin of her belly and bottom (evidently thinking of the effect of the sight upon Robert when he should enter the room), then she playfully parted the lips of her cunt and examined it closely in the glass. The titillation of her fingers brought another blush, and she seemed as if she could not resist the temptation to frig herself a little, moving a couple of digits in a restless kind of way backwards and forwards between the vermilion lips of love.

My blood was on fire, and much as I hated her, I would have liked to gamahuche her there and then. But suddenly the door opened, and Robert stood transfixed, as he exclaimed in surprise, 'Surely, Cecilia, you have lost all modesty; why have you never exposed yourself to me like that before?'

'Oh, Robert dear, how you startle me, you came up so soon and I was only just looking at the love I know you are longing to caress as soon as the light is out.'

'I really did not know you were such a charming figure, Cecilia, but now you are naked I will feast on the sight, and we won't put out the lights, my dear. I must now examine in detail every charm. By the way, I may tell you that during your absence I found some bad books of my late brother's and they so fired my imagination by the extraordinary descriptions of various modes of sexual enjoyments that I quite blushed to think of our innocent ignorance, and long to try some of them with you.'

He had almost torn his clothes off whilst speaking, and I could see his prick as rampant as possible, in fact I believe it had never lost its stiffness since our excitable bout a short time before.

He threw himself into her arms and they hugged and kissed whilst she, taking hold of his pego, slowly backed towards the bed as she tried to bring its head to the mark.

'Not there, Cecilia, love, you have another maidenhead I mean to take tonight; our plain silly way of doing it only leads to getting a lot of children, and surely my quiver is full enough of them. I'll have no more, it's positive ruination, however rich a father may be. No, no, the French style in future, do you understand, I mean to get into your bottom,' he said, as seriously as possible, yet with evident excitement.

'What a nasty idea! You shall never do that, Robert, to me!' she exclaimed, crimsoning with shame to the roots of her hair.

'But I must and will, Cecilia. Look at this book, here are all the different ways of "doing it". Why they suck each other, fuck – ah – you start at the vulgar word – but it's fuck – fuck – fuck – that's the name for it. They fuck in bottoms, under armpits, between the bubbies – another nasty name for titties – anywhere – everywhere – it's all the same to a man, all is what they call C U N T, a word I am sure you have seen somewhere in your lifetime written on shutters, doors, or even on the pavement – a deliciously vulgar word, Cecilia, but the universal toast of men when they meet in company.' I could see he was trying to make her look at a little French book, called *La Science Pratique*, with its forty pretty little plates. 'How my blood has been fired by fancying all these delightful ideas to be enjoyed when you came home.'

'Why, Robert, you are mad, I'll burn that horrible book, I won't learn their filthy ways!' snatching at the book.

'You're my wife, every bit of your body is mine to do as I please with it; don't drive me to extremities, Cecilia, or I may be rough, for I'm determined to put my prick in your arse, now at once!' trying to turn her over.

'Robert, Robert, for shame, Beatrice will hear your disgusting language. You shall never abuse me that way!' hiding her face in her hands and beginning to sob.

'But I will, and you may blubber like a child. Your tears only urge me on, if you resist I'll smack and beat you, till you are obedient!'

She struggled, but a woman's strength is soon exhausted, and at last he got her face down on the bed, with her bottom on the edge and her feet on the floor, then giving her a tremendously painful smack on her bum, he spread her legs wide apart, opened the cheeks of that glorious bottom, anointed the head of his bursting prick with spittle, also the tight-looking brown hole he was about to attack, and then pushed on to the assault of the virgin fortress.

I could hear her moan with pain as the head gradually forced its way within the sphincter muscle. 'Ah – it's pricking – oh, oh – you'll rend me, Robert – oh, pray – Ah – r – r – re. – Oh! Oh!'

At last he was in, and rested a moment or two, then slowly began his fucking motions.

Presently I could tell by the wriggling of her bottom that she enjoyed it. His hands were busy frigging her cunt in front. How excited they got, each seeming to spend at the same moment, but he kept his place, and the second finish was so excitable that they screamed quite loudly in the frenzy of emission, whilst Cecilia actually fainted away with Robert fallen exhausted on her senseless body.

Presently he recovered sufficiently to be able to apply restoratives to his fainting wife, and as soon as he had brought her round, so that she could understand what he said, proceeded to tell her 'that in future they would enjoy all the novel ideas he had found in that nice French book, no more big bellies for you Cecilia, or the anxiety of children for either of us. You must now suck my prick, till it is stiff enough again,' he said, presenting it to her mouth.

'No, no, I never can do such a dirty trick; besides, it's doubly disgusting, you have not even washed since you outraged my bottom,' she sobbed, as her eyes filled with tears, seeing no signs of compassion in his face.

'What's that to me, you've got to suck it, so go on, my dear, without all those wry faces, which only add to my fun, it's rare sport to make you submit to my fancies. I find I've been a fool ever since I was married, not to have asserted my right to do as I please with every bit of your person, cunt, arse, mouth, or bubbies; they can all afford me intense pleasure, without getting in the family way. Now go on, and I will fuck you with a fine large dildo. Mind you must swallow every drop of my spendings when it comes.'

He forced his prick between her reluctant lips, all slimy and soiled as it was from the previous *enculade*, then producing an enormous dildo, nearly twelve inches long, and big in proportion, he put a little cold cream on it, and presented the head to her notch, trying to force it in.

'Ah! No! no!! that's so awfully large!' she almost screamed, but the head was partly in, and despite her sobs, and moans of pains, he soon succeeded in passing at least ten inches of it into her distended vagina.

Her cunt was exposed towards me, so that I could see how gorged it was with that big india-rubber tool, and the sight of her slit so stretched to its utmost capacity caused quite a thrill of desire to shoot through my veins, it was almost impossible for me to prevent myself making some kind of demonstration. How I longed to be with them and join in the orgy of lust. Each shove of that tremendous affair now seemed to afford her the most intense delight. She sucked his prick in a kind of delirium, her highly wrought feelings banishing every sense of delicacy, shame, or disgust that might have previously deterred her from doing so. I frigged myself furiously, they screamed and spent, till at last both spectatrix and actors were thoroughly exhausted.

When I awoke next morning, and applied my eye to the peephole, it was just in time to see Her Ladyship awake. First she felt her cunt to see if it was all right, and not ruined by the giant dildo she had taken in the previous night. Her eyes sparkled with desire, and she repeatedly blushed as I suppose the recollection flashed through her mind. Presently throwing the sheet entirely off her husband's body, she handled his limp affair for a few moments, then putting her face down, took the head of his prick in between her lovely lips, and sucked away with evident relish, till she had him in a glorious state of fitness, and was about to treat herself to a proper St George, when Robert, who had only been feigning sleep to see what his randy wife would do, suddenly woke up, and insisted upon her applying it to her arsehole instead of her cunt, wetting it with spittle.

Slowly but surely she achieved its insertion, although to judge by her face it was evidently a painful operation. But when once in how they enjoyed that glorious bottom-fuck. Even after he had spent she rode on till he met her again, and both seemed to come at the same time, kissing each other in a frenzy of erotic madness.

My peephole afforded me the sight of many more luscious scenes between Lady Cecilia and her husband before I left town to take up my residence at Hastings for the benefit of my health.

My agent had secured and furnished for me a pretty little detached residence of thirteen or fourteen rooms, surrounded by gardens and orchards, so as to be delightfully free from the prying curiosity of my neighbours.

The household consisted of a cook and housekeeper, both young persons, not exceeding twenty-four or -five years of age, the latter being the daughter of a decayed merchant, a most pleasant and intelligent companion, but up to the time I engaged her, strictly prudish, virtuous.

Being naturally fond of young boys and girls, we had also two very pretty page-boys of about the age of fifteen or sixteen and two beautiful young girls about the same age, instead of housemaid and lady's-maid.

At first I felt considerably enervated by the little excesses I had been a party to, or witnessed, whilst staying with the new Earl, but the soft bracing air of the southern coast soon made me feel more like myself again, and long to indulge in the delicious dalliances of love, to which my warm temperament made me always so inclined.

The result was that I determined to seduce every member of my virgin household, each one of whom I believed to be thoroughly virtuous up to their entering my service.

The two youngest girls, as my special attendants, slept in the next room to mine, and had a door of communication by which the two rooms entered into the other without the necessity of going into the corridor.

I had quite a passion come over me to gamahuche these two pretty young things, and make them thoroughly subservient to my purposes.

You may be sure I was not long in putting my plans in operation as soon as I had sketched them all out in my brain. That very same evening, after my two pretty demoiselles had put the finishing touches to my toilet and left me sitting in my *chemise de nuit*, in front of a cosy fire with my feet resting on the fender, as I pretended to be reading a thrilling romance:

'Leave that door open, my dears,' I said, as they respectfully bid me good-night. 'I feel so dull perhaps I shall call for you to keep me company, if I feel that I cannot go to sleep.'

In a few minutes I heard them tittering and laughing.

'Now, girls,' I cried, 'come here this moment. I want to know what you are having such fun about. Come just as you are, no putting anything more on or waiting to hide your blushes. Annie! Patty! Do you hear?'

Afraid of making me angry, the two girls came blushing into my room just as they were, in their nightgowns.

'Well now, what is it that is amusing you so?'

'Please, my lady, it was Patty,' said Annie with a wicked look at her companion.

'Ah, no, you fibber! My lady, it was Annie began it,' retorted the other, looking quite abashed.

Nothing could be got out of them, each saying it was the other.

At last I said: 'I can guess pretty well what you two girls were amusing yourselves about; now tell me truly, were you looking at each other's privates in the glass?'

This question hit the mark, and seeing how shamefaced and blushing they both were, I went on: 'No doubt, examining to see which one showed most signs of hair on her little pussy. Let me see Annie,' as I suddenly caught the bottom of her nightdress and in an instant had it reversed over her head, so as to cover up her face and expose all the rest of her beautiful little figure. 'Why, the impudent little thing hasn't a hair to boast of! Give her bottom a good slapping, Patty!'

Patty was only too pleased to do it, and the slaps fairly echoed through the room, mingling with Annie's piteous cries to let her go.

My blood was up. The sight of her beautiful bum, all flushed and rosy under the sharply administered slaps, made me fairly lust to take further liberties. So I let the little victim go, whispering in her ear, and her tearful eyes were brightened in a moment. She darted at Patty and sooner than it takes to write was dragging her about the room fully exposed, with her head and arms secured in her reversed nightdress.

I amused myself by slapping poor Patty's pretty posteriors till they were almost black and blue, regardless of her sobbing and crying for mercy.

At last we let her go, and I took her on my lap to kiss away her tears. She soon smiled again and nestled herself to my body quite lovingly. This seemed to make her companion almost jealous as she appealed to me with a flushed face to kiss her also, which I readily did in the most loving manner, and I asked her to fetch a decanter of wine and some glasses from a cabinet, saying I felt so dull and sleepless I must have something to cheer me.

'Ah, my dear lady,' exclaimed Patty, kissing me again and again, 'you don't know how we all love you and feel for you, being left alone and unhappy. There is nothing we wouldn't do to bring a smile to your pale face.'

'Then we'll sleep together and have a romp on the bed. Only mind, you are good girls, and never tell your mistress's doings,' I replied, taking a glass of wine, and ordering them to do the same.

A second and a third glass seemed to open their eyes immensely; the least touch or joke sent them into fits of laughter. They blushed and seemed quite excited. In fact Patty, who had remained on my knee, was almost ready to faint with emotion as she caressed my face and bosom, the cause being a hand I had managed to slip under her nightdress, so that one finger had been tickling and playing with her almost hairless slit and gradually working her up to a state of excitement she was at a loss to comprehend.

'Let us all be naked. Throw off every rag, my dear ones, I want to feel your soft warm flesh next to mine, to cuddle you and feel you all over. Shall I read a pretty little piece of poetry about a potter who married your namesake, Patty?' I said, and seeing they were ready for anything, told Annie to bring me a manuscript called *The Haunted House* from a drawer in the cabinet.

'Now listen to "The Tale of a Potter" and don't laugh till it is finished. You will find it rather free but nothing more than big girls like you ought to know.' Then I commenced:

> Young Hodge, he was a worthy wise,
>   A potter he by trade;
> He fell in love with Martha Price,
>   She was a parson's maid.
>
> This Hodge worked amongst his pans,
>   His pots, his mugs, his delf;
> He said: 'A sad fate is a man's
>   When he is by himself.
>
> Now soon I'll marry Martha Price,
>   A nice snug home I've got;
> The parson soon the knot shall splice,
>   And we'll both piss in one pot.'
>
> Then Hodge he made a pretty pot,
>   And took it to his love;
> Said he: 'I've brought this pot to show,
>   I mean your love to prove.
>
> Now name the day, the happy day,
>   Whose night shall bring me bliss;
> When your sweet cunt and my stiff prick
>   Shall mingle in this their piss.'
>
> They married were within a week,
>   And Hodge he was in luck
> He took sweet Patty's maidenhead
>   With his first vigorous fuck.

Then in her arms he fell asleep,
    But started with affright;
And in the middle of the bed
    He sat up bold and white.

'Oh, love! oh, love! I've had a dream,
    A dream to cause me fright;
I dreamed we both were in my shop
    And there I hugged you tight.

I dreamed I went your cheek to kiss,
    We romped with hugs and squeezes;
When down I knocked the pots and pans
    And broke them all in pieces.'

Then Martha answered with a laugh:
    'No pots you've broke, good man;
But much I fear this very night,
    You've cracked a Patty Pan.'

And from that night unto this day
    Hodge in that crack would pop,
A prick as thick as any brick,
    But the crack he cannot stop.

So maids beware, heed well your pans.
    With this my tale is ended;
If your pan's cracked by prick of man,
    It never can be mended.

Throwing down the manuscript, I had a finger in each of their cracks sooner than it takes to write. 'What darling little pans each of you has! I long to throw you on the bed and kiss them. What do you think of mine with its soft curly hair? Only it's a broken pan, you know, my dears, as I've of course had my husband.'

'La, and was that really so nice, dear lady? Oh, I love you so, do let me look,' exclaimed Patty, slipping off my knee and kneeling between my legs to get a better sight of the object of her curiosity, which she first kissed most lovingly, and then, parting the hair, put a couple of fingers right up my cunt. This so tickled and delighted me that I leant back in the chair and pulled Annie close to my bosom as I hugged and kissed her, whilst I still had a finger in her little slit, as far as it would go. My legs also mechanically opened to facilitate inspection, as Patty exclaimed, 'How deep my two fingers can go right up and it is so warm and moist. It makes me feel I could eat it!'

In a few minutes we were all tossing on my bed in a state of nature. They laughed, screamed and blushed as I excitedly examined and kissed their respective cunnies. How my tongue revelled around their budding clitorises till they rewarded me with those first virgin emissions which are always so deliciously thick and creamy. How lovingly they both repaid all my caresses, Patty paying the most ardent attentions to my cunt, which delighted her more and more every moment, whilst Annie seemed to prefer sucking my bubbies as I gamahuched her.

'What a treat it would be to see you both lose your maidenheads at once,' I exclaimed.

'Ah! couldn't the pages do it for us, dear lady? I do love that Charlie so!' appealed Patty without consideration in her excitement.

'I'll try and manage it; but we must be careful not to let them into our secrets before I can find out how they are disposed,' I replied.

'Oh, I know Charlie is a rude, bold little fellow, wicked enough for anything if he had the chance. What do you think, I once actually caught him handling his affair in the pantry when he thought no one was looking and when I happened to enter suddenly; it was sticking out straight and red-looking at the top. His face was quite red and he seemed rather short of breath; but the impudent fellow, like the daredevil he is, shook it fairly in my face as he asked me to give him a kiss, saying: "What do you think of this, Patty? That's how it gets, when" – oh, mistress I can't tell you all he said.'

But I pressed her and at last she told me: 'It was when we had been waiting on you, mistress. "Oh, Patty," he said, "isn't she lovely, such mouth and teeth and loving eyes, I feel as if I could jump at her, I do!" '

'Very well, Master Charlie,' I laughed, 'perhaps I shouldn't so much mind if you did, when we are alone someday I will give him the chance and let you two dears know all about it. But I will first read you another song from *The Haunted House* and tomorrow I will give you a copy, and I expect both to be able to sing it soon.'

Live and Learn

Tune: 'Drops of Brandy'

When I was little, and good,
  A long time ago 'm afraid, miss;
A stiff prick was not understood,
  I was a quiet little, shy little maid, miss.

I knew but one use for my cunt,
  I knew not what joy 'twould afford me,
The sight of a cock would affront,
  And talk about fucking have bored me.

But now, oh, much wiser I've grown!
  I'll stretch my legs open for any,
My modest shy feelings have flown,
  And fucks, why, I can't get too many!

I like a stiff prick up my arse,
  Though too much of that makes you bandy.
When I look at my quim in the glass,
  It always pouts red and looks randy.

I like a fuck – morn, noon, and night,
  On every weekday and Sunday:
If I'm fucked on the Sabbath, all right!
  But I want to be buggered on Monday.

Oh! Let it be hot or be cold,
  I'm always alive for a cock, miss;
Men, fair, dark, young or old,
  Here's a hole that'll take in their jock, miss!

I can spend for an hour at a time,
  My cunt is as hot as fire, sir,
The man that says: 'Fucking is crime,'
  I say to his face, he's a liar, sir.

Then give me a prick in each hand,
   Turn my arse north, my cunt to the south;
And get all your jocks well to stand,
   One in each hole and one in my mouth;

I'll fuck and I'll suck and I'll frig,
   Until you're all quite bloody well spent, sir!
Then I'll take in the lodgers again,
   And never once ask them for rent, sir!

Hurrah! for my cunt, my best friend,
   Hurrah! for a cock to kiss, sir,
I'll fuck till this life comes to end,
   I hope too, there's fucking in bliss, sir!'

When we awoke in the morning it was too late for a repetition of our
tribadism, so I made them get up quickly and bring in breakfast,
promising to look after Master Charlie during the day.

❧❦❧

Part Six

After luncheon I ordered Charles to take several shawls and a floor-stool into the summer-house of the garden, as I wished to take a nap, and was sure the open air was more conducive to refreshing sleep than the close atmosphere of a room on a warm sunny day.

Annie and Patty exchanged significant glances as I gave the order, but my uplifted finger stopped any further manifestation of intelligence.

We had a fine large garden at the back of the house, in some parts beautifully shaded by umbrageous elms of a venerable age, especially on the banks of a small circular pond about twenty yards in diameter, where, facing the south, the summer-house stood under the trees by the side of the small lakelet.

I followed Charles as he carried out my orders, and arriving at our destination, ordered him to spread the shawls over a sofa which stood there, for fear the leather might be damp. Then he fetched a pillow, and placed the foot-stool at my feet.

I had nothing on but a loose morning-wrapper, with my chemise and drawers underneath.

'How very oppressive it is,' I exclaimed, as I languidly sank back on the couch as soon as he had prepared it, allowing as I did so, a most negligent exposure of my neck and a slight glimpse of the orbs of love beneath.

'Ah! Oh, oh! My goodness; the dreadful cramp!' I almost screamed, as bending down in great apparent pain, I pulled up the robe to rub the calf of my right leg. 'Ah, oh! what torture!'

Charles was on his knees at my feet in a moment.

'Oh, my lady, is it so very bad? Let me bend up your toes!'

'No, no, not there, rub the calf, as hard as you can, Charles, there's a good boy!' I replied, my face wincing under the pain. 'Higher, rub along my leg, the foot's no use!'

Somehow the toe of my bad foot touched his trousers just outside the most interesting part of his anatomy; the slipper had fallen off and I could feel his prick quickly harden and throb under my toes, whilst his face flushed all over, and I thought quite a perceptible tremor passed through his frame, as he went on rubbing my leg below the knee, and I need not say how my own lustful temperament was affected by the contact.

My robe had opened down the front so that he had a full view of legs, drawers and bosom, perhaps the wrinkle of love itself.

My blood was in a boil and I could no longer resist the impulse to enjoy such a beautiful Adonis.

'Get up, Charles, it's better now,' I said in a low voice, 'and pray don't tell what you've seen by accident. That cramp threw me into such an awful agony I did not know how I tossed about!'

'Dear lady, your secrets are always safe with me,' he replied, looking down bashfully as he rose to his feet. 'I could kiss the ground under your feet to prove my devotion!'

'No, you are such a kind boy that just for this once, Charles, only this once, mind, I will give you a kiss myself instead. Come closer to me! What a fine boy you are. Now don't be bashful, really I mean to kiss you, if you promise never to tell.'

'Ah, madame, how kind of a great lady to a poor page-boy like me! I shall never forget such a favour and would die for you any time!' he said with bashful excitement.

'Come then,' and I took his handsome face between my hands and kissed him repeatedly. 'Why don't you kiss me, Charles?'

'Oh, lady, may I take that liberty?' he asked, his warm lips almost sucking the breath from me, so earnest was his kissing.

'Yes, yes,' I murmured, 'you may kiss me now, dear boy! And would you be faithful, Charles, if I trusted my life, my honour to your keeping?'

'Those kisses have made me your slave forever, dear lady. Nothing could ever wring a secret of yours from me.'

'Then, Charles, I will tell you I'm in love with your figure! I know you must be a perfect Cupid, and should like you to strip quite naked, that I may enjoy the sight of a living statue. Will you do so, no one will ever know?' I asked.

His face was crimson and I could see that he actually trembled under my gaze. 'Now Charles, make haste, and if you do that for me I'll give you a sovereign and a new suit of clothes.'

Slipping off his jacket I began to unbutton his trousers. Turning them down, my eager hands wandered under his shirt, feeling the firmness of the ivorylike flesh of his deliciously rounded buttocks whilst my eyes did not fail to detect how his linen stood out in front and was saturated with his spendings.

He seemed to understand me now and almost quicker than I can write it, he was naked as Adam in Paradise.

My roving hands took possession of his beautiful little prick, quite six inches long, and ornamented round the tight-looking balls by just a shade of curly brown hair.

'What's this, Charles, are you often wet like this?' as I called his attention to the glistening sperm on my fingers. 'What a big fellow this is, quite enough for a man. Did you ever make love with a girl?'

'No, my lady, but I wanted to try it with Patty, only she never would.'

'Then you shall with me, Charles, now. And I'll try to get Patty for you afterwards, I should so like to see you two together,' I said, drawing his prick to my lips and sucking it deliciously for a moment or two till I felt he was getting near a second spend.

'Now, sir, kneel down and kiss me,' I said, letting him go as I reclined on the sofa and opened my legs whilst his hands opened the slit in my drawers and exposed the lips of my cunt to view. His mouth was glued to it in a moment, and ah! oh! how his lascivious tongue made me spend in a second or two whilst my unslippered foot was rolling his prick on his thigh. But I was afraid of losing the next emission of his love juice, so I gently drew him over my body and directed his dart of love into my cunt.

He was hardly up to his business, but the instinct of nature seemed to prompt him to shove in.

What ecstasy as I felt the slow insertion of his virgin prick! How it seemed to swell inside the luscious sheath which received it lovingly.

At first we lay motionless, billing and cooing with our lips, till I began a slight motion with my buttocks, to which he was not slow to respond.

How I enjoyed that boy! The knowledge that I had a really virgin prick within me added such a piquancy to my enjoyment that I fairly screamed from excess of emotion as I spent and felt his balsam of life shoot into my longing womb.

He had to fuck me three times before I would let him dress and go about his business. He had been with me over two hours, but the time was well spent in making love and worming out of him all about himself and the other page who slept with him, Sam, who although good-looking had so much Indian blood in him that his complexion was almost black.

In answer to my questions Charlie informed me that they often played with each other, and rubbed their cocks together till the thick white stuff squirted out, and he added: 'Dear lady, would you believe it, his affair is two inches longer than mine; besides, it is the blackest part about him!'

'Do you think he would like a game with us?' I asked.

'Oh, certainly. He is just the fellow! It was he who taught me all I know, and I must tell you what he told me, that his last master, Colonel Culo, who had brought him over from Calcutta, had him sleep in his cabin all the way home and seduced him by handling and sucking his prick, which was so nice that at last Sam let the Colonel fuck him in the bottom-hole. The Colonel wasn't very big, you know, and easily got into him by using a little pomade. Then, when Sam left him because the Colonel was afraid he might get about his daughters if he kept him in his service, he was presented with a present of fifty pounds. He often wants me to let him get into my bottom as he said it felt very nice, but I never would go further than playing with cocks.'

'Well then, this very night, about an hour after all the rest are in bed, bring him with you to the girls' door. You will find it ajar and mind only to come in your shirts and be sure not to disturb the cook and housekeeper.'

With these orders I kissed and let him go, then went in to dress for dinner.

Just before we went to bed I treated Cookie and the housekeeper to a good glass of port in which I put a rather stiff narcotic to make them sleep well so that in case our revels with the two pages should prove noisy they would be too sound asleep to hear anything of it.

Patty and Annie were all nervous excitement and expectation after I told them of my arrangement. We were all naked and they hot as possible, and could not resist pressing their naked bodies against me, while with tears and blushes they expressed their fears of the pain of losing their troublesome virginities.

At last I heard a slight noise in their bedroom which so startled them that they flew to go and hide themselves underneath the bed, whilst I opened the door and entering their room, which was in darkness, found my two young men in the dark hesitating to tap at the door.

'Slip off your shirts and slippers,' I whispered in a low voice. 'Feel, I am quite naked myself, all is to be free between us now,' as my hands groped for their pricks. I found them to be as stiff as possible, and could not resist pressing their naked bodies against my own belly, where the contact of their throbbing pricks had such an effect on me that selecting Sam by the size of his affair, I backed towards the girls' bed and drew him upon me. What a luscious bit it was! So large that my cunt was fairly gorged with the delicious morsel, which spent almost before it was well into me. My arms held him firmly round the waist as my body rested against the edge of the bed so that without withdrawing he had to go on with the delicious fuck, and I begged Charlie to put his prick into Sam's behind, to make him do his work well with me. The latter was nothing loath, and although the want of lubricant was rather an obstacle, Charlie soon succeeded in spite of his wincing and flinching a little.

The effect was to give my cavalier quite double energy. My hands passed behind him and played with Charlie's prick and appendages as he fucked Sam's bottom delightedly.

This was another virgin prick I was enjoying. Fancy taking the maidenheads of two handsome youths in one day. It fired me with the most lustful sensations! How my cunt throbbed on his glorious black prick. How we spent in torrents of that elixir of love which makes us die in ecstasy at each fresh emission. What heavenly joys to spend together, as we did, three times without withdrawing. I knew such excesses were only tending to shorten my life, but reason is powerless to resist the attraction of such Cytherian joys.

At last it was finished and we entered my room where the lights of a dozen candles showed everything to the best advantage. The figures of the two youths reflected in the looking-glasses round the room seemed to fill my apartment with lusty young fellows, half dark and half fair, all with limp and glistening pricks, just as they had withdrawn from the combat of love.

'Listen, my dears, cannot you hear the heavy breathing of the two girls under my bed? I'll wager they've been frigging each other whilst we had that glorious fuck in the other room!' I exclaimed. 'But let us first refresh our affairs with a cold douche and have a glass of champagne! Then see if we won't drag them out in the light, my boys!'

We laved ourselves, and a couple of glasses apiece immensely revived our flagging energies. I had a nice little dog-whip with a long lash on it. So telling the boys to lift up the curtains of the bed, I slashed under on the surprised and timid beauties so effectually that I had only time to give about half a dozen cuts before they sprang from their concealment and ran screaming round the room as I followed and plied my whip smartly over their tender bottoms. The sight of the thin weals which every cut drew on their tender skin, the shrieks of pain and the blushing effects on both faces and bums, so excited us that the boys' pricks stood again immediately and I longed to see the two pages ravish them as roughly as possible. Yes, I confess, that at that moment I felt awfully cruel and should have liked to see them suffer the most dreadful agonies under their defloration.

I know that with many men their delight is intensified if they can only inflict pain on the victims they ravish, but for a woman to gloat over such a sight is almost incomprehensible. Yet it is so, I was literally mad with lust for blood and torture!

At last I made them kneel down and kiss the boys' pricks as they begged of them to take their maidenheads.

Charlie had Patty and Sam had Annie. I ordered them to lay the girls on the soft Turkey carpet in the middle of the room with pillows under their buttocks. Then my two young champions, kneeling between their legs, opened the lips of the girls' spending cunts and proceeded to insert the heads of their pegos within the vermilion clefts of the victims.

It was a most delightful sight for me as I witnessed the blushes and enjoyed every painful contortion of their faces as the pricks were ruthlessly shoved into them under the influence of my whip, which I used without pity to push the boys on to victory. At last it was done and I could see that the boys had spent into them and I was sorry it was so soon over.

The tears of the girls were changed to loving smiles as by my directions they all had another wash. Then we sat down to jellies and wine, indulging in all manner of freedoms and jokes, till my young men began to feel their feet again and I could see that both of them were enjoying and eyeing me most amorously.

My blood was up and nothing would do but I must enjoy them both at once with the girls joining in the best way they could.

Sam and Charles sat on either side of me, and I could feel both pricks ready for action. So I made the former sit on the edge of the bed and take me on his lap, and as soon as I felt properly seated on the fine black prick, I called Charlie to shove his cock into me from behind, along with Sam's. This was not quite so easy to do, as Sam quite filled my sheath. Yet I was determined to have it so, and with the assistance of the girls, Charles succeeded in accomplishing my erotic fancy. Then by my orders, Annie and Patty tickled my clitoris and the lips of my distended cunt, as well as the cocks and balls of my two lovers.

Description fails me in endeavouring to picture the excessive voluptuousness of this conjunction, *trio in uno*. My profuse spendings so lubricated their pricks that they were soon quite comfortably rubbing together up and down, up and down inside my delighted cunt, and then: 'Ah! Oh! Oh! I spend! I die in ecstasy! Where am I? Ah! heavens! Oh! God, what bliss!' That is how I screamed out and then almost fainted from excess of emotion, only to awaken directly to find them also in the frenzy of their emission.

The excitement was so great that my champions retained their stiffness and kept their place whilst the girls, not to be outdone, jumped up on the bed, and Patty, turning her bottom to my face, buried Sam's face between her thighs as she pressed her cunt to his mouth for a gamahuche, with Annie straddling and lying over her to present her cunt and bottom to my lascivious tongue, which did not fail to seize the opportunity to revel both in her cunt and little wrinkled pink bum-hole.

This went on until sheer exhaustion compelled us to separate, and how I hugged and kissed them all, when at last I let them retire to their respective rooms.

Next day I was very ill and the day after that a medical man had to be called in, Patty going by my express desire to a doctor with very limited practice who I thought would not be exhausted by his lady patients.

As soon as he arrived my servants all retired and left us alone.

'My dear lady,' said Dr Loveshaft, 'what has brought you to this state of unnaturally prostrating excitement? Tell me all. Don't keep anything back if you wish me to do you any good.'

'Oh, doctor,' I replied in a whisper, 'pray, put out the light, the fire is quite enough to see by, and put your ear close to my lips. I can only whisper my confession, and don't want you to see my blushes.'

This was done and his face was close to mine when I threw my arms nervously round his neck and drew his face to my feverish lips and kissed him wantonly, saying:

'I want love; there's no one to love me. Oh! Oh! Fuck me first and physic me afterwards. I know you must be a gallant man, and mine's a real case of nymphomania!'

Whilst one hand still held him in a most amorous embrace, the other wandered to his prick, which my impassioned appeal had brought to a sense of its duty in a moment. What a fine fellow he was too, both long and thick, as opening his trousers without resistance he let me take it.

'Throw off your clothes, there's a love of a man, and let me have this first, and the medicine afterwards,' I exclaimed, thrusting my tongue into his mouth.

He was a most amiable doctor and it was nearly an hour before the consultation was over.

I rapidly declined after this and in spite of the doctor's unremitting attentions, both to my health as well as my cunt, I grew worse and worse and had to be sent to Madeira for the winter. So I shall conclude my long tale with my adventure on shipboard on the voyage out.

My housekeeper, whom I shall call Miss Prude, went with me as companion. We had arranged to have a fine large state-cabin in the stern of the steamer, with sleeping beds, or more strictly speaking, berths for four, as I engaged Patty and Annie to accompany us as servants. At any rate, Miss Prude thought so, but I had a deep design to seduce that virtuous young lady in spite of herself. So, by a little bribery, Annie was induced to stay behind and let my dear Charlie take her place in female attire.

As you journey to Southampton at night, we embarked at a very early hour before daylight, my companion being with me in a first-class carriage whilst the servants travelled in another part of the train and looked after the shipment of our luggage. Miss Prude never for a moment suspected the change while she and I retired to our berths as soon as we got on board, leaving everything to the girls.

For the first two days sea-sickness quite prostrated us all, especially my companion, but on the third day she was quite lively and the supposed Annie kept as much as possible out of sight till we all retired to rest. The servants had got into their berths and appeared to be asleep. Miss Prude and myself were both undressed and sitting side by side on the ottoman. I asked her to put out the lamp and as she did so I put my arm around her waist and drew her gently down by my side.

'Isn't it lovely now we've got over the sickness? What a beautiful sensation the motion of the vessel gives. Oh, if you were but a nice young man now, my dear!' I said kissing her most amorously and thrusting my tongue into her mouth whilst one of my hands wandered under her nightdress and invaded all those delicious hairy parts, so sacred to virginity.

'Oh, for shame, my lady! How can you be so rude?' she exclaimed in a loud whisper.

Still I found she did not repulse me and from the heaving of her bosom she was evidently in considerable confusion.

'What is your Christian name, darling? Miss Prude is so cold,' I asked, between my lascivious kisses.

'Selina, but pray, don't, my lady!' she said almost with a sigh as my fingers found out her little clitoris between the pouting lips which her yielding legs had allowed me to titillate.

'What a love of a name; Selina! and you must call me Beatrice, will you – there's a darling? And we must sleep together in the same berth, there's room for both. I must kiss you all over to prove my love – even there, darling,' I said indicating her pussy with my finger, which was on the spot at the time, 'and you shall do the same to me. Or, if you don't like, you shall see how Patty loves to kiss my crack. Ah! Ah! you'll soon learn, Selina, to know what is nice, even if it seems horribly rude to think of.'

'Did you never guess, my dear,' I continued, 'why some girls are so awfully fond of each other? Well, I will tell you – it is because they are in the habit of procuring from each other all those forbidden joys which married people alone are supposed to enjoy.'

She was all a-tremble. My fingers were fairly buried in her slit, as far as they would go, and making her spend deliciously.

'Oh! Oh! I must suck it, every pearly drop that distills from your virgin recess is worth its weight in diamonds!' I said excitedly, throwing her back at full length on the ottoman, whilst I fell on my knees between her yielding thighs and glued my lips to her cunt. My tongue revelled in that thick creamy emission which only real virgins give down, for when their love-juices have for so long not been secreted, they are far more creamy than the spending of a woman is after often being fucked or frigged.

She enjoyed it immensely. How she wriggled and twisted in the excess of her excitement.

At last I got up and woke Patty. Then returning to my ladylove, I whispered in her ear: 'Selina, darling, I am going to give you a real taste of what a man is like. Patty is going to put on my dildo and fuck you with it, while she tickles my bottom-hole and you gamahuche my cunt. Won't that be a delightful conjunction, my love?'

'You frighten me, Beatrice dear. What is a dildo, will it hurt?' she whispered in a low tone.

'Exactly like a man's affair, Selina! And although it can shoot a delicious soothing emission into you at the ecstatic moment, there is no fear of getting in the family way,' I softly replied. 'Now Patty is ready, let me straddle over your face and present my cunny to your sweet lips for a sucking kiss. You will like it. It will prepare you for the unmistakable joy the dildo will give when it once gets in,' suiting the action to the word by placing myself over her.

Her blood was in a boil. She eagerly thrust her tongue into my longing cunt which almost instantly rewarded it by a copious spend which Selina seemed to relish as much as any epicurean gamahucher would have done; her legs were lasciviously wide apart, which circumstance Master Charlie was not slow to avail himself of; the position in which I was over her effectually preventing the longing virgin from seeing the impending ruin.

Opening the lips of her spending cunt gently with his fingers, the fellow cunningly frigged her with the ruby head of his prick, until poor Selina got so excited that she began to bite me and wriggle about in such an extraordinary way, as well as moan and sob out: 'Oh! Ah! shove, shove! Do push it in further, Patty dear! I feel I must have it. Oh! Oh! Ah-h! It hurts now! Pray, don't!' as he commenced to force the maidenhead in earnest. I pressed my cunt upon her mouth so that she could not scream and intensely enjoyed the pain we put her to; for she was awfully tight and Charlie was not to be denied. He pushed and rammed at her in lustful fury, spending, but still going on, till he got the whole of his manhood fairly into her sheath, then he rested for a few moments, making his prick throb in its tight receptacle till all sense of pain seemed to be lost to our victim, and the natural lubricity of her nature asserted itself once more and answered with a wanton heave of her bottom to every thrust of her partner. There seemed no satisfying her greedy cunt, now it had once got a taste of the real thing.

At last we got off her, and lighting the lamps once again, let her see the dildo for herself and guess! How astonished she was to find it was real life, instead of a hateful substitute, but she forgave us for the deception which had afforded her such exquisite pleasure.

After refreshing our parts with cold water, she thoroughly enjoyed the sight of Charlie fucking the amorous Patty, and with her own hands handled his balls and tickled them as well as Patty's cunt during their encounter.

As we could not expect to have more than another two nights on board ship, I determined to make the best of the time, especially as I had a particular fancy for good-looking youths in preference to men; and there were a couple of young middies on board I had quite fallen in love with as they had shown me many delicate attentions when I was so ill for the first few days.

A fine bright morning saw us on deck directly after breakfast.

'Good-morning, my lady,' said young Simpson raising his cap with a knowing, wistful look.

'Come here, you impudent-looking boy,' I laughed, and as he approached, said, in a whisper:

'Can you keep a secret?'

'My bosom is as safe as an iron chest, if Your Ladyship has anything to confide,' was the reply.

'I am going to leave you soon, you know, and would like to give you and young William a treat in my cabin tonight, if you can manage to come after all are retired – you are off duty then, I think?'

'Yes,' he replied, 'from 10 P.M. to 6 A.M. and you may depend on us being very quiet.'

Putting a finger to my lips as a sign of strict secrecy, I glided away from him and sat on the poop for the greater part of the day, looking at the water in dreamy anticipation of the fun I hoped for that night.

I had made ample preparation for them and bribed the stewards not to take any notice if they heard noises in my cabin, as I was going to give a little party to two or three young lady passengers before going ashore at Funchal, the port of Madeira.

After supper, myself and companions lay down to rest in our clothes, leaving the lamps burning and the refreshments all ready to hand. After a while, when all was quiet, our cabin door opened softly and the two handsome boys in their best uniforms quietly saluted us as they entered, both of them kissing me before I could rise from the couch. The door was bolted by Patty, who laughingly told them to mind how they behaved, or they would get served out. In reply to which both of them caught her and kissed her in spite of her pretended resistance.

The middies were hungry and soon did ample justice to a game-pie washed down with several bumpers of champagne as they toasted us, from the servants to myself.

I drank glass for glass with them. My veins were on fire, consumed by my lustful longings to enjoy two such handsome youths, and as soon as they had finished their repast, I begged them to sit by my side on the ottoman. And just as Simpson was in the act of sitting down I drew him upon my lap, saying with a laugh:

'What a nice baby he is to nurse, what a pretty little dear, kiss its dear mama.'

My lips met his in a long-drawn osculation which seemed to make him quiver all over with emotion as he lay on my bosom.

'Did you ever have a sweetheart, dear boy?' I asked.

'Yes; such a pretty girl at the Cape. I have rare fun with her when I go ashore.'

'What! Are you impudent enough to take liberties with her?'

'Yes, she even let me get into bed with her.'

'You impertinent little fellow to mention such a thing to me! Here, Miss Prude, and you girls, tie him up and pull down his breeches! I've got a tickler that will make his bottom smart for this!' I exclaimed, pushing him from me with great apparent disgust.

'What a lark! I should like to see them do it. Here, Peter, old boy, help us or these girls will really master me,' as he began to find himself rather overmatched.

A smile and a gesture from me only turned his chum Peter Williams to our side and it was fun to see how foolish he looked when he found himself really tied up to one of the berths and his breeches pulled down in spite of all he could do. How he blushed as they tucked up the tail of his shirt and exposed a very pretty white-skinned bum which was soon rosy enough under the hand-slapping he got from the whole party, all thoroughly enjoying the joke.

'Stand aside all of you,' I said sternly, 'and let me pay him the desserts for his impudence,' advancing birch in hand.

He was a plucky little fellow and disdained to cry out although I saw two or three big tears roll down his crimson face under my infliction, and could also see that his cock was as stiff as a poker. He was released, and without even waiting to pull his breeches up, rushed forward to help us as we stretched his friend Peter on the ottoman, and then by my direction he sat on his back, whilst I gleefully let him have a due share of the birch till he begged hard to be let off.

When they thought to adjust their clothes we all began to laugh and tease them about the beautiful red weals we could see, pulling up their shirt-tails and taking such liberties that in a short time they were quite undressed and we had two youths in a state of nature with standing pricks to look at.

'Well, I wouldn't give much for those toys of yours if that is all you have to show the girls!' I said laughingly, as I switched the parts indicated with my rod. 'Why Annie here has a better cock than any of you. We'll all strip and you shall see.'

This was the expected signal and any further restraint on our impulsive passions was thrown aside in a moment.

I think those two handsome middies had never really had a girl before and that I really took their maidenheads. In fact, I indulged in my letch for having two pricks in my cunt at once, whilst Charlie fucked Miss Prude before our eyes, till she had hysterics from excessive lubricity.

We kept it up till nearly five o'clock, fucking, gamahuching and indulging in every fancy we could think of. I even made Charlie get into my bottom with Simpson in him. Peter Williams also postillioning his companion with his prick in his fundament, whilst Miss Prude and Patty tickled and helped to excite us the very best way they could.

At last they were obliged to leave us and I may say that was the last lustful orgy I was ever able to indulge in, for my constitution broke down rapidly even during my stay at Madeira and I returned to England in the following May, since when, dear Walter, you have been my constant and loving attendant, and seen how rapidly this consumption is carrying me to my grave. Oh! I would that I had strength to do it once more and that you were my manly champion in that combat of bliss which I shall never taste again. Would to Heaven I might die in spending as I felt your very soul shoot into my vitals, but, alas! it cannot be! Still, if there is bliss in the world to be, I feel assured of an everlasting fuck.

Amen! I am unable to hold my pen any longer.

*La Rose
d'Amour*

*or The
Adventures
of a
Gentleman
in Search
of Pleasure*

*Translated
from the
French*

Chapter One

Thus every creature, and of every kind,
The sweet joys of sweet coition find.

DRYDEN

At the age of seventeen, through the mistaken but paternal fondness of my father, the Count de L—, I was still immured in an old château, on the coast of Brittany, with no society but that of my tutors, who had me at an eternal round of daily lessons, endlessly poring over dozens of musty volumes. Naturally of an indolent disposition, I became *ennuyed* to such a degree by the monotonous routine of my life that I verily believe I could not have survived three months longer had it not been for an accession of company which the old château received.

I was most agreeably surprised, while at my studies one morning, by the noise of carriage wheels driving rapidly over the stone pavement of the courtyard. I threw my book into one corner, bounded down the stairs, and met my father at the hall door; he was accompanied by my uncle, Count C—, and his two sons, who were about my own age.

In the course of the day my father told me that he was about to start for Russia as ambassador, and that after remaining at the château for a week or two, my uncle and cousins would return to Paris, taking me with them, as during his absence I was to reside with my uncle.

The next day my father, after giving me a great deal of good advice and his blessing, started *en route* for St Petersburg.

My cousins, Raoul and Julien, I found to be two as wild young colts as ever were let loose upon the inhabitants of a country village, setting at defiance everything, and leading me, who proved an adept scholar, into all kinds of mischief, whilst their father, who had some business in the neighbourhood, could not look after our conduct.

Going one day into my cousin Raoul's chamber in search of him, on opening the door, I was perfectly astounded at what I saw. There lay Raoul on the bed in the arms of one of the *femmes de chambre*, Manette, a most lusty, finely formed, rosy-cheeked wench.

When I entered the room my cousin was lying on the top of Manette, clasped in a tight embrace, a pair of large white legs crossed over his back, and from the heavings and motions of their bodies, I perceived that they were enjoying themselves in a manner altogether satisfactory; and so intent and enraptured were they, with the exercise they were taking, that they did not notice my having entered the room.

Although, during the three days my cousins had been with me, they had, by licentious conversation, uprooted all my preconceived notions of virtue in woman, so strictly had I been reared, never having been allowed to enter the company of females, not even in the village adjoining the château, that seeing the two on the bed in that manner I was so amazed that I stood at the door watching them till Raoul raised himself off the girl.

He got up, standing with his back to me, while Manette still lay with her eyes closed, her petticoat and shift thrown up, her thighs wide apart, revealing to my ardent gaze a round white belly, the bottom part of which was covered with a large growth of jet black curly hair, and lower down, between her thighs, I discovered what I had so often heard of, but never seen before – a cunt; from between the locks of curly hair that grew over the mount above, and around the dear delicious slit, I could perceive two fat and rosy lips slightly gaping open, from which oozed a little whitish-looking foam.

My senses were so confused with what I saw, and the strange emotions which had been called up in me, that I stepped forward towards the bed. The moment my step was heard Manette buried herself under the bedcovers, while Raoul came to meet me, and taking me by the hand led me up to the bed, saying –

'Cousin Louis, what have you seen? how long have you been in the room?'

I answered and told him I had witnessed their whole performance.

Raoul threw the cover off the girl, and raising her to a sitting posture, with one arm round her waist, said –

'Cousin Louis, you, who have never tasted the pleasures to be received in the arms of a pretty girl, do not know what it is to resist the temptation of making use of every opportunity and means in one's power to gratify the appetite; and see what a beautiful, charming mistress Manette is; who could deny her? Having done me the honour to invite me to her chamber last night she left me no option but to return the courtesy this evening, and take the consequence.'

I replied, 'Yes, she is very charming,' and feeling a desire to get an insight into the pleasures derived from the conjunction of the sexes, I laid my hand on the bare knee of Manette, who still sat on the edge of the bed, her clothes scarcely covering her cunt and thighs, and slipped it under her chemise till it rested on the hairy mount that overtopped the delicious slit beneath.

But Raoul stopped me, saying, 'Excuse me, cousin, but Manette is mine, at least for the present, but as I see you are anxious to initiate yourself in the mysteries of the Cyprian goddess, I think that with the help of Manette I shall be able to find you a companion for the night; can we not Manette?' said he, turning to her.

'Oh, yes,' said the girl, jumping to her feet, and assuming a smiling look, 'we will get Monsieur Louis my little sister Rose, who I am sure is a much prettier girl than myself, and she has larger and whiter breasts than I have,' said she, covering a pair of fine round white globes, which I was greedily devouring with my eyes. 'I am sure,' she went on, 'that you will be pleased with Rose, when we bring her to you tonight.'

Telling Manette that on condition she brought her sister at night to my chamber, I would be secret and mention to no one what I had seen, I retired and left them.

Going to my chamber early in the night I spent an hour in a fever of excited expectation till Manette entered the room, leading her sister by the hand. Rose was a most beautiful girl, and the moment she entered the room and the door was closed, I sprang forward, caught her in my arms, and led her to a sofa, where I sat down and drew her to my side. I unpinned the handkerchief that covered her breasts, and clasping her again in my arms covered them with burning kisses. This caused Rose to blush exquisitely and struggle somewhat to release herself from my embrace, when Manette stepped before us, saying –

'Monsieur Louis, Rose was never in company with a man before now, and of course is a little backward, but is very willing to remain with you, and left to yourselves you will, I am sure, find her all you wish; is it not so, sister?'

To which Rose replied, 'Oh yes,' and hid her face in the cushion of the sofa.

Manette told me that as wine was a great reviver of the spirits and provocative of love, she would go and bring me some, telling Rose to ply me plentifully with it. She went, and soon returned with a tray of wine, cakes, &c., and retired, wishing us 'a happy night of it'.

When Manette retired I locked the door, then drawing up a sofa to the table I led Rose to it, and seating myself by her, endeavoured to put her at her ease by not proceeding to any liberties at first, till I had plied her with some half-dozen glasses of wine. After she had drunk pretty freely, the natural vivacity of her character began to show itself in her open and free conversation. I now put my arms around her waist and neck, and pressing her close to my breast, imprinted burning kisses upon her rosy pouting lips. I then slipped one hand into her bosom, feeling and moulding her firm round bubbies. After dallying thus awhile I stooped and slipping a hand under her chemise, raised her clothes up on her knees. Squeezing and playing with her legs, I slid my hand along her thigh till my fingers rested on a bunch of silken mossy hair, which overhung the entrance of her virgin cunt.

Playing with the silken curls, twining and twisting my fingers through them, I dropped one finger lower down, and putting just the tip of it between the lips, I titillated her so well that she began to wriggle about in her seat. I could stand it no longer. I was on fire; the blood was boiling through my veins. I raised her on her feet, and began stripping her, fairly tearing her clothes off in my haste, till she stood perfectly naked before me. Ye gods! what beauties, what charms, were exposed to my ardent fiery gaze, what delicious breasts, how firmly moulded, small, yet so round and firm. I press them, kiss them, take the nipples in my mouth, I draw her to me, till feeling her naked body against me, I drop on my knees and transfer my love kisses to the lips of her luscious little hairy slit. I was in a perfect frenzy, I burned, I raged. In a trice I threw off everything, and clasping her body to mine, I raised the trembling girl in my arms, and carried her to the bed.

Placing a pillow on which to rest the plump, luxurious cheeks of her backside, I lay her down, springing on the bed by her side. I open wide her thighs, and my prick being up in arms and eager for the fray, I lay my length upon her. With the tips of my fingers I unclose the pouting lips, and with the utmost trouble insert the head of my virgin rod into the entrance of her no less virgin cunt.

No sooner did I feel the head lodged aright than I drove and shoved in with the utmost fury; feeling the head pretty well in I thrust and drove on, but gained so little that I drew it out, and wetting it with spittle, again effected lodgement just within the lips. At length by my fierce rending and tearing thrusts the first defences gave way, and I got about half-way in, but had become wrought up to such a pitch that the floodgates of love's reservoirs gave way, and I sank upon her breast in a delirium of transport as I oiled her torn and bleeding cunt with a perfect flood of virgin sperm.

Poor Rose had borne it most heroically, keeping the bedclothes between her teeth, in order to repress any cry of pain, whilst her hands clasped my body to hers, or even handled the shaft of love to assist its murderous intentions on her virginity.

As I lay panting and gasping on Rose, glowing with the fierce excitement, my eyes darting forth their humid fires, the stiffness which had perceptibly remitted, returned with redoubled vigour, and I again began to make headway into her. The sperm that I had spurted into her cunt had penetrated and oiled the dark and narrow passage, making my further entrance somewhat easier. I now recommenced my eager shoves, my fierce lunges, and I felt myself gaining at every move, till with one tremendous and cunt-rending thrust I buried myself into her up to the hilt. So great was the pain of this last shock that Rose could not suppress a sharp shrill scream, but I heeded it not; it was the note of final victory, and only added to the delicious piquancy of my enjoyment as I buried myself, if possible, yet further within the soft, luscious folds of her love sheath. We lay for a short time in the closest conjunction with each other, so that the hair on both of us was interwoven in one mass.

Putting my arm around her neck, I drew her to a yet closer embrace, and planting numberless kisses on her rosy lips and damask blushing face, which was wet with tears of suffering which the brave little darling could not prevent from starting from her lovely eyes, I drew out the head and slowly thrust it in again; my fierce desires goaded me to challenge her to a renewal of the combat. A smile of infinite love crossed her lovely countenance, all signs of past pain seemed to vanish, and I could feel the soft and juicy folds of her cunt, throbbing and clasping tightly on my enamoured prick; my movements quickened in an instant, and so exciting was the to-and-fro friction, aided by the delicious jingling of my magnificent stones against her backside, that despite all her pain, Rose was thrown into such an ecstasy that she clasped me in her arms, and throwing her legs over my back paid down her first and virgin tribute to man, forced from her by the soul-stirring motions of my rod of love, while I met her and spurted another stream of burning sperm into the utmost recesses of her fount of love, commingling our juices together and partially cooling the fires which were raging within us.

So novel, so new and exquisitely delicious, so transporting, so heavenly were the sensations, so ecstatic were the joys we both felt that we twined and writhed in each other's arms like serpents, while Rose exclaimed – 'Oh God! I die! Oh heaven! What joy, what pleasure. Oh! oh! ah! ah! – h! – h!' and ended in one long deep-drawn sigh.

With a few convulsive jerks and struggles of her delicious backside she loosened her hold, and stretching herself out with a shudder, fainted away, and I, who was at my last gasp, also sank into oblivion.

When we had recovered from our delirium I got up and poured out some wine, gave it to Rose, and tossed off a bumper myself, I then planted a soft kiss on the lips of her torn and bleeding cunt, exclaiming – 'True fount of love, sole seat of never failing joys and pleasures to man, dear, delicious, hairy little slit, from this moment my whole life and soul are forever devoted to you.'

I spent the night with Rose, in one continued round of pleasure, revelling in the full enjoyment of her virgin charms. Again and again did we renew our embraces, swimming in a sea of pleasure. So furiously did we enter into our combats of love that nature soon became exhausted, and we fell asleep in each other's arms.

In the morning when I awoke Rose was sitting up in bed, looking with anxious eyes on the now diminutive, shrunken instrument which the night before had ripped open the entrances to her virginity, robbing her of her maidenhead. When she perceived that I was watching her she threw herself into my arms and hid her face in my bosom.

Gently raising and reassuring her, I made her take hold of it, and began dallying with her breasts, tickling her, pressing them, sucking their rosy nipples, while the touch of her hand renewed in me the fires which were already springing into flame. Rose had the pleasure to see the small shrunken thing she first took into her hand spring up into a magnificent rod, smooth and polished as ivory, its large uncapped head red and glowing with the heat that was raging in it. I determined that she should reap the reward of her labour, and gather into her storehouse the rich harvest of love that was awaiting her.

Gently laying her down, and placing a pillow under the firm half-moons of her backside, I stretched open her legs to the utmost, exhibiting to my gaze the gaping lips of her cunt, ready open to receive the delicious morsel which, panting and throbbing like a high-mettled courser, raised his foaming head erect against my belly.

Laying myself down on Rose I made her take hold of my prick to put it in, but so firm and erect was it that she could barely bend its head down to the entrance. So magnificent was the erection that with all the stretching her cunt had received the night before it would not enter. Drawing myself back to wet the head within the lips, I slowly shoved it into her; she could not move, but lay quietly till I stirred her up so powerfully that we soon melted away, my deep thrusts making her feel the pleasures more sensibly, and giving her the full enjoyment of that which she had but tasted the night before.

We had barely recovered ourselves when we were aroused by a knocking at the door. Slipping on a loose *robe de chambre* I immediately opened it, and Raoul and Manette came in. I led them up to the bed, and pulling off the coverlet showed them the blushing Rose, more beautiful in the morning from the fatigues she had undergone the night past.

I called their attention to her, saying, 'Behold her chemise, see how it is dyed by the juice and crimson tide, which flowed from the parent stem after I had plucked *la rose d'amour* from my lovely Rose.'

My cousin Raoul now congratulated me. He said that he was overjoyed to have been instrumental in procuring for me such a delicious rose as Rose turned out to be; that he was sincerely glad he had been partially the cause of my being thus happily initiated into the mysteries of the divine art of love, and at the same time of my having had a virgin partner in my delicious combats.

Manette, too, congratulated her sister.

'How pleased she was to learn that she had secured such a lover as M. Louis, how happy you will be together now you have once tasted the supreme joys to be obtained in each other's embraces, sipping of the pleasures of which I am sure you will never tire.'

I now spent all my nights with Rose, sometimes in her own chamber, again in my own, and not content to wait for the night I would sometimes get her into my room in the day, and enjoy myself with her.

One day, while I was in my room with Rose – she stretched across the foot of the bed, her clothes raised up, and exposing to my view all her beauties, I standing between her legs with my prick (which was a very large one, few men being able to boast of one as large), in my hand – Manette suddenly entered the room, I having neglected to lock the door.

She got a fair view of my prick, and stood looking at it, apparently amazed at its being so big, but seeing the manner in which I was engaged, she retired.

Chapter Two

The following day in the afternoon, Manette came into my room and asked me to follow her to her chamber, whither she led, saying, 'I have something to show you that will please and satisfy you much more than your mistress could do.'

I followed her to her chamber, which after entering, she locked. I stood looking out of a window while Manette went behind the bed, the curtains of which were drawn. Hearing a light step advancing towards me I turned round, and Manette stood before me entirely naked; she sprang into my arms, clasping me round the neck, and led me to the bed, on which she seated herself.

I now saw what it was she had to show me, and being no ways loath to enter into the combat with her, to which she had invited me, I threw off my coat and waistcoat, while she let down my pantaloons, and drew out my blunt but ever-ready weapon, then falling back on the bed, drew me on top of her. My cock soon ran its full length into the soft and luscious sheath which nature intended for it. Twice before I got off her did I open the floodgates o f love's reservoir, and pour into her a stream of fiery sperm, as each time she met me, letting down the very cream and essence of her body so copiously that our thighs were bedewed with it.

From this time till my cousin left the castle did I enjoy Manette in the same manner each day.

At the end of the second week after his coming my uncle announced his departure for Paris on the following day, and told me to make all preparations to go with him. When this was announced to my cousins and myself we determined to make the best possible use of the day by spending it in the woods on the banks of a small creek, with our respective mistresses.

It was Sunday morning; Raoul, myself and Julien (for although I have not mentioned him in connection with our love affairs, it must not be supposed that he was idle in such things all the time, far from it; while Raoul and myself amused ourselves with Manette and Rose he consoled himself in the arms of Marie, one of the dairymaids, a large lusty brunette, and very good-looking, to whose bedchamber he stole every night) set out, meeting the three girls at the place appointed, they having gone on some time before us, carrying provisions and wine.

Having saluted our beauties we proceeded to arrange matters for a lunch, and sat down or rather reclined on the green sward, and discussed the merits of some of the good things they had provided for us, and after satisfying our appetites felt inclined to taste of the other good things they had left, but which were not visible.

Accordingly, as a preparatory note, we slipped our hands in their bosoms, and dallying awhile, rolled them over on their backs, but in spite of our endeavours we could not raise a petticoat, more than just to get a glimpse of a thigh, for they resisted all our endeavours to get further into matters, saying they would not consent to such naughty things in sight of each other, and if we did not behave better they would run off and leave us.

I then purposed we should undress and take a bath. 'We will strip ourselves to our shirts and then strip you and at the word of command all shall throw off their nether garments.'

To this there was some demurring on the part of our young ladies, as they felt some shame at being seen by each other thus, especially Marie, whom neither Raoul nor myself had seen till the present time, but we overruled their objections and stripped to our shirts, then each going up to his mistress, commenced unhooking and unlacing, and taking off frock and petticoats, till nothing but their shifts were left on them. I gave the word of command, 'Off shirts.' We threw our shirts off, but on looking at our girls found them still standing in their shifts.

Finding they would not take their shifts off I proposed that one after the other throw off and stand naked, each as they did so to be examined in all parts by the men, and their relative beauties compared, and to the one that would first do so to be offered a handsome diamond ring.

Manette stood forth saying that having come there to meet and enjoy ourselves with our lovers, and they having thrown off all covering, she would not spoil the sport, as she was not ashamed to let them see all that she had, for she was sure she had as pretty a leg and as sweet a little cunt as any girl in Brittany.

I was so much taken with the lusty Marie, Julien's mistress, her immense titties, her extraordinary large hips and thighs, above all her beautiful cunt, which was covered up and hidden in a most luxuriant growth of jet black hair, which hung down fully eight inches long, and from out of which peeped two large red pouting lips, which looked most temptingly luscious, that I proposed we should each, after our first bathe, change mistresses, so that each one should have enjoyed the mistresses of the other two.

To this my cousins consented – with it the girls were much pleased as Manette was very anxious to have me once more bury myself within the juicy folds and recesses of her cunt; and Marie was also very willing, as she had whispered to me while I was examining her that although she was large she had a little cunt, but that even so Julien's prick was too small to give her much pleasure when he was in her; that mine was nearly twice as large as his, and she was sure that if I would consent to try her, I would like her much better than Rose.

I now led the way into the brook, leading Rose by the hand, the others following us. Once in, we played and sportively wantoned in the water, playing all manner of tricks, plunging them in over head and ears, and provoking them in every possible way, and under pretence of washing our fair partners, we gave our hands every liberty, going over every part, the breast, squeezing and moulding their titties, their soft bellies, rubbing their thighs, their cunts, and all other parts; the girls at the same time going over us in pretty much the same manner.

As we thus stood in the water, which was only about waist deep, our engines erect, and in good working condition, with my arm around Rose's waist, I tried to insert the nozzle of my engine into the mouth of her water-tight furnace, for the purpose of putting out the fire which was raging within it, but could not succeed, as we were unable to support one another.

My attention was drawn to a considerable splashing I heard, and on looking round I perceived that Raoul and Julien had lain their nymphs down on the edge of the water, their heads resting on the bank, and had got into them in that manner, the motions of their backsides and bellies coming together making the water fly all over them.

This was an example set before us, which Rose and I could not resist, so I led her out of the water and we sat down on the grass, under the shade of a tree; there setting her across my thighs, her legs lapping around my backside, her soft, beautiful white belly rubbing against mine, I dallied with her ruby-nippled titties, firm and springing to the touch, with one hand, while with the other I tried to make out the entrance to the harbour of love, in order to make room for my masterpiece of nature, that stood reared up between her thighs, and pressed hard against her belly, as if demanding admittance and shelter within the soft and luscious sheath, which nature has so bountifully supplied to woman, and of which Rose possessed a most lovely specimen. She in a fit of humour affected to elude my efforts to gain entrance into her, trying to protract the desire she was feeling by managing her manoeuvres so that they made the fire which was burning in us rage fiercer, and redoubled my excitement.

I covered her with burning kisses, and her eyes shot forth humid fires, and, languishing, seemed to melt beneath the long dark silken lashes which half concealed them. We rolled and twined about on the green sward, locked in each other's arms, till I at last got her under, with my knees between her thighs, and I was soon fairly into her, while she, feeling the dart of love entering into the very depths of the retreat, gave up, and lay at my mercy. But the fight growing fiercer and fiercer, she soon brought me to a crisis, at the same time paying down her own tribute to man.

Closing her eyes and breathing a sigh she stretched out her limbs with a faint shudder; the muscles instantly relaxing gave me to know that she had experienced the greatest pleasure that woman is capable of receiving or man of giving.

We had not recovered out of our trance when the others came up, and slapping us on our backsides soon brought us to.

Immediately on their coming out of the water we changed partners, Raoul taking Rose; Julien, Manette; and I, Marie, and on receiving her I lay down between her beautiful legs, my cheek pillowed on the mossy hair that surmounted the gaping lips of the delicious entrance below.

Reclining thus for some time, sipping wine, eating bonbons and sweatmeats, we dallied away an hour or two, till our passions began to rise in such a manner as to be not long kept in subjection. My cousins, I suppose, thinking that being in the water added to the pleasure they received from the girls while fucking them, or from the novelty of the thing, proposed our going into the water again, and there enjoy our mistresses. They did so, but I remained under the tree with Marie. When the others got under the bank, I rose up, and spreading down all the dresses and petticoats, and making a pillow of a coat. I made a comfortable bed for Marie to lie on. I invited her to the combat. She got up and lay on the bed I had prepared for her, placing herself in an excellent position to favour my entrance. I laid myself down on her gently, she taking hold and guiding into the opening the head of the instrument which was to pierce her to the very vitals. After she had lodged the head between the lips of her cunt, I titillated her with it for a moment and then slowly drove it into her, so slowly that it was a full minute before it was all in, so tight was her cunt and so large was my prick that they were stretched and gorged to the fullest extent.

Marie's cunt was small, very small indeed, most lusciously tight, and slowly drawing my rod out to the head – the tightness of it causing so great a suction that it sent a thrill of most exquisite pleasure through the whole body – then darting it into her, and again drawing it out, and darting it in till I could no longer master myself, my motions became so rapid and vigorous that we soon let down and mixed the essence of our souls together.

Although I loved my little Rose, with her dear little cunt and all her charms, and although I found great pleasure when in the arms and enjoying the riper beauties of her sister Manette, yet the sensations of delight and pleasure I had just received from Marie were, in my mind, superior to them both.

I was the second time tasting and sipping of the sweets to be had in the arms of Marie when the rest of the party broke in upon us, but we did not mind them, and kept on till we had finished our work. After resting from our labours for some time, and our appetites being sharpened, we got our nude sirens to rearrange the luncheon, then after satisfying our appetites, and taking another bathe, we dressed and set out for home. On the way I called for a consultation as to whether our exchange of mistresses should stand good for the night or not.

Raoul answered that as we had spent the day together so we ought to do the night, for all of us to lie together in one room, and if either of the girls wished to be fucked by either of us, that she should say so, and be accommodated, and vice versa, to which we all consented.

That night we met in my chamber at eleven o'clock, the girls fetching in beds from another room, and making them up on the floor. I stretched myself naked on a pallet, and Manette ran up and lay down by me. Raoul took Marie for trial, and Julien, Rose.

After I had given the plump Manette a double proof of the powers within me, another change was made, and I got the lusty Marie. Towards daylight we were each lying with our own particular mistress, and after making all arrangements for the future we fell asleep, I in my favourite position, lying between the legs of Rose, having them thrown over me, my head pillowed on her soft white belly, my cheek resting on the silken mossy hair that surrounded her cunt.

We breakfasted at ten o'clock, after which I slipped up to Manette's room, where I found her, Rose and Marie. To each I made handsome presents, and told them if they would be true to me, that on my return from Paris, I would take and keep the whole three of them. Each one of them was anxious to have me tumble her once more on the bed, but as I could only do one they drew lots for my last fuck, which fell to Marie. She lay down across the bed, and while I let down my pants the other two girls threw up her clothes, and each raised a leg, and after I had made good my entrance they rested her thighs on my hips, so that I soon put her in ecstasy by the delicious manoeuvres of love's piston-rod. Half an hour later, I was on the road to Paris.

Chapter Three

We spent five days on the road, and if our amorous pleasures had in any way debilitated us, we were thoroughly restored to full vigour by the journey.

We arrived at the Count's hotel in Paris late in the evening, too late, so said my cousins, to give me an introduction to any of their *filles d'amour*, and after partaking of a slight supper we retired to our (at least for that night) virtuous couches.

The next day we spent at the Palais Royal, and on the Boulevards. At ten o'clock we went up to Raoul's chamber and had not been seated more than a minute or two before three beautiful girls entered, bearing trays, on which were wines, comfits, bon-bons, sweetmeats, &c. Having had them arrange these on a round table, Raoul introduced the pretty dears to me.

After the introduction we sat down to the table and passed an hour or so in drinking, eating and chatting with our lovely guests till the champagne began to get into our heads; then we were not content with kissing and feeling the bubbies of our charmers, and other little liberties, and we tried to get deeper into matters, but found ourselves repulsed by our ladies, who, on our attempting to use a little gentle force, got up and ran out of the room. No sooner were they gone than Raoul said –

'Don't be afraid, cousins, they will return shortly, and we will give them a great surprise by stripping ourselves perfectly naked.'

We did so, whereupon Raoul told me to choose which of the girls I would have for my partner for the night when they entered into the room again.

Presently the door opened, and the girls entered one after the other, all of them in as naked a state as ourselves with the exception of quantities of green gauze, which each of them was wrapped in, and which only served to heighten their charms instead of hiding any part of their bodies from our view. Their hair falling down over their shoulders in long ringlets increased their beauty in combination with the gauze, so much so that I stood perfectly bewildered, and not until my cousin spoke to me did I think of choosing a partner. But Louise, a lovely little sprite of eighteen, fair, finely formed, with a large bust, wide expanding hips, large firm buttocks, and pretty plump withal, shot forth at me such fiery glances from a pair of most bewitching dark blue eyes that I immediately chose her.

The moment I named her she ran up to me, and opening her gauze enveloped me in it with herself. No sooner had she done so than the other two were in the arms of my cousins.

We again sat down to the table, our mistresses sitting on our laps. Louise hugged up as close to my naked body as she could; her delicious fat backside resting on my thighs, her large, firm bubbies pressed against my breast, a plump little arm thrown round my neck, her soft cheek nestling against mine, her rosy pouting lips glued to mine, in burning, fiery kisses, were enough to set on fire the soul of an anchorite, and as if this was not enough the bewitching little devil parted her thighs, and slipping her hand between them, caught hold of my prick, which had been rooting up against her backside, trying to find some hole or other in which to put his head and hide himself, and drawing it up between her thighs put the head of it between the fat juicy lips of her already spending cunt, rubbing the head between the nymphæ till I became so much excited that I told her if she did not want me to spill my liquor on her thighs she must let me in, as I could not possibly contain myself much longer.

Finding that she had worked me up to the pitch that suited her purpose, Louise raised one leg, and giving it a swing, threw it over my head, making herself revolve on her own 'axass', bringing her round, soft and smooth belly against mine. Being now seated crosslegged, she raised herself on her toes, and taking fresh hold of my prick, lodged the head of it in her cunt, then letting her weight fall upon me, impaled herself on it, piercing herself up to the very quick. Thus engaged she moved herself up and down; so rampant was I that I gave way before Louise was quite ready, but feeling the hot juice flooding the recesses of her cunt brought down her second tribute in time to mix with mine. We kept glued together, till my pego drawing itself up into littleness, fell out from the juicy folds of its nest.

Louise got up, and ran out of the room, soon followed by the two other girls, who I now saw had been engaged in the same game that

Louise and myself had been playing. In a short time they returned, and we sat drinking till a late hour.

My amorous little devil of a partner had at last got me so excited that I proposed we should not go to bed for the night. My mistress, taking a light, led me to her chamber, which it was easy to see was fitted up as a sanctuary for love alone, a place in which nothing else was done or thought of. We first refreshed ourselves by bathing the most excited parts in icy cold water, then full of undiminished vigour, I carried her to the bed. We spent the night in one continued round of voluptuous pleasure.

The time thus passed for two weeks, without any other variety than occasionally slipping into the rooms of the mistresses of my two cousins and enjoying them for an hour or so during the day.

At last, Raoul advised me not to engage myself with either of the girls for a few days, as I should require all my vigour renewed, for he was going to introduce me to an establishment rivalling anything heard of in the *Arabian Nights Entertainments*, an establishment of girls, supported by the nobility alone, the admission fee to which was one thousand francs. In it, he said, there were the most beautiful females in all France. He repeated his caution to me about holding any sexual intercourse with either of our girls, as I must do honour to his recommendation, that being a stranger about to be initiated I would be obliged to perform in public the first round with the girl I should choose for the night.

On the evening of the third day after my cousin's announcement I went with him to the house in which the orgies were celebrated. It was a large and gloomy-looking mansion, situated in the Rue St Honoré. We arrived at the gate, and were admitted by the porter. Crossing a paved courtyard we ascended a broad flight of stone steps, and my cousin, giving his name to the doorkeeper, led the way through a dimly lighted hall, into a small, neatly furnished apartment at the left-hand side, in which he left me for a few minutes, as he said, to bring in the examining committee. He returned very soon, accompanied by three gentlemen, to whom he introduced me, saying my desire was to become a member of the club.

The initiation was very simple; it merely consisted in my handing over to them the entrance fee of one thousand francs, and one thousand francs more for the benefit of the house.

I was then led up another large flight of stairs, and invited into a dressing-room. They there informed me that I must adopt the costume of the house, which was simply a large dressing-gown open in front, put on over the shirt. I stripped as they did, and we were soon *en règle*. Being led to a pair of large folding doors, which noiselessly opened at our approach, I was almost blinded by the flood of light which streamed through them. On my entering the room, a scene of the utmost magnificence and gorgeousness presented itself to my view, rivalling any fairy tales I had ever read. It was a large saloon of lofty height and great length, supported on both sides by rows of columns of marble of variegated hues; between the pillars supported on alabaster pedestals stood a number of masterpieces of sculpture, in the finest Carrara marble, representing nude females in every position in which could possibly be combined grace and lasciviousness.

So natural did they appear with a piece of gauze thrown across their shoulders, one would have sworn they were living witnesses, flesh and blood, so admirably was their hair chiseled out, representing the mode of wearing it by women of different countries, so well was the rounded swell of the breasts imitated, and then, further down, the short curly hair that ornamented the beautiful lifelike pouting lips below, that one were almost tempted to advance and feel if they were not living. Some, too, were most ludicrous; one I saw representing a woman, her knees slightly bent and wide apart, with a prick about halfway into her cunt. Another was made to hold in her hand, the head just without the lips of her love notch, a prick that appeared to have fallen out of her cunt, and shrunken up in her hand.

At the end of the hall there played a fountain of perfumed waters, which diffused through the room a most delicious and fragrant coolness. There were painted on the walls, pictures, the most lascivious that nature could conceive, women in every variety of posture and position, nearly all of whom were represented as fucking with a man.

But the ceiling was the *chef d'œuvre* of this gorgeous apartment. The centrepiece represented an immense cunt painted in the finest colours, from between the lips of which depended a large carved prick, with stones attached, from which hung a magnificent chandelier. On the outer side, and around the large cunt in the centre, were pricks with wings flying at it, from some of which you could see a stream of sperm spurting into the centrepiece. Again, on the outside of the ring of pricks was a circle of naked nymphs, who appeared to be in pursuit of the pricks; they seemed to be leaning forward with outstretched hands ready to grasp them; the whole thing, intermixed with gold and silver stars, and surrounded with clouds of cerulean hue, formed a most splendid scene.

In the centre of the apartment was a long table, on which was laid out a most luxurious repast, served up on gold and silver plate, which partook of a character similar to the other adornments of the room. There were chased on the seats nude figures of men and women in all shapes and positions. Here were goblets supported on a stem, shaped like a prick; others there were, the bowls in shape of a cunt, supported on legs beautifully formed, and vases of every description, one of which in particular caught my eye; it represented a nude female standing on her head, her legs bent at the knees, the feet resting on the hips, and forming the handles, the cunt representing the mouth, in which was set a bouquet of rare flowers.

After being introduced to the gentlemen present, and having time given me to notice the different beauties of the apartment, I was told that the goddesses of the establishment would soon enter to their supper, and that as they came into the room I should choose the one I most fancied, as they were all perfectly free, there being no jealousy among the men in that respect.

◆§♥◆

Chapter Four

Shortly a bell sounded, and through a side door entered a troupe of the most beautiful young girls the world could produce.

The effect on me was electric, so much beauty congregated together I could not imagine. So bewitchingly graceful did they appear as they gleefully tripped into the room, striking the most lascivious attitudes. So true to a fault were their figures, so charming was the clear transparent whiteness of their necks and faces, slightly tinted with the rose's hue, shaded by masses of rich black, auburn or chestnut hair, which waved in the light like rays of molten gold and fell in ringlets over their beautifully rounded shoulders, whilst their eyes, half-hid in the long silken lashes, beaming and sparkling with licentiousness, made them look like houris descended from the Moslems' paradise, rather than anything of mortal mould. And what served to heighten the enchantment their appearance cast over me was their dress.

Some entered dressed in pants and cymar, *à la Turque*, displaying to the utmost advantage their large busts and beautifully rounded hips.

Others (the majority) dressed in Turkish pants of fine blue or pink gauze, with a short petticoat hanging halfway to the knee, made of the same material, and which, instead of hiding any part of their bodies, only added to their beauty, and heightened every charm.

Their beautiful breasts could be plainly seen, even the rosy-tipped nipples could be distinguished as they rose and fell in undulating palpitations against their slight covering.

The shape of the legs and thighs could be seen; nay, the masses of curling hair that overhung their delicious, luscious little cunts, even the lips of which I could see – all, all was visible.

I stood thus entranced, gazing on the fairylike beings that were grouped around me, without a thought but of their extreme loveliness, till I was aroused from my state of dreamy delight by one of the gentlemen present asking me to give my arm to one of the ladies, and take her for my partner at the supper table. And if after supper I should see any other lady whom I might prefer to my first choice, I should be at full liberty to take her.

All that I could do in answer was to gaze around on them with a half-bewildered look, till a beautiful creature came up to me, and with a smile, putting her arm in mine, her lustrous dark eyes beaming with the very spirit of luxuriousness, asked if I would not accept her as my companion for the night.

I answered her by putting my arm around her taper waist, and drawing her into a close embrace, imprinted on her lips a dozen burning kisses, which she returned with equal ardour.

Leading the way to the table, we seated ourselves on a sofa (there being no chairs, but a sofa for each couple) and the repast commenced.

No sooner had we taken our seats than an unseen band struck up, playing the most beautiful and seductive airs; and as the dessert came on, a large curtain, which was stretched across at one end of the room, suddenly drew up, exhibiting a beautiful little stage, on which appeared four girls dancing some of the most licentious dances, throwing themselves into the most tempting postures, pirouetting till their gauze skirts stood entirely level with their navels, showing their cunts, even drawing apart the vermilion lips of those mossy temples of love by the extension of their legs, allowing us to catch a glimpse of the luscious interior which the open legs half disclosed.

After sitting at the dessert an hour or more, drinking the most exciting and heating wines with one another, on a given signal the girls withdrew to prepare for the ball, leaving us to do the same, which consisted merely in our stripping stark naked, retaining only our pumps.

I must here beg the reader's indulgence to state what I should have said before – that is, that the members of the society which held their revels in this house all belonged to the first families in the kingdom. That when any gentleman was initiated he must bring with him and present to the society some female relative, either a sister or cousin, mistress, or some beautiful female friend, so that in enjoying the relatives of other members he could have no advantage over them or their honour.

The young lady who had made herself my partner, I learned, was Mademoiselle de C—, daughter of Count C—, and sister to one of the gentlemen present. Here, on the pretence of being on a visit to each other's houses, they met once a week, and gave loose to the most unbounded licentiousness. All modesty was formally banished from the house, the most lascivious abandon being substituted in its place.

After stripping we entered the ballroom, which, like the *salle à manger*, was painted with nude figures, and instead of seats, it was furnished at the sides and ends with richly made couches stuffed with the softest down, with sprung bottoms, sheets of the finest lace, and coverlets of silk and satin, but no curtains to them, as nothing was allowed to be done in secret.

If a gentleman and his partner were tired of dancing, they could retire to a couch and play at the game of love.

On brackets against the wall, a little raised above the couches, were shelves supporting decanters of wine, trays of comfits, and other stimulating refreshments.

We had not long to wait for our partners ere they came dancing into the room, as naked as we were except for a wide scarf of light blue or pink gauze, which each had thrown over her shoulders.

If I was pleased with my partner at supper I was much more so now that I could have a fair view of her when perfectly naked. Her skin rivalled alabaster in whiteness, her beautiful full breasts sustained themselves firm and round as two globes; her well rounded shoulders tapered down into a small waist, a small foot, with an ankle expanding upwards into a fine calf, her thighs full, large and proportionately made, swelling up into a pair of large hips, while the two half-globes of her backside were equally massive and firm. Her hair, which she had combed out, hung down to her knees, while her cunt was surrounded and overshadowed by a mass of jet black hair which grew upon and around her belly as high as her navel, hanging down between her thighs some way, forming a perfect veil or covering over the dear little slit, contrasting most beautifully with the snowy whiteness of her belly and thighs.

On entering the room she ran up to me with extended arms, but I caught her, and held her out at arm's length, surveying and devouring with my eyes her every charm and beauty, and then I clasped her in a long embrace and we writhed about in each other's arms, rubbing our bellies together, till Mr Pego began to snort and prance about between her thighs, seeking for an entrance into some hospitable retreat in which to hide his impudence.

So great was the excitement raised in me by feeling her soft white belly rubbing against mine, as well as the springy mossy covering of her fount of love pressing against my rampant machine, that I would have sent him in to explore the dark little cavern concealed between her thighs, as we stood in the centre of the room, had she not prevented me.

Hardly knowing how to contain my still increasing passion, I slid between her arms, and dropped on my knees to the floor, parting with my fingers the glossy ringlets that hid a pair of rosy pouting lips, most lusciously tempting, and implanted my burning kisses on that amorous spot.

There was no time for further dalliance as the music began, and she led me away to join in the dance.

After the first cotillion I led her to a couch, and reclining on it drew her down by my side, and would soon have brought matters to a crisis had she not prevented me again, by saying that we should be obliged to enter the lists, and go through our first manual exercise on a state couch in the centre of the room, surrounded by the whole company.

Shortly after I heard the tinkle of a small bell, and immediately entered four men, wheeling in a couch of carved rosewood, covered with sheets of the finest linen, overspread with one of Brussels lace.

The committee, one of whom was my partner's brother, advanced to me and led me to the couch, while three of the ladies present took Mademoiselle de C—, and placing her on her back turned a small screw at one side of it, which, acting on springs, raised that part on which rested her beautiful buttocks, elevating them at least one foot higher than her head or feet, forming a sort of bow, and throwing up that portion of her belly and thighs which was most contiguous to the dear little cleft in the bottom of her belly.

So soon as they had arranged everything the three girls stepped back a little, and the men placed me on the top of her who was to share my sweet labour. She extended her thighs to the utmost to receive me.

After I was placed comfortably on her the gentlemen fastened us down on the couch by means of belts of india-rubber, which extended across the bed, and held us firmly on it.

I soon perceived the necessity of this, as at the least motion I made (there were such powerful springs fixed in the body of the couch) the springing caused by it would have thrown me off my partner if not off the couch.

The sweet little creature, who was lying under me, now threw her legs across my back, and clasping me in her arms, showed that she was ready for the delicious combat.

Upon these signs the girls who had placed her on the couch advanced, and one with the tips of her fingers held open the lips of her cunt, while another took hold of my stiff-stander, and pointing his head at the entrance, directed him to the opening before him. But so highly were my passions wrought up, and such a magnificent erection had I acquired, so swelled up was its large red head, and so lusciously tight and small was the entrance to the grotto of love, that it would not enter.

After two or three trials, each of which failed, the one who had hold of my driving machine, forced my backside up from off Mademoiselle de C—, and slipping her head between my thighs, took my prick into her mouth, and palating it with her tongue, wet it well with saliva, and letting it out of her mouth, again presented it at the entrance of the fiery furnace which was gaping to receive it. Effecting a safe lodgement for the head, with one vigorous thrust I buried myself in her to the very haft.

So fierce was the concussion produced by the meeting of our bodies that my magnificent stones fairly cracked against her delicious backside. With such force did I come down on her that the springs in the bed were forced low down, and resounding sent us some three feet into the air. The bed was so constructed that the springs could force the bed up from the body on which it rested.

I now felt that I was master of the field, and taking advantage of my position, gave my partner such a series of thrusts and drives – the springing of the bed driving her to meet me – our bodies came together with such a force as to make all tremble.

The spectators around us were continually calling out to us and commenting upon our performance with such exclamations as the following: 'O God, what a magnificent thrust.' 'How splendidly he drives it home to her.' 'See how deliciously their bodies meet together.' 'What a splendid prick, what beautifully large stones, how exquisitely do they flop against her buttocks,' &c.

'Ah, Mademoiselle de C—, how I envy you those glorious cods and that luxurious prick, with which you are now gorging that greedy little maw of yours,' exclaimed a lively young creature as she left her gallant's arm to approach the bed and get a fairer view of the fierce driving machine which so excited her imagination. 'Oh, how beautiful!' she said, as stooping down she caught a full view of the whole machinery in motion. 'See how the proud courser steams and smokes as he reins back his head to the starting place, and then how he makes everything foam again as he dashes onward in his mad career, towards the goal of victory!' and in her excitement she took my stones in her hand, and gently squeezed them, and brought me at once to the crisis.

Making one last lunge forward, I lay quivering and gasping on my fair partner's bosom, drenching her inmost parts with a perfect shower of the elixir of love.

My partner, who had been no ways backward in sustaining my fierce lunges and had returned them with thrusts and upheavings fully as amorous as my own, feeling the heat of the burning liquid I was injecting in her, gave way at the same time, and dissolving her very soul into a flood of sperm, opened the gates of love's reservoir, and let flow such a stream of pearly essence as never came from woman before.

After we had recovered ourselves from the delirium in which our senses were lost for a few moments, the belts which held us together were loosened.

I arose, and raised Mademoiselle de C—; as I stood her on the floor large drops of spendings fell pattering between her feet, attesting the vigour and warmth with which we had entered into the pleasure of love.

I now received the congratulations of the male part, as to the manner in which I had gone through the performance, and done such credit to our sex.

My mistress also received the encomiums of the females, all of whom envied her her good luck in having me for a companion.

Then I took the dear girl to one of the side couches and we reclined for a short time, taking wine and refreshments to invigorate ourselves for further enjoyments.

Casting my eyes around the room I observed that every couch was occupied by a couple, all of them playing the same game we had just gone through with.

My fair partner and myself arose and promenaded round the room, observing the different modes and manners of frigging which some of them adopted.

At the sight of so many beautiful women in action all at once, I thought it only right my mistress should complete the set, and leading her back to the couch, I again gave her such a delicious fuck that she could not get up for half an hour afterwards.

Shortly after the company had recovered from the transports into which they were plunged, two servants entered the room, bearing in on trays small cups of spiced chocolate, prepared in such a way as to give the drinker strength to enter the lists of love ten or a dozen times.

Fucking was now proclaimed the order of the night.

Never in the world was there so much delicious frigging done at one time by an equal number of persons. Never were there so many beautiful cunts to be seen so gorged and stuffed, and so well fucked by so many noble pricks. Never did women receive such a shower of sperm as drenched them from all quarters.

The debauch was growing to its height, the chocolate began to operate fiercely on the men. The women writhed and twined themselves about the floor, fucking, screaming and shouting in ecstasy.

The most licentious words now issued from the mouths of those females, who, on the morrow, would meet you in their salons with a demure look and virtuous countenance.

The excitement was steadily increasing. The women became perfect Bacchantes, they drank freely of the most exciting and exhilarating wines.

Suddenly they stripped the beds from off the couches, and spread them on the floor, forming one large bed, upon which they could all lie down.

The uproar increased.

Here might be seen two women contending (amicably) for one man.

Again, two men contending for one woman, till each found a place for their inflamed pricks, one in her cunt, and the other in her bottom or mouth at the same time.

The females shouted, ran after the men, throwing themselves on the bed, dragging the men on the top of them.

My loving mistress partook of the universal excitement with the rest. She was, if possible, more furious than any of her sex, mad with the extraordinary lubricity aroused within her amorous frame, twining herself in my arms, rubbing all parts of her body against mine, smothering me with kisses, nay, even pinching and biting me with force, so highly were her erotic propensities aroused, and continually calling on me by every endearing name, to frig, fuck, or give her satisfaction with my tongue.

Placing herself in the most lascivious positions, throwing up her legs and outstretching her arms, she would invite me, in the most licentious terms, to enter the amorous lists, expatiating on each and every separate beauty of her person, declaring the superior firmness of her plump bubbies, which she would press and squeeze, then on the white and velvet softness of her belly, describing all the luscious charms of her cunt, the luxurious heat contained within its juicy folds. Then turning on her belly, would display the two full and plump moons of her backside, inviting me to enter from that quarter. Then throwing her legs back, lay with the feet resting on her buttocks.

While in this position a thought struck me, and I determined to put it in execution.

Throwing myself on my back, my feet towards her head, my bare arse against hers, my prick stiff and erect as a rod of ivory tipped with red, I told my inamorata to lower her legs on my body. As she did so I had my battering ram right to the point, and she impaled herself on its head. This was a rather novel mode of fucking, but none more so than the manner in which some of the others were frigging.

The orgies of these Bacchantes partially subsided for a few minutes, when the president of the club, calling for order, put to the vote whether the lights in the room should be put out or not.

Having witnessed all that had passed, I thought this a strange proceeding, and I asked my fair partner to solve the riddle; she replied that at a certain hour at each meeting the party, both male and female, stripped themselves of every ornament. The women were not even allowed to retain combs in their hair. The men then retiring to another apartment for a moment or two, the women would put out all the lights in the room, taking care, however, to leave one burning in a small side closet; then on the ringing of a bell the men would again enter the room, in which were their mistresses, and mixing indiscriminately with them, would recommence the soft pleasures of love at once.

Neither the ladies nor their lovers were allowed to open their mouths even for a whisper, for fear of being known to each other, and it was for the same reasons everyone was obliged to lay aside every ornament, no matter what it might be, so that a brother and sister, in case they were together, could not recognise one another by any particular bracelet, ring or other ornament.

After the vote had been taken we did as I have just stated.

On our re-entering the room, which was totally dark. the door was locked from the outside by an attendant, and stumbling forward through the darkness, we met the women, who threw themselves into our arms, so that we were soon tumbling pell mell on the floor.

I got hold of a plump little fairy, and groping my way to one corner of the large bed, I placed her in a favourable position, and finding my way in the dark as well as in daylight, I revelled in the most voluptuous charms.

Oh, ye gods! how tight did her cunt clasp my prick. What a luscious suction was created by the juicy folds of her cylinder as my piston-rod shoved in and out. How gloriously she met all my thrusts by the most energetic heaves. Oh, how her fiery kisses were lavished on my cheeks and lips, as I pressed her to my bosom. And now the crisis came on, and we swam in a sea of pleasure.

I lay by her side, and broke the rules by telling her in a whisper who I was. I questioned her about her adventures in the dark.

She went on to tell me that at one of the meetings, on the lights being suddenly restored, she found herself lying in the arms of her half-brother, and that she had frequently met with her cousin also.

She said that she had known brothers and sisters, and many a pair of cousins, who had been caught in each other's arms, and that on the lights being restored, so far from quitting one another they pursued the chase till the game was run down, and enjoyed themselves as they would, had they been strangers.

She said that in order to obtain the full enjoyment of the pleasures of love, it was necessary to do away with all modesty and restraint; that man was made for woman, and woman for man. That, for her part, she considered it made no difference who the actors were, as long as the fucking was well done and enjoyed.

All her actions and movements pronounced my partner one of the most licentious of women. She played with all parts of my body; laying her head on my thighs, she would handle my stones, put the head of my prick between other lips than those nature formed to receive it, and tickling the head of it with her tongue she tried to awaken it to renewed vigour; trying every means to arouse its dormant energies, she succeeded, and casting herself into my arms, lay on her back upon me.

My pego was in a beautiful state of erection, his head rooting up between the snowy thighs of my fair burden, and furiously butting the door, demanding an entrance into the secret chamber of love. With the tips of her fingers she opened the valves that closed the rosy-tinted aperture of her cavernous recess, and inserting the head I gave rein to my courses, and for the seventh time that night did I drown myself in bliss.

So well pleased was I with my companion that, despite the attraction of the many beauties who were groping about over the room, enjoying themselves first with one man, then with another, and any of whom I might have had, I laid myself in her arms, my cheek resting on a very large round globe of flesh, her arms clasping me close to it, while her legs were crossed with mine.

In this position I fell into a sound sleep.

When I awoke the lights were blazing with great splendour, and I found the girl in whose arms I had fallen asleep engaged in a vigorous combat with a man who lay close by me.

Continuing the debauch till the approach of day, we all dressed, each one going separately, and by different routes to their residences.

I reached home, and hastening to my apartment, completely worn out from the violent exercise I had undergone, I fell into a sleep from which it was three o'clock in the afternoon before I awoke.

Chapter Five

I attended all the orgies of the club – of which I had been made a member – where new debauches were committed every week.

At each meeting my partiality for the delicious creature I had lain with last, on my initiative night, increased to such a degree that I determined to have and retain her to myself if possible.

Celestine was the daughter of the Marquis de R—. In the club she was known by the soubriquet of La Rose d'Amour, by which name I shall continue to call her.

She combined all the graces and charms peculiar to the softer sex.

She had a temptingly small foot, giving tokens of the excellent smallness of the delicious slit, which nature had placed between a pair of ripe fleshy thighs, backed by a pair of fair buttocks, beautifully rising up, swelling out into bold relief from the adjacent parts. A belly white and soft as a bed of snow, a waist slender as a nymph, a neck like a swan, small mouth, inlaid with two rows of ivory, lips rosy and pouting, cheeks soft as the velvet down of an overripe peach, languishing dark eyes, sparkling and beaming with a lascivious fire, shaded by long silken lashes, while her auburn hair fell in a profusion of ringlets over her neck and shoulders, half concealing a pair of large globes rivalling alabaster in whiteness, tipped with nipples hard and red as rose buds, in fact she was 'perfection personified'.

The day following my last visit to the club, I received a letter from St Petersburg announcing my father's death, desiring me immediately to set out for that place for the purpose of removing his remains to France.

Now, I had never seen enough of my father to have great fondness for him; what little filial affection I had was soon drowned by the ideas I had of enjoyment now I was to succeed at once to his vast fortune, so that I did not like to give up my pleasures, especially that of meeting with La Rose d'Amour.

On receiving the letter I at once proceeded to the Hotel de R—, and on enquiring for Celestine was shown into the drawing-room.

The servant returned to usher me into her mistress's boudoir, where, opening the door, I passed in, and found her reclining on a sofa, in a bewitching dishabille. Her neck was uncovered, the bosom of her wrapper open, half displaying her pretty bubbies. One foot resting on the sofa, the other on an embroidered footstool, her skirts were raised to her knee, displaying a finely rounded calf. After locking the door I read her the letter I had received, and telling her I could not part from her, implored her to leave home and accompany me on my journey, telling her that on our return to France, I would fit up my château in Brittany with all the luxury of an Eastern harem, where we might reside amid all the pleasures that love could induce, and all the luxury that wealth could purchase.

After a few short murmurs she consented, and I left her to make the necessary preparations for our departure on the morrow.

As she was to accompany me in male attire, acting as a page, I was obliged to have recourse to my faithful valet, to procure proper dresses, &c.

By eight o'clock in the evening he had everything prepared, and as we were to start at daylight, Celestine, under pretence of going to a ball, came and passed the night with me in my chamber at my uncle's.

At daylight we set off with all the speed that four good horses could give us.

My companion made a very handsome-looking boy, and was the cause of our having some very amusing adventures on our journey.

At a small town on the frontier, at which we stopped, on showing my passport to Monsieur le Maire, he insisted on our staying at his house for the night, which I at last complied with.

He was an old man about sixty, grey-haired and bald. When we arrived at his house, he sent a servant to inform his wife that there were strangers in the hall below and that he desired her presence.

In a few minutes, to our agreeable surprise, there entered the room a very charming, rosy-cheeked, vivacious-looking young woman, about twenty-two years of age.

In the course of the evening I observed by the almost scornful manner in which she regarded her husband that the union with him had been a 'marriage of convenience', and furthermore, from the glances I perceived passing between her and Celestine, I knew she wanted but the opportunity to give her husband the slip, so I determined, if the chance offered, to repay M. le Maire's hospitality by making an addition to his bald pate in the shape of a pair of horns.

On retiring for the night, my mistress informed me that she had an engagement with our host's wife. That she intended to drug a glass of wine for her husband on going to bed, which would ensure her freedom for at least ten hours, and that as soon as her husband was fast asleep she would go to her room.

Telling Celestine to undress and get into my bed, I went into the room prepared for her, and stripping myself perfectly naked, awaited in darkness the coming of the charming hostess.

After waiting for an hour I heard a light step advancing towards the room, the door opened, and she entered, and whispering Rudolph, the name Celestine had taken, advanced to the bed. Slipping the bolts in the door, I caught her in my arms, and found she was as naked as myself. In kissing her she knew immediately by my whiskers that I was not the person she expected to meet, and fearing she had made a mistake in the room, she gave a slight scream, and struggled violently to free herself.

But I retained a firm hold of her naked waist, and drawing her to the bed, explained everything to her. How that my page Rudolph was my 'chère amie', accompanying me in this disguise.

After calming her fears I lighted a taper that stood on the table and after a careful study of her beauties, while I pinched and kissed everything, especially a dear hairy little cleft at the bottom of her belly, I found her to exceed the expectations I had formed at the supper table.

She could not resist my handling her person, and freely gave herself up to my touches.

The game was getting too exciting to stand dallying very long, so turning her on her back, I plunged my weapon into a bath of hot juicy flesh, and gave her a luxurious feast of the fruit of which she had had before but a very slight taste.

Five times that night did I put her through the manual exercise of love, and five times did she die away in the most ecstatic enjoyments, the pleasures of which she declared she had only known in imagination.

It was with sincere regret that Madame le Maire parted from me at dawn of day, to join her sleeping husband, to whose brows had just been added a pair of horns. They were short to be sure, but there appeared every prospect of their branching out into large antlers.

Before leaving me she made me promise to stop on my return.

After breakfast in the morning I returned my host my sincere thanks for his hospitality, assuring him that the entertainment I had received in his house was far beyond my expectations.

I ordered my carriage, and followed by my page, took the road to Vienna.

In a fortnight more we reached St Petersburg, where, after preparing everything for my return, I determined to devote a day or two to pleasure.

At a ball given at the Imperial Palace, to which I was invited, I became acquainted with the Countess Z—, one of the most accomplished beauties at Court and the reigning belle of St Petersburg.

The Countess Caroline was a widow of twenty-three! She had been married at twenty, and about a month after her marriage her husband had been killed in a duel with an Englishman.

The Countess had a gait and look proud and haughty as a Juno, her oval face and majestic figure excited my highest admiration, and I determined to make her mine.

Entering into a conversation with her, I found that she was pleased with my company, and much more with my person.

Accomplished as she was, Caroline Z— had the vice, peculiar to all Russians, of drinking large quantities of brandy. In fact, she drank so much that knowing she lived in a large palace, with no one but her serfs, I formed the resolution of making her mine that same night.

I plied her with brandy till late in the evening, and she became so much excited as not to be able to control herself. I kept close by her side throughout the night, till the ball broke up. I humbly asked permission to be her escort home.

Engaging her in a laughing conversation, I put the question to her as we descended the palace stairs, and the giddy young creature, nearly intoxicated with brandy, at once accepted.

I handed her into the carriage, bid the driver go fast, and in a moment we were at her palace.

On alighting she invited me in – an invitation which I promptly accepted – and led me up a flight of large stairs into her own dressing-room. So much was she affected by the brandy she had drunk that she hardly knew what she was doing.

Laying off her bonnet and shawl she rang the bell, and two waiting-maids entered. Asking to be excused for a few minutes, she retired to her boudoir, followed by her attendants, and in a short time reappeared in a different dress, a loose flowing gown of rich cashmere.

Calling for lunch and brandy, she dismissed the attendants who brought it in. They retired in apparent amazement at the sight of a man being admitted into her dressing-room, and especially at that hour.

I now watched my opportunity, and pouring a few drops of liquid from a small vial I always carried about me, into a glass of brandy, I presented it to her, and she drank it off.

It ran like liquid fire through her veins, her eyes sparkled with licentiousness, her heart heaved and palpitated with the fierce desires which were consuming her.

Advancing my seat beside her own, I poured into her ears a tale of burning love. I put my arm around her waist, and finding she made no resistance, pressed her to my bosom, and planting numberless kisses on her lips, sucked the breath from her.

In a minute more she delivered herself up to me body and soul, she threw her arms around my neck, and repaid the kisses I had just given, with interest.

I rose up with her in my arms, and carried her into the boudoir, in which stood a bed in a recess. I undressed her till she stood in her shift, and then taking off my own clothes, stood in my perfect nudity. Giving Caroline a soft kiss I drew the shift from off her, and had a fair view of all her secret charms.

Leading her to the bedside I gave her the fillip on her back, and soon was buried to the very utmost notch in the most lusciously tight cunt I had ever entered.

With what fire, what enthusiasm, with what fierce upheavings did she meet and receive the piercing thrusts of my love dart.

The excitement thickens, the combat grows hotter and hotter. Heavens! what pleasure! what joy! what ecstasy! Oh, how my lively partner kept time to all my fierce desires! In what a sea of delight was I plunged! What an indescribable luxurious heat reigned in the luscious folds of her cunt! Ye gods! how often did I dart my stiffened arrow through the rich, juicy flesh of her deliciously sensitive quiver! I felt the crisis approach, our mouths met; we devoured each other's tongues;

her rosy lips, how sweet and warm! What intense voluptuousness in those amorous bites, that burning struggle of our tongues, that sought, moistened, entangled, drew back, and darted together again!

I gave her the *coup de grâce*, and so great was the flood that issued from the reservoirs of love that the precious pearly fluid flowed down her thighs as I spurted into the deepest recess of her cunt the burning sperm.

Caroline had not all the briskness and vivacity of La Rose d'Amour, her movements were languishing but more voluptuous. I turned her over and over, I touched and handled every part. I kissed her again; everything did I devour with my fiery kisses, especially the gaping lips of her cunt, which were wet with the liquid stream from the fountain of pleasure which I had poured into her.

The spark kindled, the flame blazed. We writhed and twined, over and over, in each other's arms, and the sixth time had my indefatigable courser bounding to the goal of victory without tiring. The storm grew higher, the sperm fell in torrents, but could not put out the blazing fire that raged within us.

We awoke in the morning refreshed from the fatigues of the night. Again did I survey all the charms of my lovely bedfellow. She stroked my limber instrument till it grew into a stately rod. I toyed with her enticing firm globes of alabaster, each tipped with a rosebud most lusciously tempting, which I moulded and pressed in my hand, and sucking the nipples received fresh fire.

I turned her on her back; she spread her thighs, and guided the dart which pierced her to the very vitals; we again drank of the sweets obtained in the fountain of Venus.

Swearing eternal constancy and love I left my charming Caroline, and hastened home.

I told Celestine all that had occurred, not omitting to expatiate pretty freely on the pleasure I had enjoyed while revelling in the virgin charms of Caroline Z—.

This somewhat piqued my French charmer, but on opening to her my views she consented to the arrangement proposed. I told her my intention was to fit up the château in all the magnificence of Barbaric pearl and gold, and to take, nay, in fact, steal off all the handsomest women that excited my desires very strongly, and carry them to the château, which I would have guarded by trusty followers, in fact, to make it a fortified seraglio.

I told her that she should reign as undisputed mistress of the place, and that, greedy as she was, she should never want for the peculiar flesh which she was always willing and ready to devour. I also told her to have everything in complete readiness to start at a moment's notice, while I went to see the beautiful Russian in whose arms I had passed the night.

Calling in the evening, I was led by a servant immediately to Caroline. I found her in a splendid bathroom, reclining in a bath of milk and perfumed waters.

Placing a cushion on the marble edge of the bath. I made my proposition to her of leaving Russia and going to France with me. I pictured to her imagination what should be the magnificent splendour of our abode, in which love alone should be admitted.

I described to her all the endless variety of enjoyments in which we could indulge, passing our days and nights in one uninterrupted round of pleasure.

So highly did I excite her imagination by the glowing description of the amorous life we should pass that she at once agreed to accompany us. I say us, for I had told her of my having Celestine with me, and of my intentions of possessing every woman who might take my fancy.

She entered at once into the spirit of my proposition, and made me promise to bring Celestine to her house on the following evening so that all three of us could spend the night together.

After spending the day in driving about the environs of St Petersburg, Celestine (in her male attire) and I alighted at the house of the Countess, and we were at once shown into the dressing-room of which I have before told.

Caroline was reclining on a sofa in all the charming coquetry of a *négligé déshabillé* when we entered. Instead of rising to receive us she merely tapped a silver bell which lay beside her, and two girls entered, who, taking Celestine into the boudoir, remained for a full half-hour.

What was my astonishment when she re-entered to behold her in a dress, the exact counterpart of the one Caroline had on, who as soon as she came in got up and embraced her, praising her beauty, admiring her figure, and calling her sister, and paying her every attention she could think of.

On asking my beauteous Russian how she had got the dress for Celestine, she replied that from the description I had given her she had the dress made in that short time, as she could not think of showing off her own charms to the best advantage with Celestine concealed by her male attire, saying which she opened a casket and placed on the brow of Celestine a coronet of diamonds of the first water, on her neck a necklace of pearls, and in the bosom of her dress a large rose formed of brilliants, asking her to receive them as a present from a sister.

Celestine drew from her finger a very large brilliant, and presented it to Caroline as a token of friendship, pleading her present poverty as an excuse for not being able to make a more handsome return for her elegant present.

Supper being laid in the room in which we then were, we sat down to a feast for the gods, expressly prepared for the occasion by the voluptuous Caroline. The dishes were all highly seasoned, while the wines were of the most heating and exciting kind.

After the dessert had been brought in I laid my plans again before my two mistresses.

Caroline said she would need but a week to make her preparations, as the most of her immense fortune consisted in money and jewels, which she would place in my hands to be disposed of as I thought proper, telling me to make arrangements for her leaving very secretly, for if either of her brothers should know of her intentions they would most assuredly detain her by force if in no other manner.

Having drunk enough wine to excite their desires pretty strongly, my two beauties commenced tussling me about, rolling me on the floor, and tumbling on top of me, their dresses in most admirable disorder; a pin becoming loose would expose the half of a breast whiter than snow; the flying up of a petticoat would display a well-turned calf, a knee, or a firm, fleshy thigh.

But this dalliance, acting as a provocative on their already excited lusts, could not be put up with very long. They burned for some more substantial good than that afforded by kissing and pinching, which were fine auxiliaries for increasing an appetite they could not satisfy.

Jumping up I ran into the boudoir, followed by the dear creatures, whose eyes flashed with the fires of libertinism, while their breasts rose and fell with quick heavings.

I hid under the bed, from whence they pulled me, and stripping me naked, glued their moist lips over every part of me, my erect Jacob's staff coming in for more than its share.

They stripped to their skin, and calling on me as umpire to decide on the relative beauties of their charms, as they stood before a large pier glass, handling their snowy strawberry-tipped bubbies, sleeking down the glossy curling whiskers that surrounded two pairs of the most temptingly pouting lips that ever adorned women. Since both were perfect models of voluptuous beauty and grace, although different in their kinds, I could not decide between them, but admired more and more the charms of which I was the happy possessor.

I seized on the rosy nipples of the heaving snowy hillocks, which disdaining the use of corsets, rested on their bosoms like globes of alabaster. I sucked them, I squeezed their soft round bellies against mine, I kissed everything and everywhere. I laid my kisses on the hairy mounts that overhung the delicious grottos underneath; the lips which close the mouth of the flesh slits next received their share; I am on fire! I burn! The bed receives us! I wish to push matters home at once; but no, they would bring me to the very point before I could enter.

Celestine has seized on my prick; she cannot get it into her cunt, so, determined not to lose it altogether, she takes it in her mouth, she sucks its glowing head, she rolls her tongue over the top of it. I am mad – delirious. No longer to be restrained I throw myself on to Caroline, who receives me with open legs and arms. I dart my fiery rod into her furnace, which consumes it. A few maddening thrusts, driven home with such force that I touch her to the very quick – a cry of thrilling pleasure escapes us at the same time – and all is over.

But so intense were our passions that we hardly perceived it till I felt her again moving up to me. How delicious! What voluptuous warmth pervaded her whole body. How exquisitely did the springing cheeks of her backside respond to all my motions. The little devil Celestine is playing with two large balls that keep knocking against the buttocks of my antagonist.

It is too much, I drive it home, and lie gasping and quivering on Caroline's breast, who cries out, 'Oh heavens! further in! I come – I spend! Oh – oh, God, I die! Oh, dear, what plea – pleas – pleas – ure!'

She had fainted. The delicious wrigglings of her backside, the contraction of her cunt, sucked the last drop from me.

When she recovered from the delirium in which her senses were plunged, she lay with her eyes languishingly beaming, her lips apart, with the tip of her rosy tongue slightly protruded between two rows of pearl – the very picture of voluptuous pleasure.

So plentifully had I bestowed in her the liquid treasure of love's reservoir, and so delightfully had she intermingled with mine the essence of her own dear self, that when I withdrew from her the pearly stream flowed out and ran over her thighs.

I had a short respite, receiving renewed vigour from the caresses of Celestine, whose greedy little maw was gaping wide to receive the half-erect machine which she was working at, trying to make it stand, so as to win her purpose.

Her whole body glows with an intense heat, the most voluptuous warmth reigns in every part! She burns, she imparts to me the fire which is consuming her very vitals. My ever willing and ready courser comes up to the stand, with head erect, impatient for the word.

I give him the reins, and he plunges forward in his impetuous career; on, on he speeds, nothing retards him. On, on, he rushes, nor stops till the race is run. He falters, he stops, his head droops, he pours out his very life blood, sprinkling the whole course which he has run with the precious liquid. It is finished; another faint struggle; a few convulsive jerks and it is all over. I lie panting on the heaving bosom of Celestine.

After having for the eighth time renewed my embraces with my two loves, I fell asleep, only to wake to new pleasures.

At the end of the week Caroline, having completed her business, placed in my hands upwards of three millions of francs and jewels to the value of one million more, and the following day we left St Petersburg.

The girls at my request provided themselves with a full wardrobe of male attire and we started for France, where I longed to be, to put into operation all my schemes of pleasure, which I was determined should rival, if not excel, anything of the kind ever seen or heard of in the East.

On passing the frontier of France, I directed my route to the château, where, after depositing my lovely mistresses, I kept on to Paris.

On entering the capital I drove to the most fashionable upholsterer, telling him what I wanted done and giving him *carte blanche* in respect of the expense to be incurred.

Telling the man to make everything of the very richest material money could purchase, I advanced him a cheque for one hundred thousand francs, with the privilege of drawing on my banker for more in case of need.

Giving orders to have everything fixed in one month, I started to seek out some of the members of the Club from which I had stolen Celestine.

My first visit was to the hotel of the Count de C—, for the purpose of seeing Mademoiselle de C—, or Rosalie, as I shall call her, who having been my partner in the initiative act on the night of my admittance to the club, I felt a considerable partiality towards, and determined to transplant to the château as soon as everything was fitted up in it.

On entering the hotel I was told that the Count and his lady were out; enquiring for Rosalie, I was shown into the music room, where I found her seated at a harp.

On the servant disappearing she ran up to me, and threw herself into my arms.

I led her to a sofa, and seating her on my knee, unfolded to her my intentions, stating what I had done and what I intended to do. Telling her how Celestine had accompanied me to Russia; how I had made a conquest of the charming Caroline; how I had brought them both to France, and left them at the château. I urged her by all the powers of persuasion I could employ to go with me to the château, where her life would be one continued round of luxurious pleasure.

She gave her consent to accompany me as soon as I had everything prepared for her reception.

During our conversation I was pressing and moulding her breasts, and as the dialogue gained interest my hand became more bold, and roamed everywhere.

When I had finished talking I found that in my absent-mindedness I had lain her down on the sofa, and was preparing to put her attentions of love to the proof, when an infernal servant opened the door to announce a visitor.

Ach, cursed luck! thought I, as we settled ourselves, to be thus interrupted at such a crime. But on seeing the lady enter my grief was changed to joy, for she was certainly the most voluptuous and beautiful creature my eyes ever looked on. With what dignity, what grace she crossed the room. What graceful ease reigned in every motion. A well-turned ankle, a pretty little foot, that noiselessly tripped across the floor, gave me a very good good opinion of what was to be found above the garter.

Rosalie introduced the lady to me as Laura, daughter of the Count de B—. Seeing there was no further opportunity of paying my compliments privately to Rosalie, I took my leave to make other calls.

I spent some six or eight days in Paris, leaving orders with jewellers and silversmiths for every variety of fancy articles, not forgetting to have my banker write to his agent in London, to procure me a swift sailing yacht of the largest size, fitted up in the richest manner, without regard to cost, and to be manned with a crew and willing to do any service I might name. She was ordered to be sent to the château on the coast of Brittany, where a small creek, putting in from the open sea, made an excellent harbour for a vessel.

Having finished my business, I hastened down to the château, taking with me a first-rate architect and a number of workmen.

In a short time I had converted a large saloon on the second floor into a magnificent hall. Its sides and ends were covered with flowers and evergreens, making a perpetual summer. On each side stood a row of statues of nude figures, which I had purchased in Paris. At either end played a beautiful fountain while in the centre was a large marble basin, in which played a third fountain. The figure that cast up the water was a statue of a female lying down, so arranged that she seemed to be floating on her back in the water; the *jet d'eau* burst from her cunt, and ascended nearly to the ceiling, making a shower bath for anyone who might be seated on the figure.

The side windows opened on to a balcony, which overlooked the sea.

On the opposite side of the corridor I had converted the whole suite of apartments into one large room, which as soon as the upholsterer arrived was to be furnished with fifty beds.

The suite of apartments on the same floor of the adjoining wing I had converted into one large bathing room. In this room was a marble bath, in which fifty people could bathe at the same time. A small fish pond stood in the garden. It turned into a small lake of about one hundred yards in diameter.

Chapter Six

In the course of a few weeks a vessel arrived in the creek, laden with furniture for the château, and the upholsterer presented himself to me. I took him through the building, showing him in what style I wished such and such rooms furnished.

The room of fountains was simply furnished with cushions of rich satin and silk, and musical instruments, as I intended it merely for smoking, singing, and dancing.

The other long room opposite was furnished with bedsteads of finest rosewood, inlaid with gold, silver, pearl, and even precious stones. Each bed had springs placed in it, and was stuffed with the finest down. The sheets were cambric of the finest texture, coverlets of silks and satins, beautifully worked, while over all was a spread of Brussels or point lace.

The curtains were of crimson velvet, set off with white silk. In the alcove of each bed was placed a mirror, set in a frame of silver.

The floor was covered with the richest carpets; the walls were hung with silk, on which were worked the loves of Cupid and Psyche, the rape of Europa, Leda ravished by Jupiter in the shape of a swan, Diana issuing from the bath, a procession of naked female Bacchanalians carrying the jolly gods in triumph on their shoulders, and other devices.

Instead of chairs and sofas there were cushions placed in the room, worked with pearls and precious stones, bordered with fringe of pure bullion.

Each bed stood on a raised dais of mahogany. The carpets were of the richest texture, so soft and thick that the foot sank ankle deep in them. At the far end was the state bedchamber; it was partitioned off from the other parts of the room by a curtain of blue velvet.

This apartment was furnished as a Turkish tent, the drapery (of green velvet) depending from a centrepiece of gold stars and being drawn down to the sides so as to form a perfect tent.

The bed stood in the centre of the place, it was made of beautifully carved cedar from Lebanon; the posts, head and foot boards were ornamented with designs of birds, fishes, men and women, &c., of pure gold and silver, set with precious stones. Curtains of richly wrought velvet, looped up with chains of gold, completed the *coup d'œil*.

I had placed no ornament in this apartment, so it was designed as an initiatory bed for all the beauties I could bring to the place. And although licentious pictures, statues, &c., may have an exhilarating effect upon men at times, they also, by their beauty, attract the attention from the dear creatures we might be enjoying.

Adjoining this large bedchamber I furnished a dressing-room. The walls and ceiling were inlaid with large plate mirrors, making the room one complete looking-glass. At the sides, overhead, no matter where they might look, whosoever entered it could see nothing but their reflections.

Here were placed stands and toilette table, of chased gold and silver, ivory, and pearl: all the perfumes of the East, all the cosmetics that could enhance the beauty, and give youth and fullness to those who inhabited the place, were here in profusion.

Adjoining the room of glasses was a drawing-room which looked out on the garden. The doors and windows opened on to a balcony running the full length of that side of the castle. To this room I paid more attention than to any other. The floor was covered with a carpet of purple velvet, stuffed with down. The rarest productions of the old masters adorned the walls, mirrors, framed in gold, depending from the beaks of birds wrought in silver, hung between the paintings. In each corner of the room stood a statue of one of the Graces, in the body of which was set a music box, made to discourse the sweetest music. On stands of alabaster were large vases, *chefs d'œuvre* of Dresden manufacture, containing sweet smelling flowers; while the richest spices and perfumes of Araby, burning in censers entirely concealed in niches in the wall, diffused through the room odours that enchanted the senses.

Here it was that I received my mistresses after all the rooms were furnished.

During the time the workmen were busy arranging the rooms and furniture, I had kept them in a distant wing of the château, refusing to see them till everything was finished. I had secured the services of a dozen or more lusty fellows and wenches, to serve as servants and guards to those I might wish to detain.

One of the men I made the servant of the bedchamber – so called, as he was the only male I allowed in this part of the castle. Him I sent to bring me La Rose d'Amour and the voluptuous Russian, with Rose, Manette and Marie.

When they entered I was reclining on a pile of cushions, dressed in a loose robe of rich cashmere, with a Turkish cap on my head, ready prepared for a bath, to which I intended to take them.

So soon as the door was closed on them they ran up, and falling on me, devoured me with embraces and kisses. Oh, how they caught fire at the touch of me, burned for that which I had kept them from more than a month, whilst I could scarcely restrain myself from throwing them on the floor and darting the liquid flame of love into them at once. But I restrained myself.

I took them into the garden of flowers, and showed them all my improvements there, the beautiful little lake surrounded with shrubs and trees, over the whole surface of which was a net of fine wire, which confined a quantity of rare birds.

Again we entered the château, and passed through to the bedchamber, where I showed them the fifty beds, telling them I intended to travel till I had procured fifty of the handsomest women in the world to lie in them.

From this we passed on to the bathing-room, and throwing off all covering, plunged into the perfumed waters.

After lying and wantoning in the bath for some time, I pulled the tassel of a bell, and four of the wenches I before mentioned entered to serve as waiting-maids.

We emerged from the water, and they dried our bodies and hair, and being given loose gowns, we wrapped ourselves in them, and I led my beauties to the dressing-room.

I cannot depict their astonishment on entering this apartment of mirrors. Taking their gowns, I threw them out of the door and closed it. I told them to dress in the rich clothes which lay before them.

How great was their astonishment to see themselves reflected a thousand times in the walls and ceiling! The toilet stands seemed to be in every part of the room, and it was some time ere they could get over the confusion they were in, but with the help of one another they got dressed. The dresses I had provided for them were those used by the Turks – wide, loose pants and waistcoats of satin, and short skirts, instead of the unhandy long shift.

After having dressed ourselves, I took them to the room of fountains, where we had a rich lunch. Here I opened to them my views, telling them that after one more trip to Paris, as soon as the yacht arrived which I had ordered, I intended to sail for Constantinople, where I would buy some of the most beautiful girls I could find, and also that I intended to purchase some mutes and eunuchs for my own harem, as I could not trust the females I might buy and bring with me the same as I could the ones that were now around me.

I told them I intended to take one or two of them with me in the vessel when I went, and that to be perfectly fair and impartial they should draw to see who should be the lucky ones; and also that I intended to have two of them sleep with me that night, and they must draw for that too.

I had determined beforehand that I would sleep with Celestine and Caroline, so I arranged the drawing that it came out as I wished.

At an early hour I led the way to the bedroom, followed by the five girls. It took us but a moment to put ourselves in a state of nakedness.

Oh, with what joy, what transports, I hugged their warm naked bodies to mine! How delightfully the soft, smooth, white skin of their bellies felt as they twined about in my arms! With what fervour did they fasten their moist, pouting lips to mine, while their lustrous eyes sparkled and flashed with lustful fires.

I draw the voluptuous Celestine to the bed. My passions are raised to the highest pitch. My prick is swelled almost to bursting, its vermilion head stands erect against my belly, not to be bent without danger of breaking.

Celestine is on her back, her thighs apart, showing the lips of her luscious cunt slightly open, anxiously awaiting the attack.

I precipitate myself upon her; I pierce her to the very quick. She screams with mingled pain and pleasure.

The enormous head of my prick distends the folds and lips of her cunt to their utmost stretch. The storm increases, everything trembles, the lightnings flash. the rain pours, it comes in torrents! I spend! I die! My God, what pleasure! Oh, heavens, have mercy!

We rolled, we screamed, we bit, we yelled like demons from the excess of our pleasure. Her cunt is a small lake of sperm, my prick swims in it, lolling its length. I draw it out, and the pearly liquid gushes forth, flooding her thighs and the sheets with the rich mingled essence of our bodies.

Ah, my charming Celestine, what an excess of exquisite pleasure did I experience whilst in your arms that night. Thrice did I, goaded by my fierce lusts, bedew the cunts of my two noble mistresses with a deluge of the precious liquid, bountifully supplied by the stream of pleasure from love's reservoir.

I recovered myself a little, and paid a visit to Rose, Manette, and Marie, to each of whom I did justice, always advancing to the attack with head erect and flying colours. Nor did I leave one of them without having well oiled their precious little maws with the dear liquid that women are ever looking for.

On the following morning I started for Paris, accompanied by Caroline, dressed as a page, to finish my preparation for starting to Constantinople.

After stopping at my hotel, I sallied out with my female page to call on Rosalie de C—, whom I was lucky enough to find alone.

Having embraced her, I introduced Caroline to her, asking when she would be ready to go with me to the château; she replied that she would be ready in two days.

I then enquired after her friend, the lovely Laura B—. I told Rosalie that I was determined to possess her friend Laura by some means or other, and that she must render me her assistance in securing her, and as I could think of no other plan, I proposed to Rosalie that she should go and get her friend to take an airing with her in the Bois de Boulogne, and that in a sequestrated place I would come up with them, alight from my carriage, and invite her and Laura to get out and take a walk, and that I would then throw a shawl over Laura's head, force her into my own carriage, take herself and Caroline, and set out with all possible speed for the castle.

Everything happened as I had arranged.

On coming up with Rosalie's carriage in the wood, I approached her with my invitation to walk.

I opened the door of the carriage, and as Laura passed out first, just as she reached the ground, Rosalie from behind threw a large shawl over her head, and drew the corners close around her neck, so that her voice could not be heard. I caught her up in my arms and carried her into my own carriage. Rosalie and Caroline entered immediately, and I dashed off with my fair prize at the top speed of four fine horses.

On the road to the château I stopped at no houses but those of persons whom I had brought over to my own interest.

Arrived at the place we stopped at for the night, I hurried with my companions into a large room prepared for us by a courier that I had sent in advance.

Immediately after my arrival supper was served. Dismissing all the attendants, I turned the key in the door, and for the first time since I had forced her into my carriage, I spoke to Laura.

I told her of my unconquerable love for her, of the feelings that were aroused in my heart towards her the first time that I saw her at Rosalie's house, and that I then formed the determination of carrying her off to the château. That I was determined no one else should be possessed of so much beauty, nor revel in such charms as she possessed.

I laid open to Laura all my plans. I informed her how I had fitted up the old castle, and for what purpose, telling her that she would there find Celestine C—, one of her old companions, and that Rosalie was another who willingly accompanied me.

I introduced her to Caroline Z—, telling her rank, how I had made a conquest of her, and how she had linked her fortune with mine, and followed me to France.

I dwelt at some length on the life of luxurious ease and pleasure we should lead at the château, expatiating on the endless joys and ecstasies of her living with me in all the unrestrained liberty of sexual intercourse.

Rosalie and Caroline also spoke to her of the life of pleasure they led with me, describing to her, as well as they could, the extreme luxury of lying in a man's arms and being well fucked; and used all their powers of persuasion to induce her to go with them and me peaceably to the château.

Laura, from being at first very sulky, neither eating nor speaking to any of us, became somewhat mollified, so that she partook of the supper, and answered questions put to her by my two mistresses.

After the supper was removed I called for wine, and while we sat talking and drinking I took care to make the discourse run principally upon one subject alone – that of love and its natural consequences, and the intercourse of the two sexes.

Caroline and Rosalie were very useful auxiliaries, talking with the utmost abandon, stripping and dancing about over the floor as the wine began to fly to their heads, uncovering their breasts, showing their bubbies, occasionally flirting up their petticoats, exhibiting a fine calf or knee, with other tricks, all of which tended to confuse the senses of the charming little Laura, who watched their movements all the while. I constantly plied her with wine till she became somewhat excited and a little free, making remarks on the two girls who were tussling on the floor.

I rang the bell, and ordered a bottle of white brandy, which, as soon as it was brought in, I uncorked, and pouring out glasses of it, invited my Russian to drink. She took up the glass, as did Rosalie, both declaring that Laura must drink with them. After some hesitation she took up her glass, and placing it to her lips, sipped a little of the liquor, and put it down.

Caroline and Rosalie, for the purpose of inducing the charming Laura to drink freely of the brandy, drank glass after glass of it, till Laura, from sipping, began to toss off her glass as well as any of us.

When I gave them the sign to retire for the night, Laura had become so intoxicated that she required the assistance of the other two to enable her to retire without staggering in her gait.

After they had got into their bedchamber, I stripped myself perfectly naked, and Caroline having left the door slightly ajar, I stepped into the room, hiding myself behind a bed curtain to observe the manoeuvres of my two lovely pimps.

They first undressed themselves stark naked, then did the same for the inebriated Laura. And then she stood in all her naked beauty before me, exhibiting charms to my ardent gaze, more lovely, if possible, than any I had heretofore ever enjoyed.

After my mistresses had stripped Laura of her clothes, they viewed and admired her naked beauty, praising it above that of the Venus de Milo, throwing her down on the floor, turning her over and over, squeezing her breasts, pinching her backside, opening her thighs, even the lips of the dear little niche between them. They praise its beauty, admire the lascivious plumpness of its lips, and even go so far as to lay their kisses upon it, the conversation running in praise, the while, on the pleasures she would mutually enjoy with the men who should be so lucky as to tear up the virgin defences which guarded the entrance to so delicious a little cunt.

I could now see Caroline insert the tip of her finger into the dear slit with which she was playing, and commence tickling her, while Rosalie threw her arms around her neck, and drawing her to a close embrace, kissed her, putting her tongue into Laura's mouth, which, with the frigging she was receiving from Caroline, caused her to experience the most delightful sensations, if I might judge from the exclamations and the wrigglings of her backside, as she squirmed about on the floor.

Perceiving, by the motions of Laura, that she would soon, for the first time, slightly experience the ecstatic joys which woman can only procure the full enjoyment of when in the arms of a man, I slipped out from my hiding place, and went and took the place of Caroline between her thighs (unperceived by Laura, whose face was hid in the bosom of Rosalie), and inserting my finger into her cream jug, I soon brought down a copious libation of the precious liquid with which my hand was plentifully bedewed, so freely did the liquid jet out once the sluice was opened. Crossing her thighs over my body she almost squeezed the breath from me, exclaiming in broken accents: 'Oh, now it comes! Again – oh, God! I faint. I die!'

Loosening her holds, she stretched herself out with, as usual, a gentle shudder, as the ecstasy caused her to faint away.

While Laura lay in her trance of pleasure I laid myself down in her arms, placing my cheek on her bosom, my lips touching hers, my hand still covering that dear slit, and my finger still retaining possession of its inner folds.

As I perceived Laura beginning to recover from her ecstasy, I drew her to my bosom and recommenced my titillations. I asked her if she was still angry with me for carrying her away, telling her that as soon as we arrived at the château she should enjoy all the reality of the unreal mockery she had just tasted through the agency of my fingers.

If her modesty and virtue were not entirely conquered, the motion of my finger reproduced in her the delicious sensations of pleasure from which she had just recovered, and which for the second time she was about to enjoy. She could make me no answer, but to throw her arms round my neck and glue her lips to mine.

My desires were excited to the highest pitch. I depicted to her the pleasure she would experience when, after arriving at the château, I should deflower her of her virginity, and triumphantly carry off her maidenhead 'on the head of this, dear Laura,' I said, as I took one of her hands and clasped it round my prick. 'Then,' said I, 'you will know all the joys of pleasures of a real fuck.'

'You will then,' I continued, 'experience all the sweet confusion, far different from what you now feel, of stretching wide apart your thighs to receive man between them, to feel his warm naked body joined to yours, the delicious preparatory toying with your breasts, the hot kisses lavished on them and on your lips, his roving tongue forcing its way between your rosy lips in search of yours, the delicious meeting of them, their rolling about and tickling each other as mine now does yours,' at the same time thrusting my tongue to meet hers.

'And then to feel him take his prick, and with the tips of his fingers part the lips of the flesh sheath into which he intends to shove it, putting the head of it between the lips, and gently shoving it in at first, stretching the poor little thing to its utmost extent, till, not without some pain to you, the head is effectually lodged in it. Then, after laying a kiss on your lips, he commences the attack by gently but firmly and steadily shoving into you, increasing his shoves harder and harder, till he thrusts with all his force, causing you to sigh and cry out, he thrusts hard, he gains a little at every move, he forces the barriers, he tears and roots up all your virginal defences, you cry out for mercy but receive none. His passions are aroused into madness, fire flashes from his eyes; concentrating all his energies for one tremendous thrust, he lunges forward, carries everything before him, and enters the fort by storm, reeking with the blood of his fair enemy, who with a scream of agony yields up her maidenhead to the conqueror, who, having put his victim *hors de combat*, proceeds to reap the reward of his hard fought and bloody battle.

'Now he draws himself out to the head, and slowly enters again. Again he draws out, and again enters, till the friction caused by the luscious tightness of the rich flesh which clasps tightly his foaming pego causes such delicious sensations that he is no longer master of himself.

'He lunges with fierceness into her, the crisis of pleasure approaches; he feels it coming, he drives it home to her – deeper, deeper. At last it comes – he spends.

'My God, the pleasure! His exclamations of Oh! ah! the deep drawn sighs, the short jerks of his backside, the quick motions of his rump, proclaim that the acme of pleasure has seized him, and that he is spurting into her the precious fluid which oils and cools the burning itchings of the dear little cunt, which has undergone the one painful trial to which all your sex is liable.'

During my description Caroline had taken my pego in her hands, and had been playing with and rubbing it all the time. I still kept my finger in Laura, and perceiving by the twitching of her rump that she was about to spend –

'I – oh, dear – I – now – feel it. There, I come now, I spend. Ah, oh, oh, h – ha!' and I died away on her bosom, to awake and find that Laura had wet my hand with a most plentiful effusion of nectar ravished from her by my fingers, while I had squirted over her belly and thighs a flood of sperm.

Laura, without any murmurings, gave herself up to me and the seductive friggings of my fingers without any reserve, and not till nature was perfectly exhausted did we fall asleep in each other's arms.

In the morning, when Laura awoke and found herself lying in my arms, she sprang from my side, and snatching a coverlet from the bed, wrapped herself in it, and sat down in one corner, sobbing and weeping as though her heart would break.

I attempted to console her, but she would not listen to me, and having dressed myself I went into another room, while Caroline and Rosalie tried to bring her to herself again, and they succeeded so far as to bring her out to breakfast, which was shortly afterwards served.

At the table they rallied Laura for her coyness in the morning, after having spent so delightful a night with me, jesting her about my having procured for her with my finger the exquisite pleasure which had thrown her into such delicious swoons. Telling her how, when the fit was coming on her she would throw her arms round me, squeeze my hand between her thighs, wriggle her plump little buttocks, &c.

After having drank a few glasses of wine she had completely recovered her spirits.

I went out of the room to order the carriage, and on my return I found her tussling with the other girls, they trying to throw her down for the purpose of giving her a taste of the pleasure she had enjoyed so frequently through my agency during the night.

When I entered the two called me to come and help them, while Laura begged me to rescue her from the hands of her tormentors.

Whilst they were thus calling on me the landlord entered to announce the carriage, and taking Laura by the arm, I led her out, followed by the others. We entered the carriage and drove off.

It was late in the night when we arrived at the château, on the third day of our being on the road. I retired to bed and fell asleep, with all the girls sleeping around me, determined to touch none of them, reserving all the powers within me for the purpose of doing full justice to the maidenhead of the lovely Laura.

ossgo

Chapter Seven

The morning after our arrival, on awakening. I roused up the sleeping beauties who lay around me, and led them to the bathing-apartment.

We all entered the water, and after sporting for an hour or more, we issued from it, and entering the dressing-room, made our morning toilets, the girls dressing in cymar, pants and waistcoat, such as are worn by the odalisques in the East.

This day was made all preparations on a splendid scale for the great sacrifice of the night, the taking of Laura's maidenhead.

We spent the time in roving about the park until noon: running, jumping and tussling, so as to keep an excited circulation of the blood.

The dinner, which I had ordered three hours later than usual, consisted of all the most highly seasoned dishes and of the richest and most exhilarating wines, of which we partook to a slight excess and at last rose from the table with our amorous propensities aroused to the highest pitch.

We retired to the bedchamber, and stripping ourselves we again sought the bath, which was highly scented with the most costly perfumes.

Remaining but a short time in the bath, we went to the bedchamber, and Rose and Marie having drawn aside the heavy hangings, we entered the state-apartment. Here Celestine and Manette, with towels of the finest linen, absorbed the water from the body and hair of Laura, while Rosalie and Caroline did the same for me.

While they were combing out the rich auburn tresses which floated in wavy masses over her neck and shoulders, I was on my knees before her, combing out the black silken hair which grew, with a luxuriance seldom seen in girls of seventeen, out of the fattest little hillock I ever saw and almost hid the entrance to the beautiful grotto beneath.

Having combed out her precious locks, *comme il faut*, and parted them from around the mouth of the greedy little maw, which was shortly and for the first time to partake and eat of the flesh, with the tips of my fingers I open the pouting lips and feast my eyes with gazing on the deep carnation of the luscious love-niche, in which I was soon to put the idol. I peep, gaze, look and try to get a further insight into the hidden mysteries of the deep, dark, cavernous recess; but my sight could penetrate no further than a most tempting bit of flesh, somewhat in the shape of a heart, which appeared to be pendant, like a dazzling light from the ceiling of a room, in the centre of the passage to the unexplored cavern, through the folding doors of which I was peeping.

My enraptured eyes still gaze on the tempting titbit before me, till, recalled to my senses by feeling something moving between my thighs, and looking down, I perceive the hand of Celestine clasped around my noble shaft, and slowly drawing her hand up and down it, covering and uncovering its beautiful red head with the fine white skin which lay around the neck in folds.

This at once gave an impetus to my desires, which could not be restrained. I raised up, and catching Laura in my arms, I carried her to the bed and placed her on it, the firm semi-globes of her backside resting on the edge of the bed, supported by a cushion of white satin, covered with an embroidered cloth of fine linen.

Celestine and Caroline support each a leg, while Rose and Marie jump on to the bed, and Manette and Rosalie stand on either side to support me, in case my feelings should overpower me at the close of the performance, and also to serve as pilots for me – the one to open the gate of love, the other to guide the fiery dart aright into the entrance.

Fearing somewhat for the little maid, who was to undergo the process of defloration, and knowing that the rose was not without its thorn and that the sting would at first be pretty severe, I anointed my impatient virgin-destroyer with perfumed oil, and marched to the battlefield, determined to conquer or to die.

Her legs were held apart. I enter between and plant a soft kiss on the lips which I was about cruelly to tear open, which seemed to send a thrill of joy through her.

I slightly incline forward; the tips of Manette's fingers part the rosy lips. Rosalie grasps hold of my pego and lodges the head in the entrance.

The two girls, who support her legs, rest them on my hips, and standing behind me, cross their arms with joined hands so that the ankles rest on them as on a cushion. Gathering myself up, I make one fierce lunge forward and gain full an inch.

The sudden distention of the parts causes her to scream with pain and to wriggle her rump in a manner that, instead of in any way ridding herself of me, helps me in my endeavours to penetrate still further.

I thrust harder, I penetrate, I pierce her. The blood begins to flow. I feel it on my thighs. Her buttocks are convulsively twitching and wriggling in endeavours to throw me off. In her agony she utters scream after scream.

Poor little maid, it is a rough and thorny way to travel. But once gone over, the road is ever after smooth. Again I thrust forward.

'Ah, my God!' she exclaims, 'I shall die! Have mercy on me!'

I have no pity on her and shove harder than ever to put her out of her pain and agony. I tear her open, carrying everything before me, and one last shove sends me crowned with victory into the very sanctum of love amidst the clapping of hands and the shouts of triumph by those who surround us.

No sooner was I buried in her to the extremest point than I lay quivering and gasping on her belly, spending into her womb a flood of boiling sperm.

I soon regained new life and vigour, and drawing myself out to the head, commenced a to-and-fro friction that caused no more than a few 'ahs' and deep-drawn sighs, as the sperm I had injected into her had oiled the parts and made the way comparatively easy for the dear creature who lay under me.

She now receives my thrusts and shoves with a slight quivering of her rump. She clasps me in her arms, she closes her eyes. A few energetic heaves and the dear girl feels the pleasure, despite that pain that a woman experiences in having drawn from her for the first time by a man the milk of human kindness.

I too meet her and again melt away in her, fairly drenching her with the copious draughts of the liquid I spurt into her.

At last I rise up from off my lovely victim, leaving her a bleeding sacrifice on the altar of love.

The girls gathered around Laura congratulating her on being transformed from a maid into a woman. The entrance being forced, she could henceforth drive into the boundless pleasures and joys of love without feeling pain.

They raised her up whilst cleaning her of the blood that dyed her thighs and buttocks, I took up the consecrated cushion and its bloody covering and directed one of them to prepare the bed for us. I – but no. I determined to give her a little rest, and ordering the girls to prepare a cold supper, told them to awake me in two hours, and we fell asleep in each other's arms.

After sleeping for some time, Laura awoke much refreshed, but still feeling sore from the severe battering she had received.

The table being laid alongside the bed, we reclined on it, the others sitting around the table on cushions.

Not feeling much inclined to eat, I commenced dallying with my bedfellow, railing her on the feelings she experienced while I was taking her maidenhead, till the spirit began to wax powerful within me, whereupon I laid her down flat on her back and fell with my face downward upon her, and thence followed where the spirit moved. Yes, verily, we did mighty deeds of fucking that night, and it was not until after the sixth operation, or moving of the spirit, that we lay exhausted in each other's arms and fell asleep.

In a few days after there arrived at the mouth of the creek a fine large steam-brig, which dropped anchor and sent a boat ashore with the captain, who delivered me a letter from my banker, stating who and what the officers and crew were and upon what terms they had been engaged.

I immediately walked down to the creek and going into the boat with the captain, was soon taken on board. I examined her decks, masts, etc., and then descended to the cabin, which extended my most sanguine expectations, so magnificently was it fitted up. The cabin contained six state-rooms, very large and splendidly fitted up, equalling in style and ornament the most elegant boudoir I had ever seen in Paris.

I questioned the captain, who was English, as well as the whole crew, in regard to the men on board.

He said that he and his men had been employed to serve me in any way I might think proper, so long as I did not command him to commit piracy. That he and the crew were paid enormous wages, and that they were bound and felt ready and willing to follow me to 'heaven or hell', if I but showed them the way.

On questioning the stewards, I found the brig to be well stored with all the luxuries that could be procured.

I ascended to the deck with the captain, and passing the word forward for all hands to come aft, I had a crew of most hardy and devil-may-care looking fellows around me in a trice, standing respectfully, hats in hand.

I made them a short address, laying open to them my intentions, and stating the service I required of them.

I gave the captain his orders to be in readiness to sail in two days and I returned to the château.

Summoning the steward I directed him to prepare everything for our voyage, as I determined to start in two days for Constantinople.

I then directed a page to send the women to me.

On their entering, I made them all strip to the skin and examined the cunts and several charms of each of them with a critical eye, endeavouring when all were most lusciously beautiful to select one as my *compagnon de voyage*; but not being able to choose among so many loves I left it to chance.

Taking up a dice-box, I made each throw in her turn. La Rose d'Amour and my fair Russian, Caroline, made the highest throws and I determined to take both.

After they had cast their dies, I informed them what my object was. Whereupon, Laura, my last love, who by the by was a great libertine, fell on her knees before me weeping, and begged me to take her with me.

It was impossible for me to take more than two, I told her, that it was no use to grieve about the matter as she could not go, but that I would pass all my remaining time with her.

Leaving the château in the care of my trusty stewards and followers, I embarked, taking with me over one million francs in gold, for the purpose of purchasing slaves in Constantinople.

◀§ ∂▶

Chapter Eight

After a pleasant voyage of about two weeks, I arrived at the capital of the Turkish Empire.

At the earliest opportunity I presented my letters to some of the most wealthy and influential foreigners under a fictitious name.

I soon became acquainted with many wealthy Turks and among them three or four slave-merchants.

I then hired an interpreter, and paying a visit to one of the merchants, engaged him as an agent to find out and procure me a lot of the handsomest females to be found in the market. And knowing that the poor class of the inhabitants were in the daily habit of selling their daughters, such as were handsome enough to grace the harems of the rich and lustful Turks, I directed him to send out some of his emissaries to search out all the families among the poor quarters who had beautiful girls and who would be apt to exchange them for gold.

In the course of a few days my agent called on me, stating that he was about to go on a three days' trip from the city to the house of an old broker-merchant of his who was continually in receipt of girls from the interior of the kingdom, and occasionally of a few from Circassia. That for certain reasons he never came to the city, but on receipt of any new beauties he always wrote, and he, my agent, went to his place of residence and either bargained for or took the females to Constantinople and sold them on commission.

He said that when I first called on him he wrote to his correspondent in the country, who replied that he had several very fine girls, one in particular whom he named Ibzaidu, who, he said, was fit to adorn the harem of the Grand Sultan.

I told my agent, Ali Hassan, to start immediately and to bring the lot, if they were beautiful, to the city.

In the interim of his absence, attended by my interpreter, I sauntered day and night through the streets and bazaars, endeavouring to spy out some of the beauties of the place; but all in vain. I could not catch even a glimpse of a female face.

On the evening of the ninth day from his leaving me, Ali called on me, saying that he had brought with him seven slaves, who were safe in his harem, and invited me to call at his house in the morning and examine them.

He ran perfectly wild in his praises of Ibzaidu, whom he pronounced to be more beautiful than a houri, the *ne plus ultra* of Circassian beauty.

About eleven o'clock the following day, I went to Ali's house and immediately entered on business.

He retired for a few minutes to give orders for the slaves to prepare for my visit.

In the course of half an hour a eunuch entered, made a salaam to his master, and retired.

Ali arose, and inviting me to follow, led the way into a large and elegantly furnished apartment in his harem.

On entering, I beheld six girls seated on the cushions at one side of the room, dressed in loose Turkish pants of white satin and waistcoats of rich embroidered stuff.

In the centre of the room was a couch and at one end of it stood two eunuchs. After surveying them as they sat, and noting their different styles of beauty – knowing it to be customary – I told Ali that I wished to examine them in a perfectly naked state to ascertain if they were still virgins, as he represented them to be. And also that I wished to see if the several parts of their bodies corresponded in beauty with their faces.

He immediately led one of them out on the floor beside me, and spoke a few words to her and the others in Turkish. I then made a sign for him and the eunuchs to go out and leave me alone with the females.

They retired, and taking hold of the girl's hand, I signed her to strip, which she refused to do. I entreated and urged her as well as I could by signs to do so; but she crossed her hands over her breast, refusing to do it. I clapped my hands and Ali and his eunuchs entered. I merely nodded my head to him and he pointed his finger at the girl and the eunuchs caught hold of her and in a trice stripped her naked. I then went up to her, laid my hand on her firm round bubbies, pressed and moulded them, felt her waist, rubbed my hand lower down, on to the mossy covering of her cunt; she sprang from me and catching up some of her clothes, wrapped them round her body, and sat down in one corner.

Ali stamped his foot on the floor, and the eunuchs took her and carrying her threw her on her back on the couch.

One held her down by the shoulders, while the other caught hold of one leg and Ali of the other, stretching them wide apart, I fell on my knees between them, and with my fingers opened the lips of her cunt. On attempting to insert one of them into it, and finding that I could barely force the tip in without causing her to wince and cry out and to twist her backside about, I desisted, firmly persuaded that she had her maidenhead inviolate.

Whilst they held her on the couch, I examined, felt, and kissed every part of her; and having provided myself with such things on purpose, I placed on her wrist, neck and finger, a bracelet, necklace and ring. Upon a sign they let her rise, and being given her clothes, she dressed and sat down much pleased with and examining her jewels.

I now led out another girl, and made a sign for her to undress which she took no notice of, standing with her arms crossed, and her head hanging down. I took her hands and removing them from her breasts proceeded to take off her waistcoat, and as she did not resist, I told Ali and his slaves to go out and wait outside the room.

I then stripped her of her pants and cymar and was much pleased with her beauty. I led her up to the couch and sitting down drew her to my side, handling her breasts, feeling her arms, belly, thighs, twining my fingers about in the luxurious growth of hair that overgrew the grotto underneath, to all of which she made no resistance.

At last I laid her down on her back and spreading her thighs apart, inspected her cunt, and found she was still possessed of all the signs of virginity. I also gave her jewels, such as I gave the first one, and inspected the balance in the same manner, picking out one after one.

Two I found not to be virgins, and one was bandy-legged although handsome in every other respect.

I called in Ali and enquired where the beautiful Ibzaidu was, desiring him to bring her to me.

Ali clapped his hands and two female slaves entered leading her in. Then they retired leaving her standing before me. She was enveloped in a piece of fine Indian muslin and had a veil over her face.

I raised the veil and started back in amazement at the dazzling beauty of her face.

I then caught hold of the drapery in which she was enveloped, and gently drawing it from her clasp, I threw it on one side and gazed with admiration on the most ravishingly beautiful form and figure I ever beheld.

Hers was one of those oval majestic figures, such as poets and mythologists attribute to Juno.

I much admired her rich jet-black hair which clustered in ringlets over her neck and shoulders, contrasting singularly with the dazzling whiteness of her skin. Her shoulders were finely formed and her arms, plump and beautifully rounded, would cause a sigh of desire to arise in any breast, to be clasped in their embrace. Her breasts, luxuriously large, hard and firm, white as snow-flakes, were tipped with deliciously small nipples, of that fine pink colour which so strongly denotes virginity in the possessor.

Her waist was gracefully elegant and tapering; her belly fine, round, and with the whiteness of alabaster, soft as the finest velvet down. Her hips were very large and wide, whilst her buttocks swelling out behind in two hillocks of snowy-white flesh, firm and springy to the touch, gave token of the vivacity and liveliness with which their owner would enter into the delicious combats of love.

Her thighs were of a largeness and fleshy plumpness seldom seen in a female, with the knees small, while the calf was large, in proportion to the thigh. The ankle tapering, and a foot delicately small, spoke plainly to the looker-on that the seat and centre of love, that dear part of woman which takes away the senses of all men, was of equally small and elegant pattern.

Her chin was most charmingly dimpled, her lips, full and pouting, slightly open, gave just a glimpse of two rows of ivory, which appeared set in the deep rosy flesh of her small and elegant mouth. Her nose was of the Grecian cast, her eyes of a sparkling lustrous black, and the forehead was middling high. She was, in fact, the very *beau idéal* of female beauty.

What ease and grace reigned in every part. With what a sylphlike springy motion she moved, as I led her towards the couch on which I stretched her out. There I examined minutely all her secret charms. I felt and handled every part.

Her cunt was ravishing, beyond all description. The mossy mount of Venus swelled up into a hillock of firm flesh, surmounted and covered with rich, mossy, coal-black hair, straight and fine as silk. The lips were most luscious, fat, rosy, pouting beauties. On opening them. I felt for her clitoris and found it to be extremely large, while the orifice was narrow and small indeed, apparently not larger than a girl's of eleven or twelve years of age.

'God of love!' I exclaimed on viewing it, 'here is a maidenhead that might have tempted Jupiter from Olympus, a prophet from the arms of the houris in Paradise, or an anchorite from his cell.'

Handling and examining so many lovely things had set me on fire and I could hardly restrain myself from immolating her on the altar as a sacrificial offering to the god of voluptuous love.

I drew myself away from her and signed her to rise up and resume her drapery.

I then concluded the bargain for the purchase of Ibzaidu, and for the other three I had chosen.

After settling with Ali, I told him that he must let me have the use of a part of his house, including the harem, during my stay, so that I should be able to guard safely my slaves and to have for them proper attendance. Also, that he must instantly purchase for me six or eight mutes and eunuchs, which he immediately set about, whilst I returned to my house to get my money, jewels, etc., and also to bring away Caroline and her companion.

Chapter Nine

In the evening I had arranged everything and was seated on a pile of cushions in one of the apartments of Ali's harem, my head reclining on the breast of the voluptuous Circassian, Ibzaidu, or Cluster of Pearls, as her name signified, surrounded by my other slaves whom I gave to Ibzaidu for servants; she, I was determined, should reign supreme until such time as I should find someone more beautiful.

I had opened my caskets of jewels, and adorned her wrists, arms, neck, head and ankles with jewels of massy gold of Western and Oriental workmanship, and it seemed that she would never tire of looking at and playing with them as a child would with a painted bauble.

Before night my host came in, bringing with him mutes and eunuchs, and he showed me through the suite of apartments devoted to my service, one of which I found to be a bedchamber, fitted up with the utmost elegance, containing twenty single beds.

Here it was that I slept among my concubines, or rather I should say that I lay with them, for I deserted all the others with whom I ought to have had sexual connection to repose in the arms of Ibzaidu, who, when she saw me advancing to her bedside, stretched out her arms to me and kicking off the cover, moved to the further side of the bed to make room for me.

I entered her bed, and lay with my cheek resting on her bosom the night long. And although my prick was in splendid condition, firm and erect as a rod of ivory, yet I never once thought of letting it force an entrance through the delicate and narrow passage into the inner court of the temple of love.

I spent about three weeks before I met with any more prizes, partly in the city, part of the time at the villa of Ali's on the banks of the Bosphorus in the company of Ibzaidu alone, leaving the other females in the city, under the care of the eunuchs.

During one of my visits at the villa, I was surprised one evening, while walking along the terrace of the garden, to see Ali dashing up the road at full speed, mounted on a full-blood Arabian. I descended to the gate and met him, to enquire the news, thinking that something might be wrong at the house I occupied in the city.

On enquiring, I was excitedly informed that there was a large lot of females to be sold in a few days, by order of the Grand Sultan.

Ali said they were the females composing the harem of some officer of the State who had been dead about one year, whose only heirs, two nephews, had been quarrelling about the possession of them ever since and that the Sultan had just ordered them to be sold and the proceeds to be divided among the two heirs; and he said that from reports circulating in the city, there must be some beautiful slaves amongst them, and he advised me to start directly for my own house, and that he would by bribery manage to get me a private interview with them, so that I could examine them at my leisure and choose such as I would like to have, and on the day of sale he would purchase them for me.

On the succeeding day I accompanied Ali to the house of the trader in whose keeping were the slaves.

The trader met us at the door, and took me at once into a room in which were the females. They were all enveloped in large white drapery which covered them from head to foot.

Mustapha, the trader, spoke to them, and they arranged themselves in a row round the room, then he retired, telling me that as soon as he left the room, they would all drop their mantles, and I could examine them at leisure.

Leaving me, he went out, locking the door behind him.

As I steppped up to the female nearest me she cast her covering behind her. So did the others and I feasted my eyes with a picture of voluptuousness greater than I had ever dreamt of.

There stood before me about sixty females, perfectly naked, who I think could not be excelled in any harem in the East. There were the women of Circassia with their dark flowing tresses, eyes of piercing black and skin of dazzling whiteness, mostly contrasted by the deep carnation of their lips, the nipples of their breasts and the jet-black, bushy hair that surmounted their cunts. Again, there were the languishing mild blue-eyed beauties ravished from the isles of Greece, and the voluptuous Georgians; even Africa had yielded up her sable beauties to the lusts of the sometime owner of all the lovely slaves who stood about me.

I minutely criticised each one separately, going over their respective claims to beauty with the eye of a connoisseur. Oh, how I feasted my sight on the row of lovely, luscious cunts that ran around the room. I look at, feel, touch them all, and stroke down the bushy hair that surrounds their notchs.

I became so much excited from the handling of so many cunts that I put my arm around the waist of one charming little creature, who by her looks must have been a great libertine, and led her into a small side-apartment where, presenting her with a fine gold chain which I wore, I laid her down on a pile of cushions, and twice gave her to experience the most ecstatic pleasures before I got off her.

I gave her some time to recover from the confusion I had thrown her into, ere we returned to the apartment in which the women were standing; they took no further notice of our return than to raise their heads and to look at the chain which I had hung around her neck.

I marched the one I had just been fucking with to one side and picked out ten others, among which number was one black, a young African about fifteen years of age, who still retained her virginal rose, and who was, on the whole, the most voluptuously formed female I had ever seen and apparently better fitted for enjoying the pleasure of love than any female in my possession. Her hair was quite straight and black as a raven's wing; her breasts were full and large, as though of ebony. Her waist was slender, while her hips were spread out to a width I had never before seen. Her thighs were of a largeness to put to shame anything I had ever lain with.

Having stood on one side those whom I wished to purchase, I called in the merchant and Ali and showed them to him, and as the sale was to take place the following day, I ordered him to be punctual in attendance to purchase them for me and left.

On the following day by noon Ali had conveyed to my apartments all the slaves that I had chosen that night. I put four of them to the test, giving them, for the first time, to know the difference between lying in an old goat of a Turk's arms to that of being well fucked by a young and lively Frenchman, overflowing with the precious aqua-vitae, which all women are so greedy after.

I now spent about two weeks in enjoying these new beauties that I had bought, with the exception of those who had not been deflowered of their virginal rose by the horny-headed old lecher, their late master, and those were but three out of the number.

Whilst I was thus idling away my time in the arms of my handsome slaves, my interpreter called on me one morning, and on being admitted into my presence told me that he had found one of the loveliest girls in Constantinople in the house of a poor mechanic and that on enquiry he had refused to part with her on any account, or for any amount of money; but he said it might be just possible to steal her off, if I was so inclined.

I promised him a large sum if he would procure her for me, and calling on Ali, my agent consulted with him as to the best means of bringing her off.

They agreed to go and stay about the house at night, until they saw the old man go out, and then, with the assistance of a couple of eunuchs, rush into the house, gag her, carry her out, and put her into a litter and bring her to me, all of which I approved, promising them a rich reward if they succeeded.

It was not until the third night that they were able to carry her off and I was agreeably surprised while reclining in the arms of one of my lovely slaves to see a couple of my mutes come into my room bearing in their arms the beautiful stolen prize.

I took her out of their arms, and seating her on a cushion, I uncovered her face and took the gag from her mouth. I found her to be a lovely creature as far as I could see and I began stripping her so that I might have a full view of her naked and thus of all her hidden charms.

Oh! what charms, what beauty met my fiery glance.

I had to call on several of the women to help me hold her while I was feeling and admiring her charms. I burned with desire to enjoy her, I lavished my eager kisses on every part of her body. I fastened my lips to hers. I sucked the rosy nipples of her breasts; the lips of her cunt received more than their share.

I was about to throw myself on her, but reflecting that I had determined to reserve all that had their maidenheads till after my return to France, I sprang from her, threw myself in the arms of Celestine and buried myself up to the hilt in her, just in time to prevent the liquor from spurting all over the floor.

Shortly after, Ali got me two more females, both of whom had been taken from one of the isles of the Hellespont.

I had now nearly run out of money and was preparing to start home, when, by accident, I found that Ali was reputed to have a daughter more beautiful than any female in Constantinople, and I determined to wait a while and get possession of her by some means or other.

I had not money enough left to think of offering a sum large enough to tempt his cupidity, so I made all arrangements to steal her off, for which purpose I despatched him into the country.

The same day I found out the part of the house in which Ali had shut up his daughter in the hopes of keeping her from my sight; and I made everything ready for stealing her off the same night as soon as it was dark.

I sent all my baggage and the females with the eunuchs and the mutes on board the brig.

I got a litter, and with the assistance of the interpreter whom I largely paid to aid me in the enterprise, I succeeded in gaining the apartment of Selina, whom I saw to be asleep. Without any noise we gagged her and putting her into the litter soon had her on board the brig with my other treasures, whereupon we instantly steered out of the harbour and made all haste; nor did I think myself in perfect safety until we floated once more in the Mediterranean.

Selina, on being released, at first made a great outcry at being carried off, and I kept out of her sight until we had been under weigh a couple of days, when the sea-sickness had tamed her wondrously, and I could approach her without having torrents of abuse and Turkish execrations heaped on my head. In fact, the whole of my passengers were sick, with the exception of Caroline, Celestine, and the Nubian slave.

These three attended the rest, till they got over their sea-sickness, which was not until the third or fourth day with some. Then all was mirth, jollity, luscious love.

After all were perfectly recovered, we ran up to a small, verdant but uninhabited island in the Mediterranean and lay to for one day and night.

In the evening I had let down into the water a very large sheet of canvas, made on purpose, supported at the corners by the yard-arms of the vessel, with the intention of letting the women have a bath. Ordering them to change their rich dresses for pants and shirts of plain white cotton, I took them on deck and having stationed the sailors in the boats a few yards distant from the canvas, I plunged them one after the other into the water in the belly of the sheet.

Here they amused and enjoyed themselves amazingly for an hour or more. They were then twisted up in an armchair, rigged for the purpose, and after dressing themselves, were again brought on deck, where they romped and played about like so many young kittens or monkeys.

Calling on a eunuch, I ordered him to bring up some musical instruments that I had procured in Constantinople.

Ibzaidu and two others played on the guzla and she sang some plaintive songs of home in a rich mellow voice that cast a sadness and gloom on the spirits of all, till Celestine seized the guitar and sang me some of the songs of our own dear France.

Thus we amused ourselves until late at night, having the supper brought up on the deck which we partook of by moonlight.

Stopping and enjoying myself by the way as I listed, it was nearly five weeks after sailing before I anchored in the harbour of the little creek close to the château in Brittany, where, after safely stowing away my goods, women, etc., I made preparation for that which you may know in the next chapter.

❧§❧

Chapter Ten

The first thing I did after one day's rest was to assign the eunuchs and mutes I had brought with me to their separate duties, which consisted solely in guarding and attending the females, either when in their apartment or when roving about in the garden or shrubberies attached to the château, so that they were never from under the sight of some of the slaves.

After having made these arrangements I made preparations for giving a grand entertainment to the captain and the crew of the steamer, who had conducted themselves very much to my satisfaction during the voyage, never having once intruded or infringed their privileges, always acting with great delicacy.

On the evening in the Mediterranean that I had the women on the deck to bathe, the sailors would have all retired below had I not called them back and sent them in the boats, and now I determined to repay them their good conduct by giving them an entertainment fit for princes.

In the evening I sent word to the captain and the crew to come up to the castle. In half an hour they were admitted and having shut up the women in an apartment out of the way, I showed them through the shrubberies and garden, all of which they viewed with amazement, wondering at the richness and taste displayed in the fitting up of the castle of beauties, as they termed it.

About six o'clock a servant made his appearance saying that supper was ready. I had ordered the supper to be served in the hall of the fountains and led my guests there.

We entered and sat down at the tables and directly came trooping in all the females of my harem and seated themselves opposite to the men.

After the supper was over, Ibzaidu and some of the other women I had brought from Turkey took their instruments and gave us a concert of Oriental music. After which Caroline went to the piano, and Celestine sat down to a harp and played some brilliant and lively pieces of French and Italian music. Upon which, those of my lovely slaves who belonged to the Grecian isles got up and danced the romaika and other dances peculiar to the country.

They were followed by Ibzaidu and two other Circassians, who were attired in the costumes of their native land, and danced some of the native dances.

These were in their turn followed by the Georgians, after which came my sable mistress, the Nubian, dressed in petticoats reaching the knees with an overdress of fine blue gauze.

Her dance was wild and pleasing and in throwing herself about over the floor, as her legs were bare, she would show her thighs, her bare buttocks and sometimes her black bushy notch.

Celestine and Caroline rose up and stepped out on the floor to dance, and Laura sat down at the piano.

They were dressed in short petticoats and dresses, the same as the Nubian, and performed some lascivious dances, showing every charm which nature had graced them with.

The officers and crew of the brig applauded the dancing very much.

About twelve o'clock I sent off the common seamen, retaining only the officers, five in number.

After the seamen left us the company became mixed, the officers sitting in the midst of the women, some of whom I had not frigged for a long time, and who looked with a wistful and longing eye on the men about them, and it was very clear to me that were I not present they would soon be engaged in the soft pleasures of love.

I clapped my hands and a couple of eunuchs entered and pointing out Rose, Marie, Manette and two others they led them away to an apartment I had fitted up with beds. Then I took leave of the officers, and the eunuchs took them to where they had put the five girls.

What a pleasant surprise to both parties! The men to find the beds occupied by the five girls and the girls to find the same number of men enter as there were of them. Oh, how they panted with the pleasure of the sight.

Instantly did they know why I had sent them to that apartment. After the men were gone I sent all the women to the chamber except a lovely Georgian, and repaired to an adjoining apartment to where the five couples were.

Here I had a place so constructed that I could see all that was going on in the other room without being seen.

After the men had got into the room they ran up to the beds and would have clasped the women to their breasts, but they all jumped out of bed naked, and began to undress the men, who were speedily divested of all clothing. Then what a scene of love followed!

The men threw the girls on the beds, and the girls opened wide their thighs as the men fell on their necks, and then jumped on them with pricks stiff as iron rods, piercing through the tender folds of the cunts under them, sending joy and pleasure to their very vitals, and I could judge from the exclamations and the writhing about, and the wriggling of backsides, the hot kisses and the amorous bites on the neck that not one but had received a double or triple dose of the sacred liquor injected into them. I think I never saw men and women fuck with greater zest, or derive more pleasure and enjoyment from frigging than they did.

Looking at them had such an effect on myself and companion that we were obliged to retire to the bedchamber for the purpose of enjoying ourselves in like manner.

In ascending a flight of stairs, my slave tripped, and falling hurt herself, so that on entering the room I had to seek another in whom to pour the extra liquor from the magic spring, and which was about to run over for the want of pumping.

The first bed I cast my eye on contained the luxurious Nubian slave, and I determined to offer up her maidenhead as the sacrificial gift to the god of love.

Approaching, I motioned her to rise and follow me to the state-bed whither I went.

We entered the bed together both stark naked, and placing her at once in a favourable position with a cushion under her large fat bottom, I lay my length on her and guiding the head of my prick tried to insert it between the lips of her slit, but could not succeed.

I got up, and oiling it well with ointment I again freed the entrance and succeeded in ripping and tearing up the works and barriers that defended her virgin rose, and found her a dish fit for the gods! Heavens! with what transports of delight did I squeeze her in my arms as I drove the arrow of love into the deepest recess of the luscious quivering flesh through which I had forced a passage for it.

Despite the pain which my forcible entrance into her must have caused, the moment I began working in her, Celeste, the name I had given her, began moving up to me with vigour, elasticity, and a sense of pleasure utterly impossible to be looked for in one in her situation.

So young, not quite fifteen, and she had a notch of such a lusciously tight smallness that even after entering her to the full length, it was with the utmost difficulty that I could work in and out of her; but with the suction caused by the tightness with which the flesh worked around the piston rod, I soon drew open the sluice of love's reservoir and thence gushed forth a stream of fiery fluid which completely drenched her inmost parts, causing a shudder of pleasure to run through her whole body that at once proclaimed to me that she was about to give proof of the joy and ecstasy with which she had received the terrible lance thrust which had given her such a wound and was causing her to pour down the essence of her very soul through the gaping orifice.

The oiling which her parts had received from the mutual flow of our sperm made the entrance somewhat easy, but still very tight.

Towards morning she began to realise the full enjoyment of the luscious pleasure of being well frigged as the folds of her cunt from the constant friction had stretched somewhat more, causing no more than a delicious tightness, perfectly agreeable to me and which greatly enhanced the pleasure, as the first three or four times that I entered her I found it too tight for the full enjoyment of perfect bliss, as it almost tore the foreskin off my pego when entering, thus causing pain which detracted from the pleasure.

In the morning when I descended to the breakfast table I found those whom I had sent to spend the night with the officers of the brig so sore that they could hardly walk from the tremendous battering they had received from their companions during the night.

I rode out through the surrounding country during the day and on my return in the evening in passing one of the rooms I heard considerable whispering, and listening I overheard one of the women in conversation with some men. I slyly opened the door and imagine my astonishment at beholding Caroline, Celestine, Rosalie and Laura in company with the four lubbery country-boors I had engaged at the château.

They were all lying on the floor, the girls with their clothes tossed up to their waists and the men with their pricks out of their breeches and the girls playing with them, trying to instil new life and vigour into the drooping instruments which had apparently just done good service.

Not being seen by them I retired, softly closing the door, to meditate on what I should do with the guilty ones.

After thinking over the subject for some time I came to the conclusion that I had no right to do or say anything on the subject, knowing that it was the instinct of nature which prompted them to act as they had done, and recollecting that I had promised to each of them that they should never want for that to which they were then treating themselves, I decided to say nothing about the matter, unless merely to give them all a severe fright.

After supper, as I was sitting in the midst of my girls in the hall of fountains, watching some of the Grecian women as they wound through the mazes of the voluptuous romaika, to the music of the guzla, I clapped my hands and four mutes entered.

I pointed out the four I had caught frigging with the servants and ordered the mutes to seize them.

They bound their wrists with silken sashes and led them up to me.

I put on a savage frown and accused them of having debased themselves to the embraces of menials.

This they denied and persisted in denying.

I ordered the mutes to strip them and taking a slender riding switch I began tapping Celestine with it on her bare buttocks very lightly just so as to cause them to blush till they became a beautiful carmine hue, mixed in with the clear alabaster, and they all four cast themselves on their knees before me and acknowledged their fault. I then told them that it demanded a more serious punishment and that they should receive it.

Now, I had ordered up from the village four of the finest-looking stout peasants to be found, and when I made a sign to the mutes they went out and returned leading them in blindfolded.

After they were in the room I conversed with them, and ordered some chocolate to be served which I had prepared with certain drugs that would cause their amorous propensities to rise every few minutes for four hours.

They were stark naked, and shortly after drinking, their lances stood erect against their bellies.

I then untied the wrists of the four girls and told them to lie down on cushions prepared for the purpose. I then led a man to each and put them in one another's arms, telling the men to go in. The men instantly mounted the women and for three hours kept them working in a dead heat.

Fourteen times did those men frig the women under them, changing women every now and then.

At first the women enjoyed it very much but at last got tired to death, perfectly worn out, battered and bruised to pieces, the lips of their slits gaping wide open, flabby and swollen, with a perfect little lake of sperm between their thighs.

As soon as I saw the chocolate begin to lose its effect on them I had them taken out and there lay the girls so befucked that they could hardly move hand or foot.

I myself was not idle during their performance, for I had three times dissolved myself in the Nubian slave. I spent the night in her arms, arising in the morning with the intention of husbanding myself for a couple of days, so as to be able to do justice to the maidenhead of Ibzaidu, which I intended sacrificing to my amorous and fierce desires.

Chapter Eleven

On the evening of the second day after, I made grand preparations for the event about to be celebrated. I had an elegant supper served such as would have tempted old Epicurus himself. All the inmates of the seraglio were at the table and I plied them so well with wine that not one except Ibzaidu arose from it sober.

When I gave the signal for retiring to the bedchamber they reeled and staggered about like so many drunken sailors. Arrived at the bedchamber we all stripped to the skin and catching Ibzaidu in my arms I carried her to the state-bed and threw her down on it, and being somewhat uncertain of my powers, as I had been sucked nearly dry by the Nubian, I called for and drank a cup of my magic chocolate which I knew would enable me to go through the act like a conqueror.

I gave the word and all the girls came round the bed with their instruments playing, and sang a beautiful song which I had composed for the occasion.

I made ready and getting on the bed fixed my victim in the best position, got between her thighs and giving a bunch of switches to one of the girls I directed her to lash my backside with them so as to smart much.

I took hold of my battering-ram and strove to force an entrance. The head is in, the soft flesh yields to my fierce thrusts. I drive in, she screams with pain but I heed it not. It is music to my ears. It tells me that I am about to arrive at the seat of bliss. I shove and thrust harder, everything gives way to me, the lashing on my buttocks gives me double force, and one fierce lunge sends me into the furthest extremity of her grotto and at the same moment I oil the mangled tender flesh of her dear little bleeding slit with such a stream of burning sperm as never woman sucked from man before. I thought my very prick and stones were dissolving in pearly liquid.

After resting myself on her bosom for a few moments, I found that my battering-ram was prepared for another assault and I fiercely drove him into the breach.

Three times before I got off did I spend the juice of my body into her without calling from her any return.

She lay and moaned in her agony and pain, and on looking I saw that I had terribly battered and bruised the entrance of the seat of pleasure.

I raised her up and had her put into a warm bath and after drying her I again put her to bed. After giving her some wine and taking some myself, I found that again I was in trim for another bout.

With a spring I placed myself between her thighs. I entered her, not without a good deal of hard work.

God of voluptuous love, what a heat reigned through her body!

How lusciously did the sweet flesh clasp around my rod!

A few thrusts and a few moves in and out awaken her to a sense of pleasure.

She moves up to me, she catches the fever that runs through me. Quicker, quicker she heaves up to me to meet my fierce lunges as I drive my foaming steed through her gap into the rich pasturage. She clasps me in her arms, and throws her snowy thighs around my back, the bounces of her bottom fairly spring me off her. I feel she is coming. Ah, my god, she comes – she spends! The sperm comes from her in a shower. I, too – I again – I spend! It runs from me. Great God! It's too much! I die! Oh-h! And then I breathed my spirit away in a sigh soft and gentle as a zephyr.

My God, how voluptuous, how luscious was the beautiful Circassian! What warmth! With what fire, what energy did she meet all my efforts at procuring and dispensing pleasure! How lusciously did she squeeze me when in her! How plentifully did she let down the milk when the agony of pleasure seized her!

We swam in a perfect sea of voluptuousness totally indescribable. Man cannot imagine, pen cannot describe it, it was an intoxication of delight – pleasure wrought up to agony, bliss inexpressible, more exquisitely delicious than that enjoyed by the houris of Paradise when in the arms of true Mohammedans, or that enjoyed by the spirits of the Elysian fields.

I felt considerably enervated for a day or two and refrained from again entering the lists of Venus until I had fairly set sail on my projected cruise in search of love and beauty in the Hesperian climes, where I hoped for the most exquisite pleasures in the arms of the ardent ladies of Cuba and the Spanish Main.

I coasted round and put into Bordeaux for the purpose of giving the sailors a chance of getting themselves girls.

In two days they were all mated, and we put off for Havana, intending to stop there a short time, as I had heard much of the beauty of the women of the island.

Arriving at Havana, I took some rooms at one of the best hotels, giving orders to the captain to keep the brig in sailing order so as to be able to sail at a moment's notice.

At the *table d'hôte* I noticed a handsome, vivacious brunette, evidently an inhabitant of the island. Her eyes were fairly hidden under a mass of deep black hair which overshadowed them; but I could perceive, whilst at the table, that she was continually glancing at me, and the moment my eyes met hers she would suddenly drop her eyes on the plate or look in another direction. From this I augured favourably and deemed success certain, thinking that I had made a conquest.

In the evening I attended the theatre accompanied by the captain, and both of us well armed. I there saw the lady in a box in company with a couple of elderly gentlemen. The one whom I took to be her husband was a cross-grained, ugly looking fellow.

I followed her home with the intent to win her.

In the morning I got an introduction to Señor Don Manuel Vasquer, the husband of Donna Isabel, my lovely *vis-à-vis* at the table.

I told him I was a gentleman of rank and fortune, travelling for the pleasure with a vessel of my own, and invited him down to the harbour to look at the brig.

He accepted the invitation and was very much pleased with the neat cleanliness of everything on deck, and with the luxury displayed in the fittings of the cabin.

I had a lunch set out and plied him well with champagne so that when he left the vessel, he was in very high spirits. On reaching the hotel he invited me up to his apartment and introduced me to his wife and a couple of other ladies we found with her.

I endeavoured as well as my looks could express to let her see that I had taken particular notice of her, and was much smitten by her charms.

After conversing for a short time I retired to my room to dress for dinner and penned a declaration to the Donna Isabel, declaring my passion for her and imploring her to grant me an interview, as I had read in her eyes that I was not disagreeable to her.

After dinner I joined her and her husband and slipped my note into her hand, which she immediately hid in the folds of her dress. I then went to my room to wait for an answer, which I felt sure would soon be sent to me. Nor had I to wait long, for in a couple of hours a negro wench opened the door, poked her head in to ascertain if I was in the room, threw a note to me and, shutting the door without saying a word, retired.

I hastily picked up the note and opening it found my expectations confirmed!

She granted me an interview. Her note stated that her husband would go out to his plantations the next day and that at three o'clock in the afternoon she would be alone taking her siesta.

The evening, night and morning hung heavily on me, and after dining, I retired to my room, laid my watch on the table and sat gazing at the dial to see the weary hours pass away; but as the minute-hand pointed to three, the same black wench again opened the door, poked her head in, looked round and drew back, leaving the door open.

I jumped up and followed her to the rooms of her mistress. Here I found Donna Isabel reclining in an elegant dishabille, on a sofa. She held out her hand to me in welcome, which I took and pressed to my lips.

She invited me to be seated and I placed myself on a foot-stool at her side. Taking her hand between mine, I disclosed my passion for her, imploring her not to refuse my love. At first she pretended to be much surprised that I should make a declaration of my love to her and appeared half angry. But as I proceeded with my tale of love and pressed her for an answer favourable to the passion which was consuming me, she appeared to relent, and rising from her reclining position made room for me to sit down beside her on the couch.

As I sat down by her side I dropped an arm round her waist and drawing her to my bosom I implored her to grant me her love – even to leave her husband and fly with me to some remote corner of the earth where we could while away our years in the soft dalliance of love.

I told her that her husband was an old man with whom she could not enjoy life, and from whom a young woman like herself could not receive those tender attentions, and the soft and real pleasure which she could enjoy in the arms of a young and devoted lover.

She sighed and hung her head on her breast, saying she never knew what it was to receive those delicious and tender pleasures from her husband that I had just spoken of. That from the time of her marriage to the present moment, his whole time was taken up with drinking and gambling. That he left her to amuse herself as best she could in the house, for he was so jealous that he would never allow her to go out

except in his company. She sighed again and wished that heaven had
given her such a man as myself.

I know not how it was, but when she stopped, I found one of my
hands had opened the front of her dress and slipped beneath her shift
and was moulding one of her large hard breasts, and my lips were
pressed on hers.

My leaning against her had insensibly moved her backwards till,
without our knowing it, her head was resting on the cushion of the sofa
and I was lying on top of her.

Whilst I was assuring her of eternal love and constancy and begging
her to allow me to give her a convincing proof of my tenderness and
affection, and also to let me convince her that as yet she had had the
mere shadow of the ecstatic pleasure of love, but that if she would allow
me I would give her the real substance and a surfeit of those pleasures
of which I felt convinced she had received but a taste from her
husband, I had been gradually drawing up her clothes, till my hand
rested on a large, firm, fleshy thigh. Isabel had closed her eyes, her
head hanging to one side, her lips slightly apart and her breast rising
and falling rapidly from the quick pulsations of the blood caused by her
fierce and amorous desires.

I raised her shift still higher till it disclosed to my sight a large tuft of
long black hair. I then unbuttoned my pantaloons and with a little
gentle force parted her legs, and got between her thighs.

Parting the lips with my fingers, I inserted the head of my engine of
love, and in a few moments we both died away amidst the most
exquisite transports of love.

I lay heaving and panting on her bosom while she lay motionless
under me, till finding that my stiffness had scarcely diminished and
knowing by the short motions and jerks of the head that he was once
more ready for the field and impatient for the word to start again, I
commenced moving in her.

'Beautiful creature,' I cried, 'what delicious sensations! What pleasure! My God!' said I, 'you are almost virgin. How lusciously tight your
sweet flesh clasps my rod!'

Her arms were clasped around my neck, her thighs around my back,
her moist rosy lips glued to mine. Our tongues met. With what
vivacity, what voluptuousness she moves up to me, giving me energetic
heaves for my thrusts. I feel from the increased motion of her bottom
that again she is about to dissolve herself into bliss. I too feel it.

'Ah, my God! Oh! what pleasure! I come; there, there, dear love, you
have it now – joy, love, bliss unbearable!' And I was swimming in a sea

of pleasure, in a perfect agony of bliss.

When we recovered from our delirium, I arose and drawing her clothes down slowly over her legs, I pressed her to my side. Planting a soft kiss on her pouting lips I folded her in my arms and asked her how she liked the reality after being fed for more than a year on the mere shadow of that delicious substance of which she had just largely partaken.

The answer was a kiss that sent a thrill of pleasure through every vein.

'Oh! my dear, this is nothing to what you would enjoy were you to link your fortune to mine and fly with me to France. Then we would live a life of love and pleasure such as you have just tasted. Our whole lives would be nothing but love and pleasure, morn, noon and night it would be love, all love. There should be nothing around us but love – nothing but pleasure!

Isabel rang a small bell and the same piece of ebony who had twice placed her head in and out of my chamber-door entered.

Her mistress told her to bring in some lunch and she soon returned with an elegant cold repast and some delicious wine.

After eating and drinking we again turned our attention to love. Rising from the chair I led her to the sofa, and drawing her on my knees, I stripped her dress and shift from her shoulder and loosening the strings of her petticoats toyed and played with her breasts, which were really beautiful, large and firm, and tipped with two most tempting strawberry nipples.

Nor was my companion idle, for whilst I was thus engaged she had unbuttoned my pantaloons and taken out my penis, which she admired and toyed with, capping and uncapping its red head till she had brought it to a most beautiful state of erection.

I raised her on her feet and all her clothing slipping on to the floor, she stood in all her naked beauty before me. What charms, what beauties did my eyes and lips feast on as I turned her round and round. Her soft round belly, her plump bottom and then her dear little cleft, that masterpiece of beauty, how I hugged it to me. What kisses I lavished on it, all of which she repaid with interest.

She sinks down on the floor between my legs. She caresses my pego, she presses it to her lips They pout and she puts its large red head between them. I push a little forward, it enters her mouth, she sucks it, her soft tongue rolls it over and over. She continues tickling it with her tongue. Feeling that if she continues I must spend, I jerk back and drag it from her mouth. She again wants to keep it. I lay her down on the floor with the cushions under her buttocks. I get on her with my head between her thighs, my prick and stones hanging over her face. Again she takes it in her mouth, while I put my tongue between the lips of her cunt and frig her clitoris with it.

The motion of her rump increases! I find she is about to spend and I suddenly rise up and seat myself on the sofa; she springs after me, jumps on the sofa, her cunt touching my face, and tightly clasps her arms round my neck.

She slowly let her bottom come down, till it touched the head of my pego. I directed it aright and she impaled herself on it.

A few motions and I most plentifully bedewed her with the nectar as she was paying down her own tribute to the god of love.

When she rose off me, the sperm dropped from her salacious slit in large gouts upon me, attesting the bountiful measure with which nature had endowed both of us with the elixir of life.

In the evening she sent her black to order her supper to be sent up into her rooms, and after quietly supping we retired to bed and I spent the most agreeable night that I ever passed with any woman.

Her husband returned the next day, but I found an opportunity to meet his wife in the evening and renewed for a short time the transport we had enjoyed the day before.

A few days later, her husband had invited a party of six young ladies and the same number of young men to visit his wife and take dinner with them. I also was invited.

Immediately after receiving the invitation I sent word to the captain to raise steam and be ready to sail at a moment's warning.

I joined the party at dinner and found three of the invited girls to be very handsome and the other three very good-looking.

After the dinner was over, I invited the party to visit my yacht and take an evening's excursion with me.

The husband of my mistress was very loud in his praises of the beauty of the yacht and of the rich and elegant manner in which she was fitted up and joined his solicitations to mine; the party consenting, we ordered carriages and drove down to where the yacht lay. Getting aboard we sailed out of the harbour and ran up the island.

After we were out of sight of the city, I took the captain aside and told him that towards night I wanted him to run the brig in towards the shore; and that I intended to seize the seven men and land them in a boat and make off with the women. I told him to go and speak to the . crew about the matter and have them in readiness to obey my signal.

A little before dusk, we ran close in shore at a place where there was no plantation visible. I had ordered some lumber to be strewn about the greater deck and commanded the captain to send the sailors to carry it away.

Sixteen stalwart fellows came aft and suddenly seized on the men and bound their arms and legs. I then told them what I intended to do, ordering the men at the same time to take the women below. Their execrations and implorings for the girls, who were their relatives, I would not listen to, but I had them put in a boat and sent ashore. They were unbound and let loose. The boat returned to the brig and we set sail for France.

The girls did nothing but sob and weep for a day or two but I soon brought them to their senses. Immediately after setting their companions ashore I went into the cabin, and bringing Ibzaidu and Mary out of their hiding places, I introduced them to the company.

When supper was served they all refused to sit at the table and eat. But I told them if they did not comply with all my wishes I would hand them over to the sailors to be used by them as they chose. This had its effect on them and they seated themselves at the table.

I rang a bell and two of the handsomest women belonging to the sailors entered stark naked, as I had ordered them thus to wait on table.

The Spanish girls were all about to rise up, but putting on a fierce aspect, I threatened them the first who should rise would be passed forward to the men. This had effect on them and they sat still.

Whilst the servant was pouring out the coffee I arose and went to the side-table as if to fetch something, but in reality to pour a few drops of a certain liquid into each cup of coffee.

The quantity put in each cup was enough to set any woman's amorous and licentious desires on fire.

They all drank their coffee and in about half an hour the effect was very visible as all the coyness of modesty had disappeared and they languishingly cast their lascivious glances at me, joking the servant-girls on their nudity, and whenever they came in reach of them, pinching, slapping, them, etc., so great was the effect produced by the drug I had put in the coffee.

When the supper was over and the tables were cleared, I commenced playing and tussling with them. Rolling them about on the floor and playing them a thousand amorous tricks which they repaid with interest – throwing me on the floor, falling in a heap on top of me – I would catch a kiss from them, squeeze a fine bubby, slide my hand along a thigh, or slip it under petticoats to grasp a large calf or a well-turned knee. I ordered in some wine of a very strong quality, well drugged with the love-potion. I plied them with the wine of which they drank very freely and in a couple of hours all reserve and modesty had left them.

I took the Señora – the wife I had seduced at the hotel and whose husband I had set ashore with the others – on one side and invited her to step into one of the state-rooms with me. I then asked her if she could forgive me for robbing her from her old cuckold of a husband. She threw herself into my arms and with a fervent embrace and kiss sealed my pardon with her lips.

◦§◦

Chapter Twelve

I then asked her to undress, and told her that in a moment I would return to her. I went out and gave an order to Mary and returned, finding my mistress stripped to her shift.

I undressed, and taking off my shirt, gave her a kiss, and drew her shift over her head and we both stood naked. I opened the room-door and picking her up carried her into the cabin amongst the girls.

Isabel had by this time got drunk as well as the girls who had come on board with her. With what shouts of laughter did they receive us, tickling us, pinching us, slapping us against one another, catching at my genitals and pulling the hair that surmounted the notch of my mistress, patting our bare backsides, throwing us on the floor, putting us on top of each other, etc., whilst I would catch them, pull up their petticoats, pinch their buttocks, flap the head of my enormous machine against the lips of their hairy little slits, force it into their hands and make them play with it.

I caught one and with the help of Ibzaidu and my mistress soon stripped her naked, handing her clothes to Mary, who had been ordered with Ibzaidu to put away the clothes, and who, being as naked as I, locked them up in one of the rooms when in a few minutes I had stripped the lot of them stark naked.

Oh! then what amorous, wanton tricks we sportively played each other, they tickling my large bags and stones, playing with my penis and rubbing it, I moulding their beautiful titties and with the tip of my finger tickling their cunts.

One little devil who could not have been over fourteen I made spend.

What fun this was to the rest, to see her recline her head on my shoulder, spread apart her thighs, and gasp out her exclamations of delight. Her oh's and ah's and me's, as she gave down the generous fluid which ran down my fingers and wet my whole hand.

While I was thus with my finger frigging the dear little maid, Isabel had squatted herself down between my legs and had taken my pego in her mouth and was frigging me in that way. I did not notice it until the delicious creature who was reclining on my shoulder had done spending. But I felt that I too was about to spend, and tried to draw my penis from her mouth, but she clasped her hands around my buttocks and squeezed me up close to her mouth, till my stones and bags tingled against her chin and neck.

I exclaimed: 'My God! Let go. I'm going to spend!'

But instead of doing so, she hugged me still more and tickled its head with her tongue more and more.

The crisis seized me, the short convulsive jerks of my backside announced that the fluid was coming.

'I'm spending; here it is. Ah, my God! what pleasure! How exquisite! What bliss! Oh, God, quicker! Oh, bliss! Heavenly joy! I'm spending,' and I fell to the floor fairly fainting away through excess of pleasure. My flesh quivered and danced, my whole body was in motion, as though attacked with St Vitus' dance.

Never, no, never in the world was a man so frigged by woman. Never before did man experience such voluptuous pleasure. Never was there such bliss so heavenly, so ecstatic, imparted to man by woman, as I received from my mistress as I let flow the pearly liquid into her mouth. Never did the most exquisite sucking and friction of a cunt produce the same amount of such intense ecstasy as I felt when spending. As the pearly liquid spurted from me she placed her tongue on the head, rolling it over and overthrew me into convulsions of pleasure.

It was some time ere I recovered myself, and then it was through the teasings and ticklings of my lovely tormentors. I had a pallet made on the floor of the cabin from the beds in the state-rooms, and putting the lights out, we lay down. I was in the arms of Isabel and soon well repaid her for the pleasure she had given just before.

Thrice did I spend into the most secret recesses of her notch the warm and generous fluid which acts so powerfully on women, and then composed myself for sleep.

After sleeping for I should judge about two hours, I was awakened by feeling someone rubbing and playing with my member, which was in fine standing order.

I found it was Isabel, who had her rump stuck close to the hollow of my thighs and was rubbing the head of my penis against her culo. She wet it every now and then and the sliding of it between her fat buttocks caused a most agreeable tingling sensation to pervade my whole corporeal system.

Wishing to aid her in her intentions, still pretending to be asleep, I did all in my power so far as regarded position, etc.

I clasped my arms around her waist and one thigh, which I lightly raised.

'Oh,' she said, 'you are awake and want more pleasure!'

I made no answer and guided the head of my prick to her little hole *au derrière*. I thrust forward but it would not penetrate. With her fingers she moistened its head with spittle and again placed it aright; but as it was an awkward position to lie in I rolled her on to her belly, placing a cushion under her to raise her rump high up, I opened her thighs, got between them and tried the back entrance. I forced it in. She squirmed and wriggled about gasping with pleasure and I could hardly keep in her.

Her wriggling about and the delicious contractions of her culo brought down from me a copious discharge of the electric fluid which I injected into her.

'Oh, God!' she exclaimed, 'what pleasure. I feel it rushing into me! How hot it is, my dear love. Again, and quicker. Now I come, too; it is running from me. My God! 'tis heaven! What pleasure. Ah, what lus – lus – luscious pleasure!'

The words died on her lips, as I was now fucking her in her slit, and had frigged her clitoris at the same time, thus procuring her the double pleasure.

Here was an entirely new source of pleasure opened to me by the libertinism of my new mistress. Already I had enjoyed her in three different places, and I found that she had penetrated into the inmost recesses of my breast, creating a sensation there which I felt could never be effaced by any other female.

What a luxury it was to see the wild, stupefied astonishment of the charming girls who surrounded me to find themselves lying with me stark naked, and it was somehow increased, I venture to say, by seeing me on top of Isabel, giving her an appetite for her breakfast with the morning draught which she sucked in with great delight.

They all sprang up looking for their clothes or something with which to hide their nakedness, but in vain; no clothes were to be seen, as I had them safe under lock and key.

The ravishing little creature in whose arms I had spent the night nearly laughed herself into fits at witnessing the dumb terror of the girls and commenced railing them, telling them everything that had occurred during the night, recalling to their minds all the follies and extravagances they had been guilty of, and tried to induce them to take their good luck, as she said, with fortitude, describing to them all the pleasure she had received from me during the night and begging them to submit to whatever I would desire with good grace as it was better for them. I then spoke to them, telling them where I was taking them to, and that at the least resistance made by them I would hand them back to the fierce desires of the common sailors; but on the contrary, if they acted as I wished them, everything should be well with them. That they could not form the slightest desire but what would be instantly complied with. The most delicate attentions should be paid them, and I ended by telling them of the life of luxury and blissful love they would lead with me, and on the contrary, of the dreadful life they would spend if by remaining refractory they caused me to give them away to the brutal lusts of the sailors.

This had considerable effect on them as I could see fear and horror plainly depicted on their countenances.

I then rang a bell for a servant and told her to bring me a bottle of wine, telling the girl where to get it.

When she brought it in I filled the glasses and asked the girls, who were huddled together in one corner, to come and take a glass each.

They did not stir, and putting on a frowning aspect, I commanded them to come and drink.

They came forward to the table and drank the wine.

I told them to seat themselves on the sofa while breakfast was being laid. I seated four on one sofa and attempted to lay myself down across their knees, but they all jumped up and ran into a corner. I determined to terrify them at once, so they would be perfectly subservient to my desires. Calling a servant, I sent her to call my mate, one who officiated as my valet.

When he entered the cabin I ordered the girls to resume their places on the sofa, which they tremblingly did.

Then I told the mate to seize on the first one of them who attempted to move, drag her on the deck and give her to the sailors.

I went up to them and sitting on one of them for a moment, lay down with my belly and face towards theirs. The one on whose thighs I rested my feet I bade to part her legs and with my toes I tickled the lips of her bushy notch. The one on whose thighs my cheeks rested I also made to part her legs so that I could drop my right arm between them. I then frigged her clitoris occasionally with my little finger, tickling her just inside the lips; she began to wriggle about on the sofa. The girls on whom rested my buttocks and thighs I made play, one with my stones and the other with my Jacob's staff.

At breakfast I put into the cup of one of the youngest and prettiest girls enough of the tincture of cantharides to make her libidinous desires show themselves pretty strongly.

After we had finished eating I took her to a sofa and drew her on my knees, and as the drug began to take effect on her, I took all the liberties I desired with her, kissing and sucking her pretty lips, the nipples of her breasts, handling her buttocks, frigging her clitoris, drawing my grand machine up between her thighs and rubbing the lips of her pussy, till I felt myself able to succeed in making an entrance into any place no matter how small. She the while hugged me in her arms, giving me kiss for kiss, rubbing and screwing her bottom on my thighs, giving evidence of the raging fever which was consuming that part of her.

Her companions, none of whom had seen me drop the tincture into her coffee, regarded her manoeuvres with me in perfect wonder, little thinking that they each would do the same before they were two days older.

I fixed a cushion and pillow on the sofa so as properly to support her head and bottom, and laying the lecherous little devil down I opened wide her legs and laid myself down between them. She aided me with good will in getting it well fixed, so as better to operate.

Mary and Ibzaidu came to act as pilots to steer my noble craft safe into the harbour of Cytheria. The entrance to the haven was very narrow, making the way rather difficult till Donna Isabel ran up to me and slapping me hard on the bare buttocks drove me up to the hilt, causing the delicious creature whom I was deflowering to scream out with the pain. The blood flowed from her and the sperm from me, mingling most delightfully.

Resting for a moment, I recommenced the delightful race and soon had the joy to know that the dear girl was reaching the very acme of human enjoyment whilst I at the same time again drowned my senses in another discharge of that peculiar fluid the flowing of which drowns one in such ecstacies.

Three others did I serve in the same manner before the close of the day, ravishing them of those dear little maidenheads which are of no manner of use to a woman, and of which I am particularly fond.

One I forced to give up to me her virginity by the aid of the tincture without taking away her senses. Oh! they were bliss, doubly refined, her fierce struggles to free herself from my lascivious embraces. How sweetly musical to my ears were her yells of agony and shame. With what transports did I force her to resign her sweet body to my fierce desires. How ravishing was the pleasure I felt in ripping and tearing up the tender outworks, the inner gates, the bulwarks, everything. And at last, despite her continued struggling and screaming, to drive full tilt into the very temple of Venus, triumphantly plucking off her virgin rose from its stem, causing the blood to flow in profusion. Oh, how I gloated on the ruins of all that is held dear and honourable by her sex – her virtue.

Ye gods! it was a fuck so altogether exquisitely delicious that it was a full half-hour before I was sufficiently recovered to enter again into the little grotto of Venus, the road to which I had just opened.

Lovely creature! Three times did I experience in your arms that fierce transporting pleasure which intoxicates the soul and drowns the mind in those voluptuous ecstacies which can only be experienced in the close embrace of the two sexes.

Abstaining from cohabiting with any of the girls for a couple of days, I felt my strength renewed and invigorated, and on the fifth day after carrying them off from the island, I had ravished the whole six of their dear little maidenheads I had cruelly forced them to give up to my lechery. But once having lost them, which they held so guarded, they entered into all my whims and pleasures with the passion and ardour that characterises the females of the south.

Once the Rubicon was crossed they became the greatest libertines I ever met with. They would hang round me day and night, trying every means in their power to keep my prick in a constant state of erection. They would lay me down on the floor stark naked, like themselves. They would fairly fight for the possession of my genitals. One would gently squeeze my stones, while another would be playing with my penis, which she would by the gentle friction of her soft, delicate hand bring to an erection.

Then would she precipitate herself on me and devour the rich morsel, palating it with those exquisite contractions and inward squeezings which at the time women are about to spend render the act of copulation so exquisitely delicious.

Then, when one was mounted on me, would the dear creatures show forth the full fire of their lechery.

Two of them would seize on my hands, one on each, and, running my fingers into their salacious slits, would thus procure for themselves a semblance of the pleasure their more lucky rival was enjoying and receiving from the friction of the stiffly red-tipped horn which sprang out from the bottom of my belly.

Isabel would rush into the arms of Ibzaidu, to whom she had taken a great liking. Tumbling on the floor in each other's arms they would press each other, squeeze breasts, suck nipples, force their tongues into each other's cunts. Their hands would play and twine in the bushy hair that shaded the mounts above their notches. Their fingers would slide lower down, would enter the sacred grotto, and then running them in as far as they could, they would commence the titillation, and with the finger of the left hand at the same time they would frig the clitoris, which would soon bring them to that delicious state of annihilation which causes the soul to dissolve itself in a sea of bliss.

At other times they would seize on the languishing Fanny, who yet retained her maidenhead although very anxious to be rid of it, and throw her on the sofa or floor, and while Ibzaidu would be squeezing or sucking her breasts, pressing her own lovely titties to her mouth, kissing and sucking her rosy lips, and thrusting her tongue into her mouth, Isabel would be between her thighs, frigging her clitoris with her fingers and, with her tongue between the lips, so titillate her cunt as to give her the most delicious pleasure. The dear Fanny would spend, pouring down the liquor of which she possessed a superabundance, amidst sighs, long and deep.

Nor would her hands be idle, for those who were procuring her the pleasure did not forget themselves.

They would force her hands into their own glowing furnaces and send down such a flow of liquid as would wet the hands of Fanny all over.

Then would these two try their best to procure for Fanny those pleasures which all around her were continually being received from me but of which I had as yet deprived her. But she was not long to be burdened with that which all maids are anxious to get rid of – her virginity.

Giving myself one day's rest, I lay down in the cabin by myself on a mattress. The girls always made their beds on the floor and we lay together. After I had been asleep for some time, I was awakened by feeling someone playing with my private parts. Isabel and Ibzaidu were lying on either side of me, their heads resting on my thighs. Isabel had taken that piece of flesh of which she was so fond in her mouth and was tickling it with her tongue. The other was feeling and playing with the curious bag which hung low down between my thighs, gently rubbing and squeezing the stones.

My machine was proudly erect as a mast, its red head glowing through the darkness.

'Come,' said Isabel, 'Ibzaidu has lived for five days on the shadow of the substance which the other girls have been so gorged with, and it is but fair that you should recompense her for starving, while others have been living in plenty. Come you, stand! Your prick is in fine condition. You must spend this night with her and me for I have not partaken of the flesh for some time.'

I laid Ibzaidu on her back and getting between her legs I entered my prick into her parts. The moment she felt the head within the further recesses of her cunt she spent most plentifully. I worked away in her for some time, holding back my own liquor as long as possible so as to give her as much pleasure as I could, and she spent three times more. Just as she was dissolving her very vitals into sperm, I met her and injected the seed into her womb.

I got off her and lay between the two. Without giving me any time for recruiting, Isabel commenced playing with my staff, which she hugged, pressing it to her breasts, squeezing it between them, pressing it against her cheeks, gently frigging it with her hand and, taking its uncapped head between her lips, softly biting and tickling it with the end of her tongue.

Then stopping till it sank down again, small and shrivelled up, she would take it and thrust the whole of it into her mouth, and by her exquisite palating and sucking and tickling cause it to start into life, proudly erecting its head till her little lips could hardly clasp it.

I laid her down on her belly, placing a pillow under the lower part of her body, and then entered her *au derrière*; I put my left hand under her thighs and inserted my fingers into her cunt, holding them stiff, whilst I worked in her arsehole.

The motions of her bottom, caused by the fall of my thighs against her backside, made her frig herself on my fingers. Thus did she enjoy a double pleasure.

Nor was Ibzaidu without share in this beautiful scene. She had lain down with her belly to my breast, her bush and slit rubbing against my side, with her right thigh thrown over my head.

Drawing her closer to me I kissed the lips of her cunt. I tickled her clitoris with my tongue, I put it between my lips and titillated her so deliciously with them that she died away in pleasure, at the same time that Isabel was losing her senses from the convulsive transports into which my double frigging had thrown her.

After this performance was over, we lay completely exhausted in each other's arms for about two hours, at the end of which time I began to feel myself somewhat revived.

While we were lying dormant in each other's embraces, Isabel had been describing to Ibzaidu the intense pleasure she had enjoyed when I enlarged her *au derrière*, and she prevailed on her to make me frig her in the same manner, making her lay her head between my thighs to play with my little thing and make it start into new life.

The beautiful, delicate and voluptuous Ibzaidu took my tickler in her mouth and by the tickling of her tongue and the sucking she gave it she soon made it to stand most beautifully erect, upon which she let it go.

I soon placed her in a convenient position for the attack which was to ravish her of her second maidenhead, and she was perfectly willing to surrender at once.

I placed her on her right side, partly lying on her back I then lay down on her left side and prepared to enter her. Isabel had lain herself down in front of Ibzaidu, her cunt touching her face, and her head between the thighs of her companion.

She took the head of my enormous machine into her mouth which she wetted well with spittle and then guided to its destination. But the place was so small that I made many attempts before I could penetrate.

At last I felt it enter. I shoved slowly and steadily, and at length felt it impossible to reach any further.

Ibzaidu writhed and twisted about so much after I was in her that I could hardly keep myself upon her. Isabel had put the fingers of her right hand into the cunt of the beautiful creature whom I was stroking behind, and the motions of her back as we worked together made her frig herself with them.

At the same time she put her own arms round the buttocks of Isabel, and drawing her slit up to her mouth, she put her tongue into it and frigged her so well in this way that Isabel spent before either of us, wetting the tongue and lips of the beautiful Circassian with the pearly drops.

The crisis now seized me and at the same moment the frigging of Isabel's fingers caused Ibzaidu to spend at the very moment I was squirting a stream of boiling sperm into her very vitals.

'Ah, dear sir, have mercy on me! I feel it here in me! I too – oh, goodness, I am spending! Oh, heavens, what a pleasure. I die – I spend again – again! I am spending!' She relaxed the convulsive grasp she had of Isabel's bottom. Her flesh quivered and danced and she lay convulsed with pleasure such as gods never dreamt of.

In three weeks we reached the coast and harboured in the little creek. I immediately went ashore, taking the women with me and went to the château.

Heavens! What a welcome I received. How the lively, rampant, lecherous girls crowded round, and with what embraces did they receive me. I was fairly devoured by the hungry creatures who crowded to embrace me.

And, La Rose d'Amour! Ah, dear Rose, as I pressed you in my arms and received your burning kisses, what a thrill did they not send through my whole body.

And you, beauteous Laura, how your little heart beat as I pressed your bosom to mine; what fire flashed from your languishing black eyes as you put one of my hands on your cunt and your own on my already stiff pego.

Then came Rosalie, the delicate, fair-skinned, blue-eyed Rosalie. With what fierce delight did she spring forward, light as the burning gazelle, and into my arms. What lustful fires sparkled in her half-closed eyes. Her lips meet mine – they are glued together. She forces open her mouth, her tongue meets mine. She rubs the lips of her cunt against my thigh, she clasps her arms tight, her breast rises and falls in quick succession, she wriggles her bottom, her backside convulsively jerks, and she says: 'Oh – oh! – God!' and sliding through my arms she sank upon the floor.

There, there at the further end of the room I see Caroline entering. Caroline, that very goddess of voluptuous beauty. She has heard of my arrival. She advances towards me, perfectly naked except for some pink gauze drawn round her waist – I too am naked, for the girls had stripped me on entering the room. My prick is hard and stiff, standing erect against my belly. Caroline sees it, she fixes her eyes on it, and remains perfectly still, fascinated by the charming sight. I fly to her, I take her in my arms, her emotions overpower her, she sinks on the floor on her back, she drags me with her. As she falls, her legs part and I fall between them, and five times did she spend ere she recovered from her fall.

When she rose up what a brilliancy sparkled in her eyes. Her gait was light and elastic as a fawn's.

When I rose up from my fall with the lovely Caroline, I met the gaze of the licentious Nubian, who was advancing to meet me, holding in her hand a glass of wine. She was perfectly naked and twisted and screwed her thighs together. I meet, accept the glass and drain the wine. The moment I drank it I knew that it was mixed with the tincture for exciting and creating amorous propensities.

The lovely creatures I have just been naming gathered round me, they embraced me in every part; some a leg and a thigh; others hung round my neck; some seized on my hands with which they frigged themselves; one seats herself on the floor between my legs and playfully squeezes my stones and strokes my once more rampant prick. The luscious Celeste has her arms clasped round my neck and I am about to impale her with my prick, but Fanny comes forward and urges her claim in favour of her little maidenhead, which is consuming her with a burning fever.

I clasp her in my arms and lay her down, falling upon her. One of the girls hastens to place a cushion under her bottom and then guides the dart to its sheath. I shove and thrust, and one of the girls, giving me a couple of hard slaps over my backside, drives me in up to the hilt and the sweet girl at once sucks in the delicious poison she has been longing for.

The wine which I had drunk contained so much tincture that my pego continued standing.

The Nubian next came in for a good stroking. Three times while I was in her did she spend. Caroline, Laura and Rosalie came in their turns; each received an exquisite frigging.

I then went to bathe, taking with me only four of the girls: Caroline, Celestine, Laura and Rosalie.

Whilst in the bathroom I twice more frigged Rosalie and Laura, and then dismissed them to their apartments, remaining with the other two.

I had supper brought into the bath to me, and determining to sacrifice myself to the libidinous desires of my two lovely mistresses, I drank more of the wine containing the tincture. Sufficient to enable me to give the two who were with me as much cock-broth as they could sip through the night.

After remaining in the bath for a couple of hours, we came out and went to the bedchamber.

I led them into the state-bedroom, and letting down the hangings, jumped into bed.

The two girls followed me and I was buried to my utmost length in the fiery furnace of Celestine. Four times did this amiable creature let fly her mettle and in such profusion did it come from her that the sheet under her bottom was all wet with it.

In her turn did Caroline take in and gorge her greedy little cunt with my morsel.

Thus did I spend the night, first frigging one and then the other, till they were entirely spent and worn out with the delicious fucking which I had given them.

I now determined to give up searching for any more maidenheads, and gave myself up to the dear girls I already possessed, than whom I could find none more beautiful, more voluptuous or more devoted to my capricious pleasures.

I now live happily surrounded by the sweet creatures, but I hear someone calling me from my private bed. I am in good condition, having abstained for three days. I fly to her, I jump into her arms and drown myself in a sea of bliss, in the arms of La Rose d'Amour.

❦ ❧

*Sub-
Umbra*

*or
Sport
among
the
She-Noodles*

❦ ❧

The merry month of May has always been famous for its propitious influence over the voluptuous senses of the fairer sex.

I will tell you two or three little incidents which occurred to me in May 1878, when I went to visit my cousins in Sussex, or as I familiarly call them, the 'she-noodles', for the sport they afforded me at various times.

My uncle's is a nice country residence, standing in large grounds of its own, and surrounded by small fields of arable and pasture land, interspersed by numerous interesting copses, through which run footpaths and shady walks, where you are not likely to meet anyone in a month. I shall not trouble my readers with the name of the locality, or they may go pleasure hunting for themselves. Well, to go on, these cousins consisted of Annie, Sophie and Polly, beside their brother Frank, who, at nineteen, was the eldest, the girls being, respectively, eighteen, sixteen and fifteen. After dinner, the first day of my arrival, Paterfamilias and Mama indulged in a snooze in their armchairs, whilst us boys and girls (I was the same age as Frank) took a stroll in the grounds. I attached myself more particularly to cousin Annie, a finely developed blonde, with deep blue eyes, pouting red lips, and a full heaving bosom, which to me looked like a perfect volcano of smothered desires. Frank was a very indolent fellow, who loved to smoke his cigar, and expected his sisters, who adored him, to sit by his side, reading some of the novels of the day, or tell him their love secrets, &c. This was by far too tame an amusement for me, and as I had not been there for nearly three years, I requested Annie to show me the improvements in the grounds before we went in to tea, saying to Frank, banteringly, 'I suppose, old fellow, you're too lazy, and would prefer your sister taking me round?'

'I'm too comfortable, lazy is an ugly word, Walter, but the fact is, Soph is just reading me a most interesting book, and I can't leave it,' he replied; 'besides, sissie is quite as well or better qualified than I am to show off the grounds. I never notice anything.'

'Come on, Annie,' said I taking her hand; 'Frank is in love.'

'No, I'm sure he never thinks of a girl, except his sisters,' was the reply.

We were now out of earshot, in a shady walk, so I went on a little more freely. 'But, surely you, coz, are in love, if he is not. I can tell it by your liquid eye and heaving bosom.'

A scarlet flush shot over her features at my allusion to her finely moulded bosom, but it was evidently pleasing, and far from offensive, to judge by her playfully spoken, 'Oh! Walter, for shame, sir!'

We were a good distance away by this time, and a convenient seat stood near, so throwing my arms around the blushing girl, I kissed her ruby lips, and drawing her with me, said, 'Now, Annie, dear, I'm your cousin and old playfellow, I couldn't help kissing those beautiful lips, which I might always make free with when we were little boy and girl together; now you shall confess all before I let you go.'

'But I've nothing to confess, sir.'

'Do you never think of love, Annie? Look me in the face if you can say it's a stranger to your bosom,' putting my hand familiarly round her neck till my right hand rested on one of the panting globes of her bosom.

She turned her face to mine, suffused as it was by a deeper blush than ever, as her dark blue eyes met mine, in a fearless search of my meaning, but instead of speaking in response to this mute appeal, I kissed her rapturously, sucking in the fragrance of her sweet breath till she fairly trembled with emotion.

It was just beginning to get dusk, my hands were caressing the white, firm flesh of her beautiful neck, slowly working their way towards the heaving bubbies a little lower down; at last I whispered, 'What a fine, what a lovely bust you have developed since I saw you last, dear Annie, you won't mind your cousin, will you, when everything used to be so free to each other; besides, what harm can there be in it?'

She seemed on fire, a thrill of emotion seemed to shoot through both of us, and for several moments she lay almost motionless in my arms, with one hand resting on my thigh. Priapus was awake and ready for business, but she suddenly aroused herself, saying, 'We must never stop here, let us walk round or they will suspect something.'

'When shall we be alone again, darling? We must arrange that before we go in,' I said quickly.

It was impossible to keep her on the seat, but as we walked on she said, musingly, 'Tomorrow morning we might go for a stroll before lunch. Frank lies in bed, and my sisters are keeping house this week; I shall have to mind the tarts and pies next week.'

I gave her another hug and a kiss, as I said, 'How delightful that will be; what a dear, thoughtful girl you are, Annie.'

'Mind, sir, how you behave tomorrow, not so much kissing, or I shan't take you for a second walk; here we are at the house.'

Next morning was gloriously warm and fine; as soon as breakfast was over we started for our stroll, being particularly minded by papa to be back in good time for luncheon.

I gradually drew out my beautiful cousin, till our conversation got exceedingly warm, the hot blood rushing in waves of crimson over her shamefaced visage.

'What a rude boy you have grown, Walter, since you were here last; I can't help blushing at the way you run on, sir!' she exclaimed at last.

'Annie, my darling,' I replied, 'what can be more pleasing than to talk of fun with pretty girls, the beauties of their legs and bosoms, and all about them? How I should love to see your lovely calf at this moment, especially after the glimpses I have already had of a divine ankle,' saying which I threw myself under a shady tree, close by a gate in a meadow, and drew the half-resisting girl down on the grass at my side, and kissed her passionately, as I murmured, 'Oh! Annie, what is there worth living for like the sweets of love?'

Her lips met mine in a fiery embrace, but suddenly disengaging herself, her eyes cast down, and looking awfully abashed, she stammered out, 'What is it? what do you mean, Walter?'

'Ah, coz dear, can you be so innocent? Feel here the dart of love all impatient to enter the mossy grotto between your thighs,' I whispered, placing her hand upon my prick, which I had suddenly let out of the restraining trousers. 'How you sigh; grasp it in your hand, dear, is it possible that you do not understand what it is for?'

Her face was crimson to the roots of her hair, as her hand grasped my tool, and her eyes seemed to start with terror at the sudden apparition of Mr John Thomas; so that taking advantage of her speechless confusion my own hand, slipping under her clothes, soon had possession of her mount, and in spite of the nervous contraction of her thighs, the forefinger searched out the virgin clitoris.

'Ah! oh! oh!! Walter don't; what are you about?'

'It's all love, dear, open your thighs a wee bit and see what pleasure my finger will make you experience,' I again whispered, smothering her with renewed and luscious kisses, thrusting the velvet tip of my tongue between her lips.

'Oh! oh! you will hurt!' she seemed to sigh rather than speak, as her legs relaxed a little of their spasmodic contraction.

My lips continued glued to hers, our otherwise disengaged arms clasped each other closely round the waist, her hand held my affair in a kind of convulsive grasp whilst my fingers were busy with clitoris and cunny; the only audible sound resembling a mixture of kisses and sighs, till all in a moment I felt her crack deluged with a warm, creamy spend whilst my own juice spurted over her hand and dress in loving sympathy.

In a short while we recovered our composure a little, and I then explained to her that the melting ecstasy she had just felt was only a slight fortaste of the joy I could give her, by inserting my member in her cunny. My persuasive eloquence and the warmth of her desires soon overcame all maiden fears and scruples; then for fear of damaging her dress, or getting the green stain of the grass on the knees of my light trousers, I persuaded her to stand up by the gate and allow me to enter behind. She hid her face in her hands on the top rail of the gate, as I slowly raised her dress; what glories were unfolded to view, my prick's stiffness was renewed in an instant at the sight of her delicious buttocks, so beautifully relieved by the white of her pretty drawers; as I opened them and exposed the flesh, I could see the lips of her plump pouting cunny, deliciously feathered with soft light down, her lovely legs, drawers, stockings, pretty boots, making a *tout ensemble*, which as I write and describe them cause Mr Priapus to swell in my breeches; it was a most delicious sight. I knelt and kissed her bottom, slit, and everything my tongue could reach, it was all mine, I stood up and prepared to take possession of the seat of love when, alas! a sudden shriek from Annie, her clothes dropped, all my arrangements were upset in a moment; a bull had unexpectedly appeared on the opposite side of the gate, and frightened my love by the sudden application of his cold, damp nose to her forehead. It is too much to contemplate that scene even now.

Annie was ready to faint as she screamed, 'Walter! Walter! Save me from the horrid beast!' I comforted and reassured her as well as I was able, and seeing that we were on the safe side of the gate, a few loving kisses soon set her all right. We continued our walk, and soon spying out a favourable shady spot, I said: 'Come, Annie dear, let us sit down and recover from the startling interruption; I am sure, dear, you must still feel very agitated, besides I must get you now to compensate me for the rude disappointment.'

She seemed to know that her hour had come; the hot blushes swept in crimson waves across her lovely face, as she cast down her eyes, and permitted me to draw her down by my side on a mossy knoll, and we lay side by side, my lips glued to hers in a most ardent embrace.

'Annie! Oh! Annie!' I gasped. 'Give me the tip of your tongue, love.' She tipped me the velvet without the slightest hesitation, drawing, at the same time, what seemed a deep sigh of delightful anticipation as she yielded to my slightest wish. I had one arm under her head, and with the other I gently removed her hat, and threw aside my own golgotha, kissing and sucking at her delicious tongue all the while. Then I placed one of her hands on my ready cock, which was in bursting state, saying, as I released her tongue for a moment: 'There, Annie, take the dart of love in your hand.' She grasped it nervously, as she softly murmured: 'Oh, Walter, I'm so afraid; and yet – oh, yet, dearest, I feel, I die, I must taste the sweets of love, this forbidden fruit,' her voice sinking almost to a whisper, as she pressed and passed her hand up and down my shaft. My hand was also busy finding its way under her clothes as I again glued my mouth to hers, and sucked at her tongue till I could feel her vibrate all over with the excess of her emotion. My hand, which had taken possession of the seat of bliss, was fairly deluged with her warm glutinous spendings.

'My love; my life! I must kiss you there, and taste the nectar of love,' I exclaimed, as I snatched my lips from hers, and reversing my position, buried my face between her unresisting thighs. I licked up the luscious spendings with rapturous delight from the lips of her tight little cunny, then my tongue found its way further, till it tickled her sensitive clitoris, and put her into a frenzy of mad desire for still further enjoyment; she twisted her legs over my head, squeezing my head between her firm plump thighs in an ecstasy of delight.

Wetting my finger in her luscious crack, I easily inserted it in her beautifully wrinkled brown bum-hole, and keeping my tongue busy in titillating the stiff little clitoris, I worked her up into such a furious state of desire that she clutched my cock and brought it to her mouth, as I lay over her to give her the chance of doing so; she rolled her tongue round the purple head, and I could also feel the loving playful bite of her pearly teeth. It was the acme of erotic enjoyment. She came again in another luscious flood of spendings, whilst she eagerly sucked every drop of my sperm as it burst from my excited prick.

We both nearly fainted from the excess of our emotions, and lay quite exhausted for a few moments, till I felt her dear lips again pressing and sucking my engine of love. The effect was electric; I was as stiff as ever.

'Now, darling, for the real stroke of love,' I exclaimed. Shifting my position, and parting her quivering thighs, so that I could kneel between them. My knees were placed upon her skirts so as to preserve them from the grass stain. She lay before me in a delightful state of anticipation, her beautiful face all blushes of shame, the closed eyelids fringed with their long dark lashes, her lips slightly open and the finely developed, firm, plump globes of her bosom heaving in a state of tumultuous excitement. It was ravishing, I felt mad with lust, and could no longer put off the actual consummation. I could not contain myself. Alas; poor maidenhead! Alas! for your virginity! I brought my cock to the charge, presented the head just slightly between the lips of her vagina. A shudder of delight seemed to pass through her frame at the touch of my weapon, as her eyes opened, and she whispered, with a soft, loving smile, 'I know it will hurt, but Walter, dear Walter, be both firm and kind. I must have it, if it kills me.' Throwing her arms around my neck, she drew my lips to hers, as she thrust her tongue into my mouth with all the abandon of love, and shoved up her bottom to meet my charge.

I had placed one hand under her buttocks, whilst, with the other, I kept my affair straight to the mark; then pushing vigorously, the head entered about an inch, till it was chock up to the opposing hymen. She gave a start of pain, but her eyes gazed into mine with a most encouraging look.

'Throw your legs over my back, my dear,' I gasped, scarcely relinquishing her tongue for a moment. Her lovely thighs turned round me in a spasmodic frenzy of determination to bear the worst. I gave a ruthless push, just as her bottom heaved up to meet me, and the deed was done. King Priapus had burst through all obstacles to our enjoyment. She gave a subdued shriek of agonised pain, and I felt myself throbbing in possession of her inmost charms.

'You darling! You love me! My brave Annie, how well you stood the pain. Let us lie still for a moment or two, and then for the joys of love,' I exclaimed, as I kissed her face, forehead, eyes and mouth in a transport of delight at feeling the victory so soon accomplished.

Presently I could feel the tight sheath of her vagina contracting on my cock in the most delicious manner. This challenge was too much for my impetuous steed. He gave a gentle thrust. I could see by the spasm of pain which passed over her beautiful face that it was still painful to her, so, restraining my ardour, I worked very gently; but my lust was so maddening that I could not restrain a copious spend and I sank on her bosom in love's delicious lethargy.

It was only for a few moments, I could feel her tremble beneath me with voluptuous ardour, and the sheath being now well lubricated, we commenced a delightful bout of ecstatic fucking. All her pain was forgotten, the wounded parts soothed by the flow of my semen now only revelled in the delightful friction of love; she seemed to boil over in spendings, my delighted cock revelled in it, as he thrust in and out with all my manly vigour; we spent three or four times in a delirium of voluptuousness, till I was fairly vanquished by her impetuosity, and begged her to be moderate, and not to injure herself by excessive enjoyment.

'Oh! can it be possible to hurt oneself by such a delightful pleasure?' she sighed, then seeing me withdraw my limp tool from her still longing cunt, she smiled archly, as she said with a blush, 'Pardon my rudeness, dear Walter, but I fear it is you who are most injured after all; look at your bloodstained affair.'

'You lovely little simpleton,' I said, kissing her rapturously, 'that's your own virgin blood; let me wipe you, darling,' as I gently applied my handkerchief to her pouting slit, and afterwards to my own cock. 'This, dearest Annie, I shall treasure up as the proofs of your virgin love, so delightfully surrendered to me this day,' exhibiting the ensanguined *mouchoir* to her gaze.

We now arose from our soft mossy bed, and mutually assisted each other to remove all traces of our love engagement.

Then we walked on, and I enlightened the dear girl as to to all the arts and practices of love. 'Do you think,' I remarked, 'that your sisters or Frank have any idea of what the joys of love are like?'

'I believe they would enter into it as ardently as I do, if they were but once initiated,' she replied. 'I have often heard Frank say when kissing us, that we made him burn all over'; and then blushing deeply as her eyes met mine, 'Oh! dear Walter, I'm afraid you will think we are awfully rude girls, but when we go to bed at night, my sisters and I often compare our budding charms, and crack little jokes about the growing curls of mine and Sophie's slits, and the hairless little pussy of Polly, we have such games of slapping, and romps too, sometimes; it has often made me feel a kind of all-overishness of feverish excitement I could not understand, but thanks to you, love, I can make it all out now; I wish you could only get a peep at us, dear.'

'Perhaps it might be managed; you know my room is next to yours, I could hear you laughing and having a game last night.'

'I know we did, we had such fun,' she replied, 'it was Polly trying to put my pussy in curl papers, but how can you manage it, dear?'

Seeing she fully entered into my plans for enjoyment, we consulted together, and at last I hit upon an idea which I thought might work very well; it was that I should first sound out Frank and enlighten him a little into the ways of love, and then as soon as he was ripe for our purpose, we would surprise the three sisters whilst bathing naked, and slap their naked bottoms all round; that Annie should encourage her sisters to help in tearing off all our clothes, and then we could indulge in a general romp of love.

Annie was delighted at the idea, and I promised the very next day to begin with Frank, or perhaps that very afternoon if I got a chance.

We returned to the house, Annie's cheeks blushing and carrying a beautiful flush of health, and her mama remarked that our walk had evidently done her very great good, little guessing that her daughter, like our first mother Eve, had that morning tasted of the forbidden fruit, and was greatly enlightened and enlivened thereby.

After luncheon I asked Frank to smoke a cigarette in my room, which he at once complied with.

As soon as I had closed the door, I said, 'Old fellow, did you ever see Fanny Hill, a beautiful book of love and pleasure?'

'What, a smutty book, I suppose you mean? No. Walter, but if you have got it I should wonderfully like to look at it,' he said, his eyes sparkling with animation.

'Here it is, my boy, only I hope it won't excite you too much; you can look it over by yourself, as I read The Times,' said I, taking it out of my dressing-case, and handing it to his eager grasp.

He sat close to me in an easy lounging chair, and I watched him narrowly as he turned over the pages and gloated over the beautiful plates and his prick hardened in his breeches till it was quite stiff and rampant.

'Ha! Ha!! Ha!!! old fellow, I thought it would fetch you out!' I said, laying my hand upon his cock. 'By Jove, Frank! what a tosser yours has grown since we used to play in bed together a long time ago. I'll lock the door, we must compare our parts, I think mine is nearly as big as yours.'

He made no remark, but I could see he was greatly excited by the book. Having locked the door, I leant over his shoulder and made my remarks upon the plates as he turned them over. At length the book dropped from his hands, and his excited gaze was riveted on my bursting breeches. 'Why, Walter, you are as bad as I am,' he said, with a laugh, 'let's see which is the biggest,' pulling out his hard, stiff prick, and then laying his hands on me and pulling my affair out to look at.

We handled each other in an ecstasy of delight, which ended in our throwing off all our clothes, and having a mutual fuck between our thighs on the bed; we spent in rapture, and after a long dalliance he entered into my plans, and we determined to have a lark with the girls as soon as we could get a chance. Of course I was mum as to what had passed between Annie and myself.

In the course of the evening, Frank and I were delighted by the arrival of a beautiful young lady of sixteen, on a visit to his sisters, in fact a schoolfellow of Sophie and Polly, come to stop a week at the house.

Miss Rosa Redquim was indeed a sprightly beauty of the Venus height, well proportioned in leg and limb, full swelling bosom, with a graceful Grecian type of face, rosy cheeks, large grey eyes, and golden auburn hair, lips as red as cherries, and teeth like pearls, frequently exhibited by a succession of winning smiles, which never seemed to leave her face. Such was the acquisition to the feminine department of the house, and we congratulated ourselves on the increased prospect of sport, as Frank had expressed to me considerable compunction as to taking liberties with one's own sisters.

The next morning being gloriously fine and warm, myself and friend strolled in the grounds, smoking our cigarettes, for about an hour, till near the time when we guessed the girls would be coming for a bathe in the small lake in the park, which we at once proceeded to; then we secreted ourselves secure from observation, and awaited, in deep silence, the arrival of sisters and friend.

This lake, as I call it, was a pond about four or five acres in extent, every side thickly wooded to the very margin, so that even anglers could not get access to the bank, except at the little sloping green sward, of about twenty or thirty square yards in extent, which had a large hut, or summer-house, under the trees; here the bathers could undress, and then trip across the lawn to the water. The bottom of the pond was gradually shelving, and covered with fine sand at this spot, and a circular space was enclosed with rails, to prevent them getting out of their depth.

The back door of this hut opened upon a very narrow footpath, leading to the house through the dense thicket, so that any party would feel quite secure from observation. The interior was comfortably furnished with seats and loungers, besides a buffet, generally holding a stock of wine, biscuits and cakes, during the bathing season.

Frank, having a key to the hut, took me through on to the lawn, and then climbing up into a thick sycamore, we relighted our cigarettes, awaiting the adventure with some justifiable impatience.

Some ten minutes of suspense, and then we were rewarded by

hearing the ringing laughter of the approaching girls. We heard the key turned in the lock then the sounds of their bolting themselves in, and Annie's voice, saying: 'Ah! Wouldn't the boys like the fun of seeing us undress and bathing, this lovely warm day'; to which we heard Rosa laughingly reply: 'I don't mind if they do see me, if I don't know it, dears. There's something delightful in the thought of the excitement it would put the dear fellows in. I know I should like Frank to take a fancy to me; I'm nearly in love with him already, and have read that the best way a girl can madly excite the man she wishes to win is to let him see all her charms, when he thinks she is unconscious of his being near.'

'Well, there's no fear of our being seen here, so I am one for a good romp. Off with your clothes, quick; it will be delicious in the water,' exclaimed Sophie.

The undressing was soon accomplished, excepting chemises, boots, and stockings, as they were evidently in no hurry to enter the water.

'Now,' said Sophie, with a gay laugh, 'we must make Rosa a free woman, and examine all she's got. Come on, girls, lay her down, and turn up her smock.'

The beautiful girl only made a slight feint of resisting, as she playfully pulled up their chemises, exclaiming: 'You shan't look at my fanny for nothing. La! Polly has got no hair on her fly trap yet. What a pretty pouting slit yours is, Annie. I think you have been using the finger of a glove we made into a little cock for Sophie, and told her to bring home from school for you.'

She was soon stretched on her back on the soft mossy grass, her face covered with burning blushes, as her pretty cunt was exposed to view, ornamented with its *chevelure* of soft red hair; her beautiful white belly and thighs shining like marble in the bright sunlight. The three sisters were blushing as well as their friend, and delighted at the sight of so much loveliness.

One after another, they kissed the vermilion lips of their friend's delightful slit, and then turning her on her face, proceeded to smack the lily white bottom of their laughing, screaming victim, with open hands.

Smacks and laughter echoed through the grove, and we almost fancied ourselves witnesses to the games of real nymphs. At last she was allowed to rise on her knees, and then the three sisters in turn presented their cunts to their friend to kiss. Polly was the last, and Rosa, clasping her arms firmly round my youngest cousin's buttocks, exclaimed: 'Ah! Ah! You have made me feel so rude, I must suck this little hairless jewel,' as she glued her lips to it, and hid her face almost from sight, as if she would devour Polly's charms there and then. The young girl, flushed with excitement, placed her hands on Rosa's head, as if to keep her there, whilst both Annie and Sophie, kneeling down by the side of their friend, began to caress her cunt, bosom, and every charm they could tickle or handle.

This exciting scene lasted for five or six minutes, till at last they all sank down in a confused heap on the grass, kissing and fingering in mad excitement.

Now was our time. We had each provided ourselves with little switches of twigs, and thus armed we seemed to drop from the clouds upon the surprised girls, who screamed in fright and hid their blushing faces in their hands.

They were too astonished and alarmed to jump up, but we soon commenced to bring them to their senses, and convince them of the reality of the situation.

'What rude! what lascivious ideas! slash away Frank!' I cried, making my swish leave its marks on their bottoms at every cut.

'Who would have thought of it, Walter? We must whip such indecent ideas out of their tails!' he answered, seconding my assault with his sharp, rapid strokes.

They screamed both from pain and shame, and springing to their feet, chased round the lawn; there was no escape. We caught them by the tails of their chemises, which we lifted up to enable us to cut at their bums with more effect. At last we were getting out of breath, and beginning fairly to pant from exhaustion, when Annie suddenly turned upon me, saying, 'Come, come, girls, let's tear their clothes off, so they shall be quite as ashamed as we are, and agree to keep our secret!' The others helped her, and we made such a feeble resistance that we were soon reduced to the same state in which we had surprised them, making them blush and look very shamefaced at the sight of our rampant engines of love.

Frank seized Miss Redquim round the waist, and led the way into the summer-house, myself and his sisters following. The gentlemen then producing the wine, &c., from the buffet, sat down with a young lady on each knee, my friend having Rosa and Polly, whilst Annie and Sophie sat with me, we plied the girls with several glasses of champagne each, which they seemed to swallow in order to drown their sense of shame. We could feel their bodies quiver with emotion as they reclined upon our necks, their hands and ours groping under shirts and chemises in every forbidden spot; each of us had two delicate hands caressing our cocks, two delicious arms around our necks, two faces laid cheek to cheek on either side, two sets of lips to kiss, two pairs of bright and humid eyes to return our ardent glances; what wonder then that we flooded their hands with our spurting seed and felt their delicious spendings trickle over our busy fingers.

Excited by the wine, and madly lustful to enjoy the dear girls to the utmost, I stretched Sophie's legs wide apart, and sinking on my knees, gamahuched her virgin cunt, till she spent again in ecstasy, whilst dear Annie was doing the same to me, sucking the last drop of spend from my gushing prick; meanwhile Frank was following my example, Rosa surrendered to his lascivious tongue all the recesses of her virginity as she screamed with delight and pressed his head towards her mount when the frenzy of love brought her to the spending point; Polly all the while kissing her brother's belly, and frigging him to a delicious emission.

When we recovered a little from this exciting *pas de trois*, all bashfulness was vanished between us, we promised to renew our pleasures on the morrow, and for the present contented ourselves by bathing all together, and then returned to the house for fear the girls might be suspected of something wrong for staying out too long.

After luncheon Frank smoked his cigarette in my room; the events of the morning had left both of us in a most unsettled and excited state.

'I say, old fellow,' he exclaimed, 'by Jove! it's quite impossible for me to wait till tomorrow for the chance of enjoying that delicious Rosa; besides, when there are so many of us together there is just the chance of being disappointed; no, no, it must be this very night if I die for it; her room is only the other side of my sisters'.'

I tried to persuade him from doing anything rashly, as we could not yet be certain that even excited and ready as she had shown herself, she was prepared to surrender her virginity so quickly. However, arguments and reasonings were in vain. 'See,' he exclaimed, 'the very thoughts of her make my prick ready to burst,' opening his trousers and letting out his beautiful red-headed cock, as it stood in all its manly glory, stiff and hard as marble, with the hot blood looking ready to burst from his distended veins; the sight was too exciting for me to restrain myself, the cigarette dropped from my lips, and going upon my knees in front of him, I kissed, sucked, frigged and played with his delicious prick till he spent in my mouth with an exclamation of rapture and I eagerly swallowed every drop of his copious emission. When we had a little recovered our serenity, we discussed the best plans for the night, as I was determined to have my share of the amusement, which Frank most willingly agreed to, provided he was to go first to Rosa's room, and prevail upon her to consent to his ardent suit; then when all seemed to be *en règle*, I was to surprise them in the midst of their fun, and join in the erotic frolic.

After dinner we adjourned to the drawing-room, where a most pleasant evening was enlivened by music and singing, leaving Frank turning over the leaves for Rosa and Polly, as they sang 'What Are the Wild Waves Saying?' Annie and Sophie whispered to me that they should like a short stroll in the garden by moonlight, so opening the window, we stepped out on to the soft gravel path, where we could walk with an almost noiseless tread. Papa and Mama were in the library playing cribbage, and we felt sure that Frank and Rosa would not run after us, so passing rapidly down a shady walk, with one arm round each of the dear girls' waists, and alternately kissing one and the other of them, I followed the instinct of love which allowed me to guide the willing girls into a rather dark arbour without the least demur on their part.

'How lovely the honeysuckle smells!' sighed Sophie, as I drew them both down by my side in the corner, and began a most delicious kissing and groping in the dim obscurity.

'Not so sweet as your dear little pussy,' said I, playfully twisting my fingers in the soft down around the tight little grotto of love which I had taken possession of.

'Oh! Oh! Mind, Walter dear!' she sighed softly, as she clung round my neck.

'Will you let me kiss it as I did Annie's this morning my little pet, it will give you such pleasure; there's nothing to be bashful or shamefaced about here in the dark; ask your sister if it wasn't delicious.'

ANNIE – 'Oh! let him Sophie dear, you will experience the most heavenly sensations.'

Thus urged she allowed me to raise her clothes, and recline her backwards in the corner, but this would not admit of Annie having her fair share of the game; as she was now all aflame with excited expectation, there was no difficulty in persuading her to kneel over my face as I reclined on my back at full length on the seat; lovely hands at once let my eager prick out of his confined position in my trousers, and as I commenced to suck and gamahuche Sophie, I felt that the dear Annie had taken possession of my cock for her own special benefit.

'Oh! let me kiss you, Sophie dear, put your tongue in my mouth,' said Annie, straddling over me, and putting away my excited engine of love up her own longing crack, and beginning a delightful St George; I clasped the younger girl firmly round the buttocks with one arm, whilst with my right hand I found and rubbed her stiff little clitoris to increase the excitement from the lascivious motions of my tongue in her virgin cunny.

Annie was in a frenzy of voluptuous enjoyment, she bounced up and down on my prick, and now and then rested for a moment to indulge in the exquisite pleasure of the devil's bite, which she seemed to possess to a most precocious extent, the folds of her cunt contracting and throbbing upon my swelling prick in the most delicious manner.

Sophie was all of a tremble, she wriggled herself most excitedly over my mouth, and I licked up her virgin spendings as they came down in a thick creamy emission.

'Oh! Oh! Oh!' she sighed, hugging and kissing Annie in fondest abandon. 'What is it, dear? I shall choke, Walter. There's something running from me; it's so delicious. Oh! What shall I do?'

Annie and myself met at this moment in a joint spend, which left us in an ecstatic lethargy of love, and the two sisters almost fainted upon my prostrate body.

When we had recovered a little, I sat up between the loving sisters.

Sophie, throwing her arms round my neck, quite smothered me with her burning kisses, as she whispered in my ear: 'It was indeed pleasure, dear Walter. Is that one of the delights of love, and what was Annie doing, for she was excited as I was?'

'Can't you guess, darling?' I replied, taking her hand and placing it upon my still rampant cock. 'That is what she played with.'

'But how?' whispered the innocent girl. 'She was kissing and sucking my tongue deliciously all the while, but seemed as if she could not keep still a moment.'

'She had that plaything of mine up her cunny, my dear, and was riding up and down upon it till we all fainted with the pleasure at the same time. You shall have a real lesson in love next time, and Annie won't be jealous, will you, dearest?'

ANNIE – 'No, no, we must all be free to enjoy all the games of love without jealousy. I wonder how Frank is getting on with Rosa by this time. We must now make haste back to the house.'

Sophie was anxious for more explanations as to the arts of love, but was put off till another time; and all being now in a cooler state of mind, we returned to the house, where we found Frank repeating the game of the morning, by gamahuching Rosa, whilst Polly was gone out of the room.

The red-haired beauty was covered with blushes, as she suddenly dropped her clothes on our entrance, and only recovered from her crimson shamefacedness when Annie laughingly assured her that we had been enjoying ourselves in the same manner.

'Oh! How rude and indecent of us all,' exclaimed Rosa, 'but who can resist the burning touches of a handsome young fellow like your brother; he was so impudent, and it sends such a thrill of voluptuousness through the whole frame.' With this, she commenced to sing 'It's Naughty, But It's Nice'.

The supper bell rang, and, after a light repast, we all separated to our rooms. Frank came into my chamber to join in a cigarette and glass of grog before finally retiring.

'It's all right for tonight, old fellow,' he exclaimed, as soon as we were seated for our smoke. 'I begged Rosa to let me kiss all her charms, in her own room without the inconvenience of clothes. She made some objections at first, but finally consented not to lock the door if I promised not to go beyond kissing, on my honour as a gentleman.'

He was too impatient to stop long, and, after only one smoke, cut off to his room. Undressing myself as quickly as possible, I went to him, and escorted him to the door of his lady-love; it was unlocked, and he glided noiselessly into the darkened chamber. She was evidently awake and expecting his visit, for I could hear their rapturous kissing and his exclamation of delight as he ran his hands over her beautiful figure.

'My love, I must light the candles to feast my eyes upon your extraordinary beauties. Why did you put out the lights?' She made some faint remonstrances, but the room was soon a blaze of light from half a dozen candles.

I was looking through the keyhole, and eagerly listening to every word.

'My love, let us lie side by side and enjoy feeling our bodies in naked contact before we begin kissing each other's charms.'

I could see that his shirt and her *chemise de nuit* were both turned up as high as possible, and his prick was throbbing against her belly. He made her grasp it in her hand, and pulling one of her legs over his thighs, was trying to place the head of his eager cock to the mark between her legs.

'Ah! No! No! Never! You promised on your honour, sir!' she almost screamed in alarm, struggling to disengage herself from his strong embrace. 'No! No! Oh! No! I won't, indeed!'

His previous soft manner seemed in a moment to have changed to a mad fury, as he suddenly rolled her over on her back, keeping his own legs well between her thighs.

'Honour! Honour!' he laughed. 'How can I have honour when you tempt me so, Rosa? You have driven me mad by the liberties I have been allowed. Resistance is useless. I would rather die than not have you now, you dear girl.'

She struggled in desperate silence for a few moments, but her strength was unequal to his; he gradually got into position, and then taking advantage of her exhaustion, rapidly and ruthlessly completed her ravishment.

She seemed insensible at first, and I took advantage of her short unconsciousness to steal into the room, and kneel at the foot of the bed, where I had a fine view of his bloodstained weapon, thrusting in and out of her shattered virginity. After a little she seemed to begin to enjoy his movements, especially after the first lubricating injection of his love juice. Her buttocks heaved up to meet his thrusts, and her arms clung convulsively round his body, and seemed reluctant to let him withdraw, until both seemed to come together in a luscious spend.

As they lay exhausted after this bout, I advanced and kissed the dear girl, and as she opened her eyes, I placed my hand across her mouth to stop any inconvenient scream of surprise, and congratulated her on having so nicely got rid of her troublesome virginity, and claimed my share of the fun, drawing her attention to the rampant condition of my cock in contrast to Frank's limp affair. I could see she was now eager for a repetition of the pleasure she had only just begun to taste. Her eyes were full of languishing desire as I placed her hand upon my prick.

In accordance with our previously devised arrangements she was persuaded to ride a St George upon me and my cock was inserted in her still tender cunt, with great care, and allowed slowly to get into position; but the excitement was too great for me and with an exclamation of delight I shot a stream of sperm up into her very entrails; this set her off and she began slowly to move upon me, her cunt gripping and throbbing upon the shaft most deliciously, and we were soon running another delightful course; this was too much for Frank, his cock was again as hard as iron, and eager to get in somewhere, so kneeling up behind her he tried to insert his prick in her cunt alongside of mine, but found it too difficult to achieve, then the charming wrinkled orifice of her pink bottom-hole caught his attention, the tip of his affair was wet with our spendings, and his vigorous shoves soon gained an entrance, as I was holding her fast and she was too excited to resist anything, only giving a slight scream as she found him slip inside of the part she thought was only made for another purpose. I asked them to rest a few moments and enjoy the sensation of feeling where we were, our pricks throbbing against each other in a most delicious manner, with only the thin membrane of the anal canal between them; it made us spend immediately to the great delight of Rosa, who at once urged us to go on.

This was the most delightful bout of fucking I had ever had; she made us do it over and over again and, when we were exhausted, sucked our pricks up to renewed cockstands. This lasted till the dawn of day warned us of the necessity of precaution, and we retired to our respective rooms.

Next morning Annie and her sisters rallied us upon our late appearance at the breakfast table, remarking with a pouting look that we could not care much for their company if we lay a-bed and left them to themselves for the best half of the day, and that Rosa was just as bad, for she was actually still in dishabille, taking her breakfast in her own room.

Here Mama interposed, by adding, 'Besides, Walter, I am astonished you should copy Frank's lazy ways, you who on your first arrival here were so eager for early-morning walks; look at Annie, she is not half so rosy and animated as she looked after your first walk.'

A deep flush passed across Annie's face at this allusion to our first eventful walk, when we had the adventure with the bull, but I prevented her parents' observing it by replying that residents in town were always in such a hurry to enjoy the fresh air, and that it seemed to have an extraordinary somnolescent effect upon me, as I could hardly keep my eyes open at supper time, or rouse myself from sleep in the morning.

FRANK – 'I'm glad you have found out it is not all laziness now. Walter will take my part when I assert it is the natural drowsiness of youth, which is readily induced by the keen bracing air we breathe all day.'

Papa made a few incredulous, ironical remarks about the youth of the present day, and then breakfast being over, as he rose from the table, said: 'Walter, would you mind riding a dozen miles to oblige me. Frank would not be ready to start for an hour at least; besides, I would rather trust you than him with the lady my note is for; Colonel Leslie's wife is both young and gay, and I would rather not run the risk of Frank being one day a co-respondent in the Divorce Court; and I caution *you* to take care of yourself.'

I readily assented, more especially when I noticed a shade of jealous anxiety flit across Annie's tell-tale face. The horse was already at the door, so springing into the saddle I rode off with a fluttering anticipation of something racy being likely to turn up. I shall not trouble about my reflections during this delightful hour's ride; the atmosphere was most deliciously bracing, and my thoughts were so amorously bent that when I reined up at the lodge-gate, at the entrance to the colonel's grounds, I felt that I could fuck anything in petticoats, from a witch to a gatepost; the gatekeeper soon passed me in, and I sprang from my saddle before the door of a fine old Elizabethan hall; my knock was promptly responded to by a most handsome young coloured fellow with a Hindu cast of feature.

Mrs Leslie was at home, and he begged I would excuse her coming down to the drawing-room, as she was still at her toilette, and would immediately see me in her private boudoir.

This courteous message revived all my romantically amorous ideas, with which I had indulged myself during my ride.

Ushered into the boudoir, I found the lady of the house to be a beautiful brunette of about three-and-twenty, with a most bewitching expression of countenance, whilst her large, full, dark eyes seemed to read my very soul as she extended her hand and drew me to a seat by her side, saying: 'So, you are cousin Walter, I suppose; how is it that Frank did not ride over with his papa's note? But tell him,' she added with a very arch look, 'that I was quite as well pleased to see you, and that I consider his cousin quite as fascinating as himself.'

Then, ringing the bell, she continued, 'Will you take a cup of chocolate with me after your ride? It will invigorate me for the serious business of your uncle's note,' opening a drawer and laying several bundles of papers like legal documents on the table, just as the servant entered (he was the good-looking Hindu who had first introduced me).

MRS LESLIE – 'Vishnu, bring up the chocolate, with two cups and some biscuits, and mind not to forget the flask of noyau,' remarking to me as he disappeared, 'Is he not a good-looking heathen? The colonel had him long before he married me, and I call him his principal Hindu deity; whenever I look at him it puts me in mind of Joseph and Potiphar's wife, especially now the colonel is away; do you not think it a burning shame to leave a young wife all alone by herself?'

She continued to run on in this curious way, without giving me a chance to make a reply or observation in return, as she busied herself laying out the papers, making pretence of an awful lot of business to be gone through

The servant now brought in the chocolate, &c., and was dismissed with the order to tell Annette that her mistress would be too busy for some time, and was not to be disturbed until she rang for the completion of her toilette.

My fair hostess was a most charming object as she moved about in her dressing-gown, which was rather open at the neck, so as to display the upper part of the snowy prominences of her luscious bosom, besides which I caught glimpses of her naked feet, with nothing on but the most *petite* blue satin slippers.

Presently she poured out two cups of chocolate, put in a little of the noyau, and presenting me with one of them took her seat by my side on the soft yielding sofa. 'Drink it off as I do,' she said; 'it will do you far more good than sipping and allowing it to get cold.'

We both drank our small cups at a draught, and I almost instantly felt a thrill of voluptuous warmth rush through my frame, and looking at my fair companion, saw that her eyes seemed to sparkle with a strange amorous fire.

The devil was in me; in less time than it takes to write it, my empty cup was put on the table, and my disengaged arm placed round her neck; I drew her face to mine, and imprinted several kisses on her lips and cheeks as my other hand took possession of that inviting bosom; she was covered with blushes as she exclaimed, 'Fie! Fie, sir!! how can you take such liberties when I can't help myself without dropping my cup?'

'Dear lady, excuse my liberties, and don't distress yourself, I am really greatly obliged to the cup for its assistance; how can I look upon such loveliness without being tempted, yes, tempted! driven mad by the sight of such charms; you will excuse, you will pardon my presumption, I am sure,' I ejaculated, throwing myself upon my knees before her and hiding my face in her lap, as I clasped my arms nervously round her waist and could feel her whole frame tremble with emotion.

Suddenly she seemed to start with pain as she exclaimed, 'Ah! Goodness! Oh! Oh!! Oh!! the cramp in my legs. Oh! Oh!' as the cup was thrown down by her side. 'Oh, release me, sir! Oh, Walter, excuse me, I must rub it!'

Here was a splendid opportunity to improve a lucky chance. 'Permit me, poor dear lady, you are in such dreadful pain, and I am a medical student,' I said, making bold to raise her dressing-gown and chafe her lovely calves with my eager hands; what lovely legs I now beheld, with not a vestige of anything on them; my blood was on fire, my fingers gradually wandered higher and higher, and I could not refrain from imprinting kisses on the delicious soft, pinky flesh, as she seemed rather to sigh than speak, 'Oh! thank you, pray don't, it's so indelicate, and the cramp is gone now.'

'No, no, dear Madame, the nervous contractions of your beautiful thighs convince me that it is higher up, and will return again in a few moments, unless I can relieve you; indeed you must not mind me, as I am a medical man,' I quickly replied, making bolder advances every moment, and taking advantages of the warm temperament I knew she possessed.

'You rogue, you young villain, your touches and kisses have undone me; how can I resist a handsome student? Oh, Walter, Walter, I must have you! I had only been trying to draw you out a little, never thinking you were such a young gallant; and now I am caught in my own net!'

'Ah! What a hurry. You'll spoil it all by your impetuosity; you shall never have me without first kissing the shrine of love.'

'Sir!' pushing me away, as I was endeavouring to get between her lovely thighs. 'Strip, strip, sir, I must see my Adonis, as your Venus now unveils herself to you,' throwing of her dressing-gown (which I now saw was her only article of clothing); and drawing my face down to hers, she thrust her tongue into my mouth, 'tipping the velvet' in the most delicious style of voluptuous abandon, and delightfully handling my prick and balls at the same time. It was too much for my impatient steed, my spendings flew all over her hands and body almost instantly.

'Ah! What a naughty impatient boy, to come so quickly! Pull off your clothes, sir, and let us take our fill of love on yonder bed. My husband deserves this, for leaving me open to such temptation. You dear boy, how I shall love you; what a fine prick you have, and so – so – what do they call it? – (blushing at her own words) so randy! That's what the colonel says of the young fellows. Isn't it a dreadfully rude word, Walter? But so full of meaning. Whenever he said so, I couldn't help wishing for a handsome, randy young gentleman, such as your uncle has sent me today.'

This is how she ran on, as I threw off everything, and I was as naked as herself in a trice; then, hugging, kissing, belly to belly, and handling each other's charms in every possible way, we slowly progressed towards the inviting bed in the other room; once or twice I stopped and tried to get my prick into her standing up, but she would have none of that, and at last, when her bottom rested against the edge of the bed, she ordered me to kneel down and kiss the seat of love; how my tongue searched out her fine stiff clitoris, which projected quite an inch and a half from the lips of her vagina. I sucked it in ecstasy, and titillated her sensitive organs so that she spent profusely in a minute or two, holding my head with her hands to make me go on; it was a most deliciously enjoyable gamahuche; my tongue revelled in her creamy emission, till she begged me to slip off my shirt and come on the bed and let her enjoy my fine prick. So I ended this prelude with a playful, loving bite on her excited clitoris, and then, springing to my feet, rolled with her on to the bed, her ready hand grasping my cock as I mounted on her lovely body.

'What a shame!' she sighed. 'How you have been spending, you naughty boy, you won't have much left for me now; but he's fine and stiff!' as she squeezed it in her hand, and brought the head of my affair to the mark.

I found her deliciously tight, and assured her she was quite a virgin.

'So I should be, my dear Walter, but for you. The colonel has got so little to please me with, that, tight as I am, I can hardly feel him! now your jewel of pleasure makes me feel gorged with delight!'

Her motions were as lascivious as her words. She writhed and threw up her buttocks with extraordinary rapidity and energy, whilst I was equally eager and rapid in ramming into her delicious cunt.

I was ready as if I had never spent, and we swam in a mutual emission almost immediately, both of us being so overcome by our feelings that we almost swooned in delight; this only lasted for a minute; the throbbing and contracting of the folds of her vagina on my enraptured prick awoke me to renewed efforts, and we were rapidly progressing towards another spend, when she checked me, and begged I would withdraw for a little, when she would amuse me till she felt she must have him again, and she added, 'I shall enjoy it so much more if I can make you last longer. Sit on my body, Walter dear, and lay your beautiful prick between the globes of my bosom; you shall spend there next time. I can't help telling you what a fine one it is, over and over again!'

She went on caressing it with her hand, and making her two bubbies close upon it, so that I could work between them. It was another delicious idea, but she had not exhausted all her ways of exciting me. Her other hand passed under my thigh, and I thought she was frigging herself, but it was only to wet her finger, preparatory to frigging my bottom-hole with it. This made me come again almost directly.

'Now,' said she, 'I mean to ride on you, and make it last as long as possible, so let us reverse positions.'

This was done, and she rode me and stopped alternately for about twenty minutes, when we met in a glorious flow of sperm.

'What do you think of that?' she exclaimed, as soon as she recovered her breath. 'We will get up and answer your uncle's letter now, and you shall promise to come again soon.'

Nothing of moment occurred during the evening, after my visit to Mrs Leslie, but I could see that Annie was rather piqued because I had nothing to tell her, except that I thought the colonel's lady a most charming person, and had been pressed to stay with her to luncheon before she would write a reply to my uncle's note.

Next day being the last representation of a celebrated piece at the theatre of the county town by a first-rate London company, Papa expressed a wish that we should all go in the evening, but Annie and Sophie, giving me a knowing look on the sly, declared they had already seen it once and did not care to go again. For my part, of course, I had seen it half a dozen times in town, so it was finally arranged that Frank, Rosa and Polly only would go with Papa and Mama; they had a drive of more than an hour before them, so started at 6 P.M., and as soon as they were out of sight we three started for the bathing place at the lake. It was such a deliciously warm evening, and it would be just the place for our anticipated pleasures, as I had suggested to Annie and Sophie during the day.

Bolting the summer-house door on the inside as soon as we got in, I suggested first of all to stimulate our mutually ardent desires by a bottle of champagne; this so exhilarated the two lovely girls that we indulged in a second bottle before stripping for a romp. Seven o'clock found us bathed in a flood of golden light from the declining sun, which now shone directly in upon us, this warned us to make haste and improve the opportunity, so each one assisting the others and at the same time indulging in many loving tricks and liberties, we were soon in Adam and Eve costume.

'Now,' I exclaimed, 'Annie dear, you won't be jealous if I make a woman of your sister, as we promised the other day,' taking the younger one up in my arms with my rampant cock throbbing against her belly, as I carried her to the lounger.

'What a naughty boy you are, Walter, anything or anybody for a change is what fickle men like, but I won't be jealous of Sophie, although I am of Mrs Leslie. I know you had her yesterday; that sheepish tell-tale look, sir, when you met me on your return, was enough to confirm my suspicions of what would happen when you were *tête-à-tête* with that killing lady,' she replied.

'For shame, Annie, darling, you told me yourself the other day love ought to be free everywhere; I don't deny my guilt, but will do my best to earn forgiveness now,' I said, pushing Sophie back upon the soft yielding lounger. 'Help me to ease this darling of her troublesome virginity, and I will then repay your own longing cunny for all your love and forebearance; I am sure Mrs Leslie would like to make you one of our party without any feelings of jealousy; there are so many ways of voluptuous enjoyment that if there is only one man to three girls it can be so varied as to give everyone the most intense delight.'

At this both the girls gave me rapturous kisses, with every possible assurance that they never would be selfish, and would be only too happy to extend the circle of those they could be free and loving with, adding with special emphasis, 'We are such noodles, dear Walter, we knew nothing till you introduced us to the arts of love, and as long as you can stay with us shall look to you to guide us in everything; we know it's wrong, but what heavenly pleasure there is in the loving mixture of the sexes.'

ANNIE, taking my prick in her hand – 'Now, sir I will show this gentleman the way into Sophie's cabinet of love; be firm, dear, he won't hurt you more than can be helped, and the after joy will soon drown all recollection of the first short suffering.'

SOPHIE, opening her legs as wide as possible – 'I'm all on fire to taste the real tree of love; don't spare me, Walter, dear, I'd rather die than not have it now!'

The red head of 'Cupid's Battering Ram' was now brought to the charge; Annie opened the rosy lips of her sister's cunt and placed my cock in the exact position, but her touches, together with the thoughts of the delicious titbit I was about to enjoy, caused me to spend in a moment all over her fingers and into the virgin passage in front. 'Push on, push on; now's the time to gain your victory,' she whispered; 'that will make it easier to get him in,' at the same time lifting up Sophie's buttocks with her disengaged hand, so as to make her meet my attack in a more favourable manner. My first lunge lodged the head of Mr Priapus fairly within the tight folds of the victim's vagina, and I had already won the first outworks of the virgin's defences.

Poor Sophie moaned under the sharp pain of my assault, but biting her lips to repress any cries of pain she courageously placed one hand on the shaft of my prick, as if jealous of her sister's loving help, and anxious to have the honour of herself showing me the way to achieve love's dearest triumph, or perhaps it was for fear of my withdrawing before completely accomplishing my task.

'You love!' I exclaimed, enraptured by this exhibition of pluck, 'I will soon make a real woman of you,' then pushing fiercely on, on, I gradually forced the tight sheath to dilate. Every obstruction gave way to my determined energy, and with a final plunge, I was buried to the roots of my affair, and shooting at the same moment my warm spendings into her inmost vitals. This exhausted me for a few moments, and I lay supine upon the heaving bosom of the lovely

Sophie, till I could feel Annie's fingers busy tickling my balls and feeling the shaft of my cock. Just at the same moment Sophie, who had almost fainted under the painful ordeal, opened her eyes, and with a loving smile pouted her lips as an invitation for a kiss, which I instantly responded to, almost sucking her breath away in my ardour. My excitement was now raised to the highest possible pitch by her sister's titillations, and the loving challenge of Sophie herself to renew my motions with her, by heaving up her bottom and nipping my prick in her cunny in the most delightful way imaginable.

This time I prolonged the pleasure as much as possible, beginning slowly, and often stopping to feel the delicious throbbings of cock and cunny in their delightful conjunction. 'Ach! this is indeed love; it repays for all the pain I felt at first. Oh! oh! dear Walter, it feels as if my very soul was flowing from me in ecstasy!' she almost screamed out, kissing, biting, squeezing me with all her might at the moment of emission, which I again responded to with a flow of my own sperm.

I now declared we must refresh ourselves a little before going further, so she reluctantly allowed me to withdraw. A short plunge in the lake had a most invigorating effect. I felt as strong as a giant again, then another bottle of fizz renewed our loving ardour; the girls were handling my prick, which stood again as hard as ivory. So slipping on my shirt, as I intended to be the uppermost of the trio, I laid Sophie on her back, and then telling the obedient Annie to kneel over her sister and gamahuche her in return for Sophie's doing the same by her, I mounted up behind her, saying, 'I've made a woman of your dear sister, and will now treat you, my darling, to a new sensation.' But just at that moment Sophie, who had no idea of my intentions, seized hold of my cock, saying she must kiss the dear sweet thing which had afforded her such exquisite bliss. Holding it tight in her hand, she took the head between her pearly teeth and kissed and treated him to such love bites that I soon spent in her mouth, which she greedily swallowed, with all the abandon of voluptuous enjoyment. Meanwhile, I had been frigging Annie's bottom with my two fingers, which I had managed to insert together, and that dear girl was sucking her sister's quim, and wriggling herself in the most excitable way possible.

Sophie was now going to insert my prick in her sister's cunt, but Annie, almost beside herself with excitement, exclaimed, 'No, no, my dear, put him where Walter has got his fingers; I should like to try that, it is so exciting; the very thought of it makes me mad with desire to know what it is like. His fingers have given me such pleasures that I am sure the dear thing in your hand will greatly improve the sensation!'

No sooner said than done; the obedient girl directed my cock to the beautifully wrinkled tight little brown hole of her sister's bottom at the very moment I withdrew my fingers. When I found they so thoroughly appreciated the idea I had resolved to initiate them into, and being well lubricated and as stiff as possible, I soon passed the portals of Annie's second virginity. But, Heavens, what a delicious bout we had, she bounded about so with delight, that I had to hold tight round her neck to prevent being thrown out, whilst Sophie, below, gamahuched her delighted sister, and with her right hand continued to press my balls and prick, keeping time to every insertion in her sister's bottom. We all spent together, almost screaming with delight, and then lay in a confused heap, enjoying all the sensations of our delicious exhaustion.

As soon as they could kiss and persuade my rather enervated tool into renewed stiffness, Sophie declared I must oblige her with a taste of the new-found joy, and ravish her bottom as well as her sister's.

This was another delicious love engagement, the sisters gamahuching each other with the utmost erotic ardour, whilst my delighted prick revelled in the tight-fitting fundamental of the sweet girl, who wriggled and plunged about so excitedly that I had to hold fast to keep my place.

After this, we returned to the house, and passed the time very pleasantly till the return of the party from the theatre. I was anxious to hear Frank's account of how he had got on with Rosa during the evening, and especially as they drove home.

'Walter,' he said, as we were once more alone in his room after all had gone to rest, 'I've had a most enjoyable time of it since we started. Of course, as we went, it was daylight, so Rose and I maintained a proper decorum, but at the theatre, Papa and Mama were separated from us by Polly, and we all five sat in the front row of the dress circle. How the sight of Rosa's swelling bosom (which her low-necked dress allowed me fully to see) made my prick stand at once; so I took her gloved hand and made her feel how hard and excited it was. As no one could see, she indulged me with quite a gentle frigging outside my trousers, till I spent profusely, to the great delight of the roguish beauty, as I could tell by the smile on her face and the excited looks with which she met my ardent gaze.

' "What a shame," she whispered in my ear. "I know what you have done, you naughty boy. You should have reserved it for a more favourable opportunity."

' "Look out, darling, as we drive home; see if I don't repay your kind attentions," I whispered in return.

'Both Papa and Mama were rather sleepy before the conclusion of the last act, and to make them go off, as soon as we were seated in the carriage, I offered them my flask of brandy to keep out the effects of the night air. It had a pretty good strong dose of narcotic in it, and they were soon sound asleep in their corners. Polly also pretended to be dozing.

'Rosa was on my lap directly, and my hands were at once groping their way to the seat of pleasure whilst she was equally busy unbuttoning my trousers and handling the staff of life.

'Our lips met in long-drawn rapturous kisses, which fired every drop of blood in our veins, and both were too impatient for the real business to prolong our toyings with each other's privates; besides, I felt she was already spending over my busy fingers. She had my cock in a glorious state of erection; so opening her delicious thighs as she raised her clothes, she at once impaled herself on the spike she so burned to have thrust into her. It was quite equal to the first time I fucked her. The long evening passed in expectation of what I might be able to do on our return journey: it so added to the piquancy of my arduous longings that I seemed in Heaven itself, and swimming in a very ocean of love, we spent over and over again; our melting kisses and tongue-sucking continually stimulating us to renewed exertions, till the near approach to home warned us of the necessity of bringing our pleasures to an end for a time. Even now, I tell you, Walter, my cock keeps throbbing and standing at the very thoughts of the delightful pressures she treated me to; her cunt bites so deliciously.'

In the morning, Papa and Mama had scarcely slept off the effects of the sleeping dose they had imbibed from the brandy flask of their dutiful son, and lay a-bed very late, in fact, almost to luncheon time; meanwhile, we, the younger members of the family, had privately agreed upon a plan of amusement for the afternoon and evening.

Finding that two pretty young girls of fourteen and fifteen were living close by, with an invalid mother, whilst their brother was away, being a midshipman in the Royal Navy, I proposed that Annie should send the Misses Bruce an invitation to spend the afternoon with us, *en famille*, without the least ceremony, and join us in an alfresco tea party at a little hut in the woods, which formed part of my uncle's estate.

At luncheon we informed the governor of what we had done and hoped that both he and Mama would join in our outdoor party in the woods.

'No thank you, my dears, we are too afraid of the damp grass and rheumatics. Besides, we have not yet got over the fatigue of yesterday. We will stay quietly at home and hope you may enjoy yourselves thoroughly, as we should do if we were younger,' replied the jolly, kind-hearted old gentleman.

This was exactly what we had wished for and expected; so Frank and Annie at once sent off the servants with every requisite for our open-air tea party.

About three o'clock, the two young ladies arrived, and as all were ready, we at once set off for the scene of our anticipated fun, which was a rough bower covered with flowering honeysuckle and clematis, at the end of a long, shady, private walk, more than half a mile from the house.

Frank and myself particularly attached ourselves to the two fresh young ladies as being the greatest strangers, and therefore justly expectant of the most attention.

Emily Bruce, the elder, was a charming dark-eyed brunette, her rather large mouth having a fascinating effect as you regarded her. In fact, such a display of pearly white teeth, I never saw before, and the very thought that they might perhaps be soon employed in love bites on my tender-headed prick filled me with maddening lust to possess myself of their owner.

Nor was her sister, Louisa, any less prepossessing, she being almost the counterpart of Emily, except that one could easily see there was a slight difference in age.

When we arrived at the bower, the servants were at once sent home, being told that they could clear away the things next morning, as it would be too late for them to return in the evening, and at the same time, without asking the consent of her young friends, dear Annie scribbled a pencil note to their mama, to say that if they at all were late, she would insist upon them staying with her all night, and not to make herself at all anxious on their behalf – this was quietly sent off by one of the servants.

As soon as we were alone, Frank and I, uncorking the champagne, lighted our cigars, and saying that the sun was still too warm for outdoor romping, pressed the girls to try some very mild cigarettes of Turkish tobacco.

At last Annie and Rosa set the example by lighting up, and were at once laughingly followed by the others. Our two young friends protested they never took wine. Still, they evidently sipped it with great delight, and we bantered them upon being so tied to their mother's apron strings, etc., till they began to be quite as free as my cousins and Rosa.

We had a good stock of fizz, besides sandwiches and cake, so that no one seemed at all anxious to take the trouble of tea-making.

Still we were careful that only enough should be taken to warm our friends up to a slightly excitable state, in fact, just to induce that state of all-overishness, which tingles through a young girl's sensitive frame when she feels the first vibrations of amorous desires, which she can as yet hardly understand.

Their sparkling eyes, slightly flushed faces and above all, the dazzling beauties of their teeth, as they indulged in gay laughter at our badinage, set all of us aflame. I could see that Rosa and my cousins were longing to help in enjoying these innocent and ravishing young girls.

Now a game of hunt the slipper was proposed, and we at once adjourned to the soft, mossy green sward outside the bower. This was a most delicious and excitable romp.

Whenever it came our turns, Frank and myself indulged in all kinds of quick and startling touches, which made the two little dears blush up to their eyes at first, and when we managed to catch one of them with the slipper we claimed a hearty kiss as penalty, which they submitted to with tolerable grace, yet evidently in a state of great excitement, it was all so new to them. We finished the game, had a little more champagne, then proposed a game of hide and seek in the wood, with the reservation that no one was to go too far off.

We were to be in pairs, I chose Emily, and Frank took Louisa. Polly and Sophie went together, whilst Annie and Rosa had to search for us when we called out.

It so happened that there was an old sand-pit close by, in which several years before Master Frank had amused himself by making a Robinson Crusoe's cave, and planted bushes in front of it, so that the entrance was perfectly out of sight, and no one would fancy anyone could be screened by the small amount of cover which seemed to grow on the side of the pit; this was just the place for our purpose, and it had been beforehand arranged that we were not to be found for a long time. Gliding into the cave Frank let fall the old curtain that hung at the entrance, and we were at once in the dark; the place was large enough for us all to sit together on a heap of fine soft sand at the further end.

'What a dear girl you are!' I whispered in Emily's ear, as I took a kiss in the dark, and drew her trembling body quite close by an arm around her waist. 'Pray don't,' she whispered in return, 'if you do not keep quiet I won't stop in this dark place.'

'Don't say so, it would be cruel, especially if you knew all I feel towards you, Emily dear. I must call you Emily, yes, and kiss you again and again; I love you so, your breath is so fragrant, what are you afraid of, there's nothing to fear among friends, darling,' I whispered, kissing my partner rapturously.

'Oh, ah, you take my breath away, Walter, I'm so unused to such goings on. Oh, fie, sir, for shame, you make me feel all of a-tremble, you take such liberties!' as I was working one hand inside the bosom of her dress, and getting possession of two hard round bubbies which throbbed with emotion under my loving caresses.

'It's all love, darling, and no one can see, can't you hear how Frank and Louisa are kissing; is it not delicious to think they are doing the same, and will be sure to keep our secret?'

A deep sigh was my only answer, and again our lips met in a long luscious kiss. My tongue was thrust into her mouth, and tickled the tip of her own velvety organ of speech. I could feel the nipples of her virgin bosom stick out as stiff as little cocks and whispered to her to allow me to kiss them.

'I can refuse you nothing,' she whispered; 'you are such a bold lover. I'm all in flame from head to foot at the numberless liberties you are taking with me. Ah, if Mama only knew,' she sighed, as I was now sucking her titties, and running my disengaged hand up her thighs; they were nipped tightly together, but gradually relaxed under the gentle pressure of my hand, till I actually got possession of her cunny, which I could feel was slightly covered with soft downy hair, and soon began to frig her gently with my forefinger. How the dear girl wriggled under this double excitement, and I could feel one of her hands groping outside my trousers over my bursting prick to return the pleasure I was giving her. One by one she unfastened the buttons, then her soft delicate hand soon had possession of my stiff affair, naked and palpitating with unsatisfied desire.

'Ah,' she whispered, 'I am satisfied at last! we had a servant at home, a few months ago, who slept in our room, and used to tickle and play with us. She told us that men had a long thing as hard as iron, which they pleased the ladies by shoving up their bellies, and that was how the babies were made. Do you believe it? She was always shoving her fingers into us as you are doing to me now, and – and – and,' here she hesitated and seemed to shudder with delight, just as I spent all over her hand, and I could also feel her spendings come in a warm gush over my fingers. It was delicious. Her hand first held tight the top of my throbbing prick, then gently worked up and down the shaft, lubricated by my spendings. It was indeed a voluptuous treat; I begged her to thrust her tongue into my mouth, and we continued the mutual frigging till she almost fainted away in her ecstasy.

Slightly recovering, I asked her what it was she was going to tell me about the maidservant, when she hesitated.

'Do, dearest, tell me everything,' I implored, in a loving whisper. 'We are now without reserve to each other; you can have no secrets from your loving Walter.'

'It was so funny, I don't know how she could do it, but Mary was so fond of sucking and kissing us where you have your hand, dearest,' she replied, 'but it was so nice you can't imagine how we enjoyed having her do it to us.'

'My love, my Emily, let me kiss you now, and it would be sublime if you would kiss me. I long to feel the love bites of your beautiful teeth in my Cupid's dart. Frank and Louisa are too busy to notice what we do,' I whispered in her ear, as I inclined the willing girl backwards on the soft pillow of sand and reversed my position so that we lay at full length, side by side, both of us eager as possible for the game; my head was buried between her loving thighs, with which she pressed me most amorously as my tongue was inserted in her loving slit; this was a fine gamahuche. I stirred up all the lasciviousness of her ardent temperament till she screamed with delight, and caused Frank and Louisa to enquire what we were doing, but we made no reply. She sucked my delighted prick, handled and kissed my balls, till I spent in her mouth, as her teeth were lovingly biting the head of my penis. She sucked it all down, whilst I repaid her loving attentions to the best of my ability with my own active tongue.

As soon as it was over, I took Emily by the hand, and we groped towards our companions, who, I found, were equally as busy as we had been. Frank thoroughly understood my intention; we all got together, and joined in a grope of cocks and cunnies without the least restraint, till suddenly the curtain was pulled down, and we heard the laughing voices of Rosa and Annie, as they exclaimed, 'See, here they are. What are these rude boys doing to you young ladies?'

Emily and Louisa were covered with confusion, but the girls lovingly assured them they would keep the secret, and introduce them to more fun after they had retired to bed, as it was now getting late, and we must all return to the house.

As I have before observed, the wing of the mansion in which we all slept was quite apart from the other wing in which Papa, Mama, and the servants were located, so as soon as we had retired, Frank and myself joined the girls in their room, or rather rooms, for they occupied two. The Miss Bruces blushed crimson at seeing us only in our shirts, especially as one was seated on the *pot de chambre*, whilst the other was exhibiting her charms to my inquisitive cousins before a cheval glass.

'All right,' exclaimed Annie, 'my dears, everything is free between us and the boys, but we mean to punish you for allowing the impudent fellows to presume upon such liberties with you in the cave. Your bottoms shall smart, young ladies, I can assure you,' as she produced a couple of light birch rods from a drawer; in fact, I had provided them for her, the idea having been suggested to me by reading a book called *The Romance of Lust*.

A fine large bed stood by the wall, facing another at the end of the room, but our programme only required one couch. Annie and Rosa were determined to have their enjoyment now; everyone was ordered to strip off shirt or chemise, then I horsed Emily on my back whilst Frank did the same by her sister.

Sophie and Polly were entrusted with the rods, and gaily switched us and our riders' bottoms as we trotted round the room, the sisters hardly knowing whether to laugh or cry, when a more stinging cut than usual made them cry for mercy; our pricks were as rampant as possible, and we were not in need of any extra stimulation; still the girls were very hard on our rumps, although not quite so severe with the sisters. The darling Emily had so twined her legs round me as I held them close under my armpits that her pretty feet in their bewitching little slippers were frigging my cock between them most deliciously.

The sight of our red smarting bottoms and bursting pricks was too much for Annie and Rosa, and they were inflamed by lust, so throwing themselves backward on the bed, with their legs wide open and feet resting on the floor, the two dear girls presented their quims to our charge, as with both hands they held open the lips of their delicious cunts, inviting our eager cocks to come on. We charged them at once, under the impulsive urging of the rods, gave a few delightful fucking motions, then withdrew and trotted round the room again, this we constantly repeated to prolong our enjoyment, till at last the dear girls could stand it no longer, their arms clasped us firmly, whilst the rods cut away with extra force to make us complete their pleasure; it was a most luxurious finish, we all spent with screams of delight, and lay for a few moments in a delicious state of lethargic exhaustion till we awoke to find Sophie, Polly, Emily and Louisa all rolling on the floor in the delights of gamahuching.

After this the two dear girls begged, with tears in their eyes, that Frank and Walter would make women of them, so that they might really taste the wildest delights of love.

'Then, dears,' said Rosa, with a sly laugh, 'you must kiss them, and make their exhausted cocks stiff again, and then we will lend the two boys to you.'

We sat on the bed by the side of our late fucking partners, who we kissed, fondled and frigged, whilst Emily and Louisa, kneeling between our knees, sucked our pricks up to standing point, as their hands drew back our foreskins or played with our balls.

Stiff and rampant as we were we entreated them to go on for a little longer, till we felt ourselves almost at spending point. Polly and Sophie arranged two bolsters and some pillows on the floor in the most advantageous manner; the sisters were each placed with two pillows under their bottoms, whilst their heads rested on the bolsters. Annie and Rosa then conducted us to the victims, who impatiently waited their immolation to the god of love with open legs and longing cunts. The two mistresses of the ceremonies took our pricks in hand, and directed them to the path of bliss. Emily was my partner again; she threw her legs over my back and heaved up to meet the fatal thrust which was to be the death of her troublesome virginity. I had no time to see how the others progressed, but heard a smothered shriek of agony from Louisa, as no doubt Frank achieved her fate for her; my partner was more courageous, she glued her lips to mine, sucking in my tongue in the most ardent manner imaginable, even while my prick was tearing through her hymen; my spending deluged her wounded quim, and we soon lost all thoughts of pain when we recommenced a lovely fuck, with me moving slowly at first, till her rapid motions spurred me on to faster plunges, her deliciously tight cunt holding me like a hand, in fact so tight that I could feel my foreskin drawn backwards and forwards at every shove.

'Ah! you dear fellow, push on, kill me with delight!' she screamed in ecstasy, as we came again together, and I was equally profuse in my words of endearment.

As we lay still after it was over her tight-fitting cunt seemed to hold and continually squeeze my delighted prick so by its contractions and throbbings I was ready again directly, and we ran another thrilling course before she would let me try to withdraw.

Frank and Louisa had been equally delighted with each other, and thus the two sisters lost their maidenheads almost at the same moment.

Not a day passed but we had some voluptuous games, whilst as to Rosa and Frank, they were openly engaged to be married, which was an especial gratification to the old people.

Time flew so rapidly that my visit drew to its close and we were all thinking of devising some signal display of love, to be enacted as a parting scene ere I took my departure from my uncle's hospitable and happy domicile, when one fine morning in June, who should favour us with a call, but my lovely brunette Mrs Leslie. She had driven over to invite myself and cousins to spend an entire day before the colonel's return. 'You know,' she said, turning to my uncle, 'how stiff and starch all his ideas are, and I must have one day of real fun before he comes home from Paris. Will you let them come tomorrow and stop till the next day?'

My uncle being too kind to refuse, the arrangement was made at once, Mrs Leslie stayed to luncheon, and we took an afternoon stroll in the park afterwards. From time to time her intelligent glances assured me she was anxious for a *tête-à-tête* with me, so I asked her to take my arm and we soon managed to give the others the slip, and lost ourselves in a dense copse. Sitting down on the soft mossy turf, under a shady little yew tree, we were quite hidden from observation.

'How I longed to kiss your sweet lips once more,' I exclaimed, clasping her in my eager embrace, and sucking her breath almost away in a luscious osculation.

'If that is all you thought of, sir, you have been vastly unfaithful to your protestations of love, and I should really feel awfully jealous of your pretty cousins and Miss Redquim did I not see the unruly state of the jewel in your trousers,' she laughingly replied, as she took speedy steps to release and secure the impatient prisoner in her grasp, continuing, 'I wonder how he has amused himself since that ever memorable day when I first had the pleasure of both seeing and feeling the noble fellow. Now tell me true, Sir Walter, have you seduced your cousins and their friend?'

I at once made a full confession of all our amours, and begged she would indulge us in every possible way on the morrow, as it would be the last grand chance I should have before returning to town. .

'Most delightful state of things I am sure, but what a shame not to have run over and invited me to join in your amorous festivities. Surely you knew it was just what I should have delighted in. I have a great mind to disappoint you now, only I should also be punishing myself, so come on, you naughty young fellow, and I will consider between this and tomorrow what your penance will be,' she said, reclining herself backwards, her fine dark eyes full of a humid languishing fire, which too truly indicated her voluptuous requirements.

Lifting her skirts quickly, I paid my devotions at the shrine of love by a kiss and playful bite of her clitoris, then, unable to dally any longer, placed myself between her readily yielding thighs, and was soon revelling within the soft juicy folds of her divine organ of bliss, delighted beyond expression by the throbbing compressions to which it treated me as I lay quietly enjoying the sense of complete possession, which is so delicious to contemplate, before commencing more vigorous action; our lips met again and our billing and cooing would have lasted some time had we not heard Frank declaring to Rosa and his sisters what a damned shame it was of Walter and Mrs Leslie to give them the slip, but he would find us and spoil our fun.

This caused my charming inamorata to heave up her buttocks as a challenge to me not to waste more time, so I put spurs to my steed, but none too soon, for just as we died away in a mutual spend, Frank, Sisters and Co. burst upon the scene with a triumphant exclamation of 'Here's Walter and his grass widow', and before we could recover ourselves the laughing party inflicted an awful slapping on our bottoms, till a truce was made and we all agreed to wait patiently for the morrow's party at Mrs Leslie's.

Next day, favoured by splendid weather, we were early at the colonel's residence, and the handsome swarthy Vishnu ushered us into the luxurious boudoir of his voluptuous mistress 'You have arrived early, it is scarcely one o'clock, my toilette's not yet made, but how very welcome you all are to my house, I need not trouble to say, after the frank understanding we came to yesterday, as to our amusements now you are here. The chocolate is just ready, and I have infused in it an imperceptible something (a secret, my dear, which the colonel brought from India), which will soon set all your young amorous blood in such a glow of desire that you will not know how to satisfy your intense cravings for the delight of love, and then naughty Walter shall be served out for his unfaithfulness to me.'

This speech made us all smile as we took up the small cups of delicious chocolate which Vishnu handed round and, as he disappeared, our hostess, who had nothing on but her dressing-gown, having drawn Frank to her side on the sofa, asked us, as the day was so warm, to throw aside as much as possible of our superfluous clothing, which was speedily done.

'We must have a romp before luncheon, then repose or stroll about during the afternoon, and in the evening we shall, I hope, enjoy some novel ideas I have quite set my mind upon,' she continued during the short time we took to disrobe. 'That's right, only keep on the *chemiserie* now, at night we will discard the last rag; I have no chemise to take off, so will keep on this convenient *robe de chambre*, but you may look,

Frank, if you don't think Rosa will be jealous,' as she opened the front, and displayed to his ardent gaze all the beauties of her person.

'If it makes her jealous, I can't help admiring such charms!' said Frank, 'but Rosa is far too sensible for that, and thoroughly enters into all our fun; in fact I am sure she loves Walter as well as she does me, only she can't marry both of us.'

'Ha! ha!! that accounts for Walter forgetting me; so to be revenged on them both you must have me now,' she replied, lifting up his shirt to see if he was ready. 'Why your love-dart is almost exactly the size of his,' and without more ado she was on his lap, and spitted herself on Frank's cock, throwing off entirely the *robe de chambre* that she might enjoy him without impediment.

This instantly excited the girls, who lay down in pairs for a mutual gamahuche and bottom-frig, Rosa playfully telling me to let Mrs Leslie have the double pleasure by fucking her bottom as she was riding Frank.

'Hold her tight, my boy,' I said, 'and I will let her beautiful little fundament know what it is to keep a stiff prick waiting for his turn,' as I took a little cold cream from the dressing-table, and putting some on the head of my prick, as well as on the delightful brown wrinkled hole exposed to my attack, began to slip it in at once, despite her struggles and screams that we should 'injure her' between us. Further and further I gradually worked in, till I could feel my cock rubbing against Frank's with only the thin divisional membrane between them, our joint spendings deluging both cunt and bum, spurting the warm, frothy sperm over our balls at every thrust. This was not enough to satisfy her, but she kept us at our work until we repeated our emissions with screams of delight, and rolled on the floor in a confused heap amongst the dear girls, who were so excited by the sight of our ecstasies that they were revelling in every species of tribadism to allay their lustful yearnings.

After this Mrs Leslie opened a side door, conducted us into her bathroom, where we refreshed ourselves and indulged in a variety of kissing, frigging, &c., but by her advice the girls refrained from exhausting us too much, and accepted cigarettes of Turkish tobacco to join us in a smoke, as we lighted some of the colonel's fine cigars. It was a picture worthy of any Apelles, as we could see the reflection of all our naked charms on the bathroom walls, which constituted one vast mirror of the very finest silvered glass, two rather good-looking fellows with big pricks, as rampant as could be wished, and five lovely ladies all smoking and puffing pretty curls or rings of vapoury nicotine, alternating that sober enjoyment with the more active fun of trying to burn the tips of their cunts with the fiery end of cigarette or cigar.

About half-past two, we dressed, and then took luncheon, then strolled in the grounds or on the bank of a small stream, where some of us passed the time trying our piscatorial luck, till the bell rang for dinner, which passed pleasantly enough, and about 9 P.M., we assembled in the drawing-room, for a grand erotic seance.

Mrs Leslie dismissed all her servants for the night, except Vishnu, who she said would be quite sufficient to attend to our little requirements.

The room was large and lofty, the windows closed and artistically draped with gorgeous black and gold curtains, the spaces between filled up with mirrors and branching candelabra, the opposite side of the apartment being also quite a tableau of flowers, mirrors and lighted wax candles, which shed a brilliant and yet soft luxurious effulgence over the whole scene; two doors at one end gave access to retiring rooms, where we undressed, and in a very few minutes the whole party, in a state of ravishing nudity, were grouped round Mrs Leslie, as she sat on an ottoman, awaiting her decision as to the programme.

She first persuaded us to sip a little of her chocolate, then went on to say, 'As we are five to two you will find I have a stock of fine, soft, firmly made dildoes to make up the deficiency in males, which alternated with the real article will enable us thoroughly to enjoy ourselves. First, I believe Miss is a virgin, notwithstanding all she knows and has seen; her delicate little pussy must be itching to be emancipated from the thraldom of virginity. Walter must do the service for her at once, on Rosa's lap; so now to business, as I see our gentlemen are in a beautiful state of readiness.'

Polly blushed deeply, but readily seated herself on her friend's lap with her legs wide open, presenting herself to my staff of life, whilst Rosa, passing her hands round the dear girl's waist, held open the lips of her cunny, and guided the head of my affair in the proper direction. Much as she had been frigged and gamahuched, it was a hard task; her cunt was so deliciously small and tight that in spite of her favourable position, I could only just get the head of Mr Priapus within the nymphæ before she started with the intense pain, and gave a suppressed scream of anguish, the tears starting to her eyes and trickling over her blushing face.

'Courage, darling, it will soon be over,' I whispered, kissing her excitedly, whilst Mrs Leslie encouraged me by saying, 'Sharp and quick, Walter, a good thrust will force better than those gentle pushes; gentleness is not real kindness when taking a maidenhead'; at the same moment I felt she was attacking my virgin bottom-hole behind with a well-lubricated dildo, its head being well in before I knew exactly what she was doing; this and the desire to possess Polly so stimulated me that I thrust furiously at the opposing obstacle, her heart-rending cries adding to my pleasure, and making me mad with desire. At last I was halfway in, then a fierce lunge seemed to break quite through as I, at the same time, deluged the tight passage with a copious emission.

The poor little victim had swooned, but Mrs Leslie, working her dildo behind, ordered me to let my cock throb inside Polly's tight sheath, as it would tend to bring her round, and excite her amorous sensibility to the utmost.

What delightful sensations I experienced; my prick feeling all the spasmodic contractions of her vagina, and having my bottom well dildo-fucked at the same time, I spent again under the influence of this accumulated excitement just as my partner was coming round under the influence of some cordial which had been poured down her gasping throat, whilst strong smelling-salts had been applied to her nostrils. She opened her eyes, giving a violent sneeze at the same time, which vibrated on my delighted prick, which instantly began gently to bestir itself in her tight scabbard; this roused her little by little, till throwing her arms round my neck, and returning my hot kisses with all the ardour of her nature, she cried and laughed by turns, as she begged me to make haste and complete her happiness.

By a side glance I could see Frank was in Mrs Leslie's bottom, Annie in him with a dildo, and Sophie doing the same to her sister, a perfect string of pederastic branchings from my own violated bum. It was such a scene as I had never seen before, and added additional fury to my already maddened lust. I came again and again before we finished, each spend more ecstatic than the last. The chocolate had so invigorated us, that we went through an almost interminable series of spendings, till at last nature could stand it no longer, we rolled on the floor in a confused heap and wound up in a mutual gamahuche; Mrs Leslie secured the blood-stained quim of little Polly, which she sucked till she had enjoyed the last drop of ensanguined spunk she could extract from the wounded slit of her young friend, who writhed in delight under the soothing touches of such a lascivious tongue.

It was between eleven and twelve o'clock when, just as we were recovering from a state of lethargic oblivion and thinking of some re-invigorating refreshment, the sound of carriage wheels on the gravel drive up to the house, and then a rat-a-tat-tat on the loud knocker made us all start to our feet and rush for our clothes.

'The colonel, by all that's unfortunate,' exclaimed Mrs Leslie, 'make haste or he will catch us; who would have thought of his arriving this time of night.'

The prudent Vishnu, pretending to be awaking out of his first sleep, so bungled and delayed opening the front door, that we were tolerably presentable by the time the colonel made his appearance, and whatever his suspicions may have been, he went through the formality of introduction in the most friendly way possible, the presence of so many young ladies evidently quite disconcerting him for the moment.

I afterwards learnt from his wife that under promise of secrecy she had confessed all to him, and vastly amused her husband by the account of our doings; but, at any rate, it stopped our fun at the time, and next day I was obliged to return to town, and thus bring to conclusion my sport amongst the she-noodles. Anything but 'noodles' after I had so enlightened them, they were in fact quite as knowing as Adam and Eve after they found out they were 'naked', having tasted of the Tree of Knowledge – which, in my humble opinion, meant having discovered *l'arte de faisant l'amour*.

Wordsworth Classic Erotica

❧ ❦ ❧

WORDSWORTH DISTRIBUTION

Great Britain and Ireland
Wordsworth Editions Limited
Cumberland House, Crib Street
Ware, Hertfordshire SG12 9ET
Telephone 01920 465 167
Fax 01920 462 267

USA, Canada and Mexico
Universal Sales & Marketing Inc
230 Fifth Avenue, Suite 1212
New York, NY 10001, USA
Telephone 212-481-3500
Fax 212-481-3534

South Africa
Struik Book
Distributors (Pty) Ltd
Graph Avenue,
Montague Gardens
7441 P O Box 193 Maitland 7405
South Africa
Telephone 021-551-5900
Fax 021-551-1124

Italy
Magis Books SRL
Via Raffaello 31c
Zona ind Mancasale
42100 Reggio Emilia, Italy
Telephone 0522-920999
Fax 0522-920666

Germany, Austria and Switzerland
Swan Buch-Marketing GmbH
Goldscheuerstrabe 16
D-7640 Kehl am Rhein, Germany

Portugal
International Publishing
Services Limited
Rua da Cruz da Carreira, 4B
1100 Lisboa
Telephone 01-570051
Fax 01-352-2066

Spain
Ribera Libros S L
Poligono Martiartu, Calle 1, no 6
48480 Arrigorriaga, Vizcaya
Telephone
34-4-671-3607 (Almacen)
34-4-441-8787 (Libreria)
Fax
34-4-671-3608 (Almacen)
34-4-4418029 (Libreria)

India
Om Book Services
1690 First Floor, Nai Sarak
Delhi 110006
Telephone 327 9823– 326-5303
Fax 327-8091